# EMOTIONAL EXCESS ON THE SHAKESPEAREAN STAGE: PASSION'S SLAVES

# EMOTIONAL EXCESS ON THE SHAKESPEAREAN STAGE: PASSION'S SLAVES

BRIDGET ESCOLME

B L O O M S B U R Y
LONDON • NEW DELHI • NEW YORK • SYDNEY

**Bloomsbury Arden Shakespeare**

An imprint of Bloomsbury Publishing Plc

50 Bedford Square
London
WC1B 3DP
UK

1385 Broadway
New York
NY 10018
USA

**www.bloomsbury.com**

**Bloomsbury is a registered trade mark of Bloomsbury Publishing Plc**

First published 2014



**British Library Cataloguing-in-Publication Data**
A catalogue record for this book is available from the British Library.

ISBN: HB: 978-1-4081-7966-6
PB: 978-1-4081-7967-3
ePDF: 978-1-4081-7968-0
ePub: 978-1-4081-7969-7

**Library of Congress Cataloging-in-Publication Data**
Escolme, Bridget, 1964-
Emotional excess on the Shakespearean stage : passion's slaves / Bridget Escolme.
pages cm. -- (Critical companions)
Includes bibliographical references and index.
ISBN 978-1-4081-7967-3 -- ISBN 978-1-4081-7966-6 -- ISBN 978-1-4081-7968-0 -- ISBN 978-1-4081-7969-7 1. Emotions in literature. 2. English drama--Early modern and Elizabethan, 1500-1600--History and criticism. 3. Shakespeare, William, 1564-1616--Stage history. 4. Theater--England--History--16th century. 5. Theater--England--History--17th century. I. Title.
PR658.E57E83 2013
822.3--dc23
2013020882

Typeset by Fakenham Prepress Solutions, Fakenham, Norfolk NR21 8NN
Printed and bound in India

To Gary Willis.

And moreover what can be sweeter to our thoughts than the image of a true and constant *love*, which we are assured our friend doth bear us? What happiness to have a friend to whom we may safely open our heart, and trust him with our most important secrets, without apprehension of his conscience, or any doubt of his fidelity? What content to have a friend whose discourse sweetens our cares? Whose counsels disperse our fears? Whose conversation charms our griefs? Whose circumspection assures our fortunes, and whose only presence fills us with joy and content?

Nicholas Coeffeteau, 1621

# CONTENTS

# ACKNOWLEDGMENTS

This project would not have been possible without the help, encouragement and ideas of many people and organizations. I am extremely grateful to colleagues in the Department of Drama at Queen Mary University of London, particularly to Jen Harvie, Maria Delgado and Nicholas Ridout, who have given invaluable advice and stimulating conversation in their capacities as Directors of Research, and as friends. Nick Ridout played a particularly important role in helping me to know and understand what this book needed to be. I would also like to thank Michèle Barrett, Head of English and Drama at Queen Mary, who supported me in my application for a period of research leave to complete the project, all of the School administrative team, particularly Jenny Gault and Beverly Stewart, without whose help with other aspects of my job this book would never have been completed, and Sally Mitchell and the Thinking Writing team for the wonderful Queen Mary Writing Retreats. Many thanks too to Paul Heritage and People's Palace Projects.

Many thanks also to all at Arden Shakespeare, particularly Margaret Bartley, Emily Hockley and Claire Cooper.

The work of a great many theatre practitioners – actors, directors and designers – is at the heart of this book; I would like to thank and acknowledge the work of all referenced in what follows and to mention here those who have given up their valuable time to talk or write to me in recent years – Jane Collins, Dominic Dromgoole, Peter Farley, Sunil Shanbag, Roxana Silbert. The help and stimulation of conversations with countless friends and colleagues must also be acknowledged; some of those I mention here will already understand the help and stimulation they have given; others may not realize the influence they have had. They include Frances Babbage, Bobby Baker, Roberta Barker, Christian

Billing, Warren Boutcher, Christie Carson, Ralph Cohen, Rob Conkie, Pavel Drábek, Sarah Dustagheer, Indira Ghose, Bret Jones, Farah Karim-Cooper, Eric Langley, Clare McManus, Lucy Munro, Marcus Nevitt, Stuart Hampton-Reeves, Peter Holland, Paul Prescott, Carol Rutter, Richard Schoch, Catherine Silverstone, Kim Solga, Tiffany Stern, Christine Twite, Tiffany Watt-Smith, Penelope Woods, Jan Wozniak, Zoe Svendsen, and Queen Mary undergraduate students who have taken the class 'Madness and Theatricality' during the past five years.

Material in the book has been stimulated and developed through presentation at a range of conferences, including the International Shakespeare Congress; the Shakespeare Association of America (particularly the panel session 'Academic Pressure and Theatrical Forms' organized by Jeremy Lopez and Paul Menzer at the 2012 meeting); the AHRC Network Isolated Acts and its 2012 conference 'Confined Spaces: Considering Madness, Psychiatry, and Performance', organized by Anna Harpin. I would also like to thank the librarians and archivists at the National Theatre Archive, the Shakespeare's Birthplace Trust and Shakespeare's Globe for their help and patience.

Thanks should also go to my mother Hilary Escolme, and my brother John Escolme and his partner Jussi Kalkkinen, for listening and questioning. And lastly my love and thanks to my partner Gary Willis, to whom this book is dedicated and who has not only proof-read it in its entirety but has provided unstinting support and encouragement at the most difficult points in its creation. He had always wondered why writers' partners got such profuse thanks in the Acknowledgements, and now he knows.

Bridget Escolme, London 2013.

# LIST OF ILLUSTRATIONS

# INTRODUCTION

[...] For thou hast been
As one in suff'ring all, that suffers nothing,
A man that Fortune's buffets and rewards
Hast ta'en with equal thanks. And blest are those
Whose blood and judgment are so well commeddled
That they are not a pipe for Fortune's finger
To sound what stop she please. Give me that man
That is not passion's slave, and I will wear him
In my heart's core, ay, in my heart of heart,
As I do thee.

Shakespeare, *Hamlet* (3.2.66–75)*

Prior to this eulogy on Horatio's blessed balance of 'blood and judgement', Hamlet gives his advice to the players, in which he conjures the embarrassing image of a bad actor in a wig, to warn the actors against 'tear[ing] a passion to tatters' (3.2.10) with over-emphatic gestures and too much shouting. In both art and life, then, Hamlet seems to privilege cool judgement over hot passion. The description of Horatio as 'one in suffering all that suffers nothing' suggests a complete detachment from the emotions produced by 'fortune's buffets and rewards', a stoical paradigm of self-control in the face of the slings and arrows Hamlet has already contemplated in the play (3.1.58). A similar privileging of reason over passion emerges in a range of early modern treatises on the passions. While the *apatheia* with which Hamlet credits Horatio is regularly dismissed as unnaturally blockish and un-Christian[1] much of the advice available to the early modern reader on the subject of emotion concerns its restraint and control. The reader is either advised against indulging the passions at all, or told that their expression should be moderated.[2] It is brutish to feel nothing – but to feel too much is to reduce oneself to the the level of the unreasoning animal. Whereas today, emotion in Western culture is regarded as an individuating force – when exhorted to 'express yourself' it is often emotion one is being asked to 'express' – the early modern passions are frequently described as that which makes one less of an individual. The passions are material forces barely under the control of what really makes man human: his sovereign reason. Indeed, the four examples of emotion or emotional affect/effect that head up the chapters of this book – anger, laughter, love and grief – often appear to the early modern philosophical mindset to sit along a continuum at the far end of which is madness. Anger is a potentially murderous mania; the mad laugh unpredictably and inappropriately; love leads to the sickness of 'love melancholy'; grief is the prime producer of melancholic insanity.

Hamlet's ideal of the perfect actor and his paradigm for the perfect, dispassionate friend are not the same. True, in advising the Players against 'anything so o'erdone' (3.2.21) as gestural air-sawing and vocal passion-tearing, he uses the imagery of weather in a similar vein to early modern sermons on the restraint of the passions in everyday life. For Thomas Playfere in his sermon on *The Mean in Mourning* (1595), crying is compared to the weather: too much weeping is like an economically unproductive, physically destructive storm:

> The water when it is quiet, and calm, bringeth in all manner of merchandise, but when the sea storms, and roars too much, then the very ships do howl and cry. The air looking clearly, and cheerfully refresheth all things, but weeping too much, that is, raining too much, as in Noah's flood, it drowns the whole world.[3]

'In the very torrent, tempest, and, as I may say, the whirlwind of your passion, you must acquire and beget a temperance that may give it smoothness', insists Hamlet (3.2.5–8) as he holds forth on the actor's craft. However, Hamlet does suggest that this temperance of theatrical expression is somehow to be found *in* 'the whirlwind of your passion' rather than that there should be no such whirlwind in the theatre, whereas his praise of his friend implies that Horatio has found the state of perfect stoical *apatheia*, in which misfortune and luck are regarded with equally dispassionate equanimity.

Hamlet's first encounter with the Players after their arrival at Elsinore (2.2) seems to sit even less easily with his praise of the man who is not a slave to his passions. While Polonius finds the First Player's tears for Hecuba just too much (2.2.499, 520–1), Hamlet is delighted with the actor's theatrical production of emotion and takes the tearful delivery of the Trojan battle narrative as a rebuke to his own lack of passionate action in avenging his father. So it is not that Hamlet thinks that passionate expression is only for actors: he takes the actor's example as one he should follow in his own life. Were he able to permit passion to overwhelm him as this actor can, birds of prey would be at his uncle's corpse already (2.2.581–2). And should the Player have had similar passionate 'motive and [. . .] cue' (561) for his speech as Hamlet has to support his revenge, far from turning the Player into an embarrassing, overacting Herod of a performer,

> [. . .] He would drown the stage with tears
> And cleave the general ear with horrid speech,
> Make mad the guilty and appall the free,
> Confound the ignorant, and amaze indeed
> The very faculties of eyes and ears.
>
> (562–6)

Here, over-passionate acting would be 'overdone' not in the sense of bombastic and implausible; it would rather be beyond effective, too much to bear, storm-like in a way that seems impossibly impressive in its excess. If the court were filled with men like Horatio, there would be no crimes like Claudius's, governed by lust for sex and power. But there would also be no theatre, no performance like the player's to impress Hamlet – and no one driven to passionate action in a cause either wrong or right in social life. The man who is not passion's slave does not make a very successful dramatic hero; Horatio's ability to suppress rather than to act upon his emotions, to govern himself entirely by his reason, would mean no star-cross'd lovers, enraged fathers, jealous husbands, furious warriors, jovial and self-indulgent drunks or murdering uncles. In praising the actor's art, Hamlet seems to be suggesting that there are times when people need to be as passionate in their expression and action as actors.

This is a book about 'excessive' emotion in the theatre in which Shakespeare worked, in the plays of Shakespeare and his contemporaries, and in the productions of those plays in performance today. It inevitably poses questions about what emotional excess actually is: how much or what kind of emotional expression is too much? What kinds or expressions of emotion are considered legitimate in theatrical culture and social life, what kinds or expressions of emotion are considered worthy of shame, repression and punishment? How does our own expression and reception of emotion – in the theatre and, more broadly, in our everyday lives – lead us to interpret the work of the early modern dramatists? In this book I will be exploring the cultural politics of emotion in Shakespeare's plays – and historicizing the ways in which we reproduce and receive them in the theatre. Writers and thinkers of the early modern period had all kinds of things to say about what we might call the emotions; a significant amount of it was negative, as Hamlet suggests in his positive evaluation of the reasonable Horatio. Yet people regularly came to the theatre to watch people laugh inappropriately, get murderously angry, fall madly in love and grieve inconsolably. This book contends that the early modern theatre is a place where audiences went to watch extremes of emotion and to consider when those extremes became excesses. It suggests that because of the social and political significance of the passions in early modern drama, and because of the ways in which emotion is structured politically in the plays, they are a particularly rich site for discussions of how our own society conceives of, celebrates and regulates emotion.

## EMOTION THEN AND NOW

The early modern period may have valued the expression or display of emotion in very different ways from twenty-first-century Western culture but the differences are not simple to define. A visitor to, say, one of the Royal Shakespeare Company's theatres in the UK today might regard it as just one site of legitimate and desired emotional expression. That audience member is likely to have been interpellated,[4] by films and television dramas, by advertising, by the therapeutic community, and in certain educational contexts, into what one might call an emotionally expressive being, one whose modes of emotional expression define the self. He or she may have been told by his or her schoolteachers that while expressing one's own emotions is valuable, the dramatic poetry in which Shakespeare expressed emotion is all the more so for its profundity and universality. If the kinds of anxieties around influence and mimesis expressed by the Puritan anti-theatrical tracts[5] have lasted at all over 400 years, they have shifted on to other media – films and computer games. Early modern drama, particularly that of Shakespeare, is overwhelmingly regarded by today's English-speaking cultural authorities as good for you, partly because it is supposedly so good at depicting characters' emotional expression. A recent scientific and educational agenda around 'emotional intelligence' and 'emotional literacy' has privileged emotion as part of a rationally regulated, functioning society, complicating once again a binary of reason and emotion that appears never to have been conceived of as simple in the first place. Shakespeare has played a part in this agenda, in the classroom and in training for the workplace.[6]

The theatre of Shakespeare's London was clearly valued by the state's highest authorities, yet it also held something of a precarious legal position.[7] If Hamlet's awe at the First Player's tears for Hecuba are anything to go by, the passions it portrayed were an essential part of its draw, despite the anxiety around the passions demonstrated by some of the treatises I will examine here. Are sermons such as Thomas Playfere's (see p. xiv), which describes too much weeping as destructive nature out of control, pointlessly attempting to legislate against the emotional outpourings of an essentially passionate culture which best expressed itself through its theatre? Were attempts to police the emotions through tracts and sermons no more successful than the repeatedly reimposed sumptuary laws of Elizabeth's reign, which uncover a society determined to indulge in sartorial excesses as much as an authority eager to rein them in?[8] A number of recent film and television productions in the UK have concerned themselves with the supposedly unbridled passions of this period. Popular characterizations of the 'Tudors and Stuarts' in television drama and documentary have suggested that if our own culture is exhorted to greater and greater outpourings of emotion, Shakespeare's contemporaries were even more ready to demonstrate the passions (particularly lust and anger, if Michael Hurst's *The Tudors* is anything to go by).[9] A documentary still on air at the time of writing, *Ian Hislop's Stiff Upper Lip*,[10] has characterized early modern England as a culture of wildly demonstrative shows of both anger and affection, in comparison to the repressed rigours of Victorian Stoicism that developed through the age of empire and in the English Public School (see p. 27). In the academy, 2011 has seen the publication of Richard Strier's monograph, *The Unrepentant Renaissance;* this rigorously historicist work demonstrates ways in which affect and emotion were highly valued in the dramatic, literary and religious works of the sixteenth and seventeenth centuries and points to a thriving anti-Stoical position in the art and society of the period.[11] Here, I too am going to assume that the expression of extreme emotion was something that people came to the theatre to see and hear – to take pleasure in, in fact. But rather than suggesting that it is completely mistaken to read anxiety around emotional expression in the cultural products of the early modern period, I want to argue that the theatre was a place for pushing at the boundaries of what society regarded as the legitimate expression of emotion, for interrogating and debating those boundaries.

Having begun to make claims for what this book will do in terms of early modern scholarship, I should state that one of its central purposes is to consider how actors and audiences deal with ideas about emotional excess in early modern drama today. Whether visitors to the theatre recognized a broadly similar spectrum of emotions in what they saw and heard on the early modern stage as they do now, or whether the different historical conditions in which the plays were produced and received make it impossible for us even to conceive of how early modern audiences may have felt in response to the emotions they saw and heard depicted on stage, my aim has been to draw the reader into a debate around what the theatre can do today with these historical/cultural differences and similarities. I am particularly interested in questions of how early modern audiences judged or valued the emotions they heard and saw performed and whether we judge or value differently. The language of the plays, the dramatic and literary traditions and conventions upon which they drew, the dramaturgy of the plays and the ways in which they were rhetorically structured to engage audiences, the architectural structures in which audiences were invited to engage with emotion expressed in theatrical fictions, the ideas circulating in early modern writings on the passions – all these cultural phenomena may be read in terms of what it might have been possible to feel in the early modern theatre. But if it is possible to make informed speculations about what kind of emotional expression was considered laudable or shameful, pitiable or risible, enjoyably or horribly excessive, how do we put those speculations to work in the theatre today? I hope that this book can be part of a dialogue between the theatre and the academy about the ways in which we receive and remake the cultural artefacts of the past.

## EMOTIONAL. EXCESS. SHAKESPEAREAN

### Emotional

All of the terms in the main title of this book are politically and historically contentious. The first Oxford English Dictionary (OED) citation of the adjective 'emotional' (as I have used it in the title here, to mean 'Of or relating to the emotions') is not until 1831.[12] The OED's first citation of the word 'emotion' to mean 'an agitation of mind, an excited mental state' is from 1602, though the common equivalent term to 'emotion' as it is currently conceived was 'passion' and even to name this as an 'equivalent' is to open oneself to the accusation of anachronism. As we will see, historians of the emotions have suggested that the shift from passion to emotion in common usage over 200 years reflects a shift in underlying concept, indeed a shift in somatic, psychological and cultural experience. The OED's 1602 citation does place 'passion' and 'emotion' in interesting proximity:

> 1602 T. LODGE tr. Josephus Wks. XV. iv. 388 The king entred into a strange passion…and in this emotion or rage of jealousie [Fr. *en ceste fureur de ialousie*] hardly contained he himselfe from killing his wife.

This might suggest that a shift is beginning to occur from the use of emotion to mean 'political agitation or unrest' (first OED citation 1562), or 'movement, disturbance or perturbation' (first OED citation 1594), to its current definition as of 'any strong mental or instinctive feeling, as pleasure, grief, hope, fear, etc., deriving esp from one's circumstances, mood, or relationship with others'.[13] In 1602, passions *are* movements, disturbances, perturbations of the mind. However, Lodge's use of the word 'emotion' in this context suggests that the word 'passion' has not yet accrued the positive and subjectivity-defining connotations that the word 'emotion' has in many English speaking cultures today. Thomas Dixon has pointed to anachronistic pitfalls of assuming that terms such as emotion and emotional, passion and passionate, feeling, affection and expression mean the same across history.[14] Neither can we assume that each of these terms has an equivalent in every historical period – that we are all feeling and expressing the same things across 400 years and simply naming them differently.

Here it is worth noting that the field of the history of the emotions contains an epistemological tension: broadly, between a discipline such as my own, namely Theatre and Performance Studies, which is interested in the ways in which language and history (arguably) constitute meaning, and the Sciences, whose overriding research imperative is to discover things about the material world which (arguably) pertain throughout history.

These two broad modes of inquiry need not entirely contradict one another. It is mainly only in the comic novel now that post-structuralist Humanities scholars are still be found berating scientists for their essentialism.[15] However, if a scientist were to demonstrate to me, as I have no doubt she could, that no matter what a seventeenth-century man's social class or religious belief was, he would still be flooded with adrenalin when fearful, I would reply that this material reality is not necessarily material to my interest in the cultural phenomena that produce fear, and legitimize or punish its expression. I am not so much interested in what is physically produced in moments when human beings are in the grip of strong passions. Perhaps it is humoral imbalance; unsurprisingly, writing in 2013, I do not believe this, though, like Michael Schoenfeldt, I often find that the language of Galenic medicine 'yields an [intuitively plausible] account of what it feels like to experience certain corporeal phenomena'[16]. Or it could be or hormonal and neurological activity, the science of which seems to me to be convincing. But I am more interested in which expressions or demonstrations of emotion are considered to be reasonable and legitimate in different historical and theatrical cultures, and which excessive, disapproved, shameful. I am interested in the binaries of reason and excess as they existed in the early modern period and as we read them today, and in the resultant sets of expressions and repressions, displays and hidings of emotion that are staged in the theatre and in everyday life.

Why use *Emotional Excess* in this book's title, then, when the early moderns would not have understood the phrase? Why not 'Passionate Excess', for example, to match early modern treatises on the 'passions', and to fit Hamlet's line from my subtitle? Aside from the issue of what 'Passionate' might mean to the reader today,[17] I want to retain, throughout this book, the sense of 'motion' in 'emotion' with which the early moderns would have been familiar and to take quite literally and theatrically the early idea that when in a heightened emotional state, we are 'moved'. Early modern figurations of the passions, as Thomas Dixon has pointed out, were founded upon Aristotelian concepts of rest and motion, taken up by Aquinas in his explication of the 'irascible' and 'concupiscible' passions[18] and drawn upon by the authors of the early modern treatises, such as Wright in his *Passions of the Mind in General* (see pp. 13–14, 113–14). I am interested here in the interrelationship of movement and emotion in the production of early modern drama today, and how attention to what those things meant in the theatre of the late sixteenth and early seventeenth centuries might give us interesting things to do and feel in the theatre today.

The first cited uses of the word emotion, then, before it came to be explicitly associated with human feeling, suggest political as well as somatic turbulence and movement. Underpinning all the examples of theatrical passions explored in this book is a sense in which all the passions are propulsive and political. Many of the early modern treatises on the passions figure them as turbulent movements it is impossible to control. Patience in the face of adversity is stasis, passion is movement (although melancholy, as we will see, produces a stasis of its own; see pp. 197–8). As such, the passions are a potential threat to social stability. Today, as the early moderns did, we speak of being 'moved' – but imagine someone being 'moved' by a news story or a fiction and I doubt the image conjured contains much actual movement. While 'moved' and 'moving' have become metaphors for a compassionate, often sorrowful, feeling 'towards' a person or incident, that 'towards' has lost its sense of direction, whereas 'moved' as it is used in the early modern drama is much more active: it can contain the same sense of compassionate feeling but usually results in someone being moved to do something. Burgundy's letter explaining his re-defection to the French in *1 Henry VI* reads:

> I have, upon especial cause,
> Mov'd with compassion of my country's wrack.
> Together with the pitiful complaints
> Of such as your oppression feeds upon,
> Forsaken your pernicious faction
> And join'd with Charles, the rightful King of France.
>
> (4.1.55–60)

Speaking of his father's past support of Bolingbroke, Hotspur relates that 'My father, in kind heart and pity moved,/Swore him assistance and perform'd it too' (*1 Henry IV*, 4.3.64–5). One can be moved to compassionate deeds and moved to angry ones, and even where there is no obvious move to action as a result of inner motion/emotion, being moved is associated with action and movement. 'A woman moved is like a fountain troubled' (5.2.143) says Katherine in her final speech of capitulation to her role as perfect wife. While your husband is obliged to move about the world for you, she argues, committing 'his body/To painful labour both by sea and land,/To watch the night in storms, the day in cold', the woman is fortunate enough to lie 'warm at home, secure and safe' (5.2.149–52). Women, at the end of *The Taming of the Shrew*, should stay 'unmoved' both mentally and physically – and it is difficult to extricate the two in early modern English. When Tullus Aufidius sees Caius Martius Coriolanus' tears in the face of his family's pleas and hears Martius give up the attack on Rome, Aufidius responds by telling Martius very simply, 'I was mov'd withal' (5.3.197). But in performance, Aufidius is rarely portrayed as 'moved' in the modern sense of empathetic tearfulness. His response is ambiguous – and in fact he is moved to have Coriolanus killed. Passion is motion/emotion in the early modern drama and often leads to passionate action. Emotion is thus a political issue for this period, in a way that has been masked by Western culture's current tendency to think of emotion as private and 'personal'. In what follows I consider ways in which the production of early modern drama today can re-politicize emotion for a modern audience.

My other reason for the use of the term 'emotional' in this title is connected to the equally contestable term 'the Shakespearean stage', by which I mean not only the stage of Shakespeare's historical period but the stages which continue to produce Shakespeare's work. This book is an exercise in linking theatre and cultural history to the ways in which we perform plays from the early modern period today. To make historical comparison, one inevitably start with the discourse through which one understands one's own moment, even as one acknowledges its partial inadequacy to the period studied. Using the words 'emotion' and 'emotional' acknowledges that I am writing about what audiences today would think of as having to do with 'emotion'. Having argued thus, I do not deny that the term 'emotional' has a problematic – because possibly misleading – history in the theatre. It is at the centre of a misunderstanding about acting – particularly about acting 400-year-old plays – which suggests that acting is all about how characters feel about things. But to re-politicize the emotional, to re-inflect it with its early modern sense of movement, I am going to start with this term, to which audiences in the West today feel they have a close relationship and which many assume speaks of something universal, transhistorical. I too read something transhistorical in this term – its sense of motion, even though that sense is lost to everyday usage. As we will see (pp. 193, 270n. 41), for a significant group of directors of Shakespeare today, powerful, engaging acting is underpinned not by 'emotion' in its current common sense of what we 'feel' about people and circumstances, or in the Stanislavskian sense of emotion memory (the generation of emotion for a character through remembering one's own emotions) but achieved through action, as Stanislavski also argued.[19] Stanislavski's technique of finding objectives for units of dramatic text – verbs that suggest what a character is trying to *do* with words – was intended to produce authentic emotion in the actor, readable by an audience. Read Stanislavski and his proponents and one finds a spiritual rhetoric which valorizes emotion and the inner life in ways that suggest a very different understanding of human subjectivity from an early modern one.[20] But his method of physical action propels performers towards and away from one another, like the concupisciple and irrascible passions of classical and early modern thought. Whether one moves away or towards, stays or goes, is of both political and theatrical importance and my analysis of theatrical emotion here is underpinned by this sense of emotion as movement.

**Excess**

There is significant disagreement within early modern studies about the supposed privileging of reason over passion and affection in the period – a debate, in fact, over what kinds of cultural anxieties or pleasures existed in relation to ideas of excess and the passions. As Richard Strier has cogently put it, the scholars he has called the 'new humoralists', led by Gail Kern Paster and Michael Schoenfeldt, have taken humoral theory to be central to an early modern understanding of the body, subjectivity, society and the cosmos – and how all of these might be regulated – so that for Schoenfeldt in particular, ' "the early modern regime seems to entail a fear of emotion," so that the great positive value becomes self-control, "the capacity to control rather than to vent emotion" '.[21] For Strier, Schoenfeldt overstresses the importance of reason and restraint in early modern literary culture, at the expense of attention to the evident and not particularly anxious pleasure taken in the erotic, the emotional and the culinary in Shakespeare, Herbert and Milton. On the one hand, *Emotional Excess on the Shakespearean Stage* could not have been conceived without the brilliant excavations and explorations of humours theory written by Paster and Schoenfeldt. The very notion of emotional excess in early modern drama depends upon an understanding, hugely influenced by these theorists, that the early moderns conceived of the passions *as* somatic excess. In a range of early modern discourses, humoral imbalance, which within normative bounds produced socially acceptable, or at least tolerated, emotions, also led to sickness and insanity. The passions, then, needed regulating, and while Strier has demonstrated that many of the early modern period's most significant Christian thinkers saw the passions as not only an inevitable but a desirable part of Godly life, the desirability of moderating and restraining the passions also emerges again and again in early modern writings on them.

However, I am broadly in Strier's camp when it comes to a desire to give pleasure equal weight with anxiety in an exploration of plays and performance events that were ultimately produced for people to enjoy. A still pertinent cultural materialist problematic relevant to this work was named by Jonathan Dollimore as the subversion/containment debate in the 1980s. The two sides of this debate were characterized by Dollimore, in the second edition of his *Radical Tragedy*, as British Cultural Materialists, who tended to find interrogation and subversion in the cultural products of the early modern period, and American New Historicists who were more inclined to see such potential subversions as contained within the limits permitted by early modern power structures and dominant ideologies.[22] At one end of the subversion/containment spectrum lies theatre as disruptive of social structures, norms and hierarchies; at the other, theatre as contained – indeed generated and reinforced by – these structures. In this book I engage in a different but related debate, one which I think is useful to characterize in terms of anxiety and pleasure. This is a book that uses discourses and critical tools that are indebted to Cultural Materialism, to determine the ways in which emotion was both policed and celebrated in the early modern theatre and the ways in which we use early modern drama to police and celebrate the expression of emotion today. I hope, though, that it also contains some challenges to an assumption that underpins much cultural materialist analysis of early modern drama and theatre: that the products of this theatre were challenging or subversive to early modern cultural norms, hierarchies and ideologies insofar as they demonstrated, revealed or produced *anxieties* about them. It is productive for a broadly leftist critical project if a dominant culture can be demonstrated to be anxious about the structures and norms it seeks to account for as natural, universal and stable, because then those structures and norms may be argued to be culturally constructed, contingent, inherently unstable and ultimately challengeable and changeable. The problem with the project of focusing predominantly on discovering the cultural anxieties that might emerge in the theatre production is that one is sometimes in danger of suggesting that early modern audiences went to the theatre primarily to be made to feel anxious – or perhaps that while, bewildered by a fug of false consciousness, people did in fact go there to be entertained, they inevitably left feeling thoroughly anxious and disconcerted.

There is a disjuncture between the notion of cultural anxiety and how it might somehow be immanent in cultural products and events, and the possible experiences of those who consumed or attended them. One issue here, perhaps, is that the study of actual audiences in theatres is methodologically challenging; it is easier to uncover cultural anxiety in the structures and discourses of artefacts and events, and either assume this anxiety was felt in their reception, or disregard whether or not it was. If we remind ourselves, on the other hand, of the obvious fact that within early capitalist culture, plays were written and produced to draw audiences to theatres and to give them pleasure, we are obliged, I believe, to give as much serious and as much political attention to the production of that pleasure as to the anxieties that may have emerged 'in excess' of it.

The phrase 'in excess of' has been a favourite of cultural materialist criticism and it is a useful one. It suggests that whatever hegemony is operating through or reflected in culture, things can happen, people can behave, words and actions can produce meaning beyond what a range of political authorities might desire, or even be able to consciously or linguistically conceive. In this phrase, excess is politically subversive: the word indicates that which dominant culture cannot contain, that which goes beyond and challenges monolithic meaning. Queer theory has made particularly liberating use of this notion of ideologically uncontainable excess of meaning. Eve Kosofsky Sedgwick writes:

> That's one of the things that 'queer' can refer to: the open mesh of possibilities, gaps, overlaps, dissonances and resonances, lapses and excesses of meaning when the constituent elements of anyone's gender, of anyone's sexuality aren't made (or can't be made) to signify monolithically.[23]

When people and systems with an interest in the maintenance of monolithic meaning are challenged by that which is 'in excess of' that meaning, then of course they may well demonstrate anxiety. Thus I am not arguing that anxieties around, say, hegemonic constructions of masculinity, figurations of race and alterity, or the regulation of slanderous language[24] do not exist in the early modern period and are not significant objects of study. However, rather than argue that early modern culture was predominantly stoical in its attitudes to the passions and that the performance of extreme emotion in the theatre must therefore have been received anxiously, I am going to be working on the assumption that the large number of people who attended the theatre in early modern London got pleasure from watching and hearing excesses of even distressing passions such as anger and grief. In the theatre, characters get too angry, laugh in the wrong places, commit crimes and go mad for love, cry for too long. They are sometimes condemned for it, simultaneously enjoyed for it; their emotional expression disrupts and exceeds authority, convention and the acceptable boundaries of sanity and subjectivity. The fact that this was and still seems to be immensely enjoyable for theatre audiences is partly the subject of this book.

## Shakespeare

This book's examples from recent productions are largely of works by Shakespeare, mainly because he is the early modern British playwright most produced by the British theatre. The book does not compare emotional expression in language across the works of early modern playwrights; there is no attempt to prove that one early modern author's work is any more emotionally expressive – or excessive – than another's, though the technology that may permit us to do so in very concrete terms is becoming more and more sophisticated.[25] It evidences Shakespeare's work as containing particularly interesting debates and contradictions about emotional excess and the theatre but also makes reference to other early modern dramatists.

Given how (relatively) well funded and popular with audiences the Royal Shakespeare Company is at the time of writing, given that Shakespeare's Globe manages to fill season after season of mainly Shakespeare in its reconstructed Elizabethan theatre, given that the National Theatre regularly gives over one of its main houses to a Shakespeare production that regularly sells out, the question 'Why perform Shakespeare's plays?' may have an obvious answer to many. This answer will include, for some, terms such as 'heritage', 'universal relevance' and 'the human condition'. But there is a tension between the activities and values of the theatre and the academy in the UK – and it extends to North America I think – when it comes to producing historical drama, a tension that arises particularly in the production of the works of Shakespeare. The theatre industry in the UK is highly invested in Shakespeare as a cultural brand and in continuing to produce his work in live performance. If asked about the Elizabethan and Jacobean theatre, those involved in the areas of British (or at least English) theatrical culture that receive some of the larger public subsidies and/or audiences would, I contend, be inclined to celebrate the period in which Shakespeare was writing as one of cultural and intellectual democracy – a time when theatre had a wider social demographic than it does now, a time when complex poetic dramas were enjoyed by audiences ranging from apprentices who paid a penny to stand in the yard, to the elite spectators at the indoor playhouses and at court.[26] Closely linked to this sense of a democratic period in cultural history is the notion of Shakespeare,[27] particularly, as a highly – or indeed the most – significant writer for his time and, as his co-actor and writer Ben Jonson had it, 'for all time'.[28] No matter the efforts within the academy at the end of the twentieth century to historicize the production and reception of Shakespeare, to demystify the cultural and ideological processes by which he became 'top poet' and generally to debunk bardolatry,[29] producers and audiences of Shakespeare in the theatre are still quite comfortable with assumptions about his universal relevance. While many theatre history and performance studies scholars assume that we should have a sceptically historicist attitude towards ostensible links between plays written 400 years ago and our own attitudes and experiences, the theatre industry – at least the part of it that produces Shakespeare – assumes we should celebrate these links and that we are almost bound to find them as we work on the plays in rehearsal. Theatre companies generally produce 400-year-old plays because they believe they, and particularly the plays of Shakespeare, somehow 'speak to us' now – and speak to us through common emotional languages, or better express that which we are 'feeling' now.

Here, I am not aiming to repair the supposedly transparent window on to the human condition supposedly encoded in Shakespeare's drama, which was shattered by Cultural Materialism in the the 1980s. But neither do I contend that the early modern drama simply offers us a series of passionate *faux amis*, a set of emotional expressions which we only imagine we can understand but which in fact are born of a set of ignorant and anachronistic hermeneutic assumptions. There are emotions, psychic movements towards and away from what might make people laugh or cry, in the plays of Shakespeare and his contemporaries that we can still understand and may sometimes still experience; there are both similarities and differences in how we value and legitimate those emotions. What I do want to argue is that by understanding the differences pertaining to emotional expression and its cultural valuation that exist between Then and Now, we might attempt to perform Then in a range of more exciting and challenging ways Now.[30] So because this is a book not only about early modern drama but about its recent theatrical production, I also consider here how the work of Shakespeare might interrogate and debate values and judgements around emotional expression with its twenty-first-century audiences. I argue that because the expression of the passions was a more clearly contended issue in the early modern period than it is today, in Western cultures that consider emotional expression to be generally A Good Thing, early modern drama can foreground for 'us' what I will call the politics of emotional expression. For despite the sense offered to us by a range of authorities that emotional expression is mentally healthy and key to valued self-actualization, the question of who is permitted to express what and when is surely one for every period and society.

## SOMATIC PASSIONS: ANGER

Some of the most significant and exciting recent work in the history of early modern emotions has been undertaken by scholars who have re-envisioned the early modern mind-set by drawing attention to the all-pervading sense of the somatic and its link to the physical world in early modern thought. I am thinking particularly here of Gail Kern Paster and her work on the somatic passions in *Humoring the Body*, after publication of which no writer on emotion in early modern literature should be in danger of thinking of early modern human subjects as psychological subjects with bodies attached. Paster's work suggests that the ways in which the early moderns conceived of the passions working in the body were radically different from today's psychological approaches. She explores the porous nature of the early modern body as the period conceived it, and the constant, shifting and reciprocal relationships that were assumed to exist between mind and body, reason and passion, human and world, human body and heavenly bodies. Indeed, her work challenges all of these binaries to the point where their very usefulness to describe early modern experience – particularly in terms of mind and body – are put in doubt. Paster discusses Galenic humoral theory and the ways in which the quotidian experience of its workings in the bodies of early modern men and women is encoded in cultural products.[31]

A determination to complicate binaries gives rise to awkward questions when considering a period which, while it certainly had an extraordinarily holistic understanding of how the universe worked, was also, morally and ethically, binarist in the extreme: in its understanding of good and evil, order and chaos (political and cosmological), male and female,[32] and, most significantly for this study, mean and excess, reason and passion. As we will see in Chapter One, '"A Brain that Leads my Use of Anger": Choler and the Politics of Spatial Production', the reason/passion binary is certainly widely circulated in the early modern period and posits a reasoning self that seeks continually to control the somatic excesses of the passions. In reiterating this binary I may open myself to accusations of a reactionary return to long-since debunked thinking. In *From Passions to Emotions*, Thomas Dixon suggests that a range of scholarly works on the history of the emotions published since the 1970s have sought to rehabilitate the passions from an antagonism with reason which they have reinforced and exaggerated to the point of falsifying cultural history:

> It is not the case that prior to the 1970s no one had realized that thinking, willing and feeling were (and should be) intertwined with one another. Almost everybody had realized this. Too many contemporary writers still appeal, nonetheless, to the idea [...] that either a particular individual, or school of thought, or period, or even the entire history of philosophy has been characterized by the view that the emotions (or feelings or passions) are entirely insidious and are to be subjected at all times to almighty reason.[33]

Dixon is writing primarily about the eighteenth and nineteenth centuries, so when I reply that this characterization of the 'insidious' passions that 'are to be subjected to almighty reason' is exactly how Seneca and many of his early modern antecedents wrote about the passions, especially of anger, I am in one sense dealing with a period too early to be relevant to his argument. Scholars writing about the passions in the late sixteenth and early seventeenth centuries in terms of humoral theory may both agree and disagree with Dixon: agree with him, in that in the holistic world view that contained the Galenic body cannot not explicitly permit the separation of mind and body, reason and passion that Descartes theorized in the mid-seventeenth century;[34] disagree, on the other hand, in that the notion of reason controlling the passions and their bodily sources in the humours is absolutely conceivable for the early modern mind-set, whether or not it is always as desirable as it is for Seneca and his followers, and whether or not it is actually ever possible. The human subject, then, while beset with the unpredictable workings of his or her passionate body in the world, and always dealing with the somatic circulation and imbalances of the humours, has also a duty of control of his or her somatic passions. She or he must therefore have a sense of an agent, a self, that might endeavour to do the controlling. Early modern writings on the emotions, while always assuming that the physical and the mental are concomitant and co-dependent, also assume a God-given reason that might, where appropriate, endeavour to choose to think or behave otherwise – in other directions – than in the ways his or her turbulent passions are in danger of forcing him or her.[35]

In Chapter One, I consider Shakespeare's play *Coriolanus* as a play about anger, its uses and its value. Caius Martius Coriolanus is obviously a figure whose anger is put to use by the state in time of war; this anger turns out to be useless for the business of peacetime governing. It emerges clearly in this play that the individual's control over the movement of his passions is politically expedient. I explore the play in the light of its source text Plutarch's *Lives*,[36] and Plutarch's and Seneca's essays on anger,[37] which figure anger as a terrifying force, in excess of what a community, society or state needs its members to do or to be. I then consider the ways in which Martius' anger has played out in theatrical (and non-theatrical) space in recent productions. Having suggested here that emotion is motion in the early modern drama, I argue in Chapter One that *Coriolanus* is a play in which anger moves its central figure across the stage and I explore what meanings that might produce for audiences today. Productions explored in this chapter are a *Coriolanus* at Shakespeare's Globe in London, whose lead actor has read Martius' anger in modern, psychological terms. This performance in a theatre that very clearly generates meaning spatially produced an exceptionally pro-Martius *Coriolanus*.[38] I consider the ways in which anger moves Ralph Fiennes' Martius through the spaces of war and peace in his *Coriolanus* film, in a way that more clearly politicizes Martius' 'use of anger'.[39] I end by suggesting, via two productions that generate meaning through site (Ivo van Hove's 'Roman Tragedies' *Coriolanus*[40] and Mike Pearson and Mike Brookes'

*Coriolanus* in an RAF aircraft hanger[41]) that it is possible to produce a *Coriolanus* in space, in ways that foreground a politics of anger for a modern audience.

## THE EMOTIONAL ETHICS OF BEING AN AUDIENCE: LAUGHTER

How is it possible to compare the emotional responses of early modern and current audiences? The kinds of ethical considerations that come into play in a study of living subjects make discerning possible answers to questions of emotion just as problematic for our own period, albeit differently so, as for the study of emotions in history. I have recently worked with a number of graduate students who have considered audience responses in the theatre today and who want to rise to Helen Freshwater's challenge of talking to actual audiences[42] rather than assuming audience response. Even putting aside questions of audience numbers to be surveyed and range of demographic, the scholar of theatre audiences faces some daunting challenges produced by expectation, obligation and education, which arise when an audience member is faced with a lengthy questionnaire, or a researcher with a clipboard and a form from the university's ethics committee to sign. These are not challenges I have faced here. In studying early modern theatre, we have a paucity of accounts of what audience members actually felt about the theatre they visited and we are obliged to speculate and extrapolate from these, from the ways in which plays and performance events appear to have been constructed to elicit audience response, and from the historical documents that suggest what it was possible to feel and what it was socially acceptable to express in the late sixteenth and early seventeenth centuries. This is not a book about audiences in the early modern period *per se* but it inevitably speculates about them, because it explores the ideas that may have been circulating among them and the kinds of responses that plays suggest were expected from them. Similarly, it is not about audience responses to the recent productions of early modern drama I examine, but the book inevitably references ideas that are circulating now about emotion and emotional expression and the ways in which productions have been constructed to elicit emotional response from audiences today. In Chapter Two, '"Do You Mock Old Age, You Rogues?": Excessive Laughter, Cruelty and Compassion' I do have questions to ask about the ethics of 'audiencing' or being an audience[43] that cross the early modern and the contemporary.

Laughter, of course, is not an emotion but an action, a behaviour or an expression of affect. One may be said to 'feel' anger, love and grief, whereas laughter is something one does – or emits. However, it is of particular interest to this study because it is, both commonsensically and in the discourses of science, involuntary, in excess of will and reason, something that happens as a result of emotions. It is in and of itself a somatic excess, a sound we usually make in excess of conscious decision. In asking what a historical culture finds funny, we are brought into contact with both seemingly universal and oddly alien cultural phenomena. What one culture finds funny, another will find tasteless, cruel, excessive. Yet what one might call the dramaturgical structure of laughter may be traced across history and science: laughter at the unexpected, laughter at the fall of the proud and pompous, laughter at ourselves as a means of social bonding, laughter at others as a means of social exclusion. Chapter Two takes as its object of study mad characters in the early modern drama, examines whether they may have been funny for early modern audiences (it seems clear that they were) and whether it may be possible to allow them to be so today – or whether that would simply be 'too much'. Notions of madness are central to this book, because for early modern medicine, excessive passion *was* madness and was caused by the same humoral imbalances as the passions. Mad figures in the early modern drama are excessive subjectivities, which push at the boundaries of vocal and gestural sense. They are objects, I will suggest, of both comedy and compassion, and subjects of their own dramas, into which they draw on- and off-stage audience members alike. Their presence and their interaction with audiences produce communities of laughter, framing and reframing the kinds of emotional responses it is socially acceptable to share publicly. In this chapter I consider plays that feature the incarcerated mad and foolish[44] – Middleton and Rowley's *The Changeling*,[45] Webster's *The Duchess of Malfi*,[46] Dekker and Middleton's *The Honest Whore*[47] – exploring how recent productions of the first two of these plays have dealt with the potentially embarrassing – to modern audiences – excesses of these figures. I then turn to Malvolio in his makeshift madhouse and a new play by Tim Crouch, *I Malvolio*,[48] which is structured around the framing of its audience as figures of excess and excessive laughers.

## PLEASURABLE EXCESSES: LOVE

Both the early modern period and our own fell, fall, 'madly in love'. The lover is repeatedly a real and metaphorical madperson in the early modern drama[49] and today's modern popular love song. The metaphor of love's madness segues into scientific reality for both periods: Burton and Ferrand (see pp. 15, 124–5, 139)[50] write extensively on love melancholy, while recent endocrinological studies of the somatic state of being in love have related it to states of insanity.[51] Love in both periods is an emotional state[52] that draws upon the metaphors of past scientific moments, metaphors which still seem intuitively to describe the way we feel when we are in love, or lose a lover. The metaphor of the heart as the seat of emotion is still so common today as to be almost too obvious to mention: hearts ache in love and are broken by lovers, emotionally intuitive hearts rule rational heads in matters of love, even as we understand the heart to be a pump for the circulation of the blood.[53] In the early seventeenth century, early understandings of the workings of the retina had displaced the Galenic theory of the eye beam, according to which beams emerge from an object being seen and pierce the eye of the beholder. But, as Eric Langley has pointed out, for poetry this was still the most potent metaphor for describing the way in which love 'enters' a lover, and the mutuality of obsessive focus that two lovers experience as the eye beams of each pierce the other.[54] In the early modern period a perfect, selfless love is held out to humankind by God, but human love is one of the somatic passions and gives rise to a complex and inextricable range of pleasures and anxieties in treatises on the passions and in early modern drama.

In Chapter Three, I suggest that the problem with the excesses of love in the early modern drama is not primarily love's association with bodily, ungodly lust, even though lust is differentiated from love at various points in the drama. Because love for the early moderns is one of the somatic passions (see p. 114) it partakes of all the potential problems of excess that the other passions do. Love's overpowering nature drives figures in the drama to extremes of action and inaction. It undoes the gendered subject, rendering men effeminate and turning women into active agents in their own dramas. The notion of what we might call a romantic love, which is based on sexual attraction but is less selfishly driven than 'mere' lust, certainly exists in the drama but this does not rescue love from the turbulent excesses of somatic passion. Love is un-self-ish because it undoes the self. It suggests that the undoing of reason, where reason is equated with self-control, is pleasurable. Whereas for angry Caius Martius, anger undoes that which his society finds reasonable and makes him most like himself, love in *All's Well that Ends Well* and *Antony and Cleopatra* is both unreasonable and de-individuating on the one hand and produces agency and action on the other. In Chapter Three, I focus on these two plays, in which love and lust drive men and women to various kinds of action in excess of themselves and their societal roles, without replacing the social self with a fantasy of independent selfhood as is indulged by Caius Martius Coriolanus. The title of this chapter contains Orsino's exhortation to his musicians to give him excess of the food of love, so that he may sicken of it and purge it from himself. *All's Well that Ends Well* and *Antony and Cleopatra* seem to proffer a very different concept of love from this conventional notion that in love, one can always have too much of a good thing. Custom famously cannot stale Cleopatra's infinite variety because, in this play, it is the infinite and impossible variety of the theatre, of which one can never have an excess. Taking pleasure in the unpredictable emotional worlds of other human beings, always in excess of one's own knowledge, is what love and theatre offer in these two plays.

## A POLITICS OF EMOTION: GRIEF

There is a tendency in a range of today's popular discourses – those of the media and popular science, and the everyday language that both feeds and reflects them – to suggest that emotions are a personal matter, paradoxically both felt in similar psychosomatic ways by everyone in a culture or community but at the same time uniquely a part of each individual. Theories of the history of grief have, as we will see, suggested that the early modern period was one in which a shift occurred towards the privileging of the personal expression of emotion. It was a time, for example, when funeral services began to emphasize the social standing of the deceased less and the personal grief of the bereaved more.[55] In the UK at the time of writing, the government is exhibiting an odd mix of the now traditional conservative desire to champion the individual and minimize state intervention into the pursuit of his or her needs and desires on the one hand, and a new interest in how the state might support or even bring about emotional states – particularly of happiness (see p. 221). In constructing and reflecting a politics of grief, as I contend that Shakespeare's *Richard III* and *Hamlet* do, the early modern drama is particularly well positioned to open up debates around how emotion may be valued and regulated today. The productions upon which I focus in this chapter do not suggest to me that the same kinds of dominant attitudes to emotion, or the same means of its cultural regulation, pertained to the early period as they do today. But the question of how much grief was too much, and the points in these plays which suggest that refusing to stop remembering the dead may have been a subversive act, can, I think, open up parallel and related questions for audiences of these dramas, as we enter a period when the government seems to be exercised about how happy we are.

The Royal Shakespeare Company (RSC)'s *Richard III* of 2011 to 2012[56] and the National Theatre's *Hamlet* of 2010,[57] examined in this chapter, do not reject the modern notion of emotional expression as central to the construction of the self. I have chosen them particularly because, in different ways, they draw upon traditions of theatrical realism that have individual characters' emotions at their centres. But both productions place individual character psychology within political matrixes produced by scenography (*Hamlet*) and conscious theatricality (*Richard III*), and both thus permit a consideration of emotion's expression and its repression, its excesses and its regulation. These productions foreground grief while going beyond the plausible and empathetic performance of that emotion, to explore its politics. As productions that seem highly conscious of their own uses of space, movement and proxemics, moreover, they are well placed to conclude a book that asks the reader to consider the links between emotion and motion in early modern drama.

Contemporary Western culture is concerned with the right to feel and express emotion; many of us are taught that emotional expression defines us, that it is the means by which one might 'get in touch with one's self'. The triggering of emotion is an important means of getting us to self-define through consumer choice and community allegiance, a means of producing an illusion of individual choice in a world of marketing demographics and mass media manipulation. Consider the ways in which emotions are both privileged and manipulated in contemporary life, and one may be tempted to return to Stoical *apatheia*, with its almost meditative emphasis on letting that pass which does not directly relate to the living of a virtuous life. What the theatre might do, in staging a period when the question 'how much emotion is too much?' seemed to be an important cultural and political question, is allow us both to take pleasure in the production of extreme emotion and consider it at a reasonable – or reasoning – distance.

# CHAPTER ONE

## 'A BRAIN THAT LEADS MY USE OF ANGER': CHOLER AND THE POLITICS OF SPATIAL PRODUCTION.

PETRUCHIO
I tell thee, Kate, 'twas burnt and dried away,
And I expressly am forbid to touch it,
For it engenders choler, planteth anger;
And better 'twere that both of us did fast,
Since, of ourselves, ourselves are choleric,
Than feed it with such over-roasted flesh.
Shakespeare, *The Taming of the Shrew* (4.1.158–63)

BRUTUS
Put him to choler straight; he hath been used
Ever to conquer, and to have his worth
Of contradiction. Being once chaf'd, he cannot
Be rein'd again to temperance; then he speaks
What's in his heart, and that is there which looks
With us to break his neck.
Shakespeare, *Coriolanus* (3.3.25–30)

### GETTING ANGRY AT WORK

At the time of writing, a Youtube search for the phrase 'angry at work' brings up a number of bizarre video recordings of people losing their tempers in office contexts and violently breaking office equipment. The first search result that appears has been online since December 2006 and features a man who cannot get his computer to link to a remote printer in his open-plan office. After a number of attempts at printing, the man rips his computer monitor from his desk and smashes it, screen-downwards, on to a nearby photocopier, whose buttons he presses in a frenzied parody of copying whatever is on his computer screen. The incident does not appear to have been staged. This is a large office, full of other workers sitting at their work stations or moving about the space, all of whom stop in incredulous fascination or horror at the incident. The suddenness and incongruity of this office worker's anger is, of course, comical; that is no doubt why it has been uploaded to Youtube. I also suspect that it has remained online and had close to 70,000 viewings to date, because it is vicariously pleasurable to see someone so angry that he no longer cares about the consequences of his actions, in a working environment that one might imagine is highly regulated: both overtly, by the corporation that owns the office, and socially, by those who have to work in this crowded environment. This man has become so frustrated that he no longer cares about the rules and is the undoubted hero of the piece as a result.

Daniel M. Gross, author of *The Secret History of Emotion: From Aristotle's 'Rhetoric' to Modern Brain Science*[1] would no doubt baulk at my using such an incident to open a chapter about excessive anger in early modern drama. For Gross, although

> [t]hrowing a temper tantrum or fuming or muttering curses under one's breath might strike us as a lesser degree of the same emotion exercised by a vengeful tyrant who forces a defiant subject to eat his own son for dinner [...] it would not strike Aristotle so. We would do well to pay close attention to Aristotle and his early modern relatives if we hope to see our way beyond the current platitudes of emotion.[2]

Gross goes on to explain that for Aristotle, anger is produced by social relationships of inequality, and asserts that, where a king is angry, he 'is angry because his entitlement is threatened, and without that extracognative entitlement manifest in the world around him, the king would have no angry thoughts at all'.[3] I assume that by 'the current platitudes of emotion' Gross is referring to a hazy, post-Freudian, popular cultural notion that everyone has emotions to express and that the expression of emotion is essential to self-realization, its repression psychically damaging. My claim that our Youtube office worker is the hero of his broken printer film may be read as one such platitude. It is ludicrous, perhaps, even to use the word 'hero' in this context. The office worker whose society might consider him in need of an anger management class has no objective correlative thunder to underscore his tantrum, he stands for no principles of *Romanitas*; it is meaningless to compare such an incident with the wrath of Lear in the storm or the fury of Caius Martius Coriolanus when the Roman soldiers turn back in fear from Corioles. In this chapter I am not, precisely, going to compare these things. But first I should say that although I agree with Gross that anger, both for Aristotle and his 'early modern relatives', was 'constituted…in relationships of inequality',[4] this does not mean that the anger of poor citizens was never considered in early modern discourses about anger. Second, I should explain that in this chapter I will be examining a range of recent stage versions (and one film) of Shakespeare's *Coriolanus* and exploring the ways in which, in the production of early modern drama, social attitudes to extreme and excessive emotion 'now' and 'then' are always in dialogue. The photograph in Figure 1 is from Ivo van Hove's celebrated and much-cited *Roman Tragedies* version of *Coriolanus* and appears to be an image of Caius Martius 'losing it' at work.

This chapter examines Shakespeare's *Coriolanus* and the ways in which Caius Martius' excessively choleric disposition, and recent social attitudes to and understandings of anger, come together in some recent productions of the play, to foreground anger and its social meanings across history. I have used Volumnia's assertion that she has 'a brain that leads [her] use of anger' in the chapter's title because I am interested in the notion that a potentially violent emotion might be *used*. This idea speaks to a subjectivity that we might indeed regard as 'early modern': a sense of self to be found not solely in the somatic production of the passions on the one hand, or in man's God-given 'reason' on the other, but in

Figure 1: Caius Martius Coriolanus (Gijs Scholten van Aschat) in *Coriolanus* (*The Roman Tragedies* by Toneelgroep Amsterdam), dir. Ivo van Hove. Courtesy Jan Versweyweld/BAM

the nexus between the two, in the way in which reason considers, controls, makes use of a passion like anger. The state at peace in *Coriolanus* demands this control, this use of emotion. How is it used? How might its uses in the fictional/historical power structures of early modern drama provoke productive questions for us today about the relationship between the individual and power, state, society?

## HEROIC ANGER

In an interview with *Time Out* London, Japanese director Yukio Ninagawa remarks of Toshiaki Karasawa, the lead actor in his production of *Coriolanus*,[5] that 'He's a very Stoic actor. He manages to contain himself even though he has strong passions inside, which gives him a dignity very appropriate for Coriolanus.'[6] The director of this extraordinarily beautiful and startlingly athletic production certainly has some supporters in linking Caius Martius with Stoicism. "Consider Coriolanus, the legendary fifth century BC warrior who turns against his city for banishing him', writes Nancy Sherman in her essay 'Stoic Meditations and the Shaping of Character. The Case of Educating the Military':

> He is portrayed by Shakespeare as the paragon Stoic warrior. Physically strong and detached, more at home in the battlefields than with his wife and son, his is the military man par excellence. Fearless, he sheds few tears.[7]

An anti-Stoical contemporary of Shakespeare writes of Martius as an example of Stoical uncouthness: 'Coriolanus was by nature a Stoic, and his roughness of manners is justly and worthily reproved.'[8] 'Stoical' in common parlance has come to mean one who can endure pain or hardship without complaining. This quality is in line with the Stoic notion of *apatheia*, and Martius' tendency to belittle his own injuries of course fits this description. But his inability to control his anger is in diametric opposition to Stoic philosophy on the passions and the play's narrative turns on the fact that the Roman general, unlike Karasawa in Ninagawa's description, cannot 'contain himself'. Whereas Seneca argues against Aristotle that it is reason, not anger, that should motivate 'warlike exploits',[9] Martius' personal fury at Aufidius, then at the Romans who have banished him, certainly seems to motivate Martius' plans of violent action. When it is in Martius' interests to contain his anger and behave 'mildly', he is unable to do so. When Martius reneges on his promise to lead an attack on Rome, his anger when his old enemy calls him 'traitor' (5.6.85) and 'boy' (101) leads to his death at Volscian hands. Seneca regards anger as entirely destructive and in opposition to man's true nature: 'A man is born to help other, wrath for the general ruin of all'.[10] The ideal, reasoning man will not entertain the passion of anger even for a moment. But as far as Martius himself is concerned, Martius *is* his anger: 'Why did you wish me milder? Would you have me/ False to my nature? Rather say I play/The man I am'. (3.2.14–16). Martius hardly conforms to Seneca's ideal of passionless *apatheia*: he claims barely to feel his war wounds and is impressively constant in the face of his friends and family when they beg him to save Rome, until he finally capitulates to his mother – but he is otherwise the precise opposite of the Senecan ideal, from his first rant to the Citizens in 1.1.166–87.[11]

What Ninagawa and Karasawa offer instead of Caius Martius' all-consuming anti-Stoical choler is a contained dignity appropriate to the production's *mise-en-scène*. The stage space for this *Coriolanus* was almost entirely taken up with a huge staircase, up and down which the Citizens tumbled in terror at Caius Martius' voice and presence, and over which the production's virtuosic fight scenes took place.[12] At the top of these stairs stood four formidable statues of Heavenly Kings, guardians to Bhuddist shrines, which, alarmingly, appeared further down the steps later in the production, as if the very upholders of the faith had moved into the human world to support Martius. This Samurai Martius is all tragic honour, the Citizens all cowering comedy: upon Martius' first entry, they all tumble downstairs. Reviewing Ninagawa's production in the *Guardian*, Lyn Gardner suggests that though this is, in ways she does not explain, an apolitical *Coriolanus* (perhaps she means that, unlike many productions and adaptations in the play's stage history, it doesn't have an explicit political/historical setting) it also contains a critique of violence and masculinity:

> In this Japanese-language production, Coriolanus is a deeply flawed man who is felled not by another's sword, but by a failure of masculinity and an inability to visualise a world in which it is not brute strength but humility and compromise that are required. Even in death, his empty sword hand continues to slice the air. It is like watching a clockwork toy soldier run down.[13]

But I would argue that there was little of *brute* strength in this Martius; or rather, his brutality was filtered through the mythology of Samurai honour and the elegant virtuosity of the actor's stage-fighting and acrobatic abilities. The continuing slicing of the air by Martius as he dies suggests, certainly, that he believes to the end that Warrior is the only role he can and should ever fill – and this is not a role that the political world of the play could use or contain. For this audience member, the Warrior role was not interrogated in the way that Gardner's clockwork toy soldier image implies. Rather the world of realpolitik was the smaller, the more ridiculous, for not being able to contain the myth that is Coriolanus. As several reviewers remarked, the first thing the audience is confronted with in this production its own image, reflected in designer Tsukasa Nakagoshi's huge mirrors. These also reflected the crowds and fight scenes, multiplying the figures tumbling and fighting, blurring the perimeters of the playing space. The Citizens come from the auditorium and line up to look back at us and bow before the performance begins: 'Clearly we are supposed to be one with them', remarks Howard Loxton of the *British Theatre Guide.*[14] Perhaps we, as they, were too overawed by the virtuoso performance of the Warrior finally to be permitted a critique of Martius' politics.

Would the distance between Shakespeare's England and the Ancient Rome which so fascinated its educated population have produced a similarly mythologized Coriolanus in the early seventeenth century? My answer is that the social and material reality of Caius Martius' anger may have produced a leaky, ambiguous kind of heroism, one that sometimes excites and awes, but also invites critique. I am going to suggest here that the politics of *Coriolanus*, the position the audience is invited to take on its debates and conflicts, is inflected by the positioning of Caius Martius' anger in social and theatrical space.

## CHOLER

First, I want to consider some of the ideas about anger that were circulating in early modern England. The early modern understanding of the passions as material and somatic is reflected above in *The Taming of the Shrew*, as Petruchio torments his new bride by insisting that the meat they were about to eat is burnt and that to eat it would exacerbate their 'choleric' (4.1.60) tendencies.

Burnt meat 'engenders choler' and must be avoided by those who already have a predominance of choler (or yellow bile) circulating in their bodies.[15] Petruchio and Kate are 'of themselves' already choleric (4.1.62) (hot, dry, quick-tempered), so better to fast than to make things worse. In this construction, our 'selves' comprise: what is in and of the body, including the passions, generated as they are by humoral predominance and motion; what is external to the body and might pass into and through it, like food; and, by implication, reason, which Petruchio here suggests should control the humorous predominance by choosing not to eat burnt meat.

The joke in this scene, of course, is that there is nothing wrong with the meat: Petruchio's suggestion that the hungry, exhausted Kate should fast rather than eat it is part of his ludicrous, albeit finally effective, taming game. The idea that 'being choleric' is an excuse for Petruchio and Kate's excessive anger is, it seems, to be laughed at as much as recognized by an Elizabethan audience. Like the notion that the stars control our fate, scorned by Edmund in *King Lea*r (1.2.119–33), although many of his audience may well have believed it, Petruchio's idea that the humours control 'ourselves' appears ridiculous here and is elided with his daft insistence that the meat is burnt when it is not.

This is not to claim that humoural theory is merely residual in Elizabethan thinking by the time Shakespeare wrote *The Taming of the Shrew*. But enjoyment of the play depends upon the assumption that Kate particularly, as the Shrew to be Tamed, ought not to be so angry, no matter what her physiological temperament. Recent productions have had Kate battered, or even raped, into submission[16] before she speaks her last soliloquy; others have played the final speech as a conspiracy between Petruchio and Katharina to win the bet on who has the most submissive wife; still others have made it clear that Katharina has not really been tamed at all.[17] But however distasteful we may now find the notion of willingly placing our hands beneath our husband's feet (*Shrew* 5.2.178), Elizabethan audiences may well have accepted that Kate's last speech is indicative of her newly learned ability to control herself and her choler. Psycho-physical temperament is one element in a complex matrix of selfhood in early modern drama, whereby notions of indulgence and restraint, reason and passion, free will and given temperament, 'self' and society are debated and held in tension. In this comedy, the self that is produced by humoral predominance gives way to the self that conforms to society's needs and conventions.

In this chapter I focus primarily on Caius Martius Coriolanus, whose choleric predominance cannot ultimately be controlled. He is a man whose inability to be 'rein'd again to temperance' leads to his exile, who momentarily lets himself be persuaded from his wrath by his mother and family, but who finally dies in a furious temper at the slights of his enemy Aufidius. Anger in this play is both one of the defining characteristics of this dramatic figure, and an excess, a disease, that Menenius vainly hopes can be cured (3.1.296). I am going to assume, then, that *Coriolanus* is a play about anger. I have not made a survey of recent spectators or readers of the play but I would imagine that this is not what most of them would answer in response to the question 'What is *Coriolanus* about?' 'Politics', or 'governance and citizenship' or 'the exigencies of war and peace' would, I think, be more likely answers. But conceiving *Coriolanus* as being 'about anger' does not make it any less 'about' the politics of cities in war and at peace. True, anger is Martius' personal problem. When he is angry, then he 'speaks/What's in his heart'; he is most himself and the Tribunes can bring about his downfall. Unlike Lear, who becomes less himself when overcome with anger (he goes mad, and as Bruce Smith has pointed out, loses both authority and masculine identity[18]), Martius suggests that it is the suppression of his anger that would lead to loss of individuated, male identity. For Martius, his anger must be expressed in certain situations or he will not be 'the man I am', whereas peacetime politics requires a social construction of selfhood that necessitates the controlled use of the passions.

As we have seen in the Introduction to this volume, Shakespeare's plays stage a range of attitudes to the passions and to the notions of expressing, extirpating and suppressing them which were circulating during the period, even within the one figure of Hamlet. I am going to give some attention here to the stoical notion that anger is of itself excessive – in excess of what is essential to human nature – and that its feeling and expression should be avoided at all costs, not because I consider that this how anger is staged in *Coriolanus*, but because this attitude to anger, circulating in classical writings available to the early moderns, is so alien to Western popular culture today. Popular psychology tells us that it is healthy to express anger within circumstances where it cannot permanently hurt anyone; that repressed anger will be 'acted out' elsewhere if it is not safely expressed around the time of its provocation; that violent anger expressed in criminal acts are expressions of past trauma; that anger should be 'managed' rather than extirpated altogether. Shakespeare's source for *Coriolanus*, North's Plutarch, on the other hand, has much to say about Caius Martius' anger, none of it positive. Plutarch's essay from the *Moralia* on anger takes the Stoic line that we are better off suppressing it entirely. Indeed, the whole point of a treatise on anger for the Ancients, and for the early modern writers who translated them and wrote their own treatises on the matter, is to discover 'how [it] may be pacified',[19] to find remedies for its 'fatal and tragical effects', as Nicholas Coeffeteau has it.[20] Expressing anger in safe and healthy circumstances does not appear to be one of these remedies. The very title of Plutarch's essay on the subject, translated by Philomen Holland, is 'Of Meekness, or How a Man Should Refrain Choler' or 'How to Bridle Anger'.[21] Although there are those who, in early modern/classical thinking, are naturally choleric, anger is, for these treatise writers, at the same time *un*natural in that it overwhelms reason and distorts even the strongest characteristics an individual might possess, such as avarice or ambition. Plutarch writes of anger that:

> like as that malady according to Hippocrates, is of all others, worst and most dangerous, wherein the visage of the sick person is most disfigured and made unlikest itself; so, I seeing those that were possessed of choler

> and, (as it were) beside themselves thereby, how their face was changed, their colour, their countenance, their gate and their voice quite altered, I imagined thereupon until my self a certain form and image of this malady, as being mightily displeased in my mind, if haply at any time I should be seen of my friends, my wife and the little girls my daughters, so terrible and so far moved and transported beside myself.[22]

Seneca figures anger as an enemy in battle who (like Caius Martius at the gates of Corioles) must not even be allowed to enter the mind, but 'is to be driven from our borders, for when he is entered and hath gotten the gates, he taketh no condition with his captives'. This is because the mind cannot objectively separate itself from the passions and once it has been penetrated by a passion as violent as anger, its physical constitution is materially and dangerously changed. It *becomes* anger:

> For at that time the mind is not retired neither exteriorly examineth she affections, to the intent she suffereth them not to have further progress than they should, but is changed herself into passion, and therefore can she not revoke that profitable and wholesome force [i.e. reason], which is already betrayed and weakened.[23]

Although anger infiltrates and materially changes the mind, Seneca separates mind and body in his analysis of anger, suggesting that initial provocations to anger are merely somatic and that the mind should work to calm itself rather than permitting anger to 'overleap reason':

> For if any man suppose that paleness, and trickling down of tears, and filthy pollution, or a deep fat sigh, or eyes suddenly incensed, or any such like thing, is a token of affection, and a sign of the mind, he is deceived, neither understandeth he, that these are the agitations of the body. [...] Wrath [...] is a passion; but never is a passion without the assent of the mind for it cannot be

> that without the knowledge of the mind, a man should deliberate upon revenge and punishment.[24]

There is an individual will in this discourse which can work to refuse anger entrance to the citidel of the mind/body. Although Kate and Pertruchio may be 'of themselves' choleric, anger is figured in Nicholas Coeffeteau's treatise as the passion that makes one least like oneself – and not only when that 'self' is normally virtuous and reasonable: even those of dubious moral standing such as the covetous and the ambitious behave unlike themselves when angry:

> she [choler] sometimes constrains the most covetous profusely to cast away their most precious treasure, and to make a heap of their wealth, and then to set fire on it; and many times also she forceth ambitious men to refuse and reject the honours which they had passionately affected before their despite: who doth not see that this Passion, more than any other, quencheth the light of reason.[25]

Anger is thus a physical excess and is extraneous, indeed contradictory, to the subjectivities and personal interests of individuals. The angry person is in and of himself excessive. Montaigne, following Seneca, disagrees with Aristotle that anger has its virtuous uses:

> Aristotle saith, Choler doth sometimes serve as arms unto virtue and valour. It is very likely: notwithstanding such as gainsay him answer pleasantly, it is a weapon of a new fashion and strange use: for we move other weapons but this moveth us: our hand doth not guide it, but it directeth our hand; it holdeth us and we hold it not.[26]

Plutarch, too, denies anger any part in 'action' of any 'wisdom and magnanimity', citing the unworthiness of the adversaries upon whom the choleric soul lets his anger fall:

> for surely the very actions, motions, gestures, and countenance of choleric persons do argue and bewray

> much baseness and imbecility: which we may perceive not only in the brain-sick fits that they fall upon little children, and them pluck, twitch and misuse; fly upon silly women, and think that they ought to punish their horses, hounds and mules.[27]

For these writers anger is a sickness and a weakness, not a sign of, nor an inspiration to, strength.[28]

It is possible in the late sixteenth and early seventeenth century to entertain the notion that the suppression of anger within an individual might do him or her harm. Montaigne thinks so, as we will see. But I have marshalled these stoical writings on anger to suggest that early modern dramatists and their audience are as likely to be of the opinion that mankind is better off not feeling or expressing anger at all and that Shakespeare inevitably writes an interesting tension into the figure of Caius Martius Coriolanus when he generates a dramatic figure from a passion that contemporary and classical discourses on the subject, including his own source, condemned so entirely.

## SLIGHT

Negative figurings of anger circulating in the early modern period must be read in the light of its conceptualization not only as a somatic but as a socially constructed passion. As Gross remarks, Aristotle's *Rhetoric* defines anger as 'desire, accompanied by… distress, for conspicuous retaliation because of a conspicuous slight that was directed, without justification, against oneself or those near to one'.[29] For Aristotle's society, explains Gross, '[a]nger is a deeply social passion provoked by perceived, unjustified slights, and it presupposes a public stage where social status is always insecure'.[30] Early modern tracts on the emotions propose similarly that anger is a response to publicly experienced 'injury' and that social inequality produces and intensifies the social slights that are the cause of anger. Thus Wright, in his *Passions of the Mind in General*, writes:

> The injurer's baseness augmenteth the injury, as a buffet given a Prince by a Prince were not so heinous an injury as if a base peasant had done it; because as the greatness of the prince's person ought more to be respected of a base man than of an equal Prince, so by beating him, his contempt is accounted the greater.[31]

Thirteen years after Wright, Coefetteau writes similarly of the intensity of the rage felt and expressed by the slighted ruler in his *A Table of the Human Passions*: '[I]f we should yield to a king all the honours of the world, and yet to forbear to give him the title of a king, this were sufficient to enflame his choler.'[32] Here, Coeffeteau is not writing of kings with a particular yellow bile problem but of all kings. Again, 'men of authority and command [...] if their inferiors fail to yield them the honour which they think is due unto them, they cannot endure this injury, but fall into rage; which makes them to seek all occasions to punish this contempt'.[33] 'Being disdained by the baser sort' is particularly provocative of anger as 'men of honour cannot endure but with much impatiency, to see themselves condemned by the scum of the people'.[34] However, the notion of socially induced fury may be applied, for Coeffeteau, to men of all social statuses: 'not only kings, but every private person is impatient to see himself condemned by those which are his inferiors'.[35] And even at the bottom of the social scale, where there may be no one left to be angry with, Coefetteau suggests that the lowliest private citizen may nonetheless feel and express anger at his 'present condition'.[36]

There is still a sense in Coeffeteau that those of lower social status have less of a right to anger than the rich and powerful. He advises us that we 'fly all affairs above our reach',[37] as they will make us feel oppressed, and then angry. But the notion that the common man should not get angry at his poverty or social position does not mean that he does not do so. Seneca, similarly, suggests that anyone may become angry at an injury and desire to punish the injurer: 'no man is so humble and base, who cannot hope to see justice upon his greatest adversary: we have power enough to hurt'.[38] Gross' example of the tyrant forcing a subject to eat his son is the stuff of myth and tragedy; the little man's temper at his neighbour's slight is not. But for Coeffeteau, the great man in his fury may still become the object of scornful laughter: 'how many great personages have we seen expose themselves to be a scorn of the world by the excuse of their choler?' he asks his reader, then gives the example of 'that famous Prince, who wrote letters to a Mountain, and who caused a river to be whipped, which had been an obstacle to his passion'.[39] In *Coriolanus*, the Citizens' anger at their treatment by the Patricians during the dearth is as much a subject of this play as the excessive passion of Coriolanus.

## BETTER OUT THAN IN?

Montaigne's essay *On Anger* opens with objections to that passion typical of his more stoical tendencies.[40] Like Seneca, whom Montaigne quotes liberally in this essay, and like Coeffeteau, he casts anger as the most negative and excessive of the passions. 'No passion disturbs the soundness of our judgment as anger does' he writes in his opening critique of parents who chastise their children while in the highly visceral throes of anger. 'You can see the fire and rage flashing from their eyes' he writes, drawing on Plutarch to add that 'according to Hippocrates the most dangerous of distempers are those which contort the face'.[41]

However, as his essay continues, Montaigne is more circumspect and permits the realities of social life to intrude upon the unyielding ethical stance of his opening passage; he is more forgiving of anger and those who experience it than his classical muses. He admits that he is not particularly good at controlling anger, if provoked to it by something sudden and surprising. Nor does he think it healthy to suppress one's anger if one is constitutionally choleric. In his own 'On Anger', he states that 'the most choleric and testy man of France…I ever say, he is the patientest man I know to bridle his choler; it moveth him and transporteth him with such fury and violence…that he must cruelly enforce himself to moderate the same'.[42] Rather than praise this paragon for his efforts, Montaigne remarks that 'As for my part, I know no passion I were able to smother with such temper and abide with such resolution. I would not set wisdom at so high a rate.'[43] Next, Montaigne writes of 'Another great man' who managed to keep his passions hidden for sake of displaying a 'gentle correctness' to the social world. Montaigne is concerned not for this man's position in the social world but for his personal, interior welfare:

> I told him that indeed it was much...always to show himself in a good temper; but that the chiefest points consisted in providing inwardly for himself; and that in mine opinion, it was no discreet part inwardly to fret: which, to maintain that mark and formal outward appearance, I fear he did.

'I would rather make show of my passions', maintains Montaigne, 'than smother them to my cost'.[44] Montaigne is not suggesting here that everyone's anger is equally to be valued, or that anger *per se* is to be valued at all. But suppressing one's anger entirely is figured here as the destructive opposite of purgation and the somatic is set at odds with the reason that decides whether to express or hide it.

In relation to this attitude to anger as 'better out than in', so seemingly modern and therapeutic, I am interested in a line spoken by Volumnia in *Coriolanus,* which she delivers after her confrontation with the Tribunes, when her son has been banished. She has been fended off by Brutus and Sicinius with the dismissive accusation that, in the excesses of her anger, she is mad (Sicinius: Why stay we here to be baited/With one who wants her wits? (4.3.43–4)). When the confrontation is over and the Tribunes have escaped, Volumnia declares that:

> [...] Could I meet 'em
> But once a day, it would unclog my heart
> Of what lies heavy to't.
>
> (4.3.46–8)

She seems to want to meet the sources of her heaviness daily, to experience the curative power of stirring up anger. Permitting a choleric imbalance, it seems, would 'unclog' something more painful. Note that this imagined daily confrontation would not unclog or expel the anger itself; this she intends to feed on and would like to renew repeatedly. But by getting angry, Volumnia would presumably drive out the misery of missing her son, or the pain at the injustice of his banishment, or whatever we might decide 'lies heavy' to her heart. Passionate expression is healthful to Volumnia, just as the expression of blood is 'medicinal' to her son (1.5.18).

Of course, such a statement does not necessarily suggest that there is a therapeutic discourse of anger common to early modern and twenty-first-century Western culture, in opposition to Stoical condemnations of anger. Volumnia herself admits in her very next speech that this form of 'therapy' will ultimately destroy her: in answer to Menenius' invitation to dinner she replies with the more often quoted line 'Anger's my meat; I sup upon myself,/And so shall starve with feeding' (4.3.50–51). Here it is the indulgence of Volumnia's anger that will eat her insides out, as Montaigne would put it, not its suppression. Her desire for further contretemps with the Tribunes may have appeared comically misplaced to early modern audience members with an understanding of anger as the most destructive of the passions: anger might well unclog what lies heavy to this mother's heart but replaces it with something much more destructive, as her next lines seem to acknowledge. However, the very fact that Volumnia considers that her anger may have a restorative or curative 'unclogging' purpose, and the fact that later, against the Stoics, she suggests that she has a 'brain that leads [her] use of anger', is of significance here. It has led to this chapter's interest in how anger is used in early modern drama, in how it is put to use by characters in plays and the cultures invented by them and reflected in them. Where writers from Seneca to Wright construe it as the most excessive and bestial of the passions, anger in *Coriolanus* seems to have a range of contradictory purposes as it shifts from being a humour, whereby choler and anger are interchangeable words and are constituted in yellow bile, to being what may now be described as a 'personality trait'. It is this sense of the passions and how one does or does not restrain them as integral to the self that also seems to be at play in Montaigne's essay.

## CAIUS MARTIUS' ANGER AND ITS SOURCES

In order to establish how anger is valued or eschewed as understandable or excessive in *Coriolanus*, I will next turn to Plutarch – not only to the direct classical source for the play, Thomas North's translation of the *Life of Caius Martius Coriolanus*[45] but to Philomen Holland's translation of Plutarch's *Moralia*, first printed in 1601, specifically its essay 'Of Meekness, or How a Man Should Refrain Choler. Or How to Bridle Anger'. Plutarch's account of Martius in his *Lives* discusses Caius Martius' choler extensively, whereas 'How to Bridle Anger' has not been explored as a possible influence on *Coriolanus*,[46] surprisingly, given some of the verbal echoes to be found in the two texts. In the opening to Plutarch's dialogue, the fictional Sylla compliments his friend on his newly achieved mastery over anger and asks him how he has managed it:

> when I see how that vehement inclination, and ardent motion of yours to anger, whereunto by nature you were given, is by the guidance of reason become so mild, so gentle, so tractable, it commeth into my mind to say thereunto that which I read in Homer:
>
> Oh what a wondrous change is here
> Much milder are you than you were.[47]

This opposition of anger to mildness recalls Menenius as the voice of reason in *Coriolanus*, attempting to guide Martius to behave 'mildly' following his unfortunate encounter with the Tribunes and the Citizens after the attempt to revoke his consulship (3.2.138–45).

Early in the treatise, Plutarch tells the bizarre anecdote of Caius Gracchus the orator, 'a man blunt, rude in behavior, and withal over-earnest and violent in his manner of pleading', who had his servant follow him to the lawcourts and play a 'mild and pleasant note' on a little pipe:

> when his master was a little out of tune...whereby he reclaimed and called him back from that loud exclaiming, and so taking down that rough and swelling accent of his voice...dulced and allayed the choleric passion of the orator.[48]

Plutarch's Fundanus thinks this is a splendid idea and declares that he would happily make use of such a service himself. When Shakespeare's Caius Martius, during the scene in which he protests that to behave 'mildly' would be to act a part least like himself, bitterly (and temporarily) consents to parlay with the Citizens in the marketplace, he rages:

> Away my disposition, and possess me
> Some harlot's spirit! My throat of war be turn'd,
> Which choired with my drum, into a pipe
> Small as an eunuch, or the virgin voice
> That babies lulls asleep!
>
> (3.2.111–15)

Even closer to this notion, despised by Martius, of turning from the noise of war to the sweet sound of the pipe, is Plutarch's example of the Lacedaemonians, who

> do allay the choler of their soldiers, when they are fighting, with the melodious sound of flutes and pipes; whose manner is also before they go to battle, to sacrifice unto the Muses, to the end that their reason and right wits may remain in them still, and that they may have use thereof.[49]
>
> (125)

Plutarch declares that he despises clichéd saws that provoke man to choler and he cites two, one of which suggests the following treatment for an enemy:

> Down to the ground with him, spare not his coat,
> Spurn him and set thy foot upon his throat.[50]
>
> (124)

This recalls Volumnia's vision of Martius beating Aufidius' 'head below his knee/And tread[ing] upon his neck' (1.3.47–8) – and the reversal of that image at the end of the play: *Conspirators draw, and kill Martius, who falls; Aufidius stands on him* (5.6.129 s.d.). The enraged treading upon the enemy that, in Aufidius' case, then gives way to calm and regret (as if Aufidius, in Plutarch's terms in the Anger essay, has returned to himself) does not appear in the *Lives*: Martius' life simply ends thus: 'they all fell upon him, and killed him in the market-place, none of the people once offering to rescue him'.[51]

In the echoes of each of the examples from Plutarch here, the hero of *Coriolanus* (and, interestingly given her statement about the uses of anger, his mother) seem to scorn Stoicism and its calm rationality. Plutarch suggests pipe music as an antidote to choler – Martius uses the pipe as a symbol of his emasculation; Menenius takes up Plutarch's favourite opposing term to anger – mildness; Martius scornfully promises that he will be mild, then breaks that promise; Plutarch cites a couplet about treading upon one's enemy's neck as an example of exactly the kind of irrational fury that should be avoided – Martius' mother fantasizes about her son doing the same to Aufidius and this is finally what happens to Martius in defeat. As we have seen, Martius' determined independence has been linked to stoicism (see pp. 4–5), as has his calm on saying goodbye to his family when he is banished in 3.3. In this scene, argues Robin Headlam Wells, 'Gone is the raging scorn for the feckless plebeians, and in its place is a restrained and dignified stoicism'.[53] However, even here it is uncertain how audiences may have read Martius' new-found calm; in the *Lives*, Plutarch explains at length that, at this point it was

> not that he did patiently bear and temper his evil hap, in respect of any reason he had, or by his quiet condition: but because he was so carried away with the vehemency

> of anger, and desire of revenge, that he had no sense nor feeling of the hard state he was in [...]. For when sorrow [...] is set on fire, then it is converted into spite and malice, and driveth away for that time all faintness of heart and natural fear. And this is the cause why the choleric man is so altered and mad in his actions, as a man set on fire with a burning ague.[54]

In this account, Martius' calm is an inward numbness – 'no sense of feeling' – and an outward appearance of calm produced by the choler raging within. Plutarch goes on to describe how once Martius had comforted his 'weeping and shrieking' wife and mother 'and persuaded them to be content with his chance', he went off to brood at his country residence, 'turmoiled with sundry sorts and kinds of thoughts, such as the fire of his choler did stir up'[55] and planned his revenge on Rome.

Of course, it could be argued that Shakespeare develops and departs from his source and produces a dramatic hero truly capable of recovering from moments of 'raging scorn' and achieving the dignified stoicism which Headlam Wells ascribes to him. But I am interested in the early modern possibility of a Coriolanus driven primarily by choler, to which Shakespeare was obviously exposed in reading Plutarch's narrative, and I want to turn now to questions of what actors and audiences do with such a figure and his emotional excesses – if indeed we read them as such – today.

## MARTIUS' CHILDHOOD AND THE ENGLISH PUBLIC SCHOOL BOY

I am going to examine a production which was intended by its lead actor as a psychological excavation of Martius' choleric temperament, although he does not use this early modern terminology. In the Shakespeare's Globe production of 2006, Jonathan Cake played Martius as a bombastic yet psychologically vulnerable English public school boy, 'desperate for affection

Figure 2: Caius Martius Coriolanus (Jonathan Cake), in *Coriolanus* dir. Dominic Dromgoole, Shakespeare's Globe 2006 (© Alastair Muir, 4854).

that has been denied him by his mother'.[56] This post-Freudian reading suggests that anger is the outward sign of an inward, unconscious lack or need, first experienced in childhood. The production is of particular interest to me, because in *Talking to the Audience*, I argued that the production of dramatic subjectivity in the shared lighting of the early modern public playhouse and in moments of direct address to the audience – of which there are plenty at the new Globe and in Cake's performance – occludes, or at least discourages, this kind of psychological reading.[57] Here I am going to suggest that Cake's assumptions about a mother's love and what its lack may have led to might not have been ones that an early modern audience would have recognized. I am also going to argue that in this production, the use of the relationship between the space of the stage and the space of the audience reinforced rather than challenged or complicated this reading. In Cake's reading of Caius Martius, as we will see, anger is a result of emotional repression.

Although Shakespeare does appear to be asking the audience to consider what the results of being brought up by someone like

Volumnia might have been, an early modern audience member may have regarded Martius' uncontrollable anger as stemming from the lack of a guiding male hand, rather than expressive of a need for more motherly love. Plutarch opens his 'Life of Caius Martius Coriolanus' by first mentioning the illustrious family from whence he came.[58] The first time Martius is named, it is in relation to his having been 'orphaned': he was fatherless and therefore not educated or civilized in properly masculine fashion. On the one hand, Plutarch tells us that the fact that Caius Martius was 'left an orphan by his father' and was therefore 'brought up under his mother, a widow' teaches us something: 'that orphanage bringeth many discommodities to a child, but doth not hinger him to become an honest man, and to excel in virtue above the common sort'.[59] On the other hand, on the second page of North's translation of the 'Life', which has the marginal note 'Choleric and impatient', Plutarch asserts that 'a rare and excellent wit untaught, doth bring forth many good and evil things together':

> For this Marcius' natural wit and great heart did marvellously stir up his courage to do and attempt notable acts. But on the other side for lack of education, he was so choleric and impatient, that he would yield to no living creature: which made him churlish, uncivil, and altogether unfit for any man's conversation. Yet men marvelling much at his constancy, that he was never overcome with pleasure, not money, and how he would endure easily all manner of pains and travails: thereupon they well liked and commended his stoutness and temperancy. But for all that, they could not be acquainted with him, as one citizen useth to be with another in the city: his behaviour was so unpleasant to them by reason of a certain insolent and stern manner he had, which because it was too lordly was disliked. And to say truly, the greatest benefit that learning bringeth unto men is this: that it teacheth men that be rude and rough of nature, by compass and rule of reason, to be civil and

> courteous, and to like better the mean state, than the higher.[60]

When Martius is finally refused the consulship by the people in Plutarch, he

> took it in far worse part than the Senate and was out of all patience. For he was a man too full of passion and choler, and too much given over to self-will and opinion, as one of high mind and great courage, that lacked the gravity, and affability, that is gotten with judgement of learning and reason, which only is to be looked for in a governor of state.[61]

For Plutarch, then, Martius lacks the reason and sociability that a father's education would have given him. Shakespeare, of course, makes more of the mother than Plutarch does: Volumnia is far more of a presence in the play than she is in the source and Plutarch certainly writes no domestic scene where Martius or his son's child rearing are discussed (1.3). But Plutarch's patriarchal notions of child rearing, which suggest that Martius' father would have been responsible for both the battle training and the socialization of his son, offer an alternative to the ultimately modern assumption that there is a warm, loving, socializing norm of motherhood that Martius lacks in Volumnia. Had he been brought up by a father, Plutarch insists he would have been more calm, reasonable and socially skilled; lacking this, he is noble on the battlefield but impatient and choleric in the city. Shakespeare makes nothing of the absent father but instead stages a warmongering mother who expects the reasoning self-control of the politician in her son, when she, as in Plutarch, has not taught it to him. In the Globe production, Margot Leicester's Volumnia endeavours to teach him the gestures of consensual politics too late, hilariously enacting in detailed mime how he must

> Go to them, with this bonnet in thy hand,
> And thus far having stretched it – here be with them –
> Thy knee bussing the stones [...]

> [...] waving thy head,
> With often thus correcting thy stout heart,
> Now humble as the ripest mulberry [...]
>
> (3.2.73–9)

His stout heart has never been corrected before and whether an early modern audience, knowing their Plutarch or not, considered the lack of a father in Martius' education, it is anachronistic to assume that they considered him 'desperate for affection' from his mother, as Cake suggests. This is not to say, of course, that Cake may not read the role as he chooses and stage whatever interpretation he thinks a modern audience would be able best to understand and enjoy. What interests me here is the way that this psychological reading is produced and developed in the theatrical and audiences spaces of Shakespeare's Globe.

Asked about the remarkable physical energy of his performance in *Coriolanus* at Shakespeare's Globe in 2006, Jonathan Cake at first suggests that Martius *is* warrior ire, explaining that whereas in most Shakespearean tragedies, fight scenes come towards the end of the play,

> The fighting in *Coriolanus* is at the beginning because it defines who he is, it's the playwright who's trying to show you the character. He starts off by showing Coriolanus at a battle because that's when he is in some way at his most articulate as a human being, most expressive, that's where he's happiest and most free.[62]

Later in this interview, however, Cake suggests that his first aim as an actor in preparing for the play was to make something more psychologically layered by way of a character than the 'thing of blood' his compatriots name him:[63]

> My very strong feeling about the play is that he's not a death machine by any means, in fact he's about the opposite of that. Yes, there is part of him that expresses itself through violence, but to me he seems desperate to be all the things that he criticizes and affects to despise.

> He's a child desperate for affection that has been denied him by his mother. He's desperate for friendship of other people.[64]

Cake does not use the term 'repressed' to describe Martius (though he acknowledges that he is in psychoanalytic territory, asserting that his interpretation 'would not take a Freudian psychotherapist to work [...] out'); but for this actor, Caius Martius' choler masks his true desire to be loved. Fascinatingly, Guillaume Winter, interviewing Cake, associates this desire with the commonplace notion that actors feel the same: 'You were talking about "being liked"', he says to Cake: 'Isn't it what acting is all about?'[65] It is not, it seems, easy to play an unlovable hero, so Cake constructed Martius' sneering contempt for the populace as psychological defence born of emotional neglect. He produced an English upper class boyishness for Martius that an audience, he hoped, could not help but love and forgive:

> The child is so stunted and brutalized by his mother and by the world he lives in, but at the same time it's incredibly hard to dislike a child, because they're not in possession of a fully-formed mind, they're all feeling. However badly children behave, it's impossible to write them off completely because they're ruled by their feelings.[66]

Although some felt that Cake's interpretation reduced the play's gravitas and some found it refreshing, the child, or boy-like quality of Cake's performance was marked almost universally in reviews of the production, and associated, with remarkable consistency, with the games of cricket and rugby (a link I find in my own notes taken after watching the performance for the first time). The *Daily Mail* reviewer even went so far as allocating Cake a position on the team: 'Jonathan Cake, handsome and inky-haired, plays Coriolanus as an engaging sort of brick. He reminded me of a rugby No 8, thick-skinned and always ready for a heave.'[67] The term 'brick' here, for those not familiar with the early to mid-twentieth-century English upper-class vernacular to be found in children's stories about boarding-schools, suggests a likeable and, most importantly, solidly dependable friend. An 'engaging sort of brick' neatly describes the ideal of bluff, pragmatic likeability that the British boy's public school system was supposed to produce. It was a product of Victorian economic expansion and colonialism. The ruling-class 'brick' tolerates hardship and uncomplainingly gets the job done. Recognition in the form of cups and colonies is heaped upon him but he does not demand them: he was always and only doing his job for King/Queen and Country.[68] The stereotype does not proscribe, as Cake's Martius makes very clear, a searing contempt for the lower orders if they step out of line. He gives 'his loyal friends bearhugs' and also claps on the back those willing to fight for him in 1.7, forgetting in an instant their reluctance to follow him in Corioles, but from his first contemptuous encounter with the Citizens in 1.1, it is clear that upper-class English privilege brings with it the inalienable right to separateness from and disregard for the cannon fodder that are the Citizens.

This was a highly engaging Martius. His mastery of irony and mimicry made the audience laugh in all the live and recorded performances I witnessed and he dominated the Globe stage with both his height and his restless shifts in pace: he demonstrated physically that he was always ready to move into battle rather than stand around receiving accolades. Cake certainly appeared to understand Martius as a choleric figure in Act I. It was anger that seemed to move him across the stage and on to the walkways built out into the yard for this production, to confront the Citizens in such a way as to suggest that he is constantly about to put his fists up. This portrayal need not have produced an unquestioning bias towards Martius; the critique I want to make of the production arises not from the fact that Martius could be funny and his energy refreshing. To play an English upper-class Martius as completely without likeable characteristics is to deny the fact that confident humour and mastery of public space which comes with privilege can be seductive. But the production blurred the debates around education for leadership that it opened, through its combination of a clear set of signifiers of English public school boy and Cake's intention to have his audiences read Martius psychologically and sympathetically. It elided the outspokenness of privilege and an apolitical psychological authenticity, as we will see.

For Cake, Martius' choler is a defensive front for his psychological vulnerability. This vulnerability emerged, as the reviewers comment, in the scenes with Volumnia, the mother who sent him off to war (for which the rugby-preoccupied reviewers were perhaps reading boarding-school) and for whose love he appeared to have been been fighting ever since. Margot Leicester's Volumnia was as energetic as her son and his own physical energy seemed drained by her presence. She was played with a less sinister dignity than is often seen in production and a great deal more movement. She sees, in her mind's eye, Martius 'stamp thus, and call thus' (1.3.33) and this gestural moment determined the rest of Leicester's performance. Much has been made of Volumnia's vicariously living through her son the warrior life her gender denies her.[69] Here she performed this life unlived gesturally and suggested to the end that Volumnia is willing consciously to perform rather than only and spontaneously to act upon passion, as is her son. The blatant enthusiasm for war and wounds conveyed through Margot Leicester's gestures provoked much laughter at the Globe and seemed to produce empathy for the son brought up by such a woman. Cake's energetic fury crumbled, as Michael Billington's review remarks, in the face of a mother figure even better able to possess the Globe stage than he. Much of the humour in this production arose in moments of bathos and the undercutting of bluster and high emotion by sudden shifts from grandiose to conversational tones. Nowhere was this more apparent as in Martius' line 'Mother, I am going to the market place' (3.2.131) when, after much storming about the wounds to his integrity which a capitulation to the Citizens would force upon him, the angry patrician warrior vocalizes the inevitability of his reduction to obedient son. This scene got a round of applause in several performances.

This apparent and audible empathy for the young man so put upon by an overbearing mother was at one with the empathy produced overall by Cake's psychological reading of Martius as victim of upper-class emotional abuse, the child whose angry emotions still rule him because he has been emotionally deprived but has not yet quite learned the oppressive lesson of controlling his feelings. This is a psychological reading of the history of English upper-class child rearing that has resurfaced in novels and films during the first decades of the twenty-first century; in A. S. Byatt's *The Children's Book*, even the Bohemian Wellwood family cannot resist the class-normative practice of sending away the oldest son, and the sensitive Tom runs away from the boarding-school in which older students have physically and sexually abused him, and eventually commits suicide; in *The King's Speech*, Colin Firth won his Best Actor Oscar for his portrayal of King George's attempts to overcome the stammer brought on, the film suggests, by the chronic emotional neglect and abuse considered character-building for upper-class children, seen (on brief daily display to their parents) and not heard (except by nannies whose response to non-normative personalities was physical abuse).

When Firth played George VI, the actor was already celebrated for his portrayal of the repressed upper-class male; the attempts of his Mr Darcy to fight the passion lurking beneath layers of patrician etiquette and pride achieved a cult following for the BBC's 1995 *Pride and Prejudice*.[70] The notion that a warm, emotionally expressive – or simply vocally expressive, in the case of the stammering George VI – human being has been repressed or stultified by upper-class child-rearing practices may well seem plausible to any audience member for whom the nurturing of individual personality, rather than the preparation for colonial rule, is the purpose of child rearing. But what these readings of upper-class psychology tend to privilege is an interest in the individual over an analysis of his class position; one is not encouraged to interrogate privilege but to understand that the rich have just as hard a time psychologically as the poor have materially. The *Evening Standard*'s Nicholas de Jongh had problems hearing 'the plummy, frail voice that Cake adopted' for the Globe's *Coriolanus* and which de Jongh felt he 'ought to abandon'; but this mix of plumminess and frailty is exactly what produces the effect of privileged-yet-vulnerable that made this Caius Martius so sympathetic. It is significant that the vocal frailty epitomized in George VI's stammer gained Firth much critical approval and an Oscar. A particularly strong and much-cited scene from *The King's Speech* was the moment where Lionel Logue, the King's speech therapist, encouraged him to swear. The appeal of this wild and joyous series of 'blasts' and 'buggers' and 'fuck fuck fucks' relied upon an audience's understanding that it represented the purging of a lifetime of upper-class repression and a more authentic, angry, self-expressive George than convention and upbringing had hitherto permitted. Once the audience at the Globe had encountered Margot Leicester's Volumnia, who so clearly lived through the fighting machine she had created, it was possible to interpret Martius' anger as self-expression as well as class contempt. Add this to the portrayal of the professional politicians of the piece, the Tribunes, as emotionally inauthentic and calculating at a time, as Cake points out (pp. 31–2), that much was being made in the UK of the untrustworthiness of our own politicians,[71] and there emerged a clear reading of anger as legitimate self-expression that, I would argue, exemplifies a very modern understanding of emotion as healthily in excess of society's oppressive demands.

As I have suggested, this 'engaging brick' of a Martius was highly energetic. Dynamic change in pace and quality of movement on the part of actors is even more crucial to the engagement of audience attention in this day-lit theatre than in those that create focus with stage lighting. Cake's shifts of vocal and physical dynamic, particularly when Martius was angry, set him apart from many other figures on stage, particularly the Tribunes, who wandered and mused as they plotted for their political survival but never entered the yard or moved on to the two walkways that had been built out into it, the first of the Dromgoole regime's many incursions into the space of the Groundlings. Cake would plant himself centre stage to make formal declamations to the gods or about his enthusiasm for a war that would rid Rome of its 'musty superfluity' (1.1.225), then would precipitate himself towards his enemies – be they political or national – with startlingly sudden changes of energy. The requests for the 'voices' of the people in 2.3 took place in the yard, where Martius, as several reviewers noted, would make much of 'pressing the flesh' of the audience, then wipe his hand disgustedly on the gown that was supposed to denote his humility. He happily strode out on to the walkways to confront the Citizens and rail against their liberties. Benedict Nightingale remarked in *The Times* that 'Two wooden walkways pass through the theatre's yard and on to the stage, allowing Roman citizens not merely to enter through a crowd of groundlings but to be clearly visible as they mingle with them and, in effect, become their spokesmen.'[72] Cake, certainly, enjoyed imagining audience as mob:

> when you walk on stage at the Globe you really have a mass, you have a mob, you have the populace standing in front of you, and *they are receiving just as characters in the play might.* Some of them want to convict Coriolanus, some of them want to defend him, most of them are probably undecided, just listening. (emphasis added)[73]

However, I would argue that the audience 'receive' Cake's Martius very differently from the fictional Citizens of ancient Rome. In several performances, and from what could be seen in recordings of others, Martius' disgust at having to shake hands with 'us' produced laughter, not an angry identification with the citizens he despised. It seemed that what was being enjoyed here was not the opportunity to enact participation in ancient Roman democracy, but Martius' comically unbridled willingness to fly in its face, because conforming to its conventions felt inauthentic to him. Cake was struck how this play appeals to:

> the current unhappiness and cynicism in the public today about lying politicians, about mendacity and spin…

> to see a politician standing on stage who cannot help but tell the truth, who cannot help but be himself, who cannot dissemble, however repugnant one might find his view of the world... I was struck when talking to people afterwards by how sympathetic and rather thrilling they found that ability to be truthful.[74]

As Cake's Martius strode about the yard, making the Citizens follow him to give their voices, the audience laughed, enjoying his outrageous nonconformity – and he appeared to have won the audience's voices too. It was possible to read Martius' choler, so far in excess of what is needed and desirable for a politician in his public relations with the Citizens in the play, as an appropriate anger at the perceived inauthenticity of politicians in the world of the audience.

Empathy for Martius was, then, produced by Cake's use of the Globe's stage and yard: through the character's willingness to openly express his potentially objectionable but at least, as Cake argues, spontaneous and psychologically readable anger; through direct address and a physical dynamic that suggests there is nowhere on this stage he fears to go or cannot possess; and through the actor's contact with his audience, something not permitted to the Tribunes by this production. The Tribunes plotted to change the votes of the fictional 'people' but never came among the paying ones and never addressed the audience from the stage either, as Cake's Martius did repeatedly.[75] As Peter Holland points out in his essay '*Coriolanus* and the Remains of Excess',[76] the Tribunes are repeatedly directed to 'remain' in the text of Coriolanus; they have the last word, alone together, commenting on the action, at the end of four scenes in which they appear. In this production, this gave the impression that they were removed from the passionate heat of the action. The spatial practices of *Coriolanus* at the Globe produced a particularly sympathetic Caius Martius and particularly despicable Tribunes, who always seemed too busy plotting to acknowledge us. The production foregrounded Martius as man of action, who involves the audience in the action of the play, whose excessive anger is generated both by the recognizable signs of upper-class childhood trauma and by a natural and authentic fury at the Tribunes, those that remained after the excitement of Martius' angry, humorous, authentic presence had departed. While Martius named the Citizens as a 'musty superfluity' (1.1.225) that can be consumed in the war, it was the Tribunes who treated the audience as superfluous to their politicking. While Martius likens himself to a lonely dragon, Cake's Martius played for the sympathy of the playgoers and Cake believed that he truly wants the love of the humanity about which he purports to be so cynical. The first time I saw the production, he was so successful in this bid for sympathy and theatrical attention that immediately after the banishment sequence, in 3.3, the Tribunes were booed, and when Martius and Aufidius embraced in 4.4, two young women standing behind me let out an 'Aaaaah!' of sympathy, as if this were a moment of baby-animal-like cuteness..

Caius Martius was recognizable here as a psychologically wounded public school boy, whose repressed anger emerged in contempt at scheming politicians; his excess of choler was thus rendered both sympathetic and understandable. Shakespeare's source in North's Plutarch source offers a useful alternative to the notion of emotional deprivation in Martius' upbringing: it suggests that his choleric pride has not been tempered with reason through an education in civic leadership. One might then ask the question, then: is Shakespeare's version of the narrative, with its greater role for Martius' mother, a mid point between ancient notions of the somatic passions and the necessity of tempering them with reason, and a post-Freudian understanding of anger as the affect produced in excess of repressed desire or trauma? This would, I think, be too Whiggish an interpretation of the play, in which current concerns with issues of child rearing and psychology are foreshadowed by Shakespeare. Ralph Fiennes' film of *Coriolanus*, which he directed and in which he plays the lead, suggests to me that audiences today need not necessarily be offered a Martius whose choleric subjectivity is produced by past emotional deprivation in order to engage with him as a dramatic figure. Although Fiennes was clearly interested in possible psychological readings of Martius, his film depicts anger as socially produced and as produced in social space.

## FIENNES' *CORIOLANUS* AND THE SITE-SPECIFIC SOLDIER

'Because of the Place, Because of the Locations.'

Ralph Fiennes' *Coriolanus* was filmed in Serbia and Montenegro. It attracted wide and prestigious critical attention, with article-length reviews from Stephen Greenblatt in the *New York Review of Books*[77] and Slavov Žižek in the *New Statesman*.[78] Interviewed on Serbian television and asked why he had chosen Serbia for his *Coriolanus*, Fiennes replied, 'Because of the place, because of the locations', then referred to 'atmosphere' and architecture. In his interview with blogger Andreas Wiseman, he made more explicit reference to the architectural history of the country's cities:

> But more importantly than [low shooting costs and support from Serbian authorities] is Serbia's grittiness – the bruised battered quality of some of the locations. There are great contrasts in Belgrade between weary Austro-Hungarian architecture, the old communist style and early 20th century neo-classicism.

Wiseman suggests that

> That is a large part of what makes Belgrade such a perfect location for a contemporary adaptation of this play. It is steeped in a very unique history and culture but also is representative of the world over. Belgrade functions like Shakespeare's Rome or his Plantagenet England. It is rich in a real and difficult history but it operates simultaneously as a 'U-topos', a 'no place', a place in which the artist can speculate or suggest.[79]

Fiennes, too, thought of his locations as places that 'could be anywhere'.[80] At points in the news coverage of food riots and warfare, watched by the inhabitants of this modern 'Place calling itself Rome',[81] he uses footage from other places. A vague American or Western European familiarity with news footage of the former Yugoslavia during the wars of the 1990s might indeed lead to a reductive sense that war is the same 'the world over'. However, Belgrade and its environs, with its sharply juxtaposed, visible architectural histories, the news footage of protesters and tanks outside the Serbian Parliament for the conflicts between Martius and the Tribunes and Citizens in Act 3, the Parliament building, inside and out (shooting had to take place at weekends, as the location for Martius' confirmation by the Patricians as Consul in 2.2 was Serbia's Parliament), always reference themselves, in productively awkward contrast to the political system depicted in the play. They recall Mike Pearson and Cliff McLucas' theory of 'hosts and ghosts' in site-specific theatre, whereby the 'host' site can always be seen through the 'ghost'-like performers that haunt it and in which the relationship between the two is always a 'mis-match', productive of 'fracture'.[82] Here the 'ghost' may be more productively considered as the Serbian location of this film, haunting Shakespeare production with its history of recent political upheaval and violent conflict. There is no modern political system that involves patrician approval of parliamentary members, followed by approval by whoever happens to be in the marketplace soon afterwards, followed by on-air political meetings in which that approval is withdrawn and the parliamentarian sentenced to death or banishment. In the contrasts and the gaps between actual Serbian locations and the action of this play, the viewer of this film is asked to consider what is the same 'the world over' and what is historically and geographically specific.

If the Globe's 2006 *Coriolanus* asked its audiences to consider the psychological underpinnings of anger, it also produced anger as movement in theatre space, as Jonathan Cake appeared to be propelled by his impulsive fury across the stage at his opponents – the Tribunes, the Citizens of Rome, Aufidius. Cake himself was keen to let the audience see what motivated this movement, where in Martius' past his anger came from and to suggest that it was somehow in excess of some true or essential humanity, crushed by a lack of parental affection. The site specificity of Fiennes' film does different work with anger and space, and thus asks the viewer to consider anger differently: as both socially and psychologically produced by the power structures that can make use of it. In his review of the film, Stephen Greenblatt complains that all Fiennes is capable of expressing in the central role is contempt. For Greenblatt, what Fiennes' 'mastery of nausea' misses is Coriolanus' semantic and thematic link to Cordelia in *King Lear*: both are figures who personify 'an adherence to a principle so extreme and uncompromising that it threatens the whole social order and must in effect be eliminated if life is to go on' but 'the viewer of Fiennes's film would never grasp the affinity'.[83] I disagree. What I think Greenblatt unintentionally buys into here is a critical history of realist acting and of subjectivity as self-expression, in which self-expression escapes through the fissures in the individual's often unconscious attempts to repress or hide it.[84] In both histories, Caius Martius is always lacking: he has few moments of self-revelation of this kind. I would rather argue that what the determined, set expression on Fiennes' face produces is not always contempt; sometimes it seems unreadable – and that is the point.

Greenblatt sees a Fiennes who

> throws all restraint to the winds in the horrific battle for the Volscian town of Corioles, where his crazed, unstoppable, virtually single-handed conquest of the citadel earns him his honorific sobriquet.[85]

I, on the other hand, saw a figure moving through streets and houses in a bombed-out city, who did not stop, because nobody was left able-bodied or armed enough to stop him and who was only 'crazed' in the way that his single-minded movement through conquerable space might seem to we who are not trained to it. The contemporary Western civilian imagination, perhaps, can only imagine the soldier as Seneca figures anger – crazed, unstoppable. Indeed, Fiennes himself describes the sequence in which Martius, inside Corioles, is ambushed by a soldier, fights and kills him with his knife, as demonstrating the 'sort of psycho-pathic, violent intensity of Coriolanus, [a] kind of extreme rage'.[86] But it is difficult to see what other kind of emotional state one might use to portray a killing of this kind and I want to argue that, though the film certainly emphasizes Martius' personal obsession with defeating Aufidius, it also suggests that this 'extreme rage' is hardly in excess of what is needed in warfare. In fact, when Martius does confront Aufidius in this sequence, he does not lash out at him as he is obliged to do at the soldier who attacks him without warning and against whom he must use a knife because he is unable to reach his gun. Here both men very deliberately put down their guns and prepare for arm-to-arm combat. Excessive (to civilians) wrath appears to be a function of warfare; personal enmity produces a deadly calm.

The Act 1 battle sequence in this film used supernumeraries from the Serbian anti-terrorist squad to perform the Roman soldiers and shows ways of passing through spaces of urban warfare that are in line with modern military training regarding how to give cover and how to enter buildings held by enemies. The sequence produces a very different Martius from the hero of many a theatre production who takes the city single-handed by charging off-stage and comes back covered in blood. This Martius moves in the way he has been trained to do, through an urban space that has already been blasted into near submission, peopled by the already dead and by frightened old people who haven't been able to escape. Fiennes himself was trained in the rules of urban warfare by his anti-terrorist squad extras and describes what he learned in significantly spatial terms:

> Soldiers are lean and fit. They've got to have compact efficiency in the way they move and operate. The SAJ [Specijalna Antiteroristička Jedinica] have been teaching me about efficiency of movement, about how to open up

> angles, the best way to move down corridors, and how best to handle weapons – moving the butt of the rifle from one shoulder to another, for example. It's about spontaneous efficiency. It's about drilling.[87]

Even the movement of the soldier's rifle fills a space here. This efficient movement through space in order to conquer and possess it is performed by Fiennes in such a way as to suggest extreme tension and alertness; all his unreadable fury is focused on the 'spontaneous efficiency' of killing and staying alive.

This Martius may be read, in accordance with Plutarch, as one who is at his disciplined, self-sacrificing best in battle, and at his choleric, antisocial worst in political settings.The film makes clear that Martius is both a poor producer of social space – he doesn't know how to pass through it unless he is destroying it or leaving it. He stops to take some water from an old man who offers him a bottle and it seems that he is momentarily bewildered by an act that remakes the room both men are in as social space in which a host can offer a stranger water.[88] He does his most efficient soldierly work alone and, once banished, he moves through landscapes of wintry wilderness until he reaches 'Antium', again with controlled, solitary efficiency, stopping to make camp in carefully chosen sheltered spots, pacing himself. The relatively recent history of the Former Yugoslavia and the location filming demands that the viewer asks where we are; it is the solidier, Martius, who could be anywhere. He has been trained to move through any space, to conquer it and stay alive for as long as possible to do so. Soldiers' slow, methodical movement through urban space in this film is punctuated by rapid runs for vantage or cover, the sudden breaking down of doors – and, of course, gunshot. Sound is produced very explicitly in space in this film; gunshot is recorded not solely as shot but as the whole act of using a gun – reloading, shot, kickback, bullet cases dropping from guns and clinking to the floor, limbs and guns against uniform fabric, breath – are all clearly audible. This is the sound of soldiers taking up space. *Pace* Greenblatt, and Fiennes' own commentary, his work as a soldier does not read as crazed, unstoppable fury – or if it does, it is because one is given the impression that this is the emotional state needed to carry out the work of a soldier. The foregrounding of the materiality of warfare suggests, I would argue, that the viewer reads Martius' furious energy, as he knifes his opponent in the empty house in 'Corioles', as necessary to the enterprise of conquering the city; if we read it as 'psychopathic', it is war, rather than Coriolanus' subjectivity, which is the site and cause of psychopathy.

When Martius reaches Antium, in the disguise produced by the overgrown beard and hair of his long march, he gets the opportunity to watch leadership as the production of social space as opposed to leadership as the conquering of place, or the compromised selfhood of political manoeuvring which Martius has rejected in Rome. Martius watches the socially competent Aufidius (Gerard Butler) walking through the small town. Everyone seems to know the Volscian leader; he shakes a number of hands, pats a number of backs, is asked to sit down and drink at a pavement bar. This is clearly an alien way of working to Martius, who manages to reconfigure Volscian leadership as Leadership Cult, without, of course, ever suggesting that he wants admirers. Once accepted by Aufidius, Fiennes' Martius has his head re-shaved and the the Volscian youth all do the same, drunkenly taking turns, on the eve of battle, to sit in the barber's chair in which their new leader was shaved. Ironically, the Martius who cannot bear to stand or sit still and be looked at or talked about, reconfigures Antium as the space of the patriarchal monument, in which Martius holds court in his iconic barber's chair and which only his mother can invade and fracture. In Rome, he was a reluctant living monument or taker-up of ceremonial space:[89] after leaving the Senate meeting to avoid hearing Cominius' speech in his praise, he finds himself outside in a corridor, a non-place of passing and waiting, where a cleaner wheels his trolley past him and they exchange puzzled glances. The cleaner has a role that is supposed to remain invisible, meaningless; Martius refuses meaning outside of military action. But his following in Antium suggests that his meaning *in* action is overdetermined and mythologized. Aufidius, too, is pulled into the cult of Coriolanus by envying it. When he asks 'do they still fly to the Roman?' (4.7.1) in this film, the impression is created that someone whose leadership style was highly nuanced socially is now being reduced or essentialized to something more Martius-like and monumental.

The film is not without psychological subtext but it is not dwelt upon, nor used to make Fiennes more sympathetic. He clearly still lives in his mother's house with his wife and son, and Virgilia (Jessica Chastain) is shown clearly pushed out of the relationship as Vanessa Redgrave's Volumnia is permitted to change her son's bandages, the mother's touch gentle but pragmatic and unabashed as Virgilia hovers awkwardly at the door. The wife touches her husband much more briefly and awkwardly in the marital bed. Redgrave's performance is clear and simple. She wears military uniform for public ceremony and has clearly had to pour her own military potential into her son. Young Martius is all innocence and potential; he does not demonstrate that that he is particularly like or unlike his father as yet. The butterfly-mammocking speech is cut (1.3.58–67). An obvious reference to the child Martius once was, looking up at his mother for love and approval, occurs as he kneels at her feet in their final encounter; but there are no sustained attempts to psychologize Martius and his choleric temperament. Anger renders him active and articulate in his fury at the Citizens; repression of anger renders him awkward and stumbling, as he is on the hustings in the marketplace. Fascinatingly his red, contorted, spitting visage in the face of his trumped-up banishment by a TV talk show that appears to have been taken over by the Citizens in 3.3 signifies an inarticulate fury that contradicts the articulacy with which Martius speaks 'what's in's heart' in this scene (3.3.29). This Coriolanus is pure anger, which is why I argue that Greenblatt is mistaken to see a fixed expression as inadequate to the role. Anger renders him active and productive – physically in battle and linguistically in confrontation. When angry, he appears able to produce performatives without thinking: 'I banish you' (3.3.123). The 'calm' demanded by political life renders him stuttering and awkward, a bad actor, as he also acknowledges he is when confronted by his family in Antium and is forced to feel other than angry. I read the fixed look of contempt marked by Greenblatt as the revulsion Martius feels for social interaction, because social interaction always involves compromise, whereas killing people does not. We cannot see this expression when he is covered with blood after the routing of Corioles, not because it is replaced by some self-revealing ecstasy or blood-lust revealing Maritius' inner life, but because the blood renders the face unreadable – it is a streaky red painting with oddly luminous blue eyes; it represents the action, the fighting, that has just occurred, not what Martius feels about it.

Slavov Žižek gets closer to a more productive reading of Fiennes' performance when he argues that Coriolanus is a 'fighting machine' whose lack of a class allegiance means he can 'easily put himself at the service of the oppressed'.[90] If Žižek is suggesting that Caius Martius has no class position from the outset of the film, he is wrong. Martius is a Patrician and speaks in the interests of the Patrician class. The lines of 1.3 in which Martius makes very clear his class position are not cut – he storms that the 'soothing' of the Citizens with democratic representatives has nourished rebellion (3.1.69) and that fixed look of nausea is first turned upon the Citizens who have come to demand corn at their own price (1.1.10). But while Martius can only fight on behalf of the Patricians, he is unable to represent them and refuses to be a sign in the semiotic system of the Senate. He hates the notion of performing on request and he finds standing still to be read disgusting, as evidenced by his leaving the Senate before Cominius makes his speech in praise of his deeds of war in order to secure his position as senator. It is at this point in the film that Martius, standing outside in the corridor, encounters the cleaner wheeling his trolley. He has calmly decided not to stand and be representative and ends up in a non-place, a corridor, meeting the curious glance of one of the disenfranchised. Both figures at this point are outside of Rancière's distribution of the sensible.[91] Both are therefore, for Žižek, potentially revolutionary figures.

Žižek's notion of an ideologically undetermined 'fighting machine' works with the notion of emotion as movement touched upon in the Introduction. Martius' anger at Rome propels him from Rome, then back to attack it – and Aufidius and the Volscians can make use of it. Once Martius has been banished from Rome – and has banished Rome in return – he can put himself in the service of anyone or anything. Žižek's reading is limited, though, by the way in which emotion is given social meaning in Roman culture. Roman '*virtus*', maleness and virtue, holds within it, semantically, the man who needs nothing but himself in battle – who is able, in simple terms, to stand up for himself – and the man whose meaning is socially inscribed, whose virtue stands for something inherent to Rome. Once he is banished, Fiennes' Martius becomes a free-floating signifier in the wintry no-man's land between this Rome and this Antium. When he reaches the latter, the film makes it clear that he neither understands it nor signifies within it. Thus while his plan to fight for Aufidius – who in this film appears as the guerrilla leader of a less powerful state than Rome – fits Žižek's notion of the potentially revolutionary fighting machine, outside of Rome's distribution of the sensible, he cannot stay alive in Antium for long, as here he has ceased to mean anything. The things that anger Martius most are words, namely the words 'traitor', from the Citizens, and 'traitor' and 'boy', from Aufidius. The virtuous Roman is the man who stands for – and stands up for – his country. The traitor behaves in his own self-interest, the boy is a weak dependant who does not yet stand for anything. In his fury at these insults, which strip from him the things he was willing to stand for, Martius demands that the Volscians kill him. In Fiennes' film, this happens at a checkpoint between territories, another non-place. Martius may be solitary, a lonely dragon, but his anger means nothing without an appropriate social context; he no longer belongs to the Romans and now that he has become doubly a non-subject (a boy and a traitor) to the Volscians, it is time to die. The conversations and compromises that living in a city (and governing it) involve produce a reasoning self which must control the choleric temperament for the long-term good of the city and for the enlightened self-interest of the individual. Coriolanus does not have self-control except when his choler is channelled in battle; he is only able to 'play the man he is', an excessively choleric one.

While Dominic Dromgoole's tenure at the Globe abandoned the 'original practices' productions pioneered under Mark Rylance, his production of *Coriolanus* must have seemed, to the audience members who did not have a fine-tuned expertise in Jacobean costume, very much a Jacobean one. However, as I have suggested here, it suggested particularly twentieth/twenty-first century concerns with the inauthenticity of politicians, the need for self-expression through anger and the inner pain of the repressed upper class male. Fiennes' 'modern dress' *Coriolanus* film, on the other hand, much more self-consciously draws parallels between the questions Shakespeare's culture may have been asking about the uses of anger and current concerns about the purposes and consequences of war. The inclusion of the action inside Corioles – not, of course, a scene in the play – demonstrates the training Fiennes undertook in military tactics, in which he becomes a 'thing of blood' (2.2.109), a fighting machine with death in his 'nervy arm' (2.1.160), the personification of 'spontaneous efficiency', the winner of the garland for killing the enemy. When Martius returns home to his political enemies, it is not permissible to render them powerless with the power of his tongue as he did his Volscian enemies with his weapon; his refusal to develop a political personality to control his choleric temperament finally leads to his death. Like the subjects of media stories of post-traumatic stress disorder, in the film he seems unable to communicate with his wife. Fiennes audio commentary on the film's DVD release suggested that some – mistakenly, in Fiennes' view – might read the scene when she opens a door to find his mother in the intimate act of changing those bandages as Oedipal. It rather suggested to me that the mother who brought him up to be a warrior, and who will not wince at these wounds as she regards them as trophies, is the only person off the battlefield who is permitted to approach them. The play's concerns with leadership in war versus leadership in politics, and the channelling of emotion required for both, are here paralleled by more recent concerns with appropriate behaviours for war and peace and what training for battle might do to the masculine psyche.

The distance between the politics of Shakespeare's Rome and any recent political regime that the locations may have recalled, and the additional scenes that the film included to explore the mentality of a modern soldier, demonstrated a drive to make this 400-year-old play about a 2000 year-old culture 'relevant' to a modern viewer. However, Fiennes' performance of anger in political space foregrounds the political uses of emotion and the subjectivity of leadership as I would argue the play does. In the light of a tradition of cultural materialist work on early modern drama (including my own), which claim that the open, public stage of Elizabethan/Jacobean London produces dramatic subjectivity as a public, dialogic act, it is ironic to suggest here that this film politicized the cultural production and reception of anger, where the performance of Shakespeare's Globe personalized it. This was due partly, perhaps, to the automatic alienation effect produced by the film and its placing of 400-year-old language in a recent theatre of war. However, I do still consider that it is possible to create equally productive dialogues between the 'then' and the 'now' of anger and its meanings in the theatre as well as on location in film, and I will conclude this chapter by pointing to two recent theatre productions of *Coriolanus*, both of which took a particular interest in the spaces of stage and audience, and in siting the production in ultra-contemporary corporate and military locations respectively.

## CORIOLANUS AND ANGER: SPATIAL SOLUTIONS IN THE THEATRE

**Getting Angry at Work 2: *The Roman Tragedies Coriolanus***

In Flemish director Ivo van Hove's celebrated version of *Coriolanus* (Figure 1), Gijs Scholten van Aschat's Martius is seen getting Angry at Work. The place of work here is not an office like the one pictured on the Youtube clip mentioned above: it is plusher and full of places to eat, drink, read, send emails and watch Shakespeare, live and on screen. As Christian Billing puts it, director and scenographer van Hove and Jan Versweywald

> came up with the idea of the corporate convention space: a place in which people could sit and watch TV in an anonymous environment in which the events of the world could unfold around spectators as they were having a beer or eating a sandwich.[92]

However, it read to me as an open-plan work space, one redolent of corporate efforts to blur work/life, or work/social life boundaries, in not dissimilar ways to the less luxurious open-plan office of the Youtube clip. As readers may know from having attended or read about this much-toured and much-cited production of *The Roman Tragedies* (*Coriolanus*, *Julius Caesar* and *Antony and Cleopatra*, cut to one approximately six-hour performance), audience members were invited on to the stage for substantial stretches of each performance. While there, they could regard the action from close quarters or look at it on one of the screens placed about the stage space. They were offered space to read newspapers, go online and send emails, or write text for the dot-matrix surtitles that rolled out above the stage. The food and entertainment offerings recalled what I suspect will be many contemporary workers' experience of wasting time at work.

It was while appearing in a TV debate that this Martius lost his temper dramatically and had to be prevented from fighting the Tribunes, Brutus and Sicinius. The play's (easily deflected, volatile) Citizens, who speak to the politician in his gown of humility and give or take from him their voices in a space of exchange, the marketplace, were cut, and the audience as (easily distracted, passive) consumers/workers took their place, watching 'the action' on a screen, surfing the internet or wandering about to buy food. Appearing on television is, of course, part of the work of a modern leader; it is how he appears to the people. His job is to appear, as Menenius and Volumnia make clear in *Coriolanus*, in a way that will please the viewers and convince them that their rulers are acting in their best interests. In the *Roman Tragedies Coriolanus*, the violent confrontations of Act 3 took place in front of an imagined 'people' of television viewers, who would have witnessed Martius' outburst before he was taken off air. It also took place before the spectators who had remained in the auditorium for this section of the production, and among those who had placed themselves around Martius' place of work, the media-obsessed centre of power which he would so much have preferred to exchange for the battlefield.

For its British audiences, this outburst of Anger at Work no doubt mapped Martius' inability to behave 'mildly' for the Citizens neatly on to the critiques of inauthenticity and 'spin' that have been repeatedly made against politicians in this country since the Blair government's term of office (see n. 72), and particularly since the expenses scandal of 2009, soon after the breaking of which the Trilogy played at the Barbican, London.[93] It would have been almost impossible to produce a modern-dress *Coriolanus* in 2009 without generating sympathy for a man who refuses to do what the politicians told him to. But there was also something exciting about the staging of this scene as bad behaviour in the workplace. The plush, corporate space, created to generate calm isolation for the most part, calm communication and cooperation when necessary, a space full of indications that work is just like home, had been violated by a passionately angry man who did not care if he broke the furniture. His anger was readable as both personal pathology and political heroism, both excessive because out of control and in excess of the ideological structures within which Martius must behave himself.

I witnessed Caius Martius' outburst from the stage at the Barbican. From the auditorium, with its view both of the stage and the action taking place on a large screen above it, it may have read differently, as an embarrassing and undignified outburst by someone unable to control himself when given the responsibility of appearing in front of the world on television. From the stage it was an excitingly theatrical expression of anger which suggested that the corporate world could not entirely contain political passion and, given that Martius' politics is violently anti-democratic, this may also have been read as a disturbingly reactionary moment. Interestingly, however, van Hove's was also the most sympathetic portrayal of the Tribunes I have seen in a production of *Coriolanus*, perhaps partly because we did not get to see the unnerving violence that they whip up in the play and partly due to the the tangle of media, communication and social networking devices and the array of comforts and opportunities for consumption displayed before Brutus and Sicinius as they stood with the audience and looked at the stage. They had so much to attempt to control, so many distractions and conflicting interests to play off against one another. 'Here's he that would take from you all your power' (3.1.182) warn the Tribunes in the play, and on this stage, the layered and ambiguous nature of that power made their rhetorical task a seemingly impossible one. Their first appearance – in the auditorium rather than on-stage – figured the conventional end-on seating area of the Barbican Theatre as the space of democracy, while the space of wandering and participation became both fragmented and passive. In his much-cited 'Walking in the City', de Certeau bids us leave behind the illusory wholeness of spectatorship, on offer from the top of the World Trade Center in New York and descend to the level of the walker, the social producer of space.[94] Here, the space of the spectator became something more critical and interrogatory, while the walkers were framed as passive consumers. What the shifting set of perspectives offered by this *Coriolanus* demonstrated was both the possibility of experiencing anger within a political/corporate space as Martius disrupts it, and of watching angrily, from the space of the auditorium, at first occupied by the Tribunes, but then abandoned by it as they attempt to join the mediatized space of political power.[95]

**The Anger of the People: Coriolan/Us**

I return, finally, to a site-specific *Coriolanus*: *Coriolan/Us*, directed by Mike Pearson and Mike Brookes for National Theatre

Wales in 2012, in an RAF aircraft hanger near Barry, South Wales. My interest in site-specific Shakespeare emerged from some experiments with this play in non-theatre spaces with Flaneur Productions in Minneapolis (2005 and 2006), which are documented elsewhere.[96] The promenade *Coriolanus* on which I worked demonstrated that direct address to the audience in a non-theatre space did not necessarily produce the dialectical and balanced shifts in political sympathy from Caius Martius to the Citizens and back again that I had assumed it would. There is an assumption underpinning some academic writing on site-specific work that it is in and of itself more politically progressive than theatre which takes place in a theatre with a conventionally seated audience sitting quietly (passively?) watching in the dark. Pearson's own work on site-specific practice has suggested this.[97] I had made similar assumptions and failed to predict that a Caius Martius that came among his audience to upbraid them as unruly

Figure 3: Caius Martius Coriolanus (Richard Lynch), First Citizen (John Rowley), Second Citizen (Gerald Tyler) in *Coriolan/Us* dir. Mike Pearson and Mike Brookes for National Theatre Wales, performed at RAF St Athan, 2012 (© Mark Douet/ National Theatre Wales)

citizens, then later address them as those who might empathize with his loathing of said citizens, might prove highly sympathetic. Comparable dramaturgical effects in the analysis of the Globe's *Coriolanus* are explored above.

*Coriolan/Us* conflated Shakespeare's and Brecht's *Coriolanus* texts[98] (the National Theatre Wales' production used a translation of Brecht's *Coriolanus* for the scenes featuring the Citizens, a cut of Shakespeare's play for the rest of the production); it was clearly interested in the perspective of the Citizens. Although the use of the Brecht did not evade any of the political problems posed for the liberal theatre-goer by Shakespeare's play (Brecht's Citizens are as easily manipulated by Menenius and by the Tribunes in turn as those in the earlier play) their speeches were rendered startlingly clear by their modernity compared to the source text. What this production permitted was the reading of audience as Citizens in a way that did not require them to act as supernumeraries. It staged the play as a site of anger across the spectrum of social class.

> "What is the city but the people?" demands Sicinius at one point in *Coriolanus* – National Theatre Wales makes the question the bedrock of this gripping promenade production. Here we, the audience, are the people – milling, drifting, scattering in alarm as the action plays out in our midst.[99]

It is significant that in Sarah Hemming's review here, she describes the 'us' of *Coriolan/Us* in terms of action. 'We' also spent a lot of time standing, sitting, watching, listening but I concur with Hemming that what the people watching this play *do* is inextricably part of this production's *mise-en-scene*. This is the case even though the act of direct address could not attempt to cast them as Citizens in this production, because they were divided from the action of the play and visually constructed as only ever 'audience': they were all listening to the actors' speeches on headsets. The Citizens themselves were played by only two actors, John Rowley and Gerald Tyler; they crossed the breeze-block divide between

Rome and Antium to play the Volscian citizens who kill Martius. Occasionally the numerical paucity of this crowd made them appear an oddly and naively brave set of revolutionaries setting themselves up, somewhat implausibly, against the larger group of Patricians who spoke Shakespeare and drove real vehicles across the vast aircraft hanger. But having no acted crowd or group of Citizens, only a crowd of audience addressed by two plebeians, made the casting of 'us' as plebeians more effective than in other productions where non-actors are addressed as Citizens. This was really Coriolan + Us, rather than Coriolanus, plus the play's Citizens, plus some audience members who are, usually, clearly just that, however they are addressed.[100]

Of course, this audience was also there just to watch. The only actual moment of 'participation' at the performance I attended was when we were induced to applaud the conferment of Martius' new surname (1.9.64). But in the shared light of the hanger, we were constructed both similarly and differently to van Hove's on-stage spectators. On the one hand, the audience was doing nothing in the face of the action, perhaps reminded, particularly when watching the two large screens on which one could also see the piece, of the comfortably disengaged viewing habits of the television audience watching wars in other places. Then, in tension with the construction of the audience as passive viewer, the audience were also a potential threat in the space: they peered into the caravans where the sound technology was housed and where the Patricians and Tribunes plotted their war and their peace, they crowded around Menenius' jeep that was rocked dangerously by the two Citizens, they milled about near meetings they should not have been overhearing and got in the way of battles in which they were not going to take part. The literal threat that the audience members might obstruct the proceedings, go where they were not wanted or trip over some of the ever-moving sound and lighting cables and cause a health-and-safety incident gave them a precarious power. Moreover, because each of its members wore headphones, the audience was foregrounded *as* omniscient audience rather than fictional mob

– so that when they were addressed patronizingly by Menenius or furiously by Martius, the fact of their extra-fictional power to hear, move, stay or leave made them, paradoxically, a yet more threatening mob.

This was a production that privileged the potentially excessive anger of the people and the danger that it might overturn Patrician power, over the personal anger of Caius Martius and his mother Volumnia, often the emotional centres of this play. Richard Lynch's Martius played angry contempt as effectively as Fiennes but fitted even better Žižek's notion of a fighting machine with no fundamental class interest. Ideologically he was, of course, absolutely of the Patricians – he is the logical end to their class position – but he could have come from anywhere. He was simply Rome's most effective war machine. Martius and Aufidius' famously homo-erotic meeting in Antium was played without relinquishing at any point the threat of violence between the two men. There was no sense, as in Cake's performance, that the audience was being asked to read some need for love in Martius here. Aufidius' delight at seeing Martius in his camp seemed to stem simply from the use he thought he could make of the exiled Roman. Volumnia, too, was de-psychologized by the production. There was nothing sinisterly smothering about Rhian Morgan's performance; she was, rather, simply a strong-willed, highly pragmatic Patrician woman, so confident in her class position that she could see no threat to it in revealing the manipulations of power and could not understand why Martius balked at being manipulative. The relationship between Martius and Virgilia was, again, productively difficult to read. She seemed utterly numb in his presence. They barely touched throughout the performance and the kiss in 5.1 hardly seemed the kind that would elicit the description 'long as my exile, sweet as my revenge' (5.3.45) so that the performance occasionally read startlingly against the grain of the text. Perhaps Bethan Witcomb's performance represented an impotent female anger that her husband should be constantly risking his life with so little regard for her and for their family; but the lack of an 'emotional' performance generated a strong sense that whatever the wife of a commander felt in this war, whatever the wife of a politician felt in this peace, was irrelevant to the outcomes of either.

Described by one reviewer as both vast and claustrophobic, the ugly, fume-filled aircraft hanger in which this *Coriolanus* took place was also an actual site of the production of war. St Athan is a working RAF base. The production managed to underplay the anger of individual characters in this play and to foreground the vested interests of every group involved in the politics of war and peace. The site framed the audience as a potentially angry group of disenfranchised citizens that might run amok and wreck the show, or damage the military base. This is, of course, a post-Marxist reading that Brecht would no doubt have enjoyed and whose distinctly unheroic Caius Martius Shakespeare might not have recognized. On the other hand, the potential violent force of anger is foregrounded here in ways that make sense of early modern treatises and their classical sources, all of whom seem so terrified of anger's excesses. I end with this production not only because it is the one that, in my experience as a theatre-goer, succeeded best in producing a politically radical reading of the play, but because it was apparently interested in anger as a political force, as that which makes and destroys communities of needs and interests, rather than as a means or effect of personal expression. In the next chapter I turn not to an emotion as such but to a physical effect of emotion – laughter – and consider that, too, as a phenomenon that generates and interrogates social groups and their interests in early modern drama and its production.

The conclusion I draw here concerns early modern drama and site-specific theatre. In a culture that tends to read anger as a matter of personal mental health, it is important, I think, to develop performance conventions that permit the performance of other discursive possibilities around excessive emotion. The psychological agency of Cake's Martius suggests that he Just Can't Help his Anger – even in the face of Volumnia's cold suggestion that we can use our brain to control anger when it is politically expedient. This sense of character emerging at a point where humoral predominance and social needs are in conflict certainly emerges in the play. But in the Globe's production, emotion is privileged where in the play it is of ambivalent personal and social value. In the play there are others who will not control their anger because it is not in their interests to do so: the people. The two broadly site-specific productions I have mentioned above demonstrate ways in which anger pushes at social-spatial boundaries and ways in which socio-political groups, as well as individuals, might be theatrically configured as angry, in excess of forces endeavouring to contain them. The meanings generated by the juxtaposition of 400-year-old text and 'modern' site do potentially great work in foregrounding how anger might be staged as both used by and in excess of the cultures that approve or disapprove, legitimate or warn against it.

# CHAPTER TWO

## 'DO YOU MOCK OLD AGE, YOU ROGUES?' EXCESSIVE LAUGHTER, CRUELTY AND COMPASSION

IAGO

Now will I question Cassio of Bianca
A housewife that by selling her desires
Buys herself bread and clothes: it is a creature
That dotes on Cassio; as 'tis the strumpet's plague
To beguile many and be beguiled by one:
He, when he hears of her, cannot refrain
From the excess of laughter.

Shakespeare, *Othello* (4.1.94–100)

Laughter reveals us as a social mammal, stripping away our veneer of culture and language, challenging the shaky hypothesis that we are rational creatures in full conscious control of our behaviour.

(Robert R. Provine, *Laughter: A Scientific Investigation*)[1]

FIRST MADMAN

Do you look for the wind in the heavens? Ha, ha, ha, ha! No, no, look there, look there, look there! The wind is always at that door. Hark how it blows, poof, poof, poof!

ALL

Ha, ha, ha!

FIRST MADMAN
Do you laugh at God's creatures? Do you mock old age, you rogues? Is this grey beard and head counterfeit, that you cry, 'Ha, ha, ha?'

Dekker and Middleton, *1 The Honest Whore*, (5.2.196–202)

## WHAT'S FUNNY? THE HERMENEUTIC PROBLEM OF LAUGHTER

During November 2011, I ran two workshops as part of Forum Shakespeare in Rio de Janeiro. This is a programme of events curated by People's Palace Projects, an arts organization based at Queen Mary, University of London, which creates and brokers international arts partnerships and produces arts for social justice projects.[2] One workshop was a half day at the University of Rio de Janeiro, with a group of highly able undergraduate students particularly attuned to the possibilities of applying physical theatre practices to early modern drama production. The other was a day with an equally talented and less privileged group from the Universidade da Quebradas, whose students were drawn from the favelas of Rio de Janeiro.[3] Some of these students had achieved extraordinary success against odds that many British drama students would find hard to imagine. What was impressive about both groups was their willingness to commit, intellectually, emotionally and physically, to working in a one-off class with a stranger on a 400-year-old play in translation. What was strikingly different about the two groups was their attitudes to the comic. The work concerned, as much of my practical work with students does, the relationship between performer and audience in Shakespeare,[4] and focused specifically on the gestural vocabularies suggested by Shakespeare's theatre. We worked on Ophelia's account of Hamlet's entry to her closet. We worked on Angelo's ultimatum to Isabella in 2.4 of *Measure for Measure*. The Quebradas group were markedly more comfortable with allowing their work on these scenes to be funny, while the University of Rio de Janeiro group suggested that working with direct address on a scene gave rise to the *danger* of 'turning it into a comedy'. The Rio group produced exceptionally visually creative work on these difficult texts (the translations used archaic language to produce a sense of a poetry of the past) which inclined either towards the confrontational, painful and more naturalistic, or towards the broadly gestural and comical. The Quebradas group seemed more comfortable with moves between the comical and the serious. This group were not unnerved by the notion that Shakespeare could be funny where his subject matter – madness and sexual exploitation – seemed most serious; they shifted between comic and serious modes with great ease, both as actors and audience.

There is a problem of culture and hermeneutics here, comparable to the one that has made Robert Darnton's *The Great Cat Massacre* such a popular work of cultural history. Darnton gives an account of an eighteenth-century worker's protest that involved the theatricalized killing of all the cats in their neighbourhood and explores the cultural differences that might make an act that a modern French person might deem distasteful and cruel hilariously funny to a eighteenth-century one.[5] It will not always be possible to excavate the reasons why a historical culture might find something acceptable to laugh at and something else excessive, tasteless or cruel – and because laughter is such a visceral and seemingly universal physical effect of emotion, it is tempting to assume that if audiences consistently laugh at particular moments in a historical drama today, they have 'discovered' what was funny about it to its original audiences. Both my Brazilian example and Darnton's massacred cats suggest that socio-economic as well as national and historical differences pertain to questions of what is funny and what is not, what it is considered legitimate to laugh at and what might make one stifle one's laughter. I have already called the students who were more reluctant to make a 'difficult' moment in Shakespeare funny 'more privileged' than those with seemingly less anxiety around generic propriety, and in a short article in an online edition of the

*Guardian* newspaper I tentatively suggested that those who have experienced violence and corruption might be better equipped to understand the dramaturgical structures of a play like *Measure for Measure* than those with relatively 'easy' lives.[6] I say 'tentatively', because as one of the relatively privileged, I am conscious both that this suggestion might be a patronizing generalization, and of the potential for misreading the laughter of another culture, even when its members are alive to explain it. In this chapter, nevertheless, I consider exactly the issue of what was funny to a culture whose members I am unable to question except through textual traces – and hope to produce a more nuanced argument than one which suggests that a more violent culture laughs at subjects that its more sheltered descendants might consider cruel.[7] I am going to suggest that while twenty-first-century and early modern cultures have not, of course, found all of the same things legitimate objects of humour, or all of the same things excessive, it is possible today to read the dramaturgy of humour in early modern drama in ways that challenge generic boundaries and simple binaries of humour and seriousness, compassion and cruelty across 400 years.

This chapter explores dramatic moments which suggest that some kinds of laughter are excessive, or cruel. The chapter's exemplary objects of laughter are mostly theatrical mad figures: characters who go mad as a result of trauma experienced as part of a dramatic plot, like Shakespeare's Ophelia, characters kept in madhouses, from Jacobean tragedies, and a figure who is incarcerated as mad as a joke or a punishment: Malvolio in *Twelfth Night*. I am going to suggest that where a twenty-first-century audience may find laughing at such figures in excess of the boundaries of human compassion and good taste, an early modern audience may have laughed freely. But far from suggesting that the early modern period is therefore merely an example of benighted social attitudes long since abandoned, I will argue that laughter in the early modern theatre is ambivalent and multi-directional rather than simply excessive and cruel. Laughter in the first plays I explore here is often, rather, in excess of simply explicable power relations between the laugher and the laughed at. As Albrecht Classen points out in his introduction to *Laughter in the Middle Ages and Early Modern Times*, 'Those who laugh either join a community or invite others to create one because laughter excludes and includes, it attacks and belittles but it also evokes sympathy and understanding.'[8] Some of the plays we are going to examine here shift remarkably swiftly from one kind of laughter to another.

In what follows, I am going to cite some scientific studies of laughter. Some of these studies are interested in laughter as a reflex, something involuntary that the laugher cannot help. According to Robert Provine, laughter is 'spontaneous and relatively uncensored, thus showing our true feelings'.[9] Of course our 'true feelings' about what is funny are, as the Great Cat Massacre example above suggests, socially determined – thus whereas scientists may find that laughter is invariably produced by, say, non-serious incongruities (see p. 65) and, indeed, are supported by early modern treatises on laughter, different societies and periods may find these non-serious incongruities in different places. What I have found useful about the universalizing tendency of scientific studies of laughter has been their concern with possible social bonding purposes of laughter in evolutionary history: Classen's laughter 'for sympathy and understanding'. Where the Humanities scholar might stereotype science – particularly evolutionary psychology as it is recounted in popular science – as tending to naturalize conservative continuities (above all in its explications of gender roles[10]), the studies I cite here interestingly suggest that laughter has developed for reasons connected with altruism and sociability rather than aggression and exclusivity.

## THE ANTI-COMICAL PREJUDICE

In the speech from *Othello* that opens this chaper, Iago declares that Cassio, when he hears of Bianca, 'cannot refrain' not from an excess of laughter but from 'the excess of laughter'. Thus to Iago, it seems, laughter is in and of itself an excess. Perhaps anything that does not further his desire to bring about Othello's tragedy is simply in excess of what is meaningful to this villain. Perhaps the companionable reflex of laughter – even when it is spiteful – is irrelevant to this figure with no companions. Or, in accordance with Provine's description of laughter, laughter is an uncontrollable reflex and Iago is always entirely in control of himself, Othello, and the plot of the play. To imagine Iago getting any closer to laughter than a contemptuous sneer at a man such as Cassio, would be to imagine Iago losing control. That such a figure considers laughter excessive is, of course, in laughter's defence. As we will see, there are anxieties around the ethics of laughter circulating in early modern writings – particularly around whether laughter tends to the derisive and the cruel – which Iago's implied dismissal of it might contest. If this cruel and monomaniacal villain calls laughter excessive, he might encourage his audiences to consider its social advantages. The 'mad' characters I examine here are always potentially excessive figures, their language a tumble of repetitive excesses which fails to keep within the boundaries of grammar and sense, paying no attention to sumptuary etiquette, wild haired and hatless with their stockings down-gyved. They are of particular interest here because to laugh at them may be considered inappropriate, even cruel – in excess of the social regulation of emotional expression both in the early modern period and today. But if it is villains like Iago who call laughter an excess, we should also consider its positive effects.

Philip Sidney's familiar theory of laughter from the *Apology for Poetry* is that laughter, particularly in the theatre, is potentially a cruel kind of pleasure: 'naughty play-makers and stage-keepers have justly made [it] odious'.[11] It is to be differentiated from delight, albeit that there may be artistic depictions that provoke both. '[O]ur comedians think there is no delight without laughter', declares Sidney, whereas in fact we delight 'in things that have a conveniency to ourselves or to the general nature' and 'laughter almost ever comest of things most disproportionate to ourselves and nature'. We are delighted at beauty and laugh at deformity;

we delight in 'good chances' and laugh at 'mischances'.[12] Sidney argues that it is the responsibility of the play-maker to be sure that his final intention is educational delight, rather than mere laughter, and declares:

> the great fault even in that point of laughter, and forbidden plainly by Aristotle, is that they stir laughter in sinful things, which are rather execrable than ridiculous; or in miserable, which are rather to be pitied than scorned. For what is it to make folks gape at a wretched beggar, or a beggarly clown; or, against the law of hospitality, to jest at strangers, because they speak not English so well as we do? What do we learn?[13]

Significantly, Sidney ends his discourse on the comic by admitting he has 'lavished too many words on this play matter' and explains that this is because, although he counts plays among the 'excelling parts of Poesy' and drama the most common poetic form in England, 'none can be more pitifully abused'. The theatre play has the potential, 'like an unmannerly daughter showing a bad education', to cause 'her mother Poesy's honesty to be called into question'.[14] Theatre appears to be the place where laughter causes Sidney the most anxiety. He links it with unruly female sexuality in this image of Poesy illegitimately mothering the theatre.

Less nervous about laughter than Sidney is Laurent Joubert's well-known *Treatise on Laughter*, first published in French in 1579, which repeatedly suggests that it is simply not natural (and his work largely discourses on laughter as a natural phenomenon) to laugh at what ought to be pitied: 'What we see that is ugly, deformed, improper, indecent, unfitting and indecorous excites laughter in us, provided we are not moved to compassion.'[15] His examples are accompanied by provisos which demonstrate that it is only light and inconsequential mishaps and improprieties that move us to laughter. If its subject is likely to be seriously pained or humiliated without desert, we simply will not laugh at an incident. Joubert's study is of laughter in 'real life'; Sidney has the poetic and dramatic arts as the object of his *Apology* and it is significant that the latter's attitude to laughter is more censorious. There is a danger for Sidney, which Joubert never touches upon, that poetry will induce its audiences to laugh at that which should be pitied; Joubert simply trusts that where something is pitiable, we will not laugh. Take Joubert's example of the unseemly exposure of body parts that should properly be covered in public:

> It is equally unfitting to show one's arse, and when there is no harm forcing us to sympathize, we are unable to contain our laughter. But if another suddenly puts a red-hot iron to him, laughter gives way to compassion unless the harm done seems light, and small, for that reinforces the laughter, seeing that he is properly punished for his foolishness and unpleasant foul deed.[16]

The bare arse makes the viewer laugh; a violent punishment will not – although a light punishment, well deserved, will. But in the context of poetry and stage plays, laughter at something that should be serious because pitiable is something more of a risk. Sidney is of course right to suggest that fictional violence, deception or impropriety are a great deal more likely to be laughed at than the same in social life: fiction is, in one simple sense, always inconsequential. However, I also want to suggest that it is in moments of morally dubious, improprietous and excessive laughter that spectators are asked to examine the community of laughers to which they belong, in a range of ambiguous and challenging ways. The theatre is not reality, despite Puritan fears that it might produce real emotions and have unwished-for consequences. But it has a social and material reality more complex than that railed against in the anti-theatrical tracts of the early modern period,[17] a reality produced when human subjects gather to watch actors pretending to be other human subjects and as audiences are asked to witness, react to, enjoy and accept the fictions produced by actors in spaces built for playing. The audience really laughs, and here I consider moments when an audience is indeed invited to laugh at the supposedly pitiful and wretched. I am going to suggest that the relationship between laugher and laughed-at is a more complex one in the shared light of the Elizabethan and Jacobean playhouse than Sidney's examples and concerns suggest. 'What do we learn?' asks Sidney from the scornful, bullying, inhospitable forms of laughter he describes. I will argue that we may learn much about laughing, community and communities of laughter.

In answer to Sidney's question, author of *Shakespeare and Laughter* Indira Ghose might answer: we learn, or rather we are able to convince ourselves, that we are superior to those at whom we laugh. In her chapter on 'Early Modern Laughter' she develops the concept of the community of laughers whose comic object is always outside of that community.[18] Ghose's theory may be read with Sidney's in its suggestion that there is always something ethically dubious about laughing. Her study certainly informs this chapter; however, I want to challenge the assumption (which Ghose herself complicates elsewhere[19]) that communities of laughers are always created at the expense of another – the outsider or Other whose existence confirms what it is to be an insider, part of a dominant group of subjects whose membership of the group becomes what it means to *be* a subject. Cuckold jokes, for example, are supposedly always at the expense of some other group of men likely to be cuckolded and create a sense of superiority among those laughing at them: '[t]hus jokes about cuckoldry, rather than serving as a hydraulic safety valve for anxieties, can paradoxically serve to create a sense of male bonding'.[20] Ghose ends her discourse on this type of joke by asserting that 'Cuckolds are always other people'.[21] However, the example she uses – the Duke's men's hunting song in *As You Like It* (4.2.10–19) – suggests that something more complex is going on than the kind of excluding behaviour involved in laughing at cuckolded outsiders. The 'horn' of which the men sing in their pastoral exile is, at one level, the hunting horn and the song suggests that the men are reclaiming it from its denigrated status as cuckold symbol for the manly pursuit of hunting: it is 'the lusty horn', the instrument that calls the hunt, not 'a thing to laugh to scorn', the sign of cuckoldry. But of course, by singing of the horn,

> It was a crest ere thou wast born.
> Thy father's father wore it,
> And thy father bore it.
>
> (4.2.15–17)

the overworked joke about cuckoldry and possible illegitimacy contained in the symbol is ever present, even as it is denied. In the shared lighting conditions of the early modern playhouse, songs are always extra-diagetic even when they are part of the fiction: the Duke's men decide to sing a hunting song at this point in the fiction; they also sing a song, do a turn, for the audience. In this case, the audience is being told not to laugh at the horn, even as they are being taunted as bastards, their fathers as cuckolds. If, on stage, there is a mix of singing to the audience and singing with each other, this is group bonding of a particularly interesting and shifting kind. One may argue that everyone onstage and in the playhouse is being asked to laugh at themselves, in a homo-sociality that is so confident it does not even need to point to a group of outsiders as the object of laughter. It is your father, everyone's father, who bore the horn – and, should anyone be offended, we're really only singing about hunting.[22] A theory of laughter communities that posits the necessity of an 'other' to laugh at fails to take into account the subtle pleasures of self-deprecation, which, one might argue, have been a part of English culture for over 400 years. But what I am particularly interested in arguing is that communities of laughter in early modern drama are so sharply shifting, so bewilderingly constitutive of one community then another, that an audience cannot always know how they are being interpellated: as laughers or as the laughed at.

## LAUGHTER, COMMUNITY, COHESION

Interestingly, a number of recent biological and psychological studies make no Sidnean distinction between laughter and delight, nor suggest that laughter is necessarily socially excluding. As I suggested above (p. 58), the Humanities may tend to regard science as overly concerned with evolutionary psychological readings of phenomena which fit an ultimately conservative model of survival of the fittest, so it is interesting to read Jaak Panksepp's 2000 study of the 'neural and psychoevolutionary underpinnings of joy', in which he elides laughter, joy and delight. Drawing upon research that has discovered 'laughter' as a result of tickling in primates and even laboratory rats, he suggests that 'A study of the underlying brain systems in other mammals may eventually help clarify the ancestral antecedents of joy within the human brain' and discusses the 'delighted attentions' indicated by laughter in infants at 'joyful tickling and peek-a-boo games of absence and presence'.[23] Far from assuming that all laughter has its basis in the production of social bonds by way of the exclusion of the Other, Panksepp remarks that 'It is a common but not an empirically firmly established view that the maturing human taste for humor is based, in some foundational way, on the existence of infantile joy and laughter'.[24] Panksepp assumes that laughter indicates joy and if laughing in infants begins, as he asserts, at two or three months, it is a pre-social phenomenon that develops socially and for social purposes as the child matures, rather than a purely social, community-building, Other-excluding one.

In Panksepp and Burgdorf's study of rats, the kind of chirping response to tickling that Panksepp equates to human laughter 'predicts playfulness [...]: animals that chirp most during tickling also solicit play the most'.[25] Unlike Joubert in the late sixteenth century, who dismisses tickling as 'an imitation and copy of real laughter'[26] and considers 'true' laughter to be a God-given form of release from only human woes and hardships,[27] modern science here considers tickling-induced laughter as a physical reflex of just the same kind as laughter at a joke or other intellectual stimulus.[28] For Panksepp, play is a social activity, even in rats, and what interests him seems to be the equation of the physical capacity for laughter-like chirping with this social activity. Giggly rats are the most social in Panksepp's article and in his joint study with Burdorf: rats who make the giggling sound solicit play the most. Those with a tendency to laugh are of a social, sanguine disposition in Joubert, for whom laughter 'indicates a good nature and purity of blood'[29]; the humoral type with the greatest tendency to laughter, 'sanguine people', are, moreover, 'naturally gentle, gracious, pitiful, merciful, humane, courteous, liberal, polite, affable, easygoing, accommodating, hardy, amiable, friendly and cheerful',[30] all social virtues. The most interesting adjective in this copious list is 'pitiful', given Sidney's concerns that laughter is often at those who should elicit our pity but at whom we cruelly laugh instead. For both this twenty-first-century scientist and this sixteenth-century theorist, who are considering the science and culture of laughter rather than dealing with anxieties about the theatre, laughter indicates playfulness, sociability and, by extension in human beings, empathy.

One remarkable consistency across 400 years of laughter analysis is the shared conclusion that unthreatening incongruity provokes laughter. In Matthew Gervais and David Sloan Wilson's summative article on 'The Evolutionary Functions of Laughter',

> what emerges from the [recent scientific] literature is something of a consensus that incongruity and unexpectedness underlie almost all instances of formal laughter-evoking humor. This is insofar as the perceived inconsistency between one's current and past experiences involves both a non-serious or playful frame and an alternate type of intelligibility, that is, a meaningful interpretation of some stimulus or event that is different from that which was initially assumed.[31]

Similarly, for Joubert, causes of laughter must be non-serious and conducive to a spirit of playfulness, or we will be moved to pity and cease to laugh. His examples of the humorous, too, are largely of the sudden and unexpected: a quick wit is funnier than an obviously laboured one;[32] the sudden and unintended glimpse of 'shameful' body parts 'such as seeing them through an open seam of the breeches' is funnier than their deliberate exposure.[33]

The undermining and exposure of credulity is a particularly strong source of laughter for Joubert. In an example that provokes one of his voluminous lists of adjectives, he describes as hilarious an incident wherein

> we are promised the sight of a beautiful young woman, and just as we are aroused, we are shown a wrinkled old lady with one eye, a runny nose, a thick and kinky beard and underslung buttocks, dirty, smelly, drooling, toothless, flat-nosed, bandy-legged, humpy, bumpy, stinking, twisted, filthy, knotty, full of lice, and more deformed than ugliness itself. Here there is something truly to laugh at, seeing ourselves made fun of in this way.[34]

Having one's own credulous hopes and expectations suddenly and surprisingly just as they are at their height seems to fit Gervais and Wilson's notion of 'non-serious social incongruity' very well.

Why summative articles such as Panksepp's and Gervais and Wilson's interest me is that one can read them with Joubert to challenge conceptions of laughter that emerge from Ghose's study and, as we will see, Carol Neely's work on theatrical depictions of the incarcerated mad: that laughter tends to connote and produce power and social exclusion. For Sidney, we laugh, particularly in the theatre, at those we should rather pity – the weak, the grotesque; for Ghose, laughter is always 'at' the other; for Neely, whose ground-breaking scholarship on madness in early modern drama seeks to recuperate the early modern Bedlam from its reputation as a cruel and voyeuristic theatre,[35] laughter and pity at the mad are, as we will see, diametrically opposed responses, albeit they sometimes appear on stage together. Panksepp, on the other hand, remarks that in mammals, 'laughter is most certainly infectious and may transmit moods of positive social solidarity, thereby promoting cooperative forms of social engagement'. For this kind of positive affect to take place, there need be no other to laugh at.[36] Similarly, 'non-serious social incongruity' can include laughter at the self as well as at the other, just as the butt of Joubert's humour in describing the old woman in his example appears to be those who were expecting a young one, rather than the old woman herself. One would hope that laughing at her perceived deformities within her hearing would count as an injury provocative of pity, and that Joubert would not consider it funny. However, there is a social hierarchy associated with laughter in Joubert's treatise: he suggests that one's social inferiors are less worthy of pity as they have no right to avenge themselves. Jokes based on deception or imposture in Joubert will amuse as long as one is 'careful about the place, the time and the persons':

> The deception we acknowledge as being laughable is lighter, and such that it cannot be ill interpreted, done among friends and companions, or inferiors, who cannot really be upset or ask vengeance. This is why one must choose the persons.'[37]

Perhaps Joubert considers his putative old lady one of these socially inferior non-subjects and it cannot be denied that laughter at the mistake in the hypothetical example may serve to create a community of the young, male and not-ugly, confident enough in their social standing to laugh at themselves. Panksepp does touch upon what he calls the 'dark side to laughter' in a way that Sidney may have understood, referring to 'the derisive laughter that arises from feelings of social scorn',[38] just as Ghose suggests that 'Within a group laughter may promote group solidarity, which may then be used to exhibit disdain toward others and to ostracize those outside the group'.[39] But Panksepp also points to situations in which 'too much laughter', far from producing and legitmizing cultural norms, 'can become a social problem'; fascinatingly, he cites Joubert's 1579 treatise himself, particularly its discussion of laughter and incontinence. Panksepp remarks that 'eliminative urges' accompanying laughter have been treated with the same kinds of agents that treat attention deficit hyperactivity disorder in children: 'we may wish to inquire,' suggests Panksepp, 'what such pharmacological agents do to children's sense of humour'.[40] The treatment of perceived excesses of activity in children may also repress their playful delight. What these twenty-first-century studies share with Joubert is the strong sense that laughter may have positive as well as divisive social purposes[41] – and the example of treatment of excessive laughter here suggests that it may also be something of a subversive force.

## LAUGHING AT THE MAD

In the opening passage of his chapter on 'Laughter and Narrative' in early modern comedy, Jeremy Lopez asserts that 'While the events of Elizabethan and Jacobean comedy, the outcome of its scenes and plots, are frequently unpredictable, the behavior of comic characters usually is not.' In these plays, 'the overt and widespread reliance on stock, conventional, typical characters' and their predictable behaviour 'provides an order and a system of rules that act as a kind of balance to the disorderly, even lawless manner in which the comic narrative develops'.[42] Thus it is comic plots that amuse because they play to the desire for the unpredictable and incongruous. Certain comic characters may be funny because they allow other characters and paying audience alike to bond in the cheery or spiteful safety that they are of the inside group of laughers, not part of one of the outsider categories of cuckolds, foreigners or ugly old women. Comic characters according to Lopez' description react predictably to the unpredictable. Malvolio is so 'full of self-love' (1.5.87–8) that he is bound to fall for Maria's letter plot; the comic incongruity that makes us laugh lies in the gap between his self-perception and the rest of the social world's perception of him. It is particularly amusing, then, when unpredictable things happen to those who like to find the world predictable, who seek to regulate and repress its unpredictabilities and who accept, legitimate and work to produce its social hierarchies. It is funny to see someone fall in the mud, writes Joubert, and 'the more indecorous the fall, the greater the laughter. I call it indecorous when it is not orderly or expected: for the surprise has much to do with it.'[43] It is even funnier if they are of high social status and pompous with it.

Lopez' theory of comic character holds good here, as one who did not exhibit a predictable set of behaviours connected with over-inflated pride would not be so funny when falling. The fact that Joubert finds anyone falling in the mire fairly amusing (anyone, that is, who does not horribly injure themselves so doing and thus provoke our pity) suggests that all human beings are comical in the pompous surety of the stability of the world and their control of its physical properties.

The comic stage figures I am going to discuss next, though, are by their very nature unpredictable; indeed, they are often predictable only in their unpredictability. These are the 'mad', who appear on the early modern stage as figures of comedy and of pity, and significantly as both. I am going to use them to trouble Lopez's theory of predictable characters in comedy, which I think suggests a particular kind of power relationship between the laughter and the laughed at, in which the audience is located in the comfortable position of knowing insider. The unpredictability of the mad figures examined here complicates laughter's social and theatrical meaning.

Mad figures in early modern drama are, as Carol Neely suggests in her brilliant study of gendered madness in the period, gesturally and linguistically excessive. Their language is characterized by quotation, fragmentation and repetition[44] – repetition often reflective of obsession with the trauma that has driven them to madness. In Dekker and Middleton's *1 The Honest Whore*, the mad figures in the (Italian) Bethlem monastery, of which more later, have been bereaved of lovers, lost all their goods at sea, or gone insane with jealousy; the troop of performing madmen in *The Duchess of Malfi* obsess about sex, cuckoldry and their past professions. Ophelia, of course, sings and speaks fragments of her father's death and, perhaps, her own sexual betrayal. Edgar in *King Lear* invents a madman whose past dealings with a sexually corrupt court haunt him – though his 'Tom o'Bedlam' is also a construct of, and perhaps a comment on, residual notions of madness as demonic possession.[45] Were any of these mad figures funny? And if they were, were they, then, paradigmatic of Sidney's doubts about laughter in the theatre, examples of the way in which theatre provokes us to laugh at that which Joubert assures us we never do? Mad figures in the theatre may have invited laughter at their excesses. But when those excesses have been produced by past trauma, Joubert explains that compassion overrides amusement:

> if a man who became frenzied or maniacal says and does some strange things, we cannot keep from laughing until we think about the great loss of his senses and understanding he has suffered. Then we experience compassion because of the misery, and more still if this misfortune does not come through his own fault.[46]

Ophelia's first entrance in *Hamlet* 4.5 may be read in the light of Joubert's analysis. The mad Ophelia is carefully introduced by the conversation between Gertrude and the Gentleman thus:

> QUEEN
> I will not speak with her
>
> GENTLEMAN
> She is importunate,
> Indeed distract. Her mood will needs be pitied.
> (4.5.1–2)

The audience, as well as the Queen, are prepared for a 'distract' figure and warned that pity is the appropriate response to her. The rest of the dialogue before her entrance concerns how her speech may be read by 'ill-breeding minds' (4.5.15) who 'botch the words up to fit their own thoughts' (4.5.10). The fear is clearly that Ophelia's fragmented discourses will expose the court in some way – and this introduction to her madness prepares the audience, too, to read her carefully. Interestingly, though, it is not until her second entrance in the scene, this time into the presence of her devastated brother, that anyone offers a compassionate commentary on her state, or appears clearly to be emotionally affected by it. Once she has entered for the first time, Claudius and Gertrude are reduced to splutterings of 'How now, Ophelia?', 'Nay but Ophelia', 'Pretty Ophelia' (4.5.22, 34, 56), suggesting embarrassment and social tension around her behaviour as much as compassion. Ophelia's sudden and fragmentary shifts of subject – particularly the young men who will do it if they come to it (4.5.60), inappropriate to the sane Ophelia's gendered innocence as perceived by her brother and father – might be as funny as 'Poor Tom's' leaping out at the Fool shouting fragments of Catholic superstition, or the comic non sequiturs of Malfi's mad professionals, were we not aware, to cite Joubert again, of Ophelia's great loss. What I want to suggest here is that in Ophelia's first mad sequence, the audience may be permitted momentarily to forget the death of Polonius and rather to laugh at the King and Queen's desperate attempts to contain the madwoman. She is, after all, according to the Q1 stage direction, frequently used by modern editors, a incongruous, potentially comical, performing mad figure: her hair may suggest crazed female distress[47] but she is also playing a lute (Hamlet Q1 13.14 s.d.). It is only at her second entrance that we are offered a clear commentary on her state (Claudius explains her madness as 'the poison of deep grief' (4.5.75) at her father's death and Hamlet's departure but only when she has left the stage). This is offered by Laertes, who makes clear that this particular kind of incongruity – 'is't possible a young maid's wits/Should be as mortal as an old man's life?' (101) – just is not funny. In Joubert's treatise, the move from laughter to compassion in the face of the mad has a clear chronology. In the the theatre, laughter and compassion uneasily share the stage.

## CRUEL AND KIND

As Indira Ghose's work on exclusive and excluding laughter communities might suggest, underpinning Sidney's anxiety around the laughter induced by stage comedies is an idea that troubles the scientific studies I have cited above, with their confidence in laughter as a positive social bonding mechanism, and

Joubert's notion that real pain is not risible. This is the idea that some laughter is cruel: laughing at those in pain, laughing at those who cannot help their appearance or behaviour. The wretched beggar or beggarly clown, the stranger who cannot speak English are Sidney's examples.[48] Read the words 'cruel' and 'cruelty' in early modern writings and there seems to be a broad continuity of meaning across 400 years. 'Cruel' then, as now, refers to inexplicably unkind people and actions, and suggests an inhuman lack of empathy and a pleasure in unkindness on the perpetrator's part. In early modern writing, cruelty is equated with a lack of humanity quite explicitly; to be cruel is to be less, or sometimes more, than human – and thus not to feel compassion for humanity's trials. Death, war, fate and the law can all be cruel[49] – they are abstractions, without pity or compassion. Cruelty is un-kindness, where 'kind' means like, kin and kin-like: it is the opposite kind of act or attitude to that which builds social bonds. Thus, when Hamlet says, 'I must be cruel only to be kind' (3.4.176), his line suggests that Gertrude – and the audience – will wonder at his lack of humane compassion for his distressed mother and that he needs to explain his seeming perversity. Two scenes earlier, as he plans this visit to his mother's closet, he has suggested that cruelty and naturalness are not opposed – 'Let me be cruel, not unnatural' (3.2.397) – and the double use of the word in relation to his mother seems to protest too much. The traitor Scroop is addressed by Henry V as a 'cruel,/Ingrateful, savage and inhuman creature!' (*Henry V*, 2.2.95); once rendered inhuman, he can be killed. The clown Launce in *The Two Gentlemen of Verona* is dismayed at his dog's dog-like cruel-heartedness, complaining:

> I think Crab, my dog, be the sourest-natured dog that lives: my mother weeping, my father wailing, my sister crying, our maid howling, our cat wringing her hands, and all our house in a great perplexity, yet did not this cruel-hearted cur shed one tear: he is a stone, a very pebble stone, and has no more pity in him than a dog.
>
> (2.3.5–11)

Crab has shown no compassion for the human emotion that even the cat is demonstrating at Launce's departure from his family, and the impossible image of the cat 'wringing her hands' draws attention to the very humanity of the emotions for which the dog has no compassion, a humanity that is absurdly foregrounded again and again in the speech that follows, as Launce tries to tell the story of his parting, using his shoes, staff, hat and the dog to represent the human protagonists. The idea of cats, dogs and inanimate objects expressing human emotion is as essential to the comedy as Launce's confusion as to what should represent whom.

Despite seeming historical continuities, the cultural industries that are in the business of recalling and reproducing the past have a range of contradictory attitudes to that past's perceived humanity or cruelty. The dramatic and medical treatments of mental illness that emerged from the early modern period give rise to very different iconographies of pastness 400 years later. The early modern period produced some of the most valued cultural artefacts studied in the Humanities today (plays, in particular) but its authorities also perpetuated judicial cruelties around which a whole other heritage industry has been built. While supremely articulate women – witty Beatrices and stalwart Isabellas – are to be found at Shakespeare's Globe, walk fifiteen minutes through South London to the Clink prison museum and a very different cultural reality of scolds' bridles and chastity belts is on display. Broadly speaking, those elements of 'our' past which 'we' wish to legitimate and universalize (the works of Shakespeare, for example) tend to be reproduced as 'kind', in both the senses of 'compassionate' and 'like-us'. A production of *The Merchant of Venice* – the Shakespeare's Globe production of 1998 comes to mind – tends to be roundly slammed by the critics if it seems to be inviting the audience to laugh at Shylock. While Shylock is cruel in his insistence on having his pound of flesh, he must also be seen, in modern productions, to be sorely provoked by a cruelly prejudiced Venetian gentile society, or the production will risk being dismissed as inhumane and anti-Semitic, contaminating Shakespeare's currency as universally human.

If Shakespeare's Globe, as its website proclaims, offers the theatre-goer and tourist 'Not just theatre but the capital at its very best',[50] other south London attractions relish the display of London Down the Ages at its violent worst. The Clink museum is dedicated to the prison of that name, first built on this site in 1144. Here, according to the museum's website, 'Visitors will experience a hands on educational experience allowing them to handle original artefacts, including torture devices'; the website goes on to contextualize itself geographically, culturally and historically thus: 'This area housed much of London's entertainment establishments including four theatres, bull-baiting, bear-baiting, inns and many other darker entertainments', the last of which remain unnamed but which I assume to include prostitution, which, unlike torture, is considered too dark to name for a website that offers an educational experience for all the family. I am unsure as to whether the list is intended to provoke surprise at the closeness of the seats of culture to what modern visitors would regard as crueler entertainments, or whether theatre is deliberately being contaminated by the connection – but the website's education page merrily declares:

> Whether you're looking for a fun visit to torture each other and learn of the truly horrible history or a visit filled with educational fun and learning, our tour team are able to offer it all and tailor to your own specific needs.[51]

A few hundred yards further east still, the London Dungeon attraction offers a range of theme-park rides around the cruelties and dangers of London's past, including a Torture Chamber exhibit where

> London's torturer always finds a way to get you talking, whether with the hook, the castrator, the jaw breaker, or the creeping agony of the rack. Maybe he'll loosen your tongue the hard way, with the tongue-tearer![52]

The excesses of the past in these two attractions are comically cruel and unthinkably distant from us. Where the Shakespeare trade seeks to teach us what is transhistorically human, the aesthetic of the Dungeon's website in particular, and its entrance on Tooley Street, seems to invite laughter at the ludicrous inhumanities of the past.

Another room in the London Dungeon is, at the time of writing, dedicated to 'Bedlam' and is advertised in similar spirit:

> Face the inmates of one of London's first asylums: infamous for driving the slightly eccentric to the depths of insanity! Quick, they're waking up. Move along before you cause bedlam![53]

The very inclusion of the Bethlem Hospital in the Dungeon experience suggests that it was, like the torture chambers, a cruel prison, that barbarically failed to recognize the true mental state of its inmates and whose tortures drove them mad. Interestingly, the Dungeon website both perpetuates and baulks at the historical stereotype of the visitor who comes to Bedlam to be entertained: we are being invited to do exactly that but at the same time are jokily warned to run off before the madmen wake up. Little wonder that scholars may feel the need to recuperate the early modern period for a degree of humane good intention when the past is depicted in such cartoon-like images of barbarity.[54] In the following examination of dramatic scenes in madhouses and a scene set at a makeshift madhouse, where Malvolio is incarcerated in *Twelfth Night*, I argue that the inclusion of mad figures in the early modern drama for their comic value offers us a more nuanced way into a debate around cruel laughter versus compassionate seriousness in the early modern period than the one that I have laid out so starkly here as taking place in the cultural/tourist spots of South London.

## LET'S ALL GO AND SEE THE MADFOLK

Did early seventeenth-century Londoners go to visit the inmates of the Bethlem Hospital for entertainment? The London

Dungeon exhibit draws on an assumption that they did, and a range of cultural and theatrical histories have assumed so too; Carol Neely's study of *Distracted Subjects: Madness and Gender in Shakespeare and Early Modern Culture* challenges this assumption.[55] She suggests that historical evidence for these visits before the Restoration is scant, based on five dramas in which incarcerated madpeople perform for audiences,[56] and a much-paraphrased reference to the Percy children visiting London in 1610, where they saw their father in the tower and were taken on a number of London outings, including 'The Show of Bethlehem'. This is the only existing reference, outside of a dramatic text, to a visit to the hospital supposedly for entertainment before 1632, and Neely argues that it is is unlikely to have referred to a visit to the hospital at all: the children more probably visited a Christmas entertainment – a show about Bethlehem.[57] Neely, following Andrews, points out that visits to Bethlem may have occurred for a range of purposes, including charitable donation and moral instruction.[58] Her argument is supported by the Duke in *The Honest Whore Part I*, who plans to arrive at the madhouse 'as if we came to see the lunatics' (5.1.110) but in order to make this pretence convincing tells his comrades that they must meet with 'some space of time/Being spent between the arrival each of other' (108–9) – suggesting that they must not be perceived as the mass audience of a theatrical spectacle if they are going to be allowed in.

The notion that previously held assumptions about visiting Bedlam for a laugh are anachronistic is key to Neely's recuperation of the hospital as an institution with a genuine charitable and therapeutic purpose.[59] The hospital was hopelessly underfunded and certainly resorted to cures that might be considered cruel and certainly ineffective today; but, argues Neely, 'Visiting seemed to have begun (or increased) gradually in the middle decades of the seventeenth century. It accelerates in the Restoration.'[60] How, then, to explain the earlier plays that cite this as a practice? Neely suggests that there are too few of them to form the basis of plausible evidence for it: there are only four plays that stage performing madmen in 'houses of confinement' plus an additional work, the *Duchess of Malfi*, in which madmen are brought to the Duchess' prison to perform for her before she is put to death. The scenes that there are, argues Neely, are better explained by the theatre's desire for metatheatrical innovation, vogue for satire (the madmen, as she points out, are often mad professionals, common objects of popular satire) and the need for the playing companies to deflect audience attention from the potentially socially disruptive or subversive in their plays' main plots, than in terms of a reflection of common cultural practice.[61] For Neely, the later habit of going to see the madfolk may have been life imitating art.[62]

Neely is right to suggest that fictional visits to madhouses in plays do not equate to a common practice of voyeuristic and insensitive visits to madhouses for entertainment in social life. But I want to challenge an implication that I think lies beneath her recuperation of early modern Bethlem: that compassion and entertainment are somehow opposed or contradictory and that laughter must be justified or denied if we are not to dismiss early modern attitudes to the mentally ill as cruel and benighted. 'The hospital does not confine mad-persons cruelly or indiscriminate; but stage madhouses make spectacles of them as the hospital is imagined to do', argues Neely on her opening page.[63] I want to argue that this notion of 'spectacle', with its connotations of voyeurism, imagines the Victorian freak show rather than early modern theatre. Neely points to the moments when on-stage audiences laugh together at the mad and suggests that 'these communal responses protect audiences from individual engagement with particular madpersons'.[64] But on the early modern stage, just such an individual encounter is very possible should a mad figure turn to address an individual in the audience, and at such a point there is the potential for communal laughter which, far from protecting said individual, renders the confronted audience member the object of that laughter. In revisiting the dramatic treatment of mad figures on the early modern stage here, I want to suggest that, whether or not real early modern gallants regularly or ever payed visits to Bedlam for entertainment, theatre audiences may have laughed at fictional mad figures in ways that produced complex and ambivalent relationships between madness and sanity and between fiction and culture. I am going to deal first with early seventeenth-century plays that feature incarcerated mad figures and consider some of the ways in which they have been treated in recent productions; I will then shift to a recent performance of Malvolio's wrongful incarceration in *Twelfth Night* which deals explicitly with whether an audience's laughter at this figure is in excess of compassion and good taste, and consider a recently staged reworking of the fate of that character by writer and performer Tim Crouch.

## THE DUCHESS OF MALFI

An on-stage, fictional audience for comedy inevitably gives rise to judgements about laughter, as the paying audience watch the fictional one laugh at what the former may or may not find funny. Fictional mad people are shown to the fictional sane in the three

Figure 4: The Duchess of Malfi (Miranda Henderson) in Ten Thousand Several Doors dir. Jane Collins, Prodigal Theatre at the Nightingale Theatre (Brighton, 2006 © Matthew Andrews)

dramas I am going to consider next: twice in formal shows for which the mad performers have rehearsed; once in theatrical revelations, where a madhouse keeper demonstrates his traumatized charges to visitors. The on-stage audience in *The Duchess of Malfi* is the least conventional of the three: she is presented with madmen from a local asylum as entertainment – or torture – before she is put to death by her brother for marrying against his will. *The Duchess of Malfi*'s mad clearly serve a satirical purpose for the paying audience: a doctor, a priest, a lawyer and an apothecary, each speaks the language of his profession, distorted by obsession and distraction; each profession is figured as a butt of humour. The scene draws not only on the comedy which, Joubert writes, is inherent in 'a man who became frenzied or maniacal' saying and doing 'strange things' (see p. 70) but on the stock comic trope of the proud man fallen. It is not each madman's fault, *per se*, that he has been incarcerated in the madhouse close to the Duchess' prison – but his former authority reduces the likelihood that an audience should feel pity for him, just as status and pomposity of Joubert's faller in the mire diminishes the pity offered him by his hypothetical bystanders.

First, the *Malfi* madmen perform their song, whose lyrics are primarily concerned with what a dreadful, harrowing and bestial song it is. The *dismal kind of music* arranged by Robert Johnson is disturbing and complex. As Leah Marcus points out in her Appendix to the *Arden Early Modern Drama* edition of the play, it 'makes daring use of chromatics to indicate madness' and 'invite[s] the singer to repeatedly imitate the sound of a wolf's howl'.[65] Presumably, though, the song must be well performed in order to be entertaining for the paying audience, especially one at the Blackfriars used to complex interact music, albeit supposedly a 'deadly dogged howl' designed to 'corrosive [...] [our] hearts' (4.2.61, 67). Through singing it, the performing madmen both demonstrate their complex humanity and comment on their animal-like state of distraction – 'Sounding as from the theat'ning throat/Of beasts and fatal fowl' (4.2.62–3). The song's self-referentiality confers on the madmen, I am suggesting, some of the agency and sentience of the actors who are in control of the song for their audience. Next comes the madmen's rambling satirical dialogue, during which they appear to be speaking to one another rather than performing for the Duchess, obsessing about past sexual betrayals and making grandiose, delusional claims. They may, of course, address any of their predictably unpredictable, obsessive ramblings to an audience member, some of whom, at the Blackfriars,[66] may have been sitting on the stage with the Duchess herself: this may have been both disconcerting and provocative of laughter at another spectator's expense. Is it really possible, though, that anything but the most hesitant nervous laughter could be generated by this display, given that the only on-stage audience which the paying one has to laugh with comprises the imprisoned Duchess, convinced from the beginning of the scene that she will die in this prison (4.2.11–14), and her waiting woman Cariola, neither of whom give any indication of finding the show funny?

The Duchess has just been subjected to two other grotesque theatrical shows, one performed by her brother Duke Ferdinand himself with his dead-man's hand prop (4.1.44 s.d.), the other shown with the intention that she take theatre for reality: waxworks of her dead children are revealed from behind a curtain (4.1.55 s.d). The madmen surely cannot serve simply as comic relief within the Duchess' tragedy, as the audience's pleasure in the satire and the theatrical mad behaviour and laughter must be filtered through the on-stage audience of the imprisoned Duchess. Matthew Steggle has suggested that Nicholas Brooke's notion of *Horrid Laughter in Jacobean Tragedy*, which had gone relatively unchallenged since its publication in 1979,[67] has made anachronistic assumptions about the ubiquity of laughter by early modern audiences at tragedies. Steggle suggests that our main sources of evidence for such laughter are scenes clearly separated from the main plot, or theatrical mistakes and bad performances.[68] But in a sense, these madfolk are both: their theatrical turn is a performance in its own right, for the paying audience, as well as one rehearsed for the Duchess. Brooke himself is unsure as to whether the 'funny and obscene' 'antics' of these madmen[69] would have generated comedy – 'the hideous tension of the scene may or may not permit actual laughter'[70] and it seems that recent production in the UK has been nervous about finding out.

The last major London production of the *Duchess of Malfi* at the time of writing (Old Vic, 2012)[71] cut the madmen's sequence altogether – though this was ostensibly due to the need to shorten the running time of the production. The National Theatre's last production (2003), set in a 1940s mafia-dominated Italy, had Janet McTeer as the Duchess, strapped into a chair and injected with what the subsequent lighting and sound show suggested were hallucinogenic drugs. Although the 'madmen' seemed to appear in the risers upstage (used later to seat actors after the deaths of their characters), they were there, as Kim Solga describes them, to act out 'choice bits of the movie she was forced to watch: a series of video projections on the back upstage wall chronicling the destruction of her happy family'. I am convinced by Solga's reading of this scene: 'perhaps [...] we had all been momentarily transported into her altered brain'.[72] The RSC's last production at the time of writing (2000–1) had the madmen incarcerated in a tall glass structure centre-stage, which, as the production opened, contained the partying court; then, for the madmen's scene, a rocking, muttering, white-nightwear-clad, pseudo-Victorian nightmare of an asylum.[73] At the National the madmen's words were cut altogether, at the RSC they were partially inaudible: this was a distressing scene of enforced incarceration and brutalized insanity, rather than the play's satire on the fallen professional classes.

A complex and engaging way around the fact that the madmen's satire is hard to grasp for a modern audience (distracted *non sequiturs* can be less than amusing for those who are finding 400-year-old satirical references difficult in the first place) was devised by Jane Collins, Peter Farley and Prodigal Theatre for their production in and around the Nightingale Theatre and Grand Central Bar in Brighton (2006).[74] This promenade production's audience followed *The Duchess of Malfi* through dressing-rooms and kitchens, into the theatre space, down into the pub itself, and up to an upstairs window, out of which the Duchess and her children could be seen kissing Antonio goodbye and disappearing into Brighton station in her attempt to escape her brothers' wrath. The equivalent of the madmen's sequence took place in one of the pub's bars, where the Duchess sat slumped before a little stage while her brothers put on a ghastly, misogynistic stand-up comedy routine for her and our benefit, complete with a ventriloquist's dummy dressed like the Duchess. This was a disconcerting experience for this audience member, not least because the bar was still open to drinkers who had not paid to see the *Duchess of Malfi* and who may have been wondering if this was really what the comedy's little audience considered proper Saturday night entertainment. Perhaps, while laughing at the mad is intolerable to modern sensitivities, laughing at misogynistic jokes is just uncomfortable enough. Thus Prodigal Theatre produced a *Malfi* prison scene highly adequate to the play – it both entertained and appalled, provoked pity for the Duchess and laughter in spite of that pity. Even where the comedy was genuinely amusing – it was well performed and could also be enjoyed as a parody of 1970s sexist stand-up – enjoyment was rendered awkward by the presence of the slumped and exhausted Duchess. I am not suggesting that there is a direct analogy between the kind of humour used by Ferdinand's entertainers in Brighton's Grand Central Bar and the satire of the madmen, but it produced a partially amused, partially awkward self-consciousness among the audience which never permitted us to forget that our laughter might be in danger of breaking social codes. We had to consider what it was acceptable to laugh at. It also gave the performers an agency which the helplessly incarcerated madfolk at the RSC in the late 1990s could not possibly have, a point I will return to in considering one of the mad figures in Dekker's *1 The Honest Whore*.

## THE CHANGELING

The mad of *The Changeling*'s madhouse plot are confined both in Alibius' madhouse and off-stage (until they perform their wedding dance in the modern productions discussed here). They are heard and not seen, shouting their obsessions (which are mostly with food but seem sexually inflected[75]) to the horror of Tony the natural fool – in fact the disguised Antonio, would-be lover of the madhouse keeper's wife, Isabella. The early modern period distinguished between madmen and natural fools similarly to the ways in which the mentally ill and the intellectually disabled are categorized today.[76] Alibius' house contains both, unlike the historical Bethlem, which only accepted those suffering from mental illnesses deemed curable.[77]

When the bogus fool Tony arrives at the madhouse with his accomplice Pedro, who pretends to be a relative paying for his simple cousin's confinement, he is treated as a child, to be tested and put into a 'form', in the hopes that his intellectual capacities may be improved, and though Alibius claims that 'I do profess the cure of either sort' (1.2.49) (i.e. both fools and madmen), it does not seem that there is much hope of curing Tony. Like Lear's fool, who calls his master 'Nuncle' and is threatened with the whip for pushing at the boundaries of his 'licence', Antonio's Tony is an infantilized figure, and there is much joking on the part of Alibius' assistant Lollio that if they are lucky he may improve to the point of gaining employment as a law-enforcer – a satire on the mental capacities of beadles and justices (1.2.124–31). Unusually at this point in the stage history of disguise, and unlike Shakespeare's pretended mad figures Hamlet and Edgar, who plan or put on their antic dispositions in the presence of the audience, Antonio makes his very first entrance in *The Changeling* disguised as Tony: there is no indication in the text that the audience should know that he is only acting the natural fool. It is clear, from the moment of his entrance, that he is to be recognized as someone with a mental disability: 'Save you, sir', says Pedro, bringing Antonio on-stage, 'my business speaks itself;/This sight takes off the labour of my tongue', to which Alibius replies 'Ay, ay, sir,/'Tis plain enough you mean him for my patient' (1.2.82–5). It is not possible to know whether the Antonio actor would have made the audience laugh as he made his disability 'plain enough', or even whether it would have been so 'plain' that the audience would have suspected from the outset that this was someone disguised as a fool. The early printed stage direction is *Enter Pedro and Antonio like an idiot* (1.2.78 s.d.) but it is not possible to tell whether or not this 'likeness' would have been penetrable to the audience, as most on-stage disguises in the early modern theatre were,[78] or whether an audience would have seen a genuinely bewildered figure, fearing being left behind by his 'cousin', and felt a degree of sympathy with him. My suggestion is that both were possible.

The disguised Antonio supports the gestural language of natural folly with a vocal range that includes laughter and which, though it is socially inappropriate, is indication to Lollio, following Aristotle, that he is human:

LOLLIO

Tony, Tony, 'tis enough, and a very good name for a fool.
What's your name, Tony?

ANTONIO

He, he, he; well, I thank you, cousin, he, he, he.

LOLLIO

Good boy, hold up your head. He can laugh; I perceive by
that he is no beast.

(1.2.95–9)

The natural fool is treated as a child, whereas the madmen, heard off-stage, are disfunctional, sexualized, vocally violent adults. 'Tony' is afraid that they will bite him (1.2.202). When Alibius and Lollio are discussing the show their inmates must perform for Beatrice Joanna's wedding, it is the madmen that are both men's first concern:

LOLLIO
I mistrust the madmen most; the fools will do well enough:
I have taken pains with them.

ALIBIUS
Tush, they cannot miss; the more absurdity,
The more commends it, so no rough behaviours
Affright the ladies O they are nice things, thou know'st.
(4.3.51–5)

Lollio is worried that the madmen are not as safely under his control as the fools; Alibius is more confident but, while he clearly considers that the madmen will be successfully hilarious in their theatrical mistakes (the more absurdity, the more commends it), he is also concerned that they may be too rough and frighten 'the ladies'. Where, in *A Midsummer Night's Dream*, the mechanicals' fears of affrighting their female spectators are clearly ridiculous, *The Changeling*'s paying audience have heard the madmen and may be less certain of how they should react to this show. The mad in this play clearly teeter between the comic and the frightening – and between the comic and the pitiful. When Alibius' wife Isabella is shown her other would-be lover, Fransiscus, who has chosen a madman disguise in contrast to Antonio's fool, she reacts to his delusional observations and typical *non sequiturs* with:

Alack, alack, 'tis too full of pity
To be laugh'd at! How fell he mad? Canst thou tell?
(3.2.42–3)

As Joubert instructs (see p. 70), she looks to find pity in the trauma that may have brought the madman to this state. Both the drama and the treatise suggest that it is sometimes more 'pitiful' to rein in one's laughter at the mad figure – but this assumes, of course, that s/he is also potentially funny.

As Joost Daalder points out, the critical history of *The Changeling* has been one of theatrical pragmatics versus thematic coherence: some have read the madhouse subplot as Rowley's entertaining comedy turn, essentially extraneous to the plot, while others have argued that it is a disturbing reflection on the main plot, whose supposedly sane characters are truly crazed with love and violent lust.[79] The latter interpretation is certainly the one favoured by reviewers of the Cheek by Jowl production of 2006, who praised the doubling of roles between the two plots – though several critics saw the link between main plot and mad plot as forged by the production rather than by Middleton and Rowley themselves:

> The perennial problem lies in reconciling this grim tragedy with the comic subplot in which a madhouse keeper's wife is assailed by counterfeit lunatics. But Donnellan solves this at a stroke by turning the actors in the main story into the asylum inmates.[80]

> Nothing can make the mad scenes funny, but Donnellan comes as near as anyone could to make them seem one with the main action: he doubles roles between the two plots and in one fine frenzy gets all the characters to join hands for a desperate lunatic jig. It looks like a dance of death.[81]

Significantly, both Billington and Clapp here regard the mad plot as a problem to be overcome – as irritatingly in excess of the tragedy proper – and Billington is pleased that the production's dramaturgy has 'reconciled' what he sees as the play's generic fragmentation, while Clapp is presumably assuming that what was once funny about the mad scenes is lost to current audiences and again wants them integrated into a more satisfying whole, with no fragmentary, mad excesses. One online reviewer is more overt about the unease with which a modern audience supposedly greets the mad scenes and about the assumed disjuncture between comedy and cruelty over 400 years: for David Benedict, writing for Variety.com, the play has

> one big minus: the subplot about feigned madness in a madhouse. A merciless parade of lunatics may have gone over well when it was first performed in 1624, but

> antics with antic dispositions sit uneasily with modern audiences.[82]

Here, to play mad without a worthily literary theme – the madness of love and lust – through which to read the madmen is to make of them a 'merciless parade'; the binary of benighted voyeurism in 1624 and enlightened analysis in 2006 is clear. John Peter in *The Times*, on the other hand, suggests that the madhouse plot is both a deliberate part of the play's thematic design and may be intentionally comical, albeit disconcertingly so: 'it's both a parody of the main plot and a grotesque variation on it'.[83] To imagine Middleton and Rowley discussing the thematic relevance of the latter's subplot to the former's narrative is to precipitate them into a twentieth-century literary critical seminar, and although they may well have considered the lust and violence of De Flores and Beatrice Joanna's narrative as a form of madness, what this reading of the play, via this production, does is to rescue it from the perceived vulgar and cruel excesses of its theatrical origins.

Whether the rendering of a grotesque coherence, in production, between the two plots is deliberate or fortuitous is not so much my concern as whether the violent excesses of one plot permit audience laughter at the mad excesses of the other. Billington and Clapp suggest they should not and even Peter suggests that any comedy in this production is grotesque parody rather than hilarious relief – but these critics are reviewing the 'dark' Cheek by Jowl production, which is full of recognizable tropes of hypocrisy and repression, and the theatrical iconography of psychoanalytic seriousness. Peter describes it as the play Strindberg would have written if he 'had been a Jacobean';[84] Clapp asserts that it 'is one of the first plays to show the unconscious running rampant. [...] For this drama of the unconscious, everything is turned inside out';[85] Billington calls Olivia Williams' Beatrice Joanna an 'unstable heroine', then a 'frenzied neurotic', and points out that 'Alsemero, who she weds, keeps a well-stocked library of sex manuals'.[86] For Peter, director Declan Donnellan 'reveals the play's power by ignoring its baroque flamboyance'[87] but there is certainly a theatrical-baroque sensibility in the production's references to dimly lit Catholic churches – red chairs are made into prayer stands, as Billington remarks, for the Alicante church in which Beatrice meets Alsemero and her wedding is staged at the beginning of the second half, complete with a repeated and monotonously sinister chant of 'Ave Maria Virgine'. This production offers madfolk as compulsively twitching figures played by the main cast, their dance one of desperation. Both the scenography and the depiction of the mad suggest that if there is any laughter to be had here, it should be, in the words of Brooke's seminal work on the Jacobean Tragedy, 'horrid' (see p. 80).

Despite its modern costuming and the ostensible intimacy of the reduced capacity Barbican auditorium, central to its design, this production had its audiences peering into the dark at a ghastly historical 'other', a vision of another era's (Jacobean? Freudian?) instability and insatiability. The most recent UK production of the play at the time of writing, directed by Joe Hill-Gibbons for the Young Vic,[88] was a much more brightly lit affair, even more blatantly 'modern', with its score of contemporary popular music (including the wonderfully sick-humorous choice of Béyonce's 'Single Ladies' for the wedding dance, providing a grim reference to the finger with a 'ring on it'[89] that features so nastily in the play) and its sex scenes featuring strong-smelling strawberry trifle (the bed trick encounter between Alsemero and Diaphanta was staged in this production and, as dramaturg Zoe Svendsen remarks, this was not food as a metaphor for sex, but a staging of food-sex itself[90]). Where Cheek by Jowl's production was read by the reviewers as taking place in the dark unconscious of the Jacobean psyche, this production took place, very consciously, in the Young Vic studio and later its main house, in the lit presence of the paying audience, some of whom were seated on the stage, and whom were addressed directly, particularly unnervingly by De Flores as he commented in soliloquy and 'aside' on his passion for and progress with Beatrice Joanna. For Cheek by Jowl's production at the Barbican the audience was, I suggest, distanced from a world of historical, foreign, Catholic excess; at the Young Vic the performers appeared determined to implicate the audience in the excesses of soundscape, death and strawberry trifle.

As in Cheek by Jowl's production, the mad plot was doubled with the main plot and came together in the dance of the fools and madmen, to the pop song which horribly recalled what had recently happened to Alonzo's finger. The dance included a parody of a traditional wedding party – speeches, eating, toasting, chatting were all choreographed into the dance, as was sex between De Flores and Beatrice Johanna, her foamy modern white wedding dress flying over her head as he forced her on to her wedding banqueting table. As in Cheek by Jowl 2006, the wedding dance brought mad and main plot together and the performers were one and the same – but instead of a dance full of recognizable tropes of the disturbed and theatrically maniacal, this was a slickly paced dance of a performance, of the kind teenagers may have learned from a Béyonce video. It was as if Alibius and Lollio had laughed about what fun it would be to get the madfolk to do a popular 'R'n'B' routine, one which the rich young crowd at the wedding also happened to know. The movements were only rendered macabre and desperate by the audience's knowledge of the plot and the fact that De Flores' rape of Beatrice is choreographed into them, with Beatrice returning to the dance proper immediately afterwards. This dance was not 'dark' – it was lively, tightly choreographed, brightly lit and hugely enjoyable – but disturbing nevertheless. It suggested that the wedding ceremony was but an empty social form, and that because all love in excess of its meaningless conventions is illegitimate here, love must inevitably turn to violence and chaos in the society that imposes weddings upon daughters. It suggested that the audience's enjoyment of this play might be in excess of their moral sensibilities and, sure enough, one is invited to both laugh and squirm as strawberry jelly turns from a food fetish to the guts spilling from the murdered characters of the last scene: not dark humour but sick humour.

Reviewers offered similar comments to those made about the 2006 production, concerning the thematic coherence of mad and main plots. Billington makes a direct comparison: 'I was won over by a production that, like Declan Donnellan's 2006 version, suggests madness is the play's real theme'[91] and writes that 'It seems natural that the actors in the main story should reappear in the truncated sub-plot, in which a madhouse doctor's wife fends off her own suitors'. Charles Spenser in the *Telegraph* says of the subplot:

> It's poor stuff in comparison with the main play, but in this production, with the suitor feigning the symptoms of cerebral palsy, mangling his language and writhing in his wheelchair sporting a grotesque pink plastic safety helmet, it certainly taps into the sick heart of a play about madness and desire.[92]

Antonio's disguise as the natural fool tapped into the humour of the playground (the imitation of cerebral palsy recalls children's cruel mimicking of the same) and the grown man is both infantilized and brutalized by the pink safety helmet he has been given, and protected by it, as he is repeatedly rapped over the head with Lollio's truncheon. The moment at which Antonio reveals himself to Isabella as a suitor gave a retrospective permission to have laughed at his 'Tony' act: we were only laughing at this ludicrous imitation of the disabled, not at the disabled themselves.

'This may not be the purest of Jacobean revivals but, in an uninterrupted 110 minutes, it captures perfectly the play's atmosphere of mad excess', writes Billington at the end of his review.[93] But if one does choose to take, for a moment, the purity of a production's Jacobean-ness as a measure of its success, this production's mix of galleried seating and a number of stage-sitters, its direct address to the audience and close proximity of actor and audience, and the music/dance interlude that works as both slick entertainment and commentary on the narrative, make this more of a 'Jacobean' revival as Cheek by Jowl's psychoanalytic one. The implication of seating 'the audience on all four sides of the action in either boxed-off galleries at ground level or looking down from the high balcony', argues Paul Taylor in the

*Independent*, is that 'we are like prurient visitors to Bedlam',[94] taking up once more the assumption that all gazing at the mad was, and is, 'prurient', in excess of humanity and good taste. But I suggest that the audience for this *Changeling* are not offered the safety of the 'prurient' gaze – if such a gaze existed at the time this play was written. This audience rather is constructed as a group of playgoers at the early modern playhouse; they are not simply permitted to gaze at the mad and the helpless but are addressed by figures with agency in the violent action to which they are witness. As we will see, in the an earlier play featuring a madhouse plot, *The Honest Whore Part 1*, actual mad figures in the early modern drama – rather than characters pretending to be mad or characters whose passions verge on insanity – can be given a comparable theatrical agency.

## *THE HONEST WHORE*

Part 1 of this two-part drama[95] contains a substantial Bethlem Monastery sequence (this particular Bethlem is situated outside Milan), in which the much put-upon Candido, a linen draper, is incarcerated by his wife, who pretends he is mad and has him committed to the asylum in order to provoke him to an anger that he frustrates her by refusing to vent. The asylum is visited in turn by two young lovers who hide there: to get married and escape the disapproving father of the bride. When this father, the Duke of Milan, discovers their plot, he and his followers arrive at the madhouse, intent on stopping the marriage. This is the exchange between the Duke and his followers, in which a visit to the madmen is posited, quite literally, as a pastime:

DUKE
Castruchio, art thou sure this wedding feast
Is not til afternoon?

CASTRUCHIO
So 'tis given out, my lord.

DUKE
Nay, nay, 'tis like. Thieves must observe their hours;
Lovers watch minutes like astronomers.
How shall the interim hours by us be spent?

FLUELLO
Let's all go and see the madmen.

ALL
Mass, content.

(*1 Honest Whore*, 5.2.100–6)

This unhesitating chorus of enthusiasm for the idea suggests to me, *pace* Neely, that watching the mad may have been considered a fun thing to do, though the aforementioned passage in which the Duke insists that the party does not arrive in a crowd suggests that treating the mad as theatre may have been considered suspiciously indelicate.[96] When faced with their first madman, the visitors' reaction is one of pity and compassion:

DUKE
How fell he from himself?

ANSELMO
[the friar who runs this Bethlem Monastery] By loss at sea.
I'll stand aside: question him you alone,
For if he spy me, he'll not speak a word
Unless he's thoroughly vex'd.[97]

*He reveals an old man wrapped in a net*

FLUELLO
Alas, poor soul!

CASTRUCHIO
A very old man.

DUKE
God speed, father.

(5.2.173–9)

Once this traumatized merchant gets into his stride, however, and begins to spout the fragmentary memories, repetitions and imagined encounters that typify mad discourse in the drama, presumably while getting more and more tangled up in his net, the party clearly begins to find him entertaining:

> 1ST MADMAN
> [...] Stay, stay, stay, stay, stay – where's the wind, where's the wind, where's the wind, where's the wind? Out, you gulls, you goose-caps, you gudgeon-eaters! Do you look for the wind in the heavens? Ha, ha, ha, ha! No, no! Look there, look there, look there! The wind is always at that door – hark how it blows – poof, poof, poof!
>
> ALL
> Ha, ha, ha!
>
> (5.2.194–9)

The madman behaves as if the gallants are part of the scene of his trauma, directing them where to look for the ever-present wind that has wrecked his ships. At first, this audience behave as a community of laughers, external to the scene; but the madman insistently draws them in, first by confronting their laughter and denying that his plight is mere theatre, then by disrupting the social hierarchy of the occasion. His response at being laughed at is to upbraid the gallants for their lack of respect for an elder: 'Do you laugh at God's creatures?' he demands. 'Do you mock old age, you rogues? Is this grey beard and head counterfeit, that you cry, "Ha, ha, ha?"' (5.1.201–3). Having thus ticked off these young puppies and accused them of laughing as if at a play, where his beard might be counterfeit, and thus, of course, implicating the paying audience in the disrespectful laughter, he takes on the epithet of father his on-stage audience has given him and, moreover, the authority of the father figure, as he turns abruptly to the gallant Pioratto and asks, 'Sirrah, art not thou my eldest son?' (203). Falling in with the joke Pioratto agrees that he is, to which the madman retorts that indeed he is not, as he looks quite different. It is to the Duke the madman turns next, addressing him with the demeaning 'Sirrah' (207), minutely examining – and then insulting – the state of his hands, to the amusement of the gallants.

Having brought the gallants into close physical proximity to him and implicated them in his comical insults at their lord's expense, the madman calls upon the Duke to 'Kneel down, thou varlet, and ask thy father blessing' (215). And once the whole party is clustered around him, he is back in the scene of the shipwreck, with his audience as his fellow sailors, and then as his enemy:

> If you love your lives, look to yourselves. See, see, see, see, the Turks' galleys are fighting with my ships! Bounce goes the guns! 'Oooh!' cry the men. Romble romble go the waters. Alas! There! 'Tis sunk, 'tis sunk! I am undone, I am undone! You are the damn'd pirates have undone me! You are, by th' Lord, you are, you are, stop 'em, you are!
> (221–6)

Within one short sequence, the madman's audience can pity, laugh at and interact with him. The madman is, at one moment, seemingly helplessly entrapped in his net, a theatrical spectacle, while the next moment he has the power to pull his spectators into a comic dialogue with him, the jokes of which are very much at the spectators' expense, and then into the narrative space of his trauma. The madman forms and reforms communities of laughers; particularly interesting here is the way in which he remakes social hierarchy by getting the Duke to kneel to him and the gallants to laugh at the Duke. His unpredictability is disarming – to a group which has already been literally disarmed at the door of the madhouse, where the very reason given for their having to hand in their swords is the unpredictability of the inmates:

> ANSELMO
> Yes, you shall,
> But, gentlemen, I must disarm you then.

> There are of mad men, as there are of tame,
> All humour'd not alike: we have here some,
> So apish and fantastic, play with a feather,
> And tho 'twould grieve a soul to see God's image
> So blemish'd and defac'd, yet do they act
> Such antic and such pretty lunacies,
> That spite of sorrow they will make you smile;
> Others again we have like hungry lions,
> Fierce as wild bulls, untamable as flies,
> And these have oftentimes from strangers' sides
> Snatch'd rapiers suddenly and done much harm,
> Whom if you'll see, you must be weaponless.
>
> (5.2.153–66)

In this prologue to the Bethlem scene, the mad are no more subsumable into one humour – or stereotype – than the sane. Anselmo suggests that watching them will conflate pity and smiling. The speech neatly reverses Joubert's analysis who writes that 'we cannot keep from laughing' at the madman 'until we think about the great loss of his senses and understanding he has suffered. Then we experience compassion because of the misery, and more still if this misfortune does not come through his own fault'.[98] For Joubert, we laugh at the madman's predictable behaviour until we remember his suffering; in Anselmo's speech, compassion is the assumed state when first confronting the mad, smiling the inevitable reaction to the theatricality of the madmen's 'antic and…pretty lunacies'. The scene suggests that it was thinkable for the early moderns to find a madman amusing and simultaneously to empathize with him – indeed, to have a complex and shifting relationship with him as a human subject.

The reciprocity between performer and audience demonstrated here is also a condition of the early modern playhouse and it is worth reconsidering here the indoor playing conditions in which early modern dramas featuring the incarcerated mad were produced. Dekker and Webster's *Northward Ho* was performed at Paul's by Paul's Children; Fletcher's *The Pilgrim* at court and then at the Blackfriars by the King's Men; Middleton and Rowley's *The Changeling* at the Cockpit by Lady Elizabeth's Men. Two plays featuring the incarcerated mad, including *The Honest Whore*, were played in outdoor, public amphitheatres; nevertheless, *The Duchess of Malfi* was in the King's Men's repertoire when they owned the Blackfriars (and Webster's irritation at the way in which his tragedies were received by the commoner crowd out of doors is clear from his preface to *The White Devil*[99]), while *The Honest Whore* itself, first performed at the Fortune by the Prince's Company in 1604, was one of only two plays of Dekker's to be revived for indoor showing – by Queen Henrietta's Men at the Cockpit around 1635.[100]

The good-humoured confrontation and flattery by teasing, used by Shakespeare when he jokes about noisy groundlings and mad Englishmen in *Hamlet*, is in particularly strong evidence in plays written with the private playhouses in mind, sites of entertainment where the rich and fashionable have their behavioural and sartorial habits dramatized and satirized. Sarah Dustagheer has argued persuasively that speeches such as Jonson's prologue to *The Devil is an Ass,* in which the playwright complains of stage-sitters restricting the playing space to the size of a 'cheese trencher' (Prologue, 8) and tells players to move out of their sight lines when they have finished speaking,[101] shows the artist reclaiming the stage space from recalcitrant playgoers rather than deliberately drawing attention to them in order to please them.[102] I have no doubt that there is some genuine exasperation at play on Jonson's part here, just as there may have been in Shakespeare's advice to those clowns inclined to show off to those less interested than they should be in necessary questions of the play. What interests me here, though, is what Tiffany Stern[103] and Ralph Cohen[104] have noted as an indoor playhouse tendency to include audiences quite explicitly within the theatrical form and fictional content of the theatre event. Nova Myhill, in her study of 'Spectators as Spectacle in the Caroline Private Theatres' argues that inductions featuring gallant stage-sitters suggest 'that the experience of playgoing is as subject to judgment as the plays themselves' by this elite audience of self-appointed critics.[105] What we have in *The Honest Whore*'s madhouse sequence is an audience for the madmen made up of the kinds of gallants who may have sat on the stage at the play's 1635 revival, attentive and empathetic one moment, raucous and disrespectful the next, always inclined to find jokes at the expense of another in their party hilarious. Myhill concludes that the on-stage audience staged by (and mingled with the real on-stage audience in) the Inductions written by Jonson and Brome 'ultimately expands the frame of the play to include the entire theater, placing the theater audience on display in the terms of the playwright rather than the reverse'.[106] The fact that in its original incarnation this play probably played at the Globe suggests that the scene's shifts from laughing at the mad to laughing at those who laugh at them was of comic value anywhere. Nevertheless, it is interesting to consider the ways in which proximity to the stage and the particular audience demographic of the private playhouse might conspire here to turn a self-constituting – and perhaps self-satisfied – in-group of laughers into a group laughing at themselves along with a distinct 'other', the madman.

## MALVOLIO

The mad figures we have considered thus far stage a fascinating uncertainty around permissible and excessive laughter and about what kinds of behaviour and laughter are in excess of what is properly human. I want now to consider the implications of this argument about shifting sympathies and comic excess for a Shakespearean text, *Twelfth Night,* via a recent play about Malvolio. Of course, Shakespeare did not write a madhouse scene as such: *Twelfth Night*'s scene of incarceration is one of false imprisonment in a makeshift madhouse. It is of particular interest here in the light of a historical interest, in theatre production, in stripping the scene of its comedy.

The image shown in Figure 5 is of Malvolio incarcerated as a madman by his gulls. It advertises not a production of

*Twelfth Night* but a staged court case, *Malvolio's Revenge*, in which Olivia appeals against the millions of dollars' worth of damages Malvolio has won in a successful suit against the 'False imprisonment, violation of constitutional rights, and...intentional infliction of emotional distress' inflicted upon him by Sir Toby *et al.*[107] This courtroom drama could stand as a parody of what Becky Kemper argues is an anachronistic interpretation of Malvolio's incarceration as an extremely cruel abuse: the showing of Malvolio through a prison grate became a scenic convention from the 1850s.[108] In her article subtitled 'Reclaiming the Humor in Malvolio's Downfall', Kemper follows C. L. Barber's warning against rendering Malvolio too pitiable,[109] and argues that the sight of Malvolio tortured and broken is a theatrical anachronism that 'can so sour the final moments of the play that they ultimately rob the audience of a satisfying conclusion'.[110] She also suggests that in comparison to the historical cultures of punishment and treatment of the mentally ill in Elizabethan and Jacobean England, Malvolio is let off very lightly: merely deprived of light

Figure 5: Malvolio (Ted van Griethuysen) in *Twelfth Night* (Shakespeare Theatre Company, 2008), used to accompany a review of *Malvolio's Revenge* (Shakespeare Theatre Company Mock Trial, Sidney Harman Hall, Washington, DC, 2009) (by kind permission of Shakespeare Theatre Company © Carol Rosegg)

and visited by a comedy priest, as opposed, say, to having his leg chained to the floor and being beaten with brambles, the fate suffered by the wife treated as mad, as a punishment for scolding, in Barnaby Riche's 'Two Brethren and Their Wives', a possible source text for *Twelfth Night*.[111]

Kemper lists the following examples of modern productions in which the incarceration scene is staged as 'nothing short of torture':

> Henry Irving's 1884 production put the steward in 'a dungeon worthy of fidelio'. Jacques Copeau in 1914 preferred the image of Malvolio's desperate fingers clawing at a grate. Bell Shakespeare company in 1995 had Malvolio stuffed in a portable dumpster that Feste beat with a baseball bat. In 2005, Dian Denley of the Globe Center Australia paraded a black-hooded Malvolio onstage, echoing Iraq's Abu Ghraib Prison.[112]

She points, as have other scholars, to the folio stage direction for the scene 'Malvolio, *within*', reminding us that the audience never actually see Malvolio during this scene, and to the fact that, though Sir Toby suggests binding him, this humiliation would not have been staged in the early modern playhouse. As David Carnegie has also marked, the convention of a visible Malvolio in his makeshift madhouse emerged on the mid-Victorian pictorial stage.[113] For Gayle Gaskill, 'the shadow of this representational staging still falls over the dark house scene' and she adds Bill Alexander's RSC production of 1987 (Malvolio: Anthony Sher) and Trevor Nunn's 1996 film (Malvolio: Nigel Hawthorne) to Kemper's list of pitiable Malvolios, pointing in particular to how the conventions of film close up invite an emphasis on the 'psychology of humiliation' in the play.[114]

The *Malvolio's Revenge* mock trial was produced by the Shakespeare Theatre Company of Washington, DC, but its lawyers were real. Malvolio's lawyer was former US Solicitor General Paul Clement, who made a passing joke about his defence of Guantanamo imprisonments without trial during the performance.[115] The linking of Malvolio's treatment to a particularly raw and current form of inhumanity could not have been clearer. In the productions listed by Kemper, the audience is asked to recognize that the joke against Malvolio has finally transgressed the boundary between comedy and cruelty and that they should stop laughing at him and empathize. If this treatment of the 'mad' Malvolio is indeed an anachronism, it is one that *Malvolio's Revenge* clearly enjoys enormously and which the performance tradition instigated by Irving asks its audiences to take very seriously.

How does the fate of Malvolio relate to the ambivalent theatrical treatments of the incarcerated mad figures discussed above? The wrongly incarcerated Malvolio is a stage mad figure in more ways than one. Like *The Duchess of Malfi* madmen after him, he is a member of the upstart professional classes whom the audience love to hate (interestingly, of course, *The Duchess of Malfi* is a play about an aristocratic woman who actually does marry her Steward[116]). Malvolio has imagined serving the lust of his mistress' heart as Edgar, in *King Lear*, imagines that his Poor Tom has done. And if Kemper and the scholars she cites are right and the audience never see him once he is incarcerated, Malvolio is like the mad figures in *The Changeling* subplot, who shout their mad fragments from off-stage and are attended to and upbraided by an on-stage carer. The joke of the sane man wrongly incarcerated, who cannot prove his sanity because everything he does and says seems to confirm his madness, is repeated in the fate of Candido, in *The Honest Whore,* imprisoned in the madhouse as part of his wife's plan to provoke a manly anger from this impossibly calm and cheerful husband, and in Fletcher's *The Pilgrim* (1621),[117] where the saintly Alina's furious father Alphonso is reconciled to his daughter's marriage as in *The Honest Whore* and is also cured of his excessive anger. In *The Pilgrim*, as in *The Honest Whore*, a father is made to reconsider his authoritarian demands when his daughter's marriage for love is approved by a higher authority. Alphonso's daughter Alinda's clever serving lady Juletta convinces the Master of a madhouse that the King wants Alphonso incarcerated. At first, the tyrant-father's fury at not being able to find his runaway daughter, then at being taken for a madman, confirms to the Master of the house that the angry gentleman does indeed deserve his incarceration – but Alphonso's anger subsides as he actually begins to doubt himself:

MASTER
Ye are dog-mad: you perceive it not,
Very far mad: and whips will scant recover ye.

ALPHONSO
Ha! Whips?

MASTER
Aye, whips, and sore whips, and ye were a Lord sir, if ye be stubborn here.

ALPHONSO
Whips? What am I grown?
[...]
I do not perceive I am so; but if you think it –
Nor I'll be hanged if it be so.
*Irons brought in*

MASTER
Do you see this sir?
Down with that devil in ye.

ALPHONSO
Indeed I am angry
But I'll contain myself: O I could burst now,
And tear myself, but these rogues will torment me:
Mad in my old days? Make mine own afflictions?
(4.1.19)

Through being taken as mad, Alphonso learns to 'contain' the anger that has been the scourge of his daughter and an object of ridicule for the audience throughout the play. I include this passage here because it demonstrates a very different dramaturgical and thematic purpose for a false incarceration from that in *Twelfth Night,* wherein Malvolio's equally comic flaw of pride reduces him to the plight of a madman but is far from redeemed by the last scene. Malvolio will never see that he has 'ma[de] [his] own afflictions' and swears revenge on the on- and off-stage communities of laughers that have made him their object. One may assume that audiences of 1602 and 1621 respectively are intended to laugh at both of these self-deluded figures – but the 'satisfying conclusion', to recall Kemper, that *The Pilgrim* offers is that the deluded are brought to self-containment. All Malvolio seems to be brought to is anger at the fact that he has been duped and an understanding that we have all laughed at him.

Much late twentieth-century criticism of *Twelfth Night* has been determined to offer audiences and readers a 'dark' ending to-*Twelfth Night*, and has read Malvolio's last line as a serious disruption to the play's celebratory ending.[118] In this reading, the audience is told that it has been enjoying itself too much and is made to face the cruel community of excessive laughers it has become. But this can only work if Malvolio has been seriously abused in his makeshift madhouse. If the audience has not seen him, if Sir Topaz has been enjoyably ridiculous and the audience has only been provoked to the mildest of pity for Malvolio, or indeed simply enjoyed the incarceration scene for its ludicrous and unnecessary theatricals – Malvolio continues to be risible when he, determinedly unredeemed to the end, offers revenge as an ending to this play instead of comedy.

My reading places the play at the conservative end of the subversion/containment debate recalled in the Introduction to this volume (p. xxvi). I argue that we cannot assume an early modern audience would have considered Malvolio's treatment excessive at all and I suggest that what *Twelfth Night* does is generate communities of laughers at Malvolio's expense.[119] He is a ludicrous social climber with ideas above his station and it is for this that he his punished; in laughing at him, the audience is constructed as a community that understands it is ludicrous for the 'Lady of the Strachy' to marry 'the yeoman of the wardrobe'

(2.5.37–8). The fact that Sir Toby Belch recognizes that the whole joke has gone too far (4.2.64–70) suggests that he recognizes the trouble that the joke will cause for him rather than, necessarily, its cruelty. Thus *Twelfth Night* may be read as a comedy of social othering that is certainly unkind to the social climber but suggests that ostracization and contempt are exactly what he deserves. The play un-kinds Malvolio, makes it clear he is not one of us. It is impossible to know what an early modern audience may have felt when Malvolio declares he will be revenged on the whole pack of them. I am suggesting here that it may not have felt implicated in some dreadful psychological torture, or particularly sorry for the fallen proud man at all.

## I, MALVOLIO

*I, Malvolio* is a play by Tim Crouch that rereads *Twelfth Night* in terms of laughter and its excesses. It tells the story of the play from Malvolio's perspective and its audience is presented, from the play's opening moments, with Malvolio as both a victim of

Figure 6: Malvolio (Tim Crouch) in *I Malvolio*, Unicorn Theatre, 2011 (© Bruce Atherton and Jana Chiellino)

early modern shame punishments and the inmate of an imagined asylum from a dark and unspecified past. The piece is one in a series written and performed by Crouch, in which he retells four Shakespeare plays from the perspectives of what he calls minor characters (*A Midsummer Night's Dream* is narrated by Peaseblossom, *The Tempest* by Caliban, *Macbeth* by Banquo). In an online interview, Crouch asserts that he is giving these characters a voice that Shakespeare does not permit them, suggesting that he is in some way subverting or undoing the power politics of the plays in question.[120] The production is of particular interest here because throughout the hour-long monologue, all addressed to the audience, Malvolio/Crouch repeatedly makes the audience laugh, something that is predicted in the stage directions of the published text of *I, Malvolio*. He then repeatedly comfronts them with accusatory questions and upbraids them for their laughter:

> I am locked away in hideous darkness. Without light, without toilette.
> *He shows the audience his behind. The audience laughs.*
> Find that funny still? Is that the kind of thing you find funny?
> Oh such fun, you think. A sport royal, I warrant.
> You bullies. You big bullies.[121]

This Malvolio is a figure disgusted by the excesses both of his world and the one he is addressing, which he assumes to be one and the same – excesses that include Belch's drinking and carousing, Viola's cross-dressing (which he dismisses as completely inexplicable, the actions of a mad woman), and all the indulgences the audience members may like to partake of: he aggressively suggests that they all enjoy dropping litter, spitting, drinking, smoking, laughing at those who are different to themselves, and, most repulsively to him it seems, going to the theatre, a place, he insists, where people might enjoy watching a man like Malvolio hang himself.[122] He also repeatedly claims not to be mad.

Malvolio is dressed for most of the performance as just the kind of victim of abuse to which Kemper and Neely might object in their revisions of the end of *Twelfth Night* and the historical treatment of inmates of Bedlam respectively. He wears filthy, in parts bloody, off-white 'combinations', full of holes which suggest that someone has poked at him with something sharp, or burnt him with cigarettes. The garment has a split in the behind through which it may be seen, when he first bends over, that he has soiled himself – presumably out of fear at some unspeakable treatment or because he has not been given anywhere to relieve himself in his prison. Large toy flies are attached to him. On his back is a sign which reads 'Turkey Cock' and underneath it another reading 'Kick Me'. His head wear seems to represent something between said turkey and the familiar horns of the cuckold; beneath his chin is a red turkey's wattle on an elastic strap. It is clear that he has been subjected to some charivari-like display, shown to the world as an object of contempt.[123] His costume speaks a history of the social pariah, from the receiver of the theatricalized medieval shame punishment, still part of legislative practice in Shakespeare's lifetime,[124] through the Victorian asylum inmate to the modern day, homeless victim of abuse.

Despite – or perhaps because of – the grim visuals, Malvolio's audience is constructed and reconstructed as a group that enjoy laughing at him, even as they are upbraided for doing so. My own experience as an audience member was of laughing openly at Malvolio's pompous accusations that we were all part of a cruel, decadent and chaotic society conspiring to incarcerate one of its only decent members, abruptly followed by genuine moments of pity for this figure, and moments of repulsion – not so much at his vilely soiled attire but at his desperate love for Olivia, of which more later.

This Malvolio figure contains two comic stooges: the proud man fallen and the social misfit. Crouch performs the play in two versions, one for its originally intended audience of 11+ and one for adults (the main differences being the strength of the swearing the piece contains and the amount of exposure offered by the character's underwear, with some improvised differences that change from performance to performance). The intended audience of young people is encoded in both versions: in Crouch's opening encounter with them, he accuses them of litter dropping. He has screwed up and abandoned Maria's forged letter, which he has been reading and rereading as the audience enter, and then fires his accusatory questions at them:

> I'll just drop this here, shall I? Is that what you'd do? In the absence of a bin. This thing here. Yes? Just leave it here. Dump it here. Let it rest and blow about. Let someone else pick it up, shall I? Someone else, shall I?
>
> Is that what you'd do, is it? That the kind of thing you'd get up to? The kind of thing you'd like? Is it?[125]

The questions develop into a rant against the litter droppers and spitters of this world, those who would reduce an ordered society to filth and chaos. Whether the audience largely comprise members who are younger than this Malvolio or not, he treats them as an authoritarian's nightmare of the younger generation, which in an adult audience generates giggly rebellion. He insists that by the end of the evening he will have been revenged on the whole pack of us and suggests that this is what the audience is: a pack, a cruel community of laughers in whose interest it is to 'other' its weaker members, laugh at his misfortune. Malvolio's monologue shifts at one point to a diatribe against the theatre:

> The theatre. Where we can drink and smoke and fornicate and squeal with delight and give access to our baser feelings and care not a jot for any decent human sensibility. Look. Look. LOOK. Look at yourselves. LOOK AT YOURSELVES. With a ghastly rictus of amorality frozen on your ugly faces. This is how you look. Like this. And this. You are all as bad as each other. All of you. ALL. ALL.[126]

He admits to having Puritan tendencies – he wants the theatres closed – and suggests that we are all ghastly voyeurs who would happily kick 'the funny man' until he bleeds, or watch him hang himself: he sets up a noose, gets one spectator to hold the rope while another readies herself to pull away his chair, then tells us he is not going to give us the sensationalist satisfaction of seeing him die. When I attended the production, he asked a man in the front row what his name was and offered a comic construction of what might happen when 'Andrew' went home after the performance – 'You're home early Andrew! – Oh yes, it finished early – he hanged himself.'

A critique of audience passivity has been central to Crouch's recent work[127] but I want to suggest here that if his intention is to make us reconsider our tendencies to bully and exclude in our acts of comic spectatorship, or to shake us from our roles in wider culture as passive onlookers to violence against difference, this is not quite the way in which this performance works upon the mainly adult audience with whom I watched the piece and for which it was not originally written. For this audience, the moments when Crouch very obviously appears to want to bring us up short in our laughter, and to consider whether we really would happily kick a man when he is down, produced what I read as the silence of mild embarrassment at being preached to, rather than a genuine reappraisal of cultures of spectatorship. I refer particularly to when Malvolio suggested that as a pack of laughers, we would laugh at anyone who is different from ourselves. The performance was, I would argue, more successful in implicating its audiences when it let them laugh and laugh again at a range of comic objects, from the primitively scatalogical (we laughed at the sudden appearance of Malvolio's arse, as Joubert suggests we should) to the pitiful (some laughed at Malvolio's story of failed love and humiliation, even at his repeated assertion that his imagined requited love had brought him the only happy moments of his life, though others let out an 'Aah!' of sympathy), to the pompous (we laughed, like Toby Belch, at Malvolio's condemnation of the excesses of social life and are cast as the carnivalesque bringers-down of the social order). The audience at the production I attended, then, both laughed and pitied as Joubert suggests we do – and laughed at the piteous, as Sidney (and Crouch's Malvolio) fears that theatrical comedy encourages us to do.

Crouch's nuanced portrayal of the awkward, pompous social misfit recalls a transhistorical archetype stretching from Malvolio himself, to Jane Austen's Mr Collins, to BBC TV's Basil Fawlty at his most snobbish: he is the socially inept social climber who desires the obvious signifiers of social success but misreads more nuanced social semiotics – most importantly, those that indicate how he himself is being read. Malvolio begins this play in the full realization that he has been made a laughing-stock, then proceeds to demonstrate how and why. He accuses his audience of caring little for his upright, ordered social view of the world, casting them as teenage rebels even when the majority are adults; he accosts them in an embarrassing leopard-print thong, in the kind of awkward burst of sexual enthusiasm that we assume must have revolted Olivia. 'A kind of innocence irradiates Malvolio's joy' at finding Maria's letter, argues Robert H. Bell of Shakespeare's figure: 'What loser has not dreamed that the last will be first? Let him without foolish fantasies cast the first stone.'[128] But what Crouch's piece suggests is that it is easy to forget any kinship with Malvolio in our own joy at being 'big bullies'. Malvolio has been punished for being a poor reader – of Maria's trick letter and of social semiotics;[129] he who cannot read the signs is, to all intents and purposes, what Malvolio insists he is not: mad – and risible. Crouch's Malvolio, like Iago in my opening quotation, considers laughter an excess in and of itself – part of a society of Belch-like decadence, material excesses, and sensation-seeking behaviours in excess of decency, propriety and kindness. What Crouch's production succeeds in doing, I suggest, is to offer its audience space in which to watch themselves laugh from within a range of laughter communities. Crouch suggests by implication that *Twelfth Night* may just have let us laugh at him.

What implications does Crouch's performance have for productions of *Twelfth Night*? For Crouch, in the end, it can have none, because as he suggests, it is giving Malvolio a voice that in the play he does not have. In one sense it offers exactly the reading of

Malvolio's plight that Kemper objects to. It suggests that, far from being a subtle interplay of performer and audience, spectator and object of spectacle that is contained within the madhouse scenes I have explored here, *Twelfth Night* is a play that allows us to laugh in self-satisfied superiority at the social climber. The mad figure on the early modern stage is an object of laughter, a generator of laughter, a laugher. Whether the wrongly incarcerated Malvolio may be seen in his improvised madhouse or not, it is clear that he cannot, as *The Honest Whore*'s madman can, look back and laugh at those who are looking at him and laughing. He is in darkness, in a separate space from his on-stage tormentors and his paying spectators. Considering the possibility of laughing at the mad in the early modern drama – so very far in excess of compassion and good taste for our reviewers of *The Changeling* – has reconfirmed my sense that performing early modern drama now has the potential to locate the audience in an oddly disturbing reciprocal relationship with traditionally and stereotypically constructed 'others'. It may also, as Crouch is suggesting *Twelfth Night* does, reconfirm such boundaries and stereotypes. *Twelfth Night* may have a more satisfying dramaturgical structure for a modern reviewer than the Jacobean dramas featuring the incarcerated mad: one cannot imagine a theatre company being praised for forcing a Shakespeare comedy into literary acceptability, as we have seen in the reviews of the 2006 *Changeling*. But modern production's need to show that its audiences have been guilty in laughing at Malvolio, that we have demonstrated 'the excess of laughter' and become a cruel pack, worthy of the abused man's revenge, suggests that the laughter it generates may be relatively contained and comfortable. *The Honest Whore*'s madman gets to ask his laughing on- and off-stage audience, 'Do you mock old age, you rogues?' (5.2.201–2), rather like Crouch's Malvolio as he asks us, 'You enjoy that sort of thing, do you? Makes you laugh, does it?' *Twelfth Night*'s Malvolio only gets to storm off-stage, swearing that he will take an impossible revenge.

It is logical that a comedy should punish an anti-comical figure like Malvolio, who, like Iago, might decry 'the excess of laughter'.

But his ultimate punishment, our laughter, regulates the disconcerting shifts in spectatorial power that laughing at and with the mad offers in the other plays I have considered here. Stephen G. Breyer, the 'real' judge at the Shakespeare Theatre Company's mock appeal against Malvolio's damages, finally decided in favour of Olivia: "'No liability,' he said. 'And the reason is: I don't like Malvolio'.[130] The raucous, laughable, shifting excesses of the mad characters considered here may not permit such a simple and self-contained judgement.

# CHAPTER THREE

## 'GIVE ME EXCESS OF IT': LOVE, VIRTUE AND EXCESSIVE PLEASURE IN *ALL'S WELL THAT ENDS WELL* AND *ANTONY AND CLEOPATRA*

ENOBARBUS
[...] Octavia is of a holy, cold and still conversation.

MENAS
Who would not have his wife so?

ENOBARBUS
Not he that himself is not so; which is Mark Antony.
Shakespeare, *Antony and Cleopatra* (2.6.122–6)

When Menas suggests that every man wants his wife holy, cold and still of conversation, Enobarbus demurs, figuring Antony, and by implication Cleopatra, as worldly, hot and shifting in comparison to Caesar's obedient and self-sacrificing sister. The ideal of womanhood in a range of early modern writings is the one Menas attributes to Octavia – but Enobarbus knows that such an ideal would not suit Antony. In *Antony and Cleopatra*, and in *All's Well that Ends Well*, love between sexual partners is framed as an excessive passion: one which is both socially problematic and theatrically pleasurable and which undoes gendered conventions of constancy, balance and restraint. As we will see, some critical accounts of love in Shakespeare have endeavoured to separate love from lust, framing lust as a violent and troublesome passion, love as a heightened spiritual state beyond the somatic. While there is no doubt that 'mere' lust often figures in early modern drama as violently excessive and excessively selfish, I am going to argue that love, too, has its anxiety- and pleasure-producing excesses. Love, in the plays under discussion here, is always in danger of undoing a version of subjectivity in which virtuous reason controls the boundless excesses of the early modern mind/body. Superficially, Helena and Cleopatra are on opposite ends of the spectrum of early modern archetypes of love and of female virtue. Compare their effects on their respective beloveds: Shakespeare's Cleopatra is the 'triple-turn'd whore' of legend (4.12.13) and the partner in Antony's double adultery; she is twice the cause of his defeat in battle and her play-death leads to his actual demise. Helena sleeps only with her rightful husband; her own false death, on a pretended holy pilgrimage, serves to bring Bertram to a right understanding of her value as a wife. Helena is good for Bertram, where Cleopatra is ultimately very bad for Antony. Cleopatra's love, the more notoriously excessive, ends in death and is matched in excess and in death by Antony's. Excessive love for Helena is something never clearly experienced by Bertram; indeed, by the end of the play, her own excessive and, some might argue, selfish passion, could be said to have cured him of youthful excesses, just as her medical knowledge cures the King of France's fistula. However, Helena's love is, as we will see, figured as excessive in a number of ways that make a comparison with Cleopatra's productive. The plays offer the excesses of love as primary sources of theatrical pleasure, while hedging the passion about with moral provisos and punishments. They explore and celebrate the excesses of love in ways that trouble some of the categories of reason and passion that are at work in the early modern period – and bring them, so to speak, into play. Both of these women act according to a love which exceeds the boundaries of ideology and reason.

## LOVE AS A PASSION

First, I want to turn to the question of whether love may usefully be considered as an emotion at all. David Schalkwyk suggests that it is a reductive mistake to describe it as one of the embodied, humoral passions of classical or early modern thought – or to categorize it as a set of neurological and endocrinological phenomena and responses, as Schalkwyk suggests modern science has recently attempted to do. He argues that love is not an emotion *per se* but 'a form of behaviour over time', involving a range of emotions, and suggests that humoral concepts of love are figured as both anachronistic and excessive in Shakespeare. Of Orsino and his conception of a humoral Love, whose excesses must be purged and which women are typologically incapable of feeling (*Twelfth Night* 1.1.1–3, 2.4.94–104), Schalkwyk writes:

> Embodiment of and spokesman for humoral theory, Illyria's duke is the sign of the excessive, the anachronistic, at a remove from reality. Almost every critic of the play has observed that Orsino's love is a fantasy. Humoral theory helps us to give a greater degree of precision to the endlessly repeated undergraduate cliché that Orsino is not in love, but rather in love with love itself. He is in love with himself as the paradigmatic embodiment of humoral psychology, and the dialogic nature of the play presents other characters who embody and enact a different concept of love.[1]

According to Schalkwyk's nuanced and convincing argument, love as a gendered, somatic passion, with all the problems of excess the passions generate, is an anachronistic notion which *Twelfth Night* supersedes. He cites early modern treatises on the passions, pointing particularly to way in which Thomas Wright's 'whole register and style' in *The Passions of the Mind* 'changes abruptly' when he turns to the subject of love.[2] 'These dry discourses of affections, without any cordial affection, have long detained & not a little distasted me', writes Wright of the other passions he has been exploring: cordial affection seems to be of a different order. Nevertheless, Wright's appeal to God, 'the soul, and life of all true love',[3] at the opening of his chapter on the subject suggests that love makes him just as nervous as the other passions. 'Now that I come out towards the borders of love', writes Wright, in a passage cited by Schalkwyk,

> give me leave, O loving God, to vent out and evaporate the effects of the heart, and see if I can incense my soul to love thee entirely...and that all those motives which stir up mine affections to love thee, may be means to inflame all their hearts, which read this treatise penned by me.[4]

When Wright 'come[s] to the borders of love', that most all-consuming of passions, he must ask God to help him turn all of it on to God himself. For Wright is not about to discourse primarily on the love of God but on human love. The very inflammatory madness that Schalkwyk argues is 'divine'[5] is one of Nicholas Coeffeteau's list of passions – 'pity, fear, bashfulness, or shame, love, hatred, desires, Choler and the rest', and Coeffeteau defines all of them as phenomena 'which are accompanied with some notable defect'.[6] Their disease-like, troublesome, excessive quality is what make passions passions – and love is one of them. Human love can be benevolent, a selfless compulsion to 'will good to some one, not for our own private interest',[7] and Coeffeteau defines it separately from desire – which is always for that which is absent. He writes of love as selfless friendship, in the beautiful passage I have used in the dedication to this book. However, he still clearly feels that human love needs policing by reason, just as do the other passions:

> Human Love is a Passion which should follow the motions of reason, and which being guided by the light of the soul should only embrace the true good, to make it perfect: for containing himself within these bounds, it should no more be a violent & furious passion, which fills the world daily with so many miseries by her exorbitant and strange disorders.[8]

Love *should* follow the motions of reason...it should *not* be a violent and furious passion. But Coeffeteau's very statement of what love should not be in this passage suggests that love does often stray into the realms of the exorbitant, strange and disordered. The construction of love as passion and disease emerges even more clearly in Ferrand's *Erotomania*, a treatise on love melancholy, which, having asserted that their are two broad kinds of love, 'the one divine, the other common and vulgar',[9] calls upon the ancients to support his argument that love is yet another of the unreasonable passions:

> love being a mixt disease, both of the body and the mind; I shall furnish my self with precepts out of *Plato,* and with medicines from *Aesculapius,* in the cure of Love Melancholy, being such as I have gathered out of *Hippocrates,* the Prince of Physitians: Intending to handle Love no otherwise, then as it is a passion, or violent perturbation of the Mind, Dishonest, and Refractory to Reason.[10]

Love, for Coeffeteau, contains something substantially different from the other passions, something divine: but human love can still be listed as a passion or affection, as it clearly is for Ferrand – and thereby may be figured, in its excessiveness, as a disease.[11]

## SHAKESPEARE AND LOVE, SHAKESPEARE AND SEX

As Paul A. Kottman points out in his study of *Romeo and Juliet*, recent scholarship has figured early modern dramatic love in terms of its social limits, so that the paradigmatic historicist interpretation of that play is of a 'dialectical tension between the lovers' desires and the demands of society'.[12] Love in the early modern drama is perhaps embarrassingly excessive in these terms, as the plays are full of lovers who appear ready to let their love exceed society's demands. Other recent studies have taken seriously the notion of a love – particularly in Shakespeare – that transcends social demands and boundaries and seem keen to separate love from sex, in ways that might lead one of Kottman's historical materialists to accuse them of a naive moral idealism. Stanley Wells concludes his chapter on 'Sex and Poetry in Shakespeare's Time' in his book *Shakespeare, Sex and Love* thus:

> So perhaps we can say that Shakespeare succeeds in writing verse which [...] can certainly appeal to a homoerotic readership but which transcends the boundaries of subdivisions of human experience to encapsulate the very essence of human love. As we might have expected of him.[13]

This essence of love, Wells suggests, goes beyond the 'light-hearted eroticism' or 'voyeuristic pleasure' of some of the other poets he is examining, 'to a profound expression of a 'hallowed' love that [...] knows no limits'.[14] For Wells here, the 'very essence' of human love is something quite other than the muddy somatic appetites that both blur and subdivide human subjectivity for the early moderns. In its 'essence', love transcends the debates around the interests and ideologies, which are inherent in its construction for a scholar such as Dympna Callaghan, cited by Kottman.[15] It is startling to consider the fact that Wells' and Callaghan's analyses of *Romeo and Juliet* were written within fifteen years of one another. For Wells Shakespeare's sonnets express a 'profound' love that is not merely erotic or visual: it is 'hallowed', spiritual. Wells reads *Romeo and Juliet* as somehow less universal than the Sonnets, because more explicitly heteronormative – but again in Wells' concluding paragraphs, Shakespeare's work is about a love that transcends the physical:

> In the end the play becomes an elegy for wedded love, a condition in which sex, while it is important, is subsumed in celebration of a spiritual as well as a physical unity.[16]

Wells ends a number of his chapters by assuring the reader in some way that it is something other, or more profound, than sex that Shakespeare is writing about when he writes of love – and ends the chapter on 'Sexual Desire' with the assertion that 'Rape is the ultimate consequence of lust, the very opposite of love. Yet the physical act is identical.'[17] This he restates in his conclusion, where he suggests that Shakespeare 'knew the dangers of of mistaking animal desire for higher passion'. But, happily, Shakespeare 'knew too that sex is an essential component even of the higher forms of human love, that it can lead to a sublime realization of the self in a near-mystical union of personalities, such as he figures forth in his poem "The Phoenix and the Turtle" '.[18] The attempt to redeem lust from what is supposedly its 'ultimate consequence', rape, reinforces manichean binaries of sex and love, physical and spiritual. Although other critics are not often as explicit about their privileging of the spiritual, the notion of a selfish, desiring, physical lust that is superficial and fleeting and could be for any sex object, and a love that is more lasting, 'profound', individuated and ultimately virtuous is an undertone for a number of recent writings about Shakespeare and love. 'Love and lust are generally polar opposites in Shakespeare,' argues Maurice Charney, 'and lust is associated with villains.' This is a continuing theme in the Sonnets, Charney goes on to argue, and in *Venus and Adonis.* In his drama, Charney asserts, 'All of Shakespeare's villains are lustful because they believe only in the natural order' and he cites *Lear*'s Edmund: 'Thou nature are my goddess' (1.2.1).[19] Thus 'nature' is figured by both Edmund and Charney as base and animalistic – excessive in its lack of restraint. But the early modern theatre cannot figure love as either pure, villainous, bodily lust or as sublime spiritual union, uncontaminated with the somatic. Human love is a 'passion', and as we have repeatedly seen here the passions are inescapably natural and somatic.

Of particular interest here is David Scott Kastan's article '*All's Well that Ends Well* and the Limits of Comedy' in which he points out that whatever early modern defenders of the theatre may say about the moral benefit of reading or watching comedy (it exposes vice and folly – Sidney; it offers light relief to the busy mind, making the worker more productive after the recreation it provides – Heywood[20]), the happy endings of stage comedies belie these attempts to render them moral reflections of the 'real world':

> This willingness to gratify human desires in the face of the evidence of human experience discomforts those

> who demand moral utility from art. Bacon complains that 'the Stage is more beholding to Love than the Life of Man'.[21]

Yet, later in the article, it seems that Kastan too demands moral utility from art, where he suggests that in the 'problem comedies', the audience is emphatically reminded that life is not comedy, through Shakespeare's deliberate over-contrivance of the happy ending:

> In the problem comedies the contrivance is the characters' own and is throughout too self-regarding, too un-responsive to the needs and desires of others, to permit our delight. We are forced to recognize that comic triumph is not innocent, that event usually will not yield to desire without some other desire yielding to event; that is, we are forced to contest the claim that 'all's well that ends well.'

If love is selfish, we cannot delight in it, and for Kastan, Helena's love in *All's Well* is only too selfish:

> though Helena finally does earn Bertram's love, she succeeds through a tenacity too nearly predatory to be completely attractive or satisfying.[22]

Kastan goes on to demonstrate repeatedly that the comic resolution to the play is pointedly inadequate to the plot and suggests that the psychological integrity of the figures in *All's Well* cannot be compelled to yield to comic form, just as Bertram cannot be compelled to love. What I am going to argue here is that a love which is in excess of self can be therefore condemned as selfish in Kastan's terms, because it overwhelms the consideration of both self and other. Both attractive and potentially satisfying, it is also problematically amoral – both for Shakespeare's culture and our own, albeit in differently inflected ways.

I am not going to argue, in opposition to Wells and Charney, that Shakespeare and his contemporaries do not differentiate in any way between love and lust. When Bertram swears to Diana 'I love thee/By love's own sweet constraint, and will forever/ Do thee rights of service' (4.2.15–17), an early modern audience would no doubt have been more likely to trust Diana's cynicism – 'Ay, so you serve us/Til we serve you' (4.2.17–18) – than Bertram's oaths. Once Bertram is tricked into believing he has had sex with Diana, he leaves her and is ready publicly to dismiss her as a whore. His declaration in the last scene of the play that he will love Helena 'ever, ever dearly' (5.3.315) is clearly of a different order. Despite Juliet's comic references to male lust ('What satisfaction can thou have tonight?' (2.2.126)), *Romeo and Juliet* makes it clear that Romeo's 'bent of love be honourable,/ [His] purpose marriage' (2.2.143–4), thus differentiating it from the lust that a Bertram feels for a Diana (or, perhaps, that Romeo felt for Rosaline). In the two plays explored here, love is certainly more than 'mere' sexual desire and is certainly more complex and sympathetic than the villainous lust experienced by an Edmund or an Iago. But this does not ultimately mean that it is without its dangers and abilities to disrupt.

## *ALL'S WELL THAT ENDS WELL*

Love in *All's Well* can be something of a problem, and I am going to argue here that this is because its excesses push at the boundaries of gendered propriety for its central female figure, rather than because of any essential qualities or faults that render the play more generally a 'problem play'. The pseudo-genre of the 'Problem Play' has been contested in scholarly discourse, since Boas labelled *All's Well*, *Measure*, *Troilus* and *Hamlet* thus in 1896,[23] borrowing from the term used to describe the social problems staged by Ibsen and Shaw, and since W. W. Lawrence reduced the 'problem' to the three comedies in 1930.[24] Even as it emerged, the usefulness of the term to categorize a range of generically slippery and/or morally challenging plays by Shakespeare was being interrogated: 'It has been perpetually redefined' by writers after Boas, asserts Peter Ure in 1961.[25] Ure's introductory solution to the vagueness of the term is to take on the vagueness of another scholar and

> borrow the warning that Dr Tillyard placed in the forefront of his book on the subject: 'I use the term vaguely and equivocally [. . .] as a matter of convenience. . . to achieve the necessary elasticity and inclusiveness.'[26]

However, in the paragraph following the one cited by Ure, Tillyard used the term in fairly inelastic fashion, to praise *Hamlet* and *Troilus and Cressida* as 'problem plays because they deal with and display interesting problems' (which perhaps sums up the ways in which scholarship now regards all the plays categorized thus), while asserting that *All's Well* and *Measure* are problem plays 'because they *are* problems'.[27] Boas tells his late Victorian readers that 'All these dramas introduce us into highly artificial societies, whose civilization is ripe unto rottenness' and that 'Amidst such media abnormal conditions of brain and emotion are generated,'[28] and Tillyard takes up the theme of the problem play as cognitive abnormality when he asks his reader to 'consider the connotations of the parallel term "problem child"'. 'There are at least two kinds of problem child' asserts Tillyard, the first being 'the genuinely abnormal child, whom no efforts will ever bring back to normality'. *All's Well* and *Measure* are 'like [this] first [. . .]: there is something radically schizophrenic about them' (10).

Society as artificial and rotten; abnormal conditions of the brain and emotion; if Boas describes their content accurately, then these plays are packed with the problems that most fascinate the late twentieth- early twenty-first-century cultural materialist critic or historian of the emotions, rather than being 'problems' in themselves. As the pseudo-genre's critical history progresses, the problems posed by these plays increasingly demonstrate, for literary scholars, Shakespeare's daring experimental bent. Even the 'problem' of genre marked by Boas and Lawrence had been recuperated by 1974, when Anne Barton stood up for generic instability, describing the 'clash between those opposing elements of fairy tale and realism, of romance motivation and psychological probability' as a disturbing but deliberate part of *All's Well*'s design, rather than as a problem of muddled genre. *All's Well* and *Measure for Measure* raise 'doubts as to the validity of comedy as an image of truth', she argues in her introduction to the *Riverside Shakespeare*'s *All's Well.*[29] It complicates genre and this is not a problem. It is significant that two years ago at the time of writing, G. Beiner called his monograph exploring *All's Well, Measure* and *Troilus Generic Tension as Exploratory Mode* and suggests that while each play has a 'vital relationship with the normative genre' the plays are part of a European dramatic 'poetics of generic tension'.[30]

However, if the problem child has become the child genius for the academy, newspaper reviewers of the Shakespeare's Globe production in 2011[31] still conformed to the notion that the seeming generic and psychological contradictions of this play still make it unwieldy and unpopular – and some conflate the complex history of the 'problem play' in criticism with a simpler notion that these are just faulty comedies. Whereas a scholar such as Bloom may now assume that for 'Modern readers (sic) [...] The marriage of Helena and Bertram is a punishment, not a happy ending, and it is a complex authorial challenge to readers demanding a complex critical response',[32] newspaper critics certainly see the play's resolution as problematic in the theatre, chiefly because of the problem that is Bertram. Tillyard's notion of the play as 'problem child', irredeemably 'abnormal', and the idea that Bertram is at the centre of this problem,[33] still emerges in journalistic criticism of the play. For Charles Spenser, self-consciously blunt in the *Daily Telegraph*, *All's well* is 'usually classed among Shakespeare's so called "problem plays", the main problem in my view being that it's not much cop'.[34] It is 'a knotty problem play' for Paul Taylor,[35] 'one of Shakespeare's most beguiling but least-loved plays' for Michael Billington[36] and 'one of Shakespeare's most charmless comedies [...] made up of improbable liaisons, arbitrary decisions, brutal exposures and mechanical resolutions' for Susannah Clapp.[37]

Having given the stock warning about problem plays, many reviewers of the Globe production praised it warmly for its interpretation of Bertram, who appeared to have 'feelings' for Helena from the outset, which he was unable to express until he believed that he has lost her in death. Sam Crane looked longing and bewildered in the presence of Ellie Piercy's Helena, as the former left for France and even after he had rejected her before the French court. The extracts below demonstrate that if Bertram can be made sympathetic, the 'problem' is solved:

> The problem with the play is always Bertram, who seems a snobbish rotter on rejecting marriage to Helena on the grounds that she is 'a poor physician's daughter'. Sam Crane plausibly plays him as a callow youth heavily influenced by the laddish military ethos and half in love with the woman he spurns: even when, after their imposed union, he tells Helena to 'haste to horse' he gives her a long, lingering look filled with quiescent desire.[38]

> Most productions (of this very rarely staged piece) present a Bertram who is noxious in his selfishness. Not here. Sam Crane gives us a hero who is sunk in a self-hating depression and who, although he knows that Helena could be the answer to his prayers, can't overcome the rooted self-dislike that would allow him to woo her.[39]

> Bertram can come over as a cad, but Crane makes him immature and conflicted, trying on poses for size. He clearly nurses unarticulated feelings for Helena, which renders him more appealing and makes sense of her pursuit of him.[40]

The implication is that, for an audience today, Bertram demonstrates an unappealing, snobbish self-centredness in his rejection of Helena, and her 'pursuit of him' – and the love that drives it – therefore makes no 'sense'. The Globe production reinvented Bertram, so that his change of heart at the end of the play was prefigured from his first stage encounter with Helena, and their final reunion produced a self-authenticating, mentally healthy and therefore 'truer' Bertram, who had always loved Helena but was just too far 'sunk in a self-hating depression' or too 'immature and conflicted' to admit it to himself. If the play, to return to Tillyard, is mentally ill – 'there is something radically schizophrenic about [it]' (see p. 120) – this production sites that illness in Bertram and cures him.

The *Financial Times* review suggests that love is difficult for a theatre audience to accept when its object is unsympathetic: a plausible heroine could not love a 'cad', so her pursuit of such a Bertram is implausible. However, this assumption emerges from a moral framework concerning love and its meanings that this play does not necessarily fit. In fact, it makes perfect sense for Helena to love a 'cad'; as early as medieval stories of love such as Boccaccio's that were circulating in translation in early modern England (and which, of course, Shakespeare used as his sources), love is sudden, manifests itself suddenly and physically and is physically overwhelming. Afflicted with love, one may be expected to use one's god-given reason to combat it – but this is exceptionally difficult. Here is Boccaccio's Amorous Fiammetta, in Bartholomew Young's English translation of 1587, describing the moment when she falls in love with the young man she sees at a religious festival, a 'cad' indeed, who eventually proves her downfall. I quote it at length as it brings us back, via so many examples, to the somatic nature of the passions in writings still circulating in the early modern period:

> a shining light issuing from out his clear eyes, and running by a most subtle and fine beam, did meet and hit directly against mine, which contending to pass further by what secret way (I know not) suddenly went penetrating to my very heart, which fearing their violent entrance, and calling to it all her exterior forces, left me altogether pale and cold. But their abode was not so long there, but the greatest fear was past, and then were they welcomed with a hot and burning passion: whereupon the foresaid forces returning to their

> places again, brought with them a certain heat, which driving all paleness quite away, painted my face like the vermillion Rose, and made me burn as hot as fire: And yet beholding from whence all this did proceed, I could not but breathe out a sorrowful sigh. And from that hour forward, my thoughts were occupied in nothing else, but meditating of his brave personage, and apparent virtues, and especially in imagining how to please him.[41]

Although Fiammetta's description bypasses the liver, which André du Laurens later asserts is an essential part of the somatic process of setting 'concupiscience on fire',[42] love is figured, as in Du Laurens' discourse, as a material force, capable of physically piercing the body of the one in love when she looks at the lover. The description of the 'most subtle and fine beam' which Fiammetta's lover emits accords with Galen's theory of vision, whereby beams physically emerge from the object of vision and pierce the eyes of she who looks. By 1621, Burton is still asserting, in the 'Love Melancholy' chapters of the *Anatomy*, that 'the most familiar and usual cause of love is that which comes by sight, which conveys those admirable rays of beauty and pleasing graces to the heart'. The eyes

> as two sluices let in the influences of that divine, powerful, soul-ravishing, and captivating beauty, which, as one saith, "is sharper than any dart or needle, wounds deeper into the heart; and opens a gap through our eyes to that lovely wound, which pierceth the soul itself" (Ecclus. 18.) Through it love is kindled like a fire.[43]

By 1604, Johannes Kepler's *Optics,* which produces something closer to modern science's understanding of vision, had been translated into English. Kepler suggests that vision occurs 'through a picture of the visible things on the white, concave surface of the retina'.[44] For Kepler, the labour of looking is done by the looker; in Galen, that which is seen sends forth its beams for the looker to receive. Beauty, post-Kepler, is indeed in the eye of the beholder. It is interesting, then, that Burton writes of love at first sight in terms of extramissive vision. Eric Langley points out a 'slippage either side of the century, where old and new conceptions of vision compete, coexist or become confused' and that 'One such slippage, where the theory remains in circulation, can be observed in poetry's treatment of the eye'.[45] Indeed, Langley remarks that to his knowledge there is

> not a single poem from the erotic narrative tradition that fails to utilize the 'transpiercing eye[beams]' tradition of extramissive theory; it would appear that not one poet in this tradition can resist the 'furious dart[s]' of eyebeams, and that [n]o armour might be found that could defend [their lovers from the] 'Transpearcing rayes of Christall poynted eyes.'[46]

One might argue that it can hardly be illuminating to compare sudden passion, this love at first piercing, with Helena's, which has grown with her, through her lifelong close proximity to Bertram – or indeed to cite Fiammetta, when Shakespeare uses another Boccaccio source for his play, the story of Giletta of Narbonne, translated in William Painter's *Palace of Pleasure*.[47] What I want to point to here is the materiality of the process of falling in love as it is described here and the reference at the end of the Fiammetta passage to the beloved's 'apparent virtues'. If a more recent definition of 'apparent' is accidentally assumed here, then the passage may be read as a knowing satire on the superficiality of a sudden love. But the use of the word to mean 'only seeming, appearing to be one thing while possibly being another' does not occur until 1846.[48] 'Apparent' here, from the French 'appearing' (the original spelling is 'apparant'), means visually evident, all too clear. And the appearance of the lover can never remain superficial, on the surface – it enters Fiammetta very literally, turning her cold then hot, forcing an audible expression of love from her: the excess of love's heat must be literally expressed in a sigh. Although Helena, we are repeatedly reassured, is a figure of moral rectitude not to be compared with the likes of Fiammetta, Helena's love, too, is figured as both visually constructed and excessive.

In the first scene of *All's Well*, Helena describes her unrequited love for Betram, whom she is about to lose sight of altogether when he leaves for Paris, as excessive at every turn. Love obliterates her. She is 'undone' without Bertram. She must 'die for love' like the hind who loves the lion. She understands that her 'fancy' is 'idolatrous', suggesting in this word (coming as it does immediately after her description of her repeatedly drawing him in her heart) that she is in love with an image. Like the idolatrous Catholic, she must 'sanctify his relics' (1.1.99), a choice of imagery that both recalls and undoes the notion of love as a spiritual good. Later, when she confesses her love to Bertram's mother, the Countess of Rousillon, the boundless excess of her love and its idolatry are again her subjects:

> Yet in this captious and inteemible sieve
> I still pour in the waters of my love
> And lack not to lose still. Thus, Indian-like,
> Religious in mine error, I adore
> The sun that looks upon his worshipper
> But knows of him no more.
>
> (1.3.199–204)

Helena's agency shifts fascinatingly in her description of her love. In her first soliloquy, she complains that her 'imagination carries no favour in it but Bertram's' and she describes the process of looking at him as one of drawing, deliberately inscribing him on to the 'table' of her heart. Where Fiammetta suggests repeatedly that there was nothing 'she', her moral, willing self, could do about her physical, material fall (her fall in love, and from virtue), Helena's first soliloquy is full of self-blame. The metaphor of drawing Bertram in her heart suggests conscious deliberation. Then, in the above speech, the notion of the idolatrous gaze suggests a helpless ignorance. Helena is like an 'Indian' who believes naively that the sun takes notice of him – but she is simultaneously knowing and sophisticated in her ability to analyse herself thus. Helena tells the audience, and later the Countess, that she just can't help herself and yet blames herself for not being able to apply reason to the idolatrous excesses of love.

Helena's passion for Bertram is hedged about with repeated yet ambiguous figurings of her virtue. In the first scene of the play, inherited 'dispositions', education and Helena's own efforts give the Countess great 'hopes' of her turning out well (1.1.39–44), though she is also rebuked in this same scene for excessive mourning of her father ('Moderate lamentation is the right of the dead;/ Excessive grief the enemy to the living' (54–5) Lafeu opines, unoriginally). Excessive show of feeling is in danger of looking showy, and although most editors point out that 'affect' in the Countess' warning ('no more, lest it be rather thought you affect a sorrow than to have it', 51–2) does not have the same connotations of affectation or hypocrisy as it does later in the seventeenth century (1661 is the OED's first citation of this meaning), the idea of showing more sadness than one actually feels surely prefigures the later definition, especially as Helena defends herself with the assertion that she does affect (show) a sorrow but 'I have it too' (53). In fact this excess of sorrow, as the audience soon discovers, is for Bertram because he is leaving for the French court, and not for her departed father.

The discussion of given and attained qualities continues in the Countess' advice to Bertram. Whereas Helena's given gifts are her 'dispositions', to which she adds by responding well to a good education, Bertram's are his father's 'shape' and his 'blood' – though when the Countess exhorts that his 'blood and virtue/Contend for empire in thee' (61–2) she is also making the unintended prediction that his heated young blood will, for the greater part of the play, win over his virtue; and concern with what is due to his 'blood', in the aristocratic sense, is what leads to his blindness regarding Helena's virtues when he rejects her later in the play.

The play opens, then, with a variety of exhortations to a pair of young people to be good, virtuous and moderate – to control themselves, in fact. The remainder of the Countess' speech to her son is a Polonius-like call to moderation and balance in friendship and conduct. Helena is introduced to the audience as both an inherent and self-made good girl – while she weeps embarrassingly all over the stage. For Kathryn Schwarz, 'Helena becomes [in the collective critical memory] a type of the disorderly woman, her conservative course of action knocked out of bounds by an excess of desire'[49] and, indeed, the Countess' assurances of her virtue are also knocked out of bounds, in the very scene in which the audience is offered them. When Bertram has taken his leave and the advice-giving adults have exited, Helena gives the soliloquy which acknowledges that she is not the dutiful daughter she seems. The speech recalls Hamlet's following the exit of his father's ghost, and is the diametric opposite to Hamlet's promises. Hamlet vows to remember his father; Helena has 'forgot' hers. Hamlet promises to obliterate from the 'tables' of his memory everything he has learned through his childhood, 'all trivial fond records,/All saws of books, all pressures past/That youth and observation copied there' (1.5.99–101) and to replace them with his father's memory and vengeance. Helena confesses that she has only Bertram copied in her 'heart's table' (1.1.94).

Helena's declaration of her love for Bertram is framed dramaturgically with warnings about excess, echoing the anxieties around the excesses of young female love that hover in the introductory passages of the source text, where Boccaccio/Painter's Gilletta of Narbonne 'fervently fell in love with Beltramo, more than was meet for a maiden of her age'.[50] Having been marked by the Countess and Lafew as a virtuous young woman in danger of mourning excessively, she confesses to her excessive love for Bertram; we then meet Parolles, the epitome of louche and disreputable excess, sometimes compared, albeit as a less likeable, or less self-aware, version, to Falstaff[51] – a liar, fool and coward (1.1.101–2) whose language is all sexual innuendo and whose 'soul [...] is in his clothes' (2.5.44).

After two of the play's older generation – the Countess and Lafew – have set up a supposedly clear moral framework whereby its young people may be judged, Helena's conversation with

Parolles is highly morally ambivalent. It begins with her odd comment that his bad qualities suit him very well when virtue does not seem so very appealing: 'when virtue's steely bones/ Look bleak i'th'cold wind' (1.1.104–5). Her sententia that 'full oft we see/Cold wisdom waiting on superfluous folly' (1.1.105–6) seems to favour neither side of the wisdom/folly binary and virtue's cold steeliness does not seem nearly as attractive as the lively, fallacious arguments about virginity that Parolles throws at Helena in response to her oddly sudden question about protecting her virginity:

> You have some stain of soldier in you; let me ask you a question. Man is enemy to virginity; how may we barricado it against him?
>
> (1.1.112–14)

In introducing the subject of how virginity may be protected, she prefigures the dangers to body and reputation to which she is about to expose herself on the journey she is planning by the end of the scene – and having set Parolles off on his predictable ramble about how keeping one's virginity is unnatural, she soon departs from her theme of keeping it, to that of 'los[ing] it to her own liking' (150–1).

Helena's discourse on virginity ensues, with its notoriously cut-off line, the missing part of which Ewan Fernie has fascinatingly ignored in his entry on the speech to the 'BloggingShakespeare' website. Where most editors gloss the speech by explaining that Helena is referring to the court when she speaks of a place where Bertram will find everything from a 'mother, a mistress, and a friend' to 'his faith, his sweet disaster' (1.1.167, 173), Fernie assumes that it is her virginity where they are to be found. In imagining herself completely given over to Bertram's love, she becomes a place of infinite variety and capacity. I find this reading – and the tone which Fernie is able to adopt when Blogging rather than writing for academic peer review – compelling, despite his somewhat perverse determination to ignore most editors' insistence on missing text: 'For though we might very well assume that becoming HIS would be to become a lesser thing,' writes Fernie of Helena,

> that's probably not how it appears to any impassioned inamorata, and maybe we should listen to experience a bit. So, imagine BEING—
>
> > His humble ambition, proud humility,
> > His jarring-concord, and his discord-dulcet,
> > His faith, his sweet disaster!
>
> Is there not an Ariel-like mobility, beauty and freedom in such a varied and textured life? … It's greatly to Helena's credit that she, unlike Troilus, can go BEYOND the fear of losing distinction in her joys. And we're very far from any kind of school-girl (or boy) sentimentality here. Consider that ecstatic ASCENT toward 'his sweet disaster'! Self-gifting doesn't end in saccharine union, but more of an amoral, Dionysian delight.
>
> Doesn't it make you SHIVER?[52]

Even if one insists on the missing line that would link Helena's virginity and the court to which Bertram is travelling, it is difficult to deny that Helena is imagining being the things she envisions Bertram will find at court, or at least links herself somehow with them. What I find particularly productive here is the way in which, read like this, the speech produces what Fernie calls an 'amoral, Donysian delight', one which suggests a self-fulfilment to the point of the obliteration of self and a love in excess of social convention. Such a conceptualization of Helena's excessive love permits both the seeming selfishness of Helena's demand that Bertram become her husband whatever he thinks of her – and the seeming self-sacrifice of the quest she undertakes.

Of course, there is no uncontainable, self-undoing love in Bertram for Helena. In promising to love her 'ever ever dearly' (5.3.315) once he fully understands what she has done to win him, it seems that he is learning love, as opposed to desire for social status or lust for the physically attractive. But his conversion is sudden and he never describes the nature of how that might 'feel' to him, as Helena repeatedly does. Over the course of *All's Well*, Bertram must learn to be less like Parolles, to settle down and marry a virtuous maid. While he learns that love is more than 'just' lust or a means to social betterment, his love is contained by social convention where Helena's reads repeatedly as in excess of it. The pleasure to be taken by the audience in the figure of Helena is that she *is* in love with a 'cad' (see p. 122); this love is comically excessive and illogical, involves visually driven lust as well as a sometimes selfless love (indeed, to separate these is to figure them falsely). It both empowers Helena to describe herself and to behave with an agency in excess of that which would have been permitted to any of her potential female audience members when the play was first produced – and it undoes her, to use her term, entirely. Love in *All's Well* – and in *Antony and Cleopatra*, as we will see – is paradoxically both self-undoing and self-intensifying.

The reviews of the Globe's *All's Well* quoted above suggest that in order for this play to be satisfying to its audiences, the union of the central figures must be a companionate marriage of individuals who understand – and have fallen in love with – each other's positive personal qualities. I argue that it is only a modern audience who leaves the theatre wondering how Helena will get along in marriage with a snobbish lecher who has both rejected her and dismissed the other woman he has declared love for as a 'common gamester to the camp' (5.3.188). I am not suggesting that an early modern audience would not have sympathized with Helena as Bertram disparages her social status and physical attractions, or that it would not have condemned his treatment of Diana. But the early modern Bertram is an embodiment of the excesses of youth, his energies are directed, quite conventionally, towards fighting, novelty and lust, so I suggest that his sudden shift to maturity and an appreciation of Helena's virtues at the end of the play would not have been too sudden to palates in 1603. The revelations of the last scene literally change Bertram, even when he has just dismissed Diana as a whore because he considers her beneath him. His change may be implausible for an audience who believes in fixed personality but quite reasonable for a culture for whom selfhood is always a struggle between reason and the passions. Suggesting that Bertram really loves Helena all along, as the Globe's 2011 production did, serves to underplay the passionate irrationality of Helena's love which is essential to the play's theatrical pleasure.

Helena's love represents a different kind of excess from that of Bertram's youthful 'blood': an excessive love that can only thrive fictionally, theatrically. While Bertram's journey to the French court and then into battle may plausibly have happened to a wealthy young man in early modern Europe, a real young woman would have been hopelessly vulnerable and compromised had she undertaken the risky journey Helena does. In order to undertake it in the play, she must be protected by an idealized virtue that an off-stage counterpart would have been unable to safeguard. Moreover, and more importantly for my argument here, Helena is in fact a more excessively passionate figure than Bertram and her passion must be contained throughout the play by repeated assurances that she is virtuous (*All's Well* contains the most frequent combined use of the words 'virtue' and 'virtuous' of the Shakespearean canon, with *Measure for Measure* coming a close second). Her passion is a source of comic, theatrical pleasure for the audience and though it is presented in one sense as the moral opposite of Bertram's lust for Diana, it is just as irrational and excessive. For David Scott Kastan (see p. 117), Helena's love is too selfish to be pleasurable and her contrivance of a happy ending suggests that Shakespeare's 'problem play' is thus problematizing comedy's happy endings generally. But I want to turn now to a production – or adaptation – of *All's Well*, which de-problematizes the play and permits a celebration of Helena's excessive love.

## SUNIL SHANBAG/ARPANA THEATRE'S *ALL'S WELL THAT ENDS WELL*

Arpana Theatre's *All's Well* is an adaptation in Gujarati, *Maro Piyu Gayo Rangoon*, produced in 2012 for the theatre's 'Globe to Globe' season of Shakespeare's plays in 37 languages. It prompted the disconcerted final comment by reviewer Andrew Dickson that 'In this most problematic of comedies, you're left wondering: what's the problem?'[53] A number of commentators have written about the questions around theatre and interculturalism provoked by this festival, and the ways in which a range of the productions negotiated the cultural imperialist histories of Shakespeare in their countries through their versions of Shakespeare.[54] Arpana's production, set in India *circa* 1900, was particularly interesting in this regard. When Bharatram (Bertram) falls for Alkini (Diana) in this version, she is in a precarious economic position as part of an opium-trading family because the British have just banned her business, making her easy prey to a young man who offers to buy up her surplus stock in exchange for her chastity. Peter Kirwan comments that the bedtrick plot 'was figured as two women's near-desperate attempts to assert self-determination under the oppressive conditions of class hierarchy and imperial rule'.[55] However, he also argues that this political history was ultimately 'an undertone to what was, fundamentally, a joyful comedy' and the production is an important case study for this chapter, because its celebratory tone convincingly counters the history of critical problematization of this play, a problematization so universal and determined that a critic who denies the 'darkness' and difficulty of *All's Well* opens herself up to the accusation of misreading – at least by theatre critics, as we have seen.

Using the nineteenth-century popular theatrical form of Bhangwadi, this production was revelatory in its ability to tell this story in such a way as to render almost meaningless the anxieties around consistency of genre and subjectivity that have labelled *All's Well* a 'problem play'. It is not that this production transformed its source text into something comically comfortable or painless, though Bhangwadi is described in the Globe to Globe publicity as a popular, perhaps escapist form that mixed music, dance and acting and 'originally catered for an audience of daily wage labourers in the 19th century'.[56] But the play's setting made sense of Bharatram (Chirag Vora)'s desire to leave his home and family and grow up. The social conventions governing the behaviour of the young male in this society meant that Bharatram did not question its class boundaries and more obvious rewards, and failed to see what might make him more lastingly happy. Bharatram was just as snobbish as any recent British Bertram, just as dismissive of Heli/Helena (Mansi Parekh) when he expressed his dismay at being married off to her. But he was a plausible product of his national and historical culture, and the actor's portrayal of his excitement and enthusiasm at leaving the conventions of home and childhood for what seemed to him like adult freedoms in Mumbai made him a more sympathetic Bertram than others I have seen; there was no need here to make him secretly in love with Helena from the start in order for him to be a flawed but not entirely dislikeable figure.

In this version of the play, Bharatram puts himself not into the service of a king but of his uncle Gokuldas (Utkarsh Mazumdar), a rich merchant. He is excited to go to and try for a fortune in Mumbai – then with Parolles' (here Parbat, played by Satchit Puranik) encouragement, escapes from his marriage to Heli to Rangoon, rather than to any neighbouring wars. Audience members of British origin may have assumed that his distaste for Helena/Heli is entirely caste-based – but Vora also gave the strong impression that Heli is part of a youth Bharatram wants to leave behind in a search for excitement, independence and the opportunity to cash in on the burgeoning wealth of the early twentieth-century city. He patronizes her as he might a little sister, telling her excitedly of the trip he is to make; his ignorance of her love, pitifully obvious to the audience, is comical but plausible.

Andrew Dickson's generally positive review of this *All's Well* in the *Guardian* called the performances 'broad brush' (see p. 137), suggesting that his expectations of subtlety in the acting of this 'problem play' were not quite met. But in the source text, there is nothing subtle about Helena's love for Bertram as she describes it in soliloquy. It is powerful, overwhelming, irrational and manifests itself gloriously in the facial expressions of Mansi Parekh's Heli, who is ever-ready to share her passion with the audience in speech and song. She is an intensely sympathetic figure because she is in love, and in a culture whose elders arrange marriages for its youth, the fact that the patriarch she has cured arranged her a marriage to the man she loves was as delightful to her as Bharatram's refusal of her was short-sighted and immature, despite the fact that the suddenness of the announcement made his dismay understandable. The Globe audience's audible delight at Heli's entrance in traditional Hindu wedding gear seemed a conventional response to a bride's entrance, enabled by the fact that at this point in the play we were clearly being asked to love Heli and were positioned as keen for her to obtain her heart's desire.

In an interview with Andrew Dickson before the Globe performances, director Sunil Shanbag says of potential responses to Bharatram:

> I'm generalising, but the Gujarati audience is a fairly conservative one [...] I think they're going to feel that he is a victim, because he got pushed into this marriage. But hopefully they'll respond to her strength also: she's decided this is the man she loves, and she goes after it. Everything is going to be ambivalent.[57]

After the production's run, Shanbag commented that a strong Heli was well received by audiences both at the Globe and for the production's run in Mumbai and cities in Gujarat. Shanbag noted that the response to the wedding scene in India was similar to that at the Globe – 'the same response at every show', an 'audible gasp when she emerges in her bridal finery...partly because it is a beautiful dress changed into in quick time' but also, he suggested, because audiences 'feel Heli is being justly rewarded' with a magnificent wedding to the man she loves. The director goes on to explain the positive reception of Heli in terms of women audience members enjoying a woman's resourcefulness: 'it is the woman in an average Gujarati home who chooses which play the family will see, so Gujarati theatre friends who saw our previews said that our strong Heli would in fact work well for us'; but also in terms of more recognizably traditional expectations around gender and marriage:

> I think the perception is that Bharatram is responsible for his own situation by being blind to what seem obvious advantages in a relationship with Heli. Kunti, his mother, is worried Bharatram will marry either an 'educated city girl' or an English 'memsahib', and she extols the virtues of a traditional Indian wife. This is familiar to Gujaratis who have a tradition of migration – indeed the Gujarati audience at the Globe probably found this very close to their own experience![58]

So Heli is both extolled by Kunti as a traditional Indian wife and leaves the safety of her home to find her husband and win him with a bed trick. The cultural context maps beautifully on to the source text's emphasis upon Helena's feminine virtue which frames the daring and exposing nature of the quest for Bertram.

Bhangwadi is a theatre form dependent upon interaction with the audience and this production clearly drew on this in creating a Helena/Heli on to whom an audience could project their own versions of romance. Her style of performance may recall, for European theatre-goers, the Lecoq or Gaulier-trained physical theatre performer who, in the mode of the clown, shares his or her figure's most delightfully painful emotions with the audience and renders him/herself empathetically vulnerable in their presence. Embarrassment played 'out' in this way is hilarious, ridiculous and also highly sympathetic; it is, I would argue, at the heart of Helena's first soliloquy when she admits to the audience that, hopeless though it is, she loves Bertram. The tearful exasperation of Heli, as Bharatram gleefully tells her of his forthcoming journey to Mumbai, is revealed to the audience even as Bharatram is blind to it and the conspiracy of emotion into which we are invited to enter with her is seductive.

Heli also sings her love, as is conventional in the Bhangwhadi musical theatre form, another empathy-producing convention for the lover figure. The songs and Mansi Parekh's highly engaging, emotive acting, albeit 'broad brush' by standards of theatrical realism, worked to produce empathetic reaction in the audience, in a way that may have recalled for its English-speaking audiences the production of affect in Western musical theatre. Although scenographically, linguistically and economically, this *All's Well* – performed on the open stage at the Globe, using close translation of Shakespeare's language – could not have been more different from a West End or Broadway 'show', a comparison is productive with what Millie Taylor calls the 'voluptuous excess and self awareness' of the musical, which, argues Taylor, 'allows audiences to access the transcendental pleasures of emotional attachment, intelligent interpretation [and] nostalgic recreation'.[59] Journalist, playwright, director and performer Sohailia Kapur writes of the essential difference between the Western musical 'where there is a distinction between spoken dialogue and song' and the tradition of musical theatre that has developed from Indian folk theatre, 'where there is no difference between songs and dialogues'. Fascinatingly, she cites Shanbag's work in musical theatre as bringing together rural and urban traditions, 'in a uniquely urban-Indian idiom, distinct from both the western musical as well as Indian folk styles'. Despite arguing for the independence of work like Shanbag's from either tradition, Kapur cites Swanand Kirkire, where he asserts that 'Musicals are pure entertainment and have the power of bringing common people to the theatre', suggesting a commonality between the forms. 'But one has to do something meaningful', continues Shanbag, and, writes Kapur, he 'continues adapting and writing new musicals in his unique urban-rural genre'.[60] Shanbag's *All's Well* offers emotional attachment (particularly to Heli), intelligent interpretation (of *All's Well*) and 'nostalgic recreation' (of the young, rural woman in love, the perfect wife for Bharatram as far as his mother is concerned) and permits this 'problem play' its elements of 'pure entertainment' while still offering the audiences the pleasures of interpretation and interrogation of gender and social class. The pain, then, of Bharatram's rejection of Heli when it is announced that he is to marry her is produced in the audience by the fact that once she has 'won' him, she believes the play already to have reached its conventional happy ending, its musical theatre closure. In this version, she is not on-stage when Bharatram expresses his distaste for the match, so when she enters in her wedding dress she is all glowing expectation, while the audience knows the rejection that is to come. What Heli has done by the end of the play is convinced Bharatram of her intelligence and resourcefulness – and she produces a satisfying closure that the audience have already had held out to them in the wedding scene.

What this production marks are the play's questions of gender, virtue and love's excesses, rather than anachronistic psychological problems around the plausibility of Helena's love for a man who initially insults her. Although Heli's love is only marginally in excess of her class/caste,[61] her actions are most certainly in excess of her cultural position as a young woman. Her love is comically, though poignantly, passionate. This version of *All's Well* is a complex yet thoroughly comic version that both relies on an audience recognizing certain cultural conventions unquestioningly – such as the notion that marriage is always positive for a play's heroine. The mix of genre and narrative convention that has been the play's 'problem' in its critical history is rendered unproblematic by the Bhangwadi form, which is in excess of the play's political realism – its setting under British colonial rule and the opium trade. In the source text, Bertram is a 'realistic' gendered archetype; Helena's daring in taking off on her travels is less anchored in social reality – she is a figure from a folk-tale rather than a recognizable type from early modern English – or early nineteenth-century Indian – social life.[62] This production makes it clear that in coming together with Heli, Bharatram too can step out of the social constructs that make him, and marry outside of his class/caste. Although Kunti can rest safe in the knowledge that he has married a 'traditional' Indian wife rather than a city girl or an English woman, Heli is a figure who publicly sings the excesses of her love, cures kings and demands a young man in marriage because she is in love with him.

I have suggested in the opening to this chapter that the excesses of love – and not only of lust – are a problem for early modern culture and theatre. Coeffeteau and Ferrand figure love as a disruptive disease like the other passions (see p. 115); Helena's love for Bertram in *All's Well* has to be repeatedly hedged about with reassurances of her virtue. However, *All's Well that Ends Well* demonstrates that in the theatre, love's excess can figure as the primary source of the audience's theatrical pleasure and exceed gendered conventions of virtue. In Arpana's production, the swiftness of Bharatram's 'conversion' to loving Heli matters little; in fact, his downcast appearance when her supposed death is announced suggests that he is beginning to miss and to value the home he had been trying to escape. What appears to engage the audience is the fact that Heli's overwhelming passion for him, sung, danced and spoken, the source of our theatrical pleasure, wins him in the end.

## *ANTONY AND CLEOPATRA*

*All's Well*'s Helena is a woman of modest means and excessive passion. She is resourceful in her quest for Bertram's love. Cleopatra, as she appears in Plutarch and Shakespeare, is a figure of sexual and material excess: she is the serial lover of the leaders of the known world, the riches rolled out to Caesar from a carpet.[63] She legendarily seduces Antony using her almost infinite resources; unlike Helena, she is a figure whose material means match her passions. A number of notorious film depictions of Cleopatra have endeavoured to match Plutarch/Enobarbus' description of the Egyptian queen on the Cydnus:[64] they are 'spectaculars', whose budgets recall the glorious excesses of the barge.[65] The history of Cleopatra in modern performance is one of awe and disapproval at both material and emotional excess. 'The

'Cleopatra look', writes Suzanne Osmond, 'embraces the kitsch spectacle of excessive opulence associated with the stereotypical Orientalist image of Ancient Egypt'.[66] Here is an extract from Laurie N. Ede's account of the making of *Caesar and Cleopatra*, the 1946 film of George Bernard Shaw's play. I am interested in the binary of prodigious excess and reasonableness that plays out in the first two sentences:

> *Caesar and Cleopatra* was produced by the famously prodigious Gabriel Pascal. [...] Pascal promised to bring in the star-filled *Caesar and Cleopatra* for a reasonable £430,000 on a 16-week schedule. The film ultimately cost £1.3 m, took 15 months to film and still ranks as one of the most costly failures of British film industry. Some of the problems weren't Pascal's fault; he faced constant delays wrought by air-raids, shortages of men and materials and the availability of the stars Claude Rains and Vivien Leigh. But *Caesar and Cleopatra* was undoubtedly a profligate film.[67]

Ede goes on to describe the 'prodigious' producer's 'multi-talentitis': how he packed the production company with star practitioners who had no sense of a contained role in the film-making process, leading to massively inflated fees and the excessive proliferation of design sketches for the film. Shaw's narrative depicts a sexually innocent, pre-Cydnus Cleopatra, who remembers Antony as 'A beautiful young man, with strong round arms [who] came over the desert' and restored her father to power when she was 12.[68] For Ede, this was nevertheless a Cleopatra's barge of a film (only of course the Plutarch/Shakespeare barge was a fabulous success rather than a costly failure).

The Victoria and Albert Museum's account of Oliver Messel's design work on *Caesar and Cleopatra* offers a completely different narrative of this film's production: it describes an artistic process steeped in the 'make do and mend ethos of wartime Britain'. Due to rationing and the unavailability of materials,

> Many of the props required [for *Caesar and Cleopatra*] had to be created using what was freely available. Authentic-looking antique Egyptian jewelry was created from thin wire, plastic, cellophane and bits of glass. Gold plates and ornaments were made from a combination of gilded leather and papier-mâché. Many of the costumes were contrived from Indian saris, obtained from some of the large department stores in London which where still functioning. Costume-making workshops were also badly understaffed due to the essential dressmaking workforce having left London due to bombing or on war service.[69]

These different accounts of the making of a Cleopatra film – cautionary tale of film industry extravagance in Ede's account, story of resourceful theatricality in the V and A's – are my way in to an exploration of the moral ambivalence that besets that most excessive of figures, Shakespeare's Cleopatra, in production. I particularly enjoy the contrast between these two accounts, because it recalls both Cleopatra's excessiveness and her resourcefulness, a binary that pertains to Helena too. Cleopatra fascinates (yet again) not only because of the ways in which she uses her fabulous wealth but because she is both an embodiment of passion's excess, fainting and sighing for love of Antony, and the consummate performer of her love, absolutely in control, completely resourceful.

Recent receptions of Cleopatra's theatrical passion have been inflected, I argue here, by cultural attitudes to her excesses of consumption. Displays of feeling and displays of wealth are conflated and judged together. Today, Enobarbus' description of Cleopatra's barge (the barge itself does not, of course, feature physically on the Shakespearean stage) almost inevitably recalls the Hollywood versions – or even the Las Vegas construction: the floating lounge bar Cleopatra's Barge is situated in the Caesar's Palace hotel and casino. Unsurprisingly perhaps, a number of late twentieth-/early twenty-first-century productions have endeavoured to interrogate the notion of a perpetually self-displaying Cleopatra, and simultaneously to reassure audiences that the theatre is far from a reiteration of her – and Hollywood's – conspicuous consumption. I want to suggest that the theatricality of Cleopatra's passion for Antony is potentially central to the pleasure produced by the play but that recent production has demonstrated a Roman tendency to balk at its excess. Central to my argument is a production that seems to deny that, for much of the play, Cleopatra is necessarily in love with Antony at all (see pp. 147–8). This is Janet Suzman's production for Chichester Festival Theatre,[70] which was driven by Suzman's consciousness of reading from a woman's perspective. The director's programme note to the production argues that Cleopatra's relationship with Antony may be largely politically expedient, until she realizes his worth upon his death (see p. 148). I cite the production as an example of a modern anxiety around the play's multiple misogynies – particularly the shifting but ultimately transhistorical desire for and distrust of women on display – and of excessive display and the spectacular more generally. This anxiety ironically reiterates some of the constructions of women it seeks to resist. In explaining away Cleopatra's emotional excess and positing her as a figure entirely in control of her passions, Kim Cattrall's performance of Cleopatra reinscribes the figure in a familiar reality of inevitably manipulative women in difficult man-made circumstances and, I argue, denies the play its pleasurable and interrogatory excesses.

*Antony and Cleopatra* places love in precisely the contradictory position in which it, and the passions more generally, appear in early modern philosophical treatises: though they cause violence, sickness and distress, life would be bland and humans 'brutish' without them (see Southwell, p. 169). Act 1 scene 5 begins with Cleopatra's call for mandragora 'That I might sleep out this great gap of time/My Antony is away' (1.5.5–6). Here a life without the 'fierce affections' she has for Antony is not even worth staying conscious for and the notion of a life without affections is considered explicitly in her conversation with Mardian the eunuch. He, as he explains, does in fact have them: it is he who uses the term 'fierce affections' (1.5.18) and thinks about 'what Venus did with Mars' (19), though he cannot put his thoughts into practice. Cleopatra assumes that he is currently better off than her, as his 'freer thoughts' are 'unseminar'd' and therefore 'May not fly forth of Egypt' (1.5.12–13); thus he will presumably not be in a sick state of longing for someone who is elsewhere, as she is. Here is a connection between the psychological and the somatic alien to modern concepts of the body: that thoughts may be said to have semen. Of course, take this literally and Cleopatra's thoughts must be 'unseminar'd' too, as she is female. It is significant that in the same moment that Cleopatra languishes for love, love is figured as male in its liveliness, movement and boundlessness. It is both a poison which she feeds herself and seems to grow more languorous while contemplating – yet the object of her love, Antony himself, when a messenger arrives from him, is a 'medicine' who guilds the messenger with his 'tinct' (1.5.38–9). Desire – love unfulfilled – is a sickness, which a communication from the loved one cures. Thoughts of love are both productive of extreme languor and figured as lively, life-giving semen. In the scene that follows, as Pompey discusses the state of the wars with the pirate Menas, fulfilled desire is described as just as inductive of languor as longing for the absent lover: Menas imagines Antony 'tie[d] up' with lust for Cleopatra in a 'field of feasts' (2.1.23) in which the food is both 'cloyless' (25) – never sickening – and yet brings on a 'Lethe'd dulness' (27). Antony is 'ne'er lust-wearied' but it is lust that Pompey hopes will weary Antony and slacken his desire to fight. In 1.5, Cleopatra both wants to sleep through her longing and indulge it; she thinks the eunuch is better off without the capacity for freer thought to fly off to a lover, yet by the end of the scene she is speaking of the salad days in which she loved Caesar as 'green in judgement, cold in blood' (1.5.77): before she met Antony she was neither mature in judgment nor sexuality. This pressures fascinatingly the early modern commonplace that youth is hot-blooded but lacks reason; here, as Cleopatra gains maturity and judgement, she also gains heat.

Among all these contradictory figurings of liveliness and sleepiness, excitement and dullness, it is clear that love, like Coriolanus' anger, is always potentially in excess of all control and use value. This emerges in 2.2, before the meeting between Caesar and Antony, where Lepidus urges Enobarbus to keep his master calm during the potentially tense encounter. 'Tis not a time for private stomaching', argues Lepidus, who clearly thinks that one's passions should be put in the control of one's wider interests and duties. The exchange continues:

ENOBARBUS

Every time
Serves for the matter that is then born in't.

LEPIDUS
But small to greater matters must give way.

ENOBARBUS
Not if the small come first.

LEPIDUS

Your speech is passion:
But pray you, sir, stir no embers up.

(2.2.9–13)

For Lepidus, there are 'small' and 'greater' matters, the small being the personal, the 'greater' being to do with power politics: there is a time for passion and this is not it. Enobarbus seems to have a better idea than his interlocutor what kind of play this is.

## PERSONAL AUTHENTICITY AND MATERIAL PLAINNESS

During the late twentieth and early twenty-first century, *Antony and Cleopatra* in British production became plainer. Partly, no doubt, to avoid orientalist cliché, fewer attempts were made to produce spectacular displays of Egyptian opulence, and differences between Rome and Egypt were increasingly made with simple choices of lighting, costume and large props. Even where the play has continued to be a vehicle for high/costly British production values – in the main houses at the RSC or at the National Theatre – these scenographic depictions have consciously historicized the work of theatrical reconstruction that must be done (and was done by Shakespeare) to produce this play, rather than offering the audience an unproblematically seductive and gorgeous 'East'. Alison Chitty's set for the National's 1987 production starring Judi Dench and Anthony Hopkins[71] was, for one reviewer, '[A] cunning all-purpose design of brick-red walls' which served to 'bind the two worlds of this rich epic together'.[72] Here it is the 'epic' that is rich, while the set is cunningly resourceful. It was a design that offered broken walls and single columns, synecdochic fragments of an ancient world; costumes recalled the Jacobean clothing of the play's origins as well as golden glints of a 'rich' ancient world. Reviewer Steve Grant had presumably become used to the notion that the Egyptian scenes of the play need not be depicted with overly sumptuous pseudo-Eastern exoticism, since five years earlier he had written of Adrian Noble's studio production at the RSC's Other Place:[73] 'I didn't find the play too confined in its present, rather bare, two tiered setting, while throughout Noble's fairly hectically-paced production there are enough atmospheric hints at world power in the making to cover up for lack of scenic changes.'[74] And in 1978, Peter Brook and Sally Jacobs' continuous staging of the play, which centred on simple screens, large stools and cushions, and plain and striped North African-inflected costumes,[75] is described by Richard Proudfoot as 'a healthy reaction against surviving mid-Victorian assumptions about staging and costuming Shakespeare'.[76] Proudfoot may be referring to the antiquarian re-creations of the Victorian stage, multiple scene changes or the additions of music and spectacular ballets: the rejection of any or all of these clearly signals for Proudfoot something both 'modern' and closer to Shakespeare in late twentieth-century theatre.[77] The signs of plain resourcefulness – present even in big-budget, big-design productions such as the National's of 1987 – continue into the twenty-first century as we will see, and map on to a need for Cleopatra to be more than a set of displays and seductive manipulations.

Not long into the opening scene of the RSC's 2006 production of *Antony and Cleopatra*, once the Roman messengers whom Antony dismisses too lightly have left, Harriet Walter as Cleopatra pulls off her iconic bobbed wig ('The spuriously inaccurate visual 'code' of jet black bobbed hair' as Suzanne Osmond describes it[78]) with something of a sigh of relief. She reveals her own hair in an untidy, boyish crop. It is an amusing moment, in which the Egyptian queen suggests that she is weary of all the iconic self-display involved in being Cleopatra: at this point in her life, 'wrinkled deep in time' (1.5.30), she would rather take a rest from her notorious identity[79] and just be herself. The moment recalls the masquerading strategies discussed by Osmond in her essay on representations of Cleopatra, the strategies of sex and power used by the 'femme fatale', whose 'shape shifting and putting on and taking off of costumes disguises and therefore infers a deception, a disguising of some true identity'.[80] This Cleopatra takes off her disguise to reveal 'herself' – and this warm, sympathetic but anachronistic move both reflects current popular notions of authenticity and selfhood beneath social construction and works against Shakespeare's construction of Cleopatra as a performer and producer of excessive pleasure. Just as men never tire of Cleopatra (2.2.246–8), being Cleopatra, in all her notorious excess, is something of which, I would argue, Cleopatra never tires herself. What the RSC moment suggests, via the synecdochic wig, is that Cleopatra's self-presentation is in excess of a more authentic self, a less dressed-up, less publicly recognizable one. Thus the figures Antony and Cleopatra display on the world stage are different from the selves the pair are permitted to be domestically – despite the fact that what they do when they are alone, according to Cleopatra, is continue to dress up (2.5.18–23). Production can fail to realize the playful theatricality and powerful self-objectification of Cleopatra because of a need to redeem the play and the figure from a history of conspicuous consumption, misogyny and essentially racist exoticization – a need to purge the play, its displays and its relationships of its perceived excesses.

## THE UNREADABLE DISPLAYS OF CLEOPATRA: CHICHESTER 2012

### *Chemistry*

I am generally somewhat suspicious of reviewers who complain of there being no 'chemistry' between lovers in stage plays. My experience of productions which are thus put down has often been that there has been something else to engage with – that 'chemistry' has not been the point of the production, or at least not the most interesting one – and I suspect that what reviewers often mean is that their own chemicals have not been stirred by the performers in question. However, when Lyn Gardner wrote of Kim Cattrall and Michael Pennington in the Chichester production of Janet Suzman's *Antony and Cleopatra*[81] that 'Despite some manufactured playfulness between the lovers at the beginning, there is an absence of chemistry between them, no sense that sex genuinely threatens the cold-hearted ambitions of Octavius Caesar [...] and Rome',[82] she made an important point. There is a politics of passion in this play around which Suzman decided not to centre her production. Love and sex in *Antony and Cleopatra* do threaten Roman ideology and ambition but here they seemed absent.

As a number of reviewers remarked of both this production and its first incarnation at the Liverpool Playhouse in 2010[83] (with Cattrall as Cleopatra but Jeffery Kissoon as Antony), it was clearly a deliberate decision to suggest that Cleopatra's choice of Antony may have been a purely politically expedient one – and not only in their first encounter at Tarsus, where the barge display is written as a seduction by Plutarch and Shakespeare, planned by Cleopatra before the couple have met. 'Does Cleopatra love Antony or does she love the fact that he is one of the three most powerful men in the Roman empire?' asks Claire Brennan of the Liverpool production.[84] For Paul Taylor, watching at Chichester, 'The production is keen to convey an intelligent heroine, who never really loses sight of her own political agenda through passion. She has enough nous to wince at the errors perpetrated by her bungling lover.'[85] The reviewers have clearly understood the questions that Suzman wanted to pose to her audience. In an interview before the Liverpool production she argued that she has found within the play a

> far more interesting drama than the old love-story warhorse. I'm more fascinated by Cleopatra as a political animal trying to survive in a savage world than in a tragic love affair. Is she in thrall to Antony? I find that not to be so.[86]

In her programme note to her 2012 production at Chichester Festival Theatre, Suzman writes:

> The play seemed to me to be enigmatic – magnificent but enigmatic; just how much does she love him? That he was thoroughly enthralled by Egypt's queen is expressed in detail and in depth in the play, and [he] fatally misjudges his tumultuous world because of it. Her passion for him is more veiled and often hyperbolic, after all she has a country and heirs to consider, but crystallizes thrillingly into very great and true poetry the moment he expires. How painfully true to life; so often we only realize what we have lost when it's gone. She marries him with a full heart at the end: 'Husband I come!' she cries and is soon to join him where the ghosts gaze.[87]

In thrall and enthralled. The common usages are each slightly different but Suzman suggests in her use of both terms that to be in love is to be passion's slave in a way that disempowers and belittles. She clearly does not want the answer to the question 'just how much does she love him?' to be particularly hyperbolic. Antony is 'enthralled' but Cleopatra is not 'in thrall'. Throughout the production, then, Cleopatra's political pragmatism was very much in evidence. In 1.3, her sickness and fainting were comically manipulative and very clearly used to get Antony to stay – until it is clear that there was nothing she could do to prevent his going and she dropped into the less emotive sincerity of 'you and I must part' (1.3.99). But this Cleopatra was clearly no clichéd archetype of femininity whose only intelligence lies in her ability to manipulate sexually. Suzman cites Adrian Goldsworthy's *Antony and Cleopatra* and Stacy Schiff's *Cleopatra, A Life* as a source for her reading of the character – and thereby conflates Shakespeare's version with a historical figure in need of feminist recuperation. Goldsworthy's account of Antony and Cleopatra's first meeting centres on political pragmatism: 'She needed to win over the man who could confirm or depose her, so it is reasonable to believe that she deliberately set out to seduce him and that from early on he wanted her as a lover.'[88] Schiff's project is to rewrite Cleopatra's history for a popular readership, reclaiming 'That Egyptian Woman's' story from sexist propaganda that began with the Romans. Like the Romans, writes Schiff,

> We remember her [...] for the wrong reasons. [In fact she was a] capable, clear-eyed sovereign, she knew how to build a fleet, suppress an insurrection, control a currency, alleviate a famine. [...] She nonetheless survives as a wanton temptress, not the last time a genuinely powerful woman has been transmuted into a shamelessly seductive one.[89]

To emphasize this point that Cleopatra 'has a country [...] to consider', Cattrall was to be found at a table signing official documents handed to her by all-purpose official Alexas and wearing heavy reading glasses, a comic contrast to the floating white Egyptian/Eastern signifiers of the rest of her costume. After Antony's first defeat of the play, at Actium, Cattrall's Cleopatra wept her devastation at the outcome of the misjudged sea battle. But her delivery of the question to Enobarbus – 'Is Antony or we in fault for this?' (3.13.2) – was spoken in a tone of practical curiosity: she seemed to be wondering what to do next if it emerged that she had involved herself with a leader of poor judgement. After Antony's second defeat in this production, it seemed more likely than not that Cleopatra had, as Antony suspects, instructed her forces to abandon Antony for Caesar when the battle seemed to be going the latter's way. She agreed readily to Thidias/Caesar's suggestion that she had been forced to be Antony's lover and a blank contempt descended upon her at Antony's treatment of the messenger. Her next reconciliation with him, particularly the announcement that it is her birthday, was brought about by a cartoon-like performance of 'feminine wiles'. At the mention of the birthday, Antony offered a comic 'oops' to the audience, like a man from a sitcom who has forgotten the wife's anniversary; this provoked a laugh – rather at Antony than with him, I sensed. Pennington's Antony was an old, highly manipulable man who loses his temper easily but can be lulled back to compliance by a seductive word or gesture from his much younger lover. Cattrall signalled clearly what Suzman suggests in her programme note – that Antony is 'a necessary male consort' for Cleopatra, 'sixteen years her senior, whom she sets out to seduce as she struggled to strengthen her hold on the throne'.

Suzman was pleased to find in Goldsworthy and Schiff's work on the 'real' Cleopatra 'that the fabled love affair was so much more subject to the savage exigencies of the time than the received impression of an equal balance of the passions, which still casts a filmic glow over the peerless pair'. Suzman also remarks that, as a woman director, she is 'inevitably less interested in the sex-bomb iconography for Cleopatra'. Her reading of the figure as one fully aware of the power of display – the opening of the production has her rising through a trapdoor in her white robe and gold jewelry, lifting her arms ceremoniously above her head – and for whom almost every action is a matter of political expediency, also chimes with L.T. Fitz's critique of 'Sexist Attitudes in *Antony and Cleopatra* Criticism', written in 1977, a few years after Suzman herself played the role for the RSC[90] and the production was recorded for television (1974).[91] Fitz, too, emphasizes that Cleopatra is a political leader: 'Being queen of Egypt gives Cleopatra the opportunity for splendour, to which she is not averse; but it is also (let it not be forgotten) her career.'[92]

Cattrall's less than overt performance of lust in this production may also have been an attempt to confound any conflation here of Shakespeare's middle-aged 'sex bomb' and the one played by Cattrall in HBO's *Sex and the City*. But a combination of a 69-year-old Antony (according to most readily available biographies, this makes Pennington 13 years older than Cattrall but his performance made the gap appear larger), whom we may have been hard pressed to imagine either going into battle or having very much by way of gaudy nights with his more physically lively consort, and a clear foregrounding of Cleopatra's political needs over the sexual in this production, resulted in the replacement of one old set of stereotypes with another. The 'impression of an equal balance of the passions' (which Suzman associates in her programme note with film versions of this love story) – the version of the play in which two infinitely powerful, equally irresponsible and roughly equally middle-aged figures give up control of the known world, then their own lives, because they cannot extricate political world from passionate life – is replaced by the story of a middle-aged leader who knows she is powerfully attractive to a now rather vulnerable and elderly one and uses him – plausibly and understandably given the male-dominated political systems within which she has to operate – to her own ends. 'Catrall's [sic] relationship with her women seems warmer than her relationship with her lover, with whom you feel she is more likely to share a cup of cocoa than a passionate kiss'[93] suggests Gardner; for Paul Taylor, who also makes the Chemistry point, Pennington's Antony 'seems less like a faded romantic idol than an incipiently senile embarrassment' and Taylor makes it clear not that he is sneering at the actor's age but that it is 'the interpretation and not this still-vigorous actor that is at fault here'.[94]

The problem here, for this audience member and the cited reviewers, with Suzman's challenge to the assumption of an equal passion between Antony and Cleopatra is that once one has understood that Antony is a vulnerable fool and Cleopatra a manipulative politician, it is difficult not to disengage from the pair entirely. The 'poetry' of the play to which Suzman refers in the programme, which she seems to suggest permits 'Love' to 'conquer all' in the end, is not the poetry of verbal echo, the linguistic construction of the 'mutual pair' (1.1.38) which a close reader like Ernest Schanzer found in the play.[95] In this production, Pompey (Oliver Hoare), in his tearful account of the death of his father when he confronts Antony and Caesar in 2.6, and Caesar (Martin Hutson), in his distress at Antony's betrayal of Octavia, performed more 'love' than Antony and Cleopatra; Ruth Everett's Octavia falls to the floor in weeping distress when she finally accepts that Antony is not sitting faithfully at home in Athens and Caesar holds her desperately in his arms, calling her his 'dear'st sister!' (3.6.100) in such a way as to suggest love between family members is more genuine and altruistic than the self-serving, self-centred love of lovers. Suzman – and indeed Cattrall – clearly want to locate a powerful political agency in Cleopatra, rather than leave her once again with the limited sexual agency granted to the icon of female beauty and sexual manipulativeness across thousands of years, beginning with Roman histories of Cleopatra and recycled in early modern figurings of inconstant woman. In deciding not to play it for love, the productions misses love's subversive excesses, as Gardner's review suggests.

### *Avoiding Misogyny*

The history of Cleopatra is part of a historical narrative of feminine excess that these modern productions are keen to eschew. In early modern misogynistic discourse, woman equals excess and men are in turn exasperated by and prey to her somatic and sexual excesses: woman's changeability, her lack of reasoning self-governance, her slavery to the passions and her excessive desire for self-display. The nature of woman in early modern writings is notoriously difficult to pin down – appropriately enough given her supposed wayward changeability. There is an inherent contradiction between the humoral and the social construction of the female. On the one hand, she is colder and damper than man, her temperament tending to the phlegmatic; on the other, she is supposedly dangerously lustful and remarkably quick to anger, which should indicate a hot – so choleric or sanguine – temperament: inherently unreasonable, woman does not have her passions under control. This was clearly a problem for early modern physiology. Gail Kern Paster quotes royal physician Helkiah Crooke, where he concludes in his *Microcosmographia* 'that...men are hotter than women...as well in regard of the Naturall Temper, as that which is acquired by diet and the course of life' and concludes that herein lies the predominant understanding of female temperament and humorality in the early modern period as cold, spongy, less vital and less clearly individuated than male.[96] But Crooke's conclusion is to an argument that he clearly sees as unresolved for many, and which he elucidates over five huge folio pages,[97] even where he has concluded it. The physicians and philosophers against which he argues have asserted that women are not only quicker to anger and more lascivious than men but, more positively, 'all the Faculties, Vital, Natural and Animal are in women more perfect in men' and so 'who will deny but they are also hotter than men?',[98] heat generating the vitality of all the faculties. Crooke goes on to demolish these arguments with a fury for which he finally feels the need to apologize, excusing himself in terms of the heat generated by manly scientific dispute. It is a fascinating discourse that demonstrates the biological construction of the female as the negative other to the male, which Paster has brilliantly analysed. The point I want to make here is that in deciding that women are phlegmatic types – slow, fearful, accepting of their fate – early modern humoral theory seems to invent the woman it would like to see, rather than the woman it fears – and then must reinvent her quickness to anger, wantonness and petulance in the light of her supposedly colder temperament.[99] By 1641, characteristics that supposedly exist in women which may appear to be contradictory but which are explained away humorally by Crooke are parodied by Royalist satirist Thomas Jordan as whore and saintly wife, the latter so stable in temperament as to seem comically naive.[100] In Crooke's biology, woman is the cold, faulty opposite of man. In *Antony and Cleopatra* she is his dangerously hot equal.

Thus, despite her supposedly steady, Octavia-like phlegmatism, the trope of woman as inconstant and faithless occurs repeatedly in a wide range of early modern dramas, treatises and ballads. That they are inconstant is Swetnam's first complaint against women in the epistle to the *Araignment*, where he laments his contact, as a traveller, with 'the heinous evils of unconstant women'.[101] Intrinsic to the sin of inconstancy are the evils of changeable mood, excessive lust, love of 'bravery' or fine dress (which is of course used to tempt men) and excessive anger – which women, in an account such as Dekker's *The Bachelor's Banquet* 'Pleasantly discoursing the variable humors of women, their quickness of wits, and unsearchable deceits', turn upon their husbands when they don't get the clothes they want.[102] Cleopatra's excessive, theatrical self-decoration, then, is both just like a woman – and also very much unlike the women who appear in early modern discourses seducing men into marriage then nagging them for clothes, or seducing men into sex and getting clothes for payment, if only for the simple reason that Cleopatra has all the riches of the East with which to provide for herself.

As Steven Mullaney points out, in early modern writing,

> Misogyny presents an interpretive embarrassment of riches: it is everywhere, unabashed in its articulation and so overdetermined in its cultural roots that individual instances sometimes seem emotionally underdetermined, rote and uninflected expressions of what would go without saying if it weren't said so often.[103]

But the ubiquitous stereotype of the inconstant woman is also the emotional centre of this play and pushes at the bounds of misogynistic thinking and at the simplicity of the stereotype. Inconstancy is central to the very plot structure of the play and is figured in Antony as well as Cleopatra, as he shifts from his declaration that 'there's beggary in love that can be reckon'd' (1.1.15) to his reckoning that it would be politically expedient to marry Caesar's sister. Octavius Caesar combines both the notion that women are naturally inconstant with the idea that women sometimes need to be so, when he assures Thidias that 'Women are not/In their best fortunes strong, but want will perjure/The ne'er-touch'd vestal' (3.12.29–31); it is clearly possible that an early modern audience would have assumed that Cleopatra acts in accordance with her wayward, shifting temperament and subjection to the passions, as she flirts with the first man who comes to her – Thidias – when it looks as though Antony's fortunes are finally waning. The trite expression of 'what would go without saying' about women in the early modern period is certainly said often enough in the play. But change and changeability – to replace 'inconstancy' with less pejorative terms – are also both central to the pleasures produced by Cleopatra for Antony (her 'infinite variety' (246) and theatrical shifts of temper) – and to the theatrical pleasure produced by this play. Changeability, that unfathomable fault of women in misogynist discourse, and in much Cleopatra criticism from Coleridge onward,[104] is not the subject of mere eye-rolling exasperation on the part of men (though Enobarbus' commonsensical utterances on the matter demonstrate such exasperation (see p. 156)) but the site of the play's emotional intensity. In Suzman's production, Cleopatra's changeability is given a clear material and psychological motivation that clears her somewhat of 400-year-old charges against women now distasteful to many modern audience members.

## PASSION AND THEATRICALITY

In the second scene of the play, Antony finally hears the message from Rome that, in the world's opinion, he is losing that world while he languishes with Cleopatra. He also hears that his wife Fulvia is dead. Fulvia, it seems, conforms to the 'familiarity breeds contempt' cliché that Cleopatra belies. In her now permanent absence, Antony mourns his wife – 'She's good, being gone' (1.2.131). Cleopatra appears to understand how absence works in this regard and repeatedly creates a theatrical desire and suspense in the play by absenting herself. She has done so as Antony enters in 1.2; she repeatedly faints – or pretends to; she fatally absents herself in Act 4 of the play, leading Antony to kill himself for love and loss of her. This production of desire by absence is central to Cleopatra's theatricality and to discuss it will require a definition of theatricality that strips the term of its connotations of inauthenticity. Cleopatra's 'celerity in dying', as Enobarbus jokes about it, makes her 'cunning past men's thought' (1.2.150) according to Antony, when he is trying to break off from her enchantments. But Enobarbus protests against the notion that Cleopatra contrives or puts on the excess of her passions:

> Alack, sir, no; her passions are made of nothing but the finest part of pure love. We cannot call her winds and waters sighs and tears; they are greater storms and tempests than almanacs can report. This cannot be cunning in her. If it be, she makes a shower of rain as well as Jove.
>
> (1.2.151–6)

Her expressions of love are so materially excessive that they must be real; they go beyond the physical expression of Fiammetta's sighs (see p. 124): her material expressions of love are more like the weather. Enobarbus' tone reads as both jocular and awed – and his barge speech will also demonstrate that he is very capable of awe when it comes to Cleopatra. He seems at once ironic in his defence of the authenticity of her passions and genuinely impressed by her acting.[105] Recall Hamlet's soliloquy after he has listened to the Player's speech and the real tears that the good actor is able to bring to his eyes, 'for nothing! For Hecuba!' (2.2.557–8). Cleopatra is able to 'die' at will; Enobarbus has seen her 'die twenty/times upon far poorer moment' (1.2.146–7) than Antony's leaving. The great actor can make 'a shower of rain as well as Jove' and, like Cleopatra, the actor is both a creator and a feeler of passion. In the very next scene, 1.3, Cleopatra demonstrates this celerity in dying, or at least fainting.

Enobarbus' seeming belief in Cleopatra's excessive passions rather contrasts with his sentiments in his exchange with Menas in Act 2. Here, the pair, who have previously fought each other, indulge in a little misogynistic joking about women's falsehood:

> MENAS
>
> All men's faces are true, whatsome'er their hands are.

ENOBARBUS
But there is never a fair woman has a true face.

MENAS
No slander. They steal hearts.

(2.6.99–101)

Menas suggests, as he shakes Enobarbus' hand, that he will be able to read his former combatant's face no matter what his hands do by seeming way of friendship, and Enobarbus replies with a remark that will bond them against a common enemy, the ever-faithless female. However, this is just the kind of conventional homosocial exchange that occurs in an all-male environment such as the parley with Pompey, and it highlights the male-constructed nature of this version of the female. In the rest of the play, Enobarbus is unable to reduce Cleopatra to an archetype of female 'untruth' in this way – she constructs herself in such a way as to 'beggar[...] all description' (2.2.208). There is no doubt that *Antony and Cleopatra* does reiterate some stock misogynies and mystifications around notions of woman's changeability and her concomitant seductive power. But it also stages changeability, passion and the changeability of passion in such a way as to render anxieties around them secondary to their theatrical appeal.

Of course, the binary of Roman duty and Egyptian excess could not be more clearly set up in the first scene of *Antony and Cleopatra*; the contrast has become a critical commonplace and a scenographic cliché. Philo describes Antony as having been pulled from his military responsibilities in Egypt and the general 'oe'r flows the measure' in his 'dotage' on Cleopatra; his legimate, masculine, somatic excess – his armour-busting heart – has become feminized in love: 'the bellows and the fan to cool a gypsy's lust' (1.1.9–10). The gendered and racially determined metaphors of excess could not be clearer. However, when we meet the couple, it is Antony who speaks of finding out new heaven and new earth rather than set a boundary to their love. Where Antony is determined to figure the space of the couple's love as the whole world, Cleopatra insists that in fact it is circumscribed by the realities of Antony's loyalties to Caesar and his ties to Fulvia. Cleopatra ventriloquizes Antony's obligations to Caesar with her "Do this, or this;/Take in that kingdom, and enfranchise that;/ Perform 't, or else we damn thee' (1.1.23–5). The more expansive Antony's language becomes, the more determined she seems to pull him back to the mundane realities of doing this or that, and of the messages that 'grate him' (19). Of course, the actor playing Cleopatra may decide that her provocative determination that he should attend to the messengers aims at exactly the opposite effect and that Antony knows exactly what is required of him when Cleopatra disingenuously suggests he pay more attention to Rome than to herself. But it is significant that it is Antony here who persistently figures that love as boundless and himself as only himself as he is 'stirred by Cleopatra' (44), where Cleopatra's first lines are concerned with the social contracts that are also part of Antony. The opening images of the constant, dutiful, soldierly general being turned to an immeasurably excessive dotage by this 'gipsy' are challenged from this first scene. In his article on the ways in which Roman needs and desires are projected on to the figure of Cleopatra, Jonathan Gil Harris argues that the very gendered notion of steadfast, reasoning male and changing, passionate woman is produced by Antony himself in his characterization of Cleopatra and serves to erase his own changeability:

> The impression of [Cleopatra's] 'variety' is in part created by the panoply of subject-positions she is accorded by the alternately desiring and disgusted Antony: 'enchanting queen' (1.2.125); 'my chuck' (4.4.2); 'my nightingale' (4.8.18); 'Triple-turn'd whore,' 'grave charm,' 'right gipsy' (4.12.13, 25, 28). Cleopatra's 'variety' provides the specular image – is, in many respects, the very effect – of Antony's own. His displacement onto her of his own vacillations exemplifies.[106]

In support of Harris' argument, it is also Antony who figures Cleopatra as the theatrical, pleasure-loving queen, suggesting that it is she who has instigated the game of wandering the streets to note the quality of the people: 'last night you did desire it' (1.1.56), he insists. In North's Plutarch, as I have noted elsewhere[107], this is rather Antony's regular escapade than Cleopatra's, although she occasionally accompanies him: Plutarch's Antony disguises himself to go among the people and Cleopatra joins him dressed as a chambermaid. In Plutarch, Antony, it is suggested, deliberately shows one side of himself to Egypt, one to Rome and this changeability is figured as theatrical and praised as a fine trait by the theatrical Egyptians:

> And sometime also, when he would go up and down the city disguised like a slave in the night, and would peer into poor men's windows and their shops, and scold and brawl with them within the house: Cleopatra would be also in a chambermaid's array, and amble up and down the streets with him, so that oftentimes Antonius bare away both mocks and blows. Now, though most men misliked this manner, yet the Alexandrians were commonly glad of this jollity, and liked it well, saying very gallantly and wisely, that Antonius shewed them a comical face, to wit, a merry countenance: and the Romans a tragical face, to say, a grim look.[108]

In Shakespeare's play, Antony shifts theatricality onto Cleopatra:

> Fie, wrangling queen,
> Whom everything becomes – to chide, to laugh,
> To weep; whose every passion fully strives
> To make itself, in thee, fair and admired!
> No messenger but thine, and all alone
> Tonight we'll wander through the streets and note
> The qualities of people. Come, my queen!
> Last night you did desire it. [*to the Messenger*] Speak not to us.
> (1.1.49–56)

However, I do not want to argue here that Cleopatra's theatricality in Shakespeare's play is a Roman invention but rather suggest that the expression of the passions in this play is linked to the intense pleasures of theatricality as much as the cultural anxieties the term also produces in the period.

On one level, the first four lines of Antony's speech above simply look like an overblown way of saying 'you look great when you're angry'. But Antony is also figuring Cleopatra here as an actor-like figure. Her every passion, says Antony, strives to make itself fair and admired in her: the compliment at once suggests that she exhibits all the passions admirably and that the passions are all competing to be admired through her. The great actor does look great when he's angry: all the passions are admired when he produces them. The speech also suggests that there is no humoral predominance in Cleopatra; she has everything, whereas the people they are about to watch in the streets have particular, and one assumes interestingly limited, qualities. Later, as we have seen, Enobarbus praises – albeit in equivocally jocular style – Cleopatra's 'sighs and tears'; here I suggest that Antony uncouples the idea of rapidly shifting passions from some ultimately misogynistic notion of women's changeability and instead associates them with the pleasure his paying audience is taking from emotional expression in the theatre.

In return, Cleopatra describes Antony as someone who, again like the great actor, is well able to control his passions, is able to put them to use. As she receives his gift of a pearl in 1.5 he is carrying out his duties in a fashion neither sad nor merry, as the messenger reports, and here Cleopatra both privileges the figure of he who is not passion's slave and simultaneously maintains that violent passions become the great man:

> O well divided disposition! [...]
> He was not sad, for he would shine on those
> That make their looks by his; he was not merry,
> Which seem'd to tell them his remembrance lay
> In Egypt with his joy; but between both.
> O heavenly mingle! Be'st thou sad or merry,
> The violence of either thee becomes
> As does it no man else.
>
> (1.5.56–64)

The ability to control the passions for the sake of one's work and duty is praised in the first part of the speech but in the second, Cleopatra is returning Antony's compliment of 1.1, in which all the passions strive to be admired within her. Antony, like Cleopatra, is actor-like in the way he is both able to put the passions to what use he will, controlling them where necessary, and in the way that they 'become' him. Being sad or merry is still nevertheless a matter of 'violence'. It is not the well-controlled, reasonable Christian expression of emotion that is being extolled here.

Arranging the weddings of actors, throwing up in the Senate,[109] getting beaten up in the streets, Antony in Plutarch can be both a great warrior and a figure of fun, a merry lover of comical theatricals and a serious Roman leader. In *Antony and Cleopatra*, Shakespeare takes up Plutarch's suggestion that it is only the Romans who believe that the 'comical face'[110] of Antony is not truly Antony – and the Antony of the play colludes in this construction of himself when it suits him, as when he assures Caesar he only neglected his duties in their wars 'when poison'd hours had bound me up/From mine own knowledge' (2.2.96–7). In this regard, he matches Cleopatra in her self-interested flirtation with Thidias and her suggestion that her relationship with Antony was enforced; Antony denies Cleopatra (and indeed marries someone else) when it is expedient.

What Antony does not have, either in Plutarch or Shakespeare, interested though he is in theatrical spectacle and play-acting in the former, is Cleopatra's ability to make theatrical spectacle of her own person. In Enobarbus' description, closely based on Plutarch of course, he is left all alone in the marketplace as everyone – as even the air would if it could – rushes to see Cleopatra on her barge. In Plutarch he is well known for dressing down rather than up for an occasion, although it is hinted that this may well have been part of a performance of authenticity that won him the approval of the man in the street:

> For when he would openly shew himself abroad before many people he would always wear his cassock girt down low upon his hips, with a great sword hanging by his side

> and upon that, some ill-favoured cloak. Furthermore, things that seem intolerable in other men, as to boast commonly, to jest with one or other, to drink like a good fellow with everybody, to sit with the soldiers when they dine, and to eat and drink with them soldier like: it is incredible what wonderful love it won him amongst them.[111]

Antony finally makes a poor, even comical performance of his own tragedy, in his botched suicide. Cleopatra takes time to get dressed for hers, chooses a means of death that leaves little trace upon the spectacle of her dead body and though she fantastizes that in dying she goes to join her 'husband' Antony, her decision to die seems as explicitly motivated by a determination not to be co-opted into a theatrical shame punishment devised by Caesar.

The figure of the actor is not an unambiguously positive one in the play. Cleopatra herself equates it with insincerity when she sarcastically interrupts the departing Antony's 'Most sweet queen' with 'Nay, pray you seek no colour for your going,/But bid farewell and go' (1.3.32–4); there is no need for him to decorate his departure with theatrical artistry or 'colour'. When she has had the news of Fulvia's death and is berating Antony for his lack of tears, she bitterly tells Antony to weep for his dead wife and pretend the tears are for her, Cleopatra: 'Good now, play one scene/Of excellent dissembling, and let it look/Like perfect honour' (1.3.79–81). The following exchange enrages Antony as Cleopatra continues to interrupt him as if commenting on his acting:

ANTONY

You'll heat my blood. No more.

CLEOPATRA

You can do better yet; but this is meetly.

ANTONY

Now, by my sword –

CLEOPATRA

And target. Still he mends;
But this is not the best. Look, prithee, Charmian,
How this Herculean Roman does become
The carriage of his chafe.

(81–6)

Despite the awed respect with which Antony's divine sponsor, Hercules, is treated elsewhere in the play, when the Roman soldiers of 4.3 believe they hear him leaving the general, to ironize Antony as 'Herculean' is a particularly sharp theatrical joke here: 'I could play Ercles rarely' (1.2.26) is the claim made by the notorious overactor Bottom and here Cleopatra teases Antony for his theatrical bombast. Later, however, when she is missing him, she pays him that similar compliment to the one Antony pays her in 1.1: the violence of his passion becomes no man else (1.5.62). And in 1.3, when Antony threatens to walk off-stage after the teasing exchange above, she shifts to a mode of speech that appears, by contrast to the overblown theatricality of which she accuses Antony, utterly sincere:

Courteous lord, one word:
Sir, you and I must part, but that's not it;
Sir, you and I have loved, but there's not it;
That you know well. Something it is I would –
Oh, my oblivion is a very Antony,
And I am all forgotten!

(1.3.88–93)

Cleopatra shifts from acting out a faint in anticipation of Antony's news, teasing him for acting himself and goading him to act better, to the fragile vulnerability of these lost lines, where forgetting what she wanted to say recalls the actor in the moment of 'drying'. 'When good will is showed', says Cleopatra later, when joking with the eunuch Mardian about his willingness to play billiards with her, 'though't come too short,/The actor may plead pardon' (2.5.8–9). Here Cleopatra comes too short and fails to express herself in words, and appears all the more pleasingly sincere as a result.

This scene ends with Cleopatra speaking of her 'becomings', which, she says, kill her when they do not 'eye well' to her one audience member, Antony (1.3.98–9). Then she finally retrieves her performance skills and 'becomes' the formally deferential Lady wishing goodbye to her Lord:

> [...] Your honour calls you hence;
> Therefore be deaf to my unpitied folly,
> And all the gods go with you! Upon your sword
> Sit laurel victory, and smooth success
> Be strew'd before your feet!
>
> (1.3.99–103)

Mark Rylance playing Cleopatra at Shakespeare's Globe in 1999[112] accompanied these lines with a deep curtsey. A Cleopatra otherwise inclined to move rapidly about the stage self-consciously performing herself, with Charmian and Iras attempting to place cushions in just the place where their mistress might sit, Rylance now became formal and still, heightening still further the triple performance of the woman, the boy (here man) player and queen that constitutes this figure. However, this did not make Cleopatra's farewell lines appear insincere. Like the good actor in *Hamlet*, Cleopatra delights with her performances and appears truly to feel what she performs.

## LOVE, THEATRICALITY, AUTHORITY

*Antony and Cleopatra* ends with Cleopatra wrestling the role of stage-manager in the Cleopatra show from Caesar. Although his planned leading of Cleopatra 'in triumph' (5.2.108) is to be a parade of prisoners of war rather than a judicial punishment, the parade that Cleopatra imagines she is escaping from by taking her own life entails a charivari-like entertainment, notoriously complete with the squeaking player who will 'boy [her] greatness/ I'th'posture of a whore' (5.2.219–20). It recalls the theatrical shame-punishments still residual in English legal culture and meted out particularly frequently on those deceitful, faithless, changeable women who had transgressed sexually.[113] The wrong-doers in these punishments are displayed by the law as the law has labelled them – as 'strumpets' stripped half naked or dressed in symbolic clothing with signs about their necks. Escaping such punishment, when Cleopatra displays herself in death she displays herself. It is essential to Cleopatra's self-construction as a self-authoring, theatrical figure of excess that her last performance is not stage-managed by Caesar. Caesar, despite often being played as a repressed, puritanical introvert by modern actors (no doubt because of his love of the old, puddle-drinking Antony (1.4.62–4) and his reluctance to get drunk with his friends on Pompey's boat (2.7.100–102)), is very much aware of the power of theatricality. This is confirmed not only by his plan to display Cleopatra to the world as his prisoner but by his shock at his sister's return to him as a 'market maid to Rome' (3.6.52) rather than accompanied by a suitably extravagant parade which might top the exhibition Antony and Cleopatra have just made of themselves and their children 'in the common show place' (3.6.12), much to Caesar's fury. Trees should have bent with the weight of men waiting to watch Octavia pass by, and 'expectation fainted,/Longing for what it had not', because Octavia is Caesar's sister (3.6.47–9). Caesar figures public display as productive of desire here. Like Cleopatra, he understands the erotic economy of these events; unlike Cleopatra, his understanding of them does not go beyond their use value. Cleopatra's self-display is so excessive in its theatricality and so inextricably bound up with the 'winds and waters' of her passions that it is inevitable that she would refuse to be displayed in the way Caesar intends. Her person 'beggars all description' within the discourses of early modern misogyny because the excessive, shifting, uncontrolled passions of the female do, in fact, appear to be in her control, as they are in the control of the actor in *Hamlet* who 'really' cries for Hecuba. According to this reading, Cleopatra's tragedy is that she can only maintain this excessive, self-performing agency in death.

She is a self-constructed theatrical being who defies misogynist discourses around women and 'bravery', whereby women dress up and use make-up in order to deceive men into loving them (and providing them with more bravery).[114] The description-beggaring excess of Cleopatra and her barge display reflects the enormity of her passionate theatrical range – or her range of theatrical passions.

Through 1.2 and 1.3, Cleopatra stages a range of early modern anxieties about women – that they are cunning, changeable, deceptive, lustful, that they think and behave in excess of male reason – and suggests that the multiple performances of this particular woman should be the focus of its theatrical pleasure. The play links this female changeability to acting and the active skill of changeability which the good actor must possess – and which the audience has clearly come to the theatre to enjoy. Woman's changeability is bound up in early modern misogynistic discourse with the excess of her passions, her inability to control them, her lack of reason – ultimately her lack of humanity. But the actor's changeability permits him to play any human; a good actor's 'becomings' are never tired of, they always 'eye well'. That Cleopatra is all changing passion produces her as one of those excessive femininities about which the misogynists such as Swetnam complain. But her changeable emotions figure her as an actor who is the ultimate controller of the passions – the actor can bring them on and off at will and produce real, material effects of passion in that 'sweating labour' (1.3.93). Cleopatra is a bewildering and 'enchanting' admixture of excess and control.

Helena opens *All's Well* pretending she is crying for her dead father where she is in fact crying over the departure of Bertram; she makes a speech in which she upbraids herself for the hopeless naivety of a love she cannot help. In a familiar comedic convention, she shows to the audience what she cannot tell the other characters – then she exposes her love with nearly disastrous consequences. Cleopatra, on the other hand, constantly and openly displays herself; this is not the same as 'pretending' anything – at least not to the audience. Even when sometimes she may be read as 'only acting' to manipulate Antony, the fact that she acknowledges her 'becomings' complicates misogynistic discourses around the manipulative female. Just as, for Enobarbus, she displays what a great queen she is through her barge pageant, she continually demonstrates to us how passionate she is for Antony, in the way that Hamlet's Player shows he can 'really' be passionate. Of course, Cleopatra is in love with Antony where Hecuba is 'nothing' to the Player. But the deliberate and conscious sense of self-display is comparable. Fascinatingly, because so paradoxically, Cleopatra is the ultimate willing agent, because she is so like an actor.

In both *All's Well that Ends Well* and *Antony and Cleopatra*, audiences are invited to take pleasure in the excesses of love. Love in both plays is certainly more than lust but it is not divided from it as Charney has suggested. It is troubling because it leaves one a slave to passion – but also because it seems to offer a powerful agency to the two female figures I have discussed here. For the early modern period, love compromises male reason, female virtue, and the work of fighting and leadership; it blurs gender boundaries – sending Helena out to work in her dead father's trade and Antony to the bedroom dressed in Cleopatra's attire when he should be fighting. In our own period it blurs the boundaries of sincerity and authenticity which British and North American societies like to police, particularly because of the ways in which Cleopatra's passion is figured as theatrical. It is impossible to tell when Cleopatra is acting – and when she is acting it does not mean she is not sincere. I am not denying that misogynist anxieties around female excess are not part of the language and dramaturgy of these plays – but I am arguing that Helena, Antony and Cleopatra are in excess of them. The expression of unreasonable love in *All's Well* and *Antony and Cleopatra* produces theatrical pleasure and this challenges constructions of emotional excess as shamefully feminine. Perhaps Shakespeare does not write another *Taming of the Shrew* because excess of passion is more entertaining than its taming.

# CHAPTER FOUR

## 'STOP YOUR SOBBING': GRIEF, MELANCHOLY AND MODERATION

CRESSIDA

Why tell you me of moderation?
The grief is fine, full, perfect, that I taste,
And violenteth in a sense as strong
As that which causeth it: how can I moderate it?
If I could temporize with my affection,
Or brew it to a weak and colder palate,
The like allayment could I give my grief.
My love admits no qualifying dross;
No more my grief, in such a precious loss.

Shakespeare, *Troilus and Cressida* (4.4.2–10)

Some skillful limner help me, if not so,
Some sad tragedian to express my woe:
But (oh) he's gone, that could the best, both limn
And act my grief; and 'tis for only this for him –
That I invoke this strange assistance to't,
And in the point call himself to do it;
For none but Tully Tully's praise can tell,
And as he could, no man could act so well
This point of sorrow, for him none can draw
So truly to the life this map of woe;
This grief's true picture which his loss has bred,
He's gone and with him what a world are dead.

Anonymous, *Elegy on the death of Richard Burbage*

When Cressida replies furiously to Pandarus' plea that she 'be moderate' (2.2.1) after hearing that she must part from Troilus, she insists that she *tastes* her grief. Read her speech alongside Richard II's insistence that he, too, tastes grief and one might assume that Cressida's declaration is part of a discourse of somatic passion quite unremarkable in the early modern period. Richard's tasting of grief is, after all, one of the feelings and experiences he lists as common to all men. The deposed King uses it to insist, albeit with a bitter irony, that he is a man as other men are:

RICHARD
For you have but mistook me all this while:
I live with bread like you, feel want,
Taste grief, need friends: subjected thus,
How can you say to me, I am a king?
(3.1.174–7)

Grief here is such a palpably physical passion and such an ordinary part of the human condition that it seems logical to describe it as being apprehended in the mouth, like daily bread. Cressida, however, brings a culinary precision to her tasting of grief. It is as if she is being asked by her uncle to water down that which tastes properly strong, and even in the extremity of her grief she is able to speak of its fullness and perfection, how its strength is appropriate to its cause – her love for Troilus. This seems a fitting description for grief in the theatre, where the audience has come to see grief finely, fully and perfectly depicted on-stage. Whereas early modern religious and philosophical thought stresses the proper place of moderate grief – Jesus wept, after all, and it would be inhuman not to respond feelingly to life's tragedies – moderation of grief was nevertheless a crucial Christian and politically correct undertaking in the early modern period: Robert Southwell declares that 'not to feel sorrow in sorrowful chances, is to want sense, so not to bear it with moderation, is to want understanding, the one brutish, the other effeminate'.[1] Mourning must be undertaken within a cosmological context which makes our human griefs both insignificant and part of a god-given state of things, in the face of which we must acknowledge our helplessness. For example, a national loss as cataclysmic as that of Elizabeth I must be seen through the proper joy of the next succession: the first of Mavericke Radford's *Three Treatises* on the succession, *The Mourning Weed*, *The Morning's Joy* and *The King's Rejoicing*, advises that

> according to the sundry turnings and movings of these higher spheres (having all one *primum movens*, God the whole monarch of heaven and earth), all other inferior Spheres, are moved, turned about or changed. [H]ence cometh alterations in kingdoms; hence cometh changes of Kings and Princes.[2]

A sermon such as Thomas Playfere's *The Mean in Mourning* (much copied, according to his rather irritable dedicatory epistle), lists the times that Christ said to his followers 'weep not', and, as we have seen (p. xiv), compares excess of weeping to the destructive excesses that he figures as both part of and as against nature. Jesus was

> Forbidding thereby immoderate weeping, which is condemned, *in nature; in reason; in religion. In nature,* the earth when it rejoiceth, as in the summer time then it is covered with corn, but when it hath too forlorn, & sorrowful a countenance, as in the winter time, then it is fruitless, and barren. The water when it is quiet, and calm, bringeth in all manner of merchandise, but when the sea storms, and roars too much, then the very ships do howl and cry. The air looking clearly, and cheerfully refresheth all things, but weeping too much, that is, raining too much, as in Noah's flood, it drowns the whole world.[3]

G. I. Pigman marked a cultural shift from an intolerance of grief at the death of loved ones and advice against its indulgence in the slightest degree, to the acceptance of this passion in moderation, over the sixteenth and seventeenth centuries.[4] However, even in this more grief-tolerant period, grief is linked with madness via the somatic continuum of melancholy, or black bile, so that in early modern discourse it is always in danger of overwhelming both body and reason. As we will see, whether the melancholic state is considered to be primarily physical and dispositional, or whether physical disease is thought to be brought about by emotional perturbation, it is assumed that when it comes to sorrow, there is a reasoning self that should endeavour to prevent grief from becoming immoderate and which is always in danger of being obliterated by melancholy.

Nevertheless, Cressida's immoderate weeping is fine, full and perfect: to her, it tastes just as it should. Of course she is, notoriously, soon to be unfaithful to Troilus, so that it may occur here, to audience members or readers who know her story, that she will be well able to 'moderate' both her love and grief before very long. But her insistence here on a perfect reflection of love and grief, of cause and effect, of grief as taste, does not seem to me to contain an ironic reference to her future conduct, or if it does, as Linda Charnes might suspect after her study of Cressida's *Notorious Identity*,[5] the irony is dramatic and may be understood by the audience at the same time as they witness an in-the-moment utterance of perfect sincerity from Cressida. The use of the taste metaphor here rather suggests that grief over loss is somehow a pain to be enjoyed – and in this chapter I am going to argue that the early modern theatre depends on depictions of extremes of grief and sorrow for the production of theatrical pleasure, despite a number of characters recommending moderation and timeliness in the expression of grief and condemning its supposed excesses, just as a sermon might. Grief that is fine, full and perfect in the theatre can be excitingly immoderate.

In the plays examined here, moral and political tensions arise in moments where excesses of grief and sorrow subvert or obstruct cultural norms, power structures and dramatic plot. In this chapter, I argue that grief and sorrow have a potentially interrogatory, even subversive politics,[6] which, in the theatre, can be explored, staged, produced in excess of what is legitimated, valued or permitted by society and culture more generally. In what follows, I suggest ways in which the theatre both reinforces and pushes at these limits, as it deals in the limitless need to produce audience pleasure. I consider the *Henry VI* plays and *Richard III* in terms of the valuations of personal grief and political grievance they contain, and *Hamlet* in terms of the ways in which the personal and the political are conflated and complicated in connection with grief.

I acknowledge that an audience watching a production of one of these plays today may feel little of the subversive power of grief, given the different ways in which that emotion is valorized in modern Western society. A theatre-goer in the English-speaking world today is a great deal less likely than an early modern one to attend a sermon that exhorts him or her to emotional moderation in mourning, the Sunday after seeing a play that seems to depend for its success on the passionate expression of grief. Here, I am going to explore two examples of how current concerns around emotional expression might be mapped on to the political dramaturgy of the passions in early modern drama – and thus open up a politics of the emotions to a modern audience. The examples are of recent British productions, produced by the two largest publicly funded theatre companies in the UK, the RSC and the National Theatre: one of *Richard III* and one of *Hamlet*.[7] Each of these modern dress productions stages grief as a disruptive political force: disruptive because, as Cressida suggests, it both seems impossible to moderate – it is in excess of the controlling agency of reason – and because there are characters in plays who seem determined to indulge it, no matter how culturally and politically expedient it might be for them to stop their sobbing.[8] The narratives of both *Richard III* and *Hamlet* are structured around personal grief in political culture; they dramatize the politics and the policing of emotion. This makes them particularly good plays for commenting on later historical moments where politics takes an active interest in how we feel. I emphasize that this is different from saying that grief is somehow the same for all time and that a particularly powerful dramatization of it is therefore 'universal'. I would rather suggest that *Richard III* and *Hamlet* have structures which generate emotions in tension with their political contexts and may thus be made to reflect upon the politics of emotion in the audience's historical moment. Although attitudes to how much grief and sorrow it is considered proper, or legitimate, or healthy to express in public or private have clearly changed since the turn of the sixteenth century, these plays invite current audiences to consider the ways in which their own cultures and societies ask them to express and display, or control and repress, grief and sorrow.

## GRIEF AND GRIEVANCE

It is difficult to ascertain how long might have been considered too long to mourn in early modern England, at least as evidenced in drama. In aristocratic society, as Sarah Tarlow has demonstrated in her study of *Ritual, Belief and the Dead in Early Modern Britain and Ireland*, the proper expression of grief and the timing of mourning lay in moderation, with an 'increasingly sentimental attachment to the dead [growing] stronger and more acceptable over the course of the eighteenth century'.[9] Tarlow gives the example of Frances Stuart who stayed in mourning for fifteen years – from the death of her husband to her own – and writes that while, by the late eighteenth century, this would have been regarded as evidence of laudably romantic sensibility, in the first half of the seventeenth century, the Duchess' mourning 'was regarded as excessive by many of her peers who questioned its authenticity and appropriateness'.[10] Claire Gittings quotes a contemporary of Stuart's remarking that '[His] loss she takes so impatiently and with so much show of passion that many odd and idle tales are daily reported or invented of her'.[11] Over-long or over-passionate mourning was considered irreligious because it represented a railing against God's purpose and a lack of faith in redemption. In a search for accessible popular advice for the bereaved today, it would be unusual, to say the least, to receive a warning that overly passionate displays of grief might be considered insincere by one's peers – mere 'bravery' (5.2.79), as Hamlet describes Laertes' show of mourning for Ophelia. A large number of bereaved families in the UK hold Christian funerals for their loved ones even if the deceased was not a believer, or even if the mourners themselves are not – but a congregation would no doubt be surprised and offended if the celebrant suggested that overly long demonstrations of grief might offend God. A modern audience may therefore be inclined to dismiss as tactless or cruel the admonishments of Claudius and Gertrude in *Hamlet* that Hamlet is mourning for too long, or of the Countess, in *All's Well*, when she suggests that with all her public weeping, Helena might be showing more than she feels. In fact the stock saws of Gertrude and Lafew, that 'all that lives must die' (*Hamlet*, 1.2.72) and that 'excessive grief is an enemy to the living' (*All's Well*, 1.1.55), are commonsensical wisdoms of the period, which anyone may have recognized as healthful advice and proper religious duty 400 years ago. Claudius is all the more wicked for hypocritically giving sober, religious council about a death that he has violently caused but this would not necessarily have undermined his advice about moderation in mourning itself.

Lucinda M. Becker points out in her study of *Death and the Early Modern Englishwoman* that it is important not entirely to conflate the public rituals of mourning with internalized feelings of grief here:

> The Oxford English Dictionary defines 'grief' in this period as mental pain, distress or suffering; its association with loss by death has strengthened only in more recent times. [...] Grief can [...] be seen as a private affliction, not necessarily expressed to others, whilst mourning is an externalized activity that reflects grief and loss.[12]

But when the Countess suggests that Helena may be thought 'rather to affect a sorrow rather than to have it' (*All's Well*, 1.1.51–2) if she continues to weep so copiously in public, she demonstrates the close early modern relationship between feelings of sorrow and loss and their public display in mourning. Some modern editors point out that 'affect' here does not yet necessarily have the connotation of affectation, so that Helena is not suspected of 'hypocritically pretending a grief that she has never felt...but that she will be suspected of making an outward show of grief in excess of that which she now (after a lapse of time) feels'. (See p. 127)[13] However, she instantly replies in her own self-defence, in words which suggest that she feels a pejorative connotation of 'affect' here: 'I do affect a sorrow indeed, but I have it too' (1.1.53).[14] Hamlet finds himself in a similar position when asked why his grief for his father 'seems so particular' (1.2.75) when he knows full well that 'all that lives must die' (72). Helena insists that her outward expression of grief accurately reflects 'that within' (*Hamlet* 1.2.85); Hamlet suggests that 'that within' is beyond expression. Gertrude is not asking Hamlet to cast off only his 'nighted colour' (1.6.68) – his mourning dress – but to cease, 'with veiled lids' to 'seek for [his] noble father in the dust' (70–71). She is essentially telling him not only to take off the trappings and suits of official mourning but to stop looking – and thus being – so sad, as what this look of sadness suggests is that he could reverse and contradict the natural way of things and find his father down in the direction of his downcast eyes. For Claudius and Gertrude, feeling and display, grief and mourning are to all purposes as one, whereas Hamlet denies that his outward expressions of sorrow – be they sartorial (his inky cloak, 77) or somatic (his sighs of sorrow and his tears, 79, 80) – necessarily reflect what he feels at all. Hamlet's claim to have 'that within which passes show' (85) has been regarded as paradigmatic of a proto-modern psychological interiority.[15] The rest of the play, however, is concerned, as we will see, with the expression of grief, in its multiplicity of senses, and melancholy, with all its yet more complex early modern nuances, and how these emerge in the social world as outward show and political action. Hamlet begins the play by asserting that he feels more than he could ever express but struggles throughout it with the fact that his grief only produces meaning when it is externalized: interpreted or expressed.

In addition to Becker's warning about historical definitions of grief here, it is worth pointing to a historical sense closer to our 'grievance'. The OED offers as its first definition of grief

'Hardship, suffering; a kind or cause of these' but gives this sense a date of 1722. Its second definition, first cited in 1584, is as 'Hurt, harm, mischief inflicted or suffered; molestation, trouble, offence'. Third, from 1573, comes 'feeling of offense; displeasure, anger'. Shakespeare's use of the word suggests that he certainly associates grief with sorrow in loss; indeed, it is used by Shakespeare in hendiadys with the words sorrow and woe.[16] The tearful Henry VI of the trilogy, of whom more later, uses it alongside woe and in association with tears for loss, and the word grief is certainly associated with mourning among the mourning women of *Richard III*. Richard, in *3 Henry VI*, who, in claiming that hot fury at his father's killing has dried up all his tears, suggests that weeping would be the conventional reaction to grief at such a loss. The sense of grief as offence or grievance still echoes in Shakespeare's early plays, however. Somerset surely speaks more in anger than in sorrow when he speaks thus of Humphrey of Gloucester, whom he later conspires to murder:

> Cousin of Buckingham, though Humphrey's pride
> And greatness of his place be grief to us,
> Yet let us watch the haughty Cardinal:
> His insolence is more intolerable
> Than all the princes in the land beside:
>
> (*2 Henry VI* 1.1.170–4)

The noun in the plural, even more, suggests wrongs or offences to be avenged rather than sorrows at loss. The Archbishop of York in *2 Henry IV* conflates the term 'griefs' with 'offences' and complains that

> When we are wrong'd, and would unfold our griefs,
> We are denied access unto his [the King's] person,
> Even by those men that most have done us wrong.
>
> (4.1.77–9)

Indeed, Hamlet deliberately reads the plural noun as referring to political grievance when he replies to Rosencrantz' query about his 'cause of distemper':

ROSENCRANTZ

Good my lord, what is your cause of distemper? you do surely bar the door upon your own liberty if you deny your griefs to your friend.

HAMLET

Sir, I lack advancement.

(3.2.339–42)

For the rest of the play, the word is used solely in association with bereavement. But this double or shifting sense of grief as offence, and grief as sorrow at loss, is significant in a consideration of the religious obligation to moderate grief in the early modern period: to show too much grief upon the death of a loved one might suggest that one has a grievance – and given that only God can take away life, immoderate grief might indicate that one's grief/grievance is against Him. Although grief, woe, sorrow and tears are often used in association or even indeterminably in Shakespeare, the fact that grief can also connote distress at an offence makes it a more appropriate term for Cressida to use than sorrow at her imminent loss of Troilus in our quotation above. She is both intensely unhappy at the parting and furious at its injustice. Its connotation of political grievance is also partially what gives grief its dangerous political edge, as we will see.

## SOMETIMES 'TIS GOOD TO BE MISERABLE IN MISERY: GRIEF IN THE THEATRE

In the anonymous elegy on the death of Richard Burbage (perhaps better known in Collier's fraudulent version of it, complete with citings of the tragic actor's Shakespearean roles),[17] the anonymous author's opening conceit is to ask for someone to help him to 'limn and act' his grief over the death of the great actor; he then declares that the only man to 'express' such a grief is the dead actor himself. The poet calls for help from an artist who can express woe visually or vocally – the limner (a copyist painter), or an actor like Burbage himself. Grief here needs depicting in ways that are beyond the power of this elegist's written word or, it is perhaps suggested, any of the mourner's powers of expression. No one but Burbage could 'draw/ So truly to the life this map of woe': the elegist's woe as expressed in his poem is a two-dimensional map which Burbage himself could turn into a more lifelike depiction. If we are to ask, then, the purpose and value of grief as it is depicted on-stage, this elegist might answer that a great actor can help us memorialize our greatest griefs and woes. He limns, or paints them by acting them – and without his acting, we are left with the elegist's flat map – not nearly as satisfactorily close to what we might want to express if we could. Grief becomes fuller, finer, more perfect when heightened and aestheticized by the actor.

Burbage, then, expressed grief in such a way as to suggest to his audiences that their own griefs were being expressed – but not merely in the purgative sense of the word 'express'. Like the moderate grief that Cressida scorns, the elegist's expression of his very own grief will never be as properly powerful as the version of it he imagines an actor producing. The catharsis-as-purgation model of the theatrical expression of emotion makes acting the political safety valve of the theatre: it permits empathetic – perhaps kinesthetic – feeling on the part of the audience in relation to actor and action – and thus *expresses* emotion in the material sense, and disperses it for the better safety and governance of society. Wherever one stands on the long historical-critical debate on what Aristotle meant by Catharsis in the Poetics,[18] this was certainly a meaning current in early modern England.[19] Leon Golden usefully cites Milton's preface to *Sampson Agonistes*, demonstrating that as late as 1671, the purgation theory of catharsis is closely linked to somatic notions of the same:

> Tragedy is ... said by Aristotle to be of power, by raising pity and fear, or terror, to purge the mind of those and such-like passions.... Nor is Nature wanting in her own effects to make good his assertion; for so in physic things of melan-cholic hue and quality are used

> against melan-choly, sour against sour, salt to remove salt humours.[20]

Theatrical expression of emotion, however, in the model I develop here, remains excessive rather than purgative, in that in its outward show of inner movement or turmoil, it releases the passions from the boundaries of the body, or the flat map of the elegist, and into the world, to be caught, enjoyed, continued rather than purged, by others. This may seem contrary to the advice to the players given by Hamlet; Tobias Doring suggests that in describing the stage as a mirror, which offers '"virtue her own feature" or "scorn her own image" [Hamlet] does not encourage the contagious effects of real passion'.[21] Even for Doring, though, 'these aesthetic principles do not remain unquestioned' and he goes on to remind us that though Hamlet scorns the contagious laughter of clowns in the advice to the players, he mourns the loss of one of them as he hold Yorick's skull.[22] Later in this chapter I will turn again to *Hamlet*, to suggest that it contains a political dramaturgy of grief that sits in tension with common Christian and Classical saws about grief's moderation.[23]

Just as contemporary defences of the early modern theatre suggested that one might learn from the instances of folly or disaster viewed on-stage, as Stephen Pender's important article 'Rhetoric, Grief and the Imagination in Early Modern England' suggests, instances and examples of disasters and bereavements are suggested as a cure for grief in the classical writings translated into English by and during this period.[24] There are scores of these to be found in Burton's *Anatomy of Melancholy*, for example, all supposedly there to help the reader find moderation in grief:

> 'twas Germanicus' advice of old, that we should not dwell too long upon our passions, to be desperately sad, immoderate grievers, to let them tyrannise, there's *indolentiæ, ars*, a medium to be kept: we do not (saith Austin) forbid men to grieve, but to grieve overmuch.[25]

Burton insists that instances of terrible sorrow helps us to palliate our own – to express it in the purgative sense. Similarly, Cicero's *Five Questions*, translated into English in 1561, advises that examples of past griefs 'not only provides knowledge about humanity but also shows that what others have endured and do endure is endurable'.[26] However, as Pender also suggests, being encouraged to imagine the griefs of others may also exacerbate grief. Burton's extraordinary lists of descriptions of those suffering from melancholy as caused by grief give as many, if not more examples of immoderate grief, as examples of those who have controlled it, or of those who have grieved moderately, from which his readers might take courage. We may read in Burton a fortifying example of Tully (Cicero), who

> was much grieved for his daughter Tulliola's death at first, until such time that he had confirmed his mind with some philosophical precepts, 'then he began to triumph over fortune and grief, and for her reception into heaven to be much more joyed than before he was troubled for her loss.' If a heathen man could so fortify himself from philosophy, what shall a Christian from divinity? Why dost thou so macerate thyself? Tis an inevitable chance, the first statute in Magna Charta, an everlasting Act of Parliament, all must die.[27]

But by the time we have got to this point in *The Anatomy*, we have already been taken through incident upon incident of inconsolable sorrow from classical times and Judaeo-Christian example. These are inevitably more lively, one might say more theatrical, than the worthy examples of self-government which Burton offers – the one above, fascinatingly, finally shored up not only by the invocation of God's law but by medieval legislation. Burton colourfully presents to the reader's imagination the roaring and tearing of hair of the woman mad with grief, the black cloud that descended upon Achilles after the death of Patroclus, the running on swords' points and jumping into graves that are the manifestations of immoderate grief.[28] These descriptions involve physical action and lively metaphor, where their admirable moderate counterparts can, for the most part, only be denoted in terms, as with Cicero above, of what the grief-stricken have stopped doing. If the reader enjoys Burton for the stories, he engages imagination, opinion, judgement, and, as Justius Lipsius suggests, 'opinion', or false judgement, amplifies affections 'and lifteth them up as it were upon a stage to be seen'. 'The stage' here, Pinder continues,

> is the imagination. The 'wonderful effects and power' of the imagination, Robert Burton confirms, consist in 'keeping the species of objects so long, mistaking, amplifying the by continual & strong meditation, until it at length it produceth in some parties real effects, causeth this [melancholy] and many other maladies.'[29]

In Lipsius it is assumed that the reader will instantly understand how problematic the imagination, with is opinions and false judgements, is, if it is compared to the stage with its infectious heightening of 'affections'.

I have listed the particular incidents above from Burton's many, because they are incidents and characters that also appear in the plays of Shakespeare. His work appeals to its audience using the very spectacle of Ophelia entering with her hair down; of Achilles avenging Patroclus; of Brutus and Antony committing suicide on their sword's points; of Hamlet witnessing Laertes attempting to jump into Ophelia's grave, and insisting that his, Hamlet's, grief for her is greater than that of the the dead woman's brother. Such images are of the kind that made the theatre a place of uncontained imagination and griefs dangerously indulged by imitation. In a sense, then, I argue throughout this book that Plato, Polonius and the anti-theatricalists were right: the early modern theatre was a dangerous place of bodied-forth imaginings and imaginary bodies, where audiences might hear and watch actors pretending to feel and thus remember what it was to feel themselves, feel again, feel more. Even in a book such as Burton's one may argue that examples of terrible grief accrue an entertainment value beyond their intended purpose of curative example.

This may not be considered a problem in the theatre today.

While a common perception may be that the British are inclined to express grief in quieter ways than a range of other cultures, the value of emotional expression may be said to be unproblematically high in the twenty-first century. A present-day theatre-goer, even if she is a practising Christian, is unlikely to feel anxiety at the tension between calls to moderation preached to her on Sundays and her interpellation as an impassioned being in the theatre. The cultural and educational value ascribed to Shakespeare today may lead her, rather, to consider the emotions depicted on-stage as valuable because paradigmatically 'human', heightened in such a way as to teach her something about 'the human condition'. While the scare quotes in the last sentence suggest that I am cynical about such a universalist perspective, I do not want to argue that this putative theatre-goer is only imagining a connection between her own griefs and those expressed in an early modern drama. The expression of grief in Western culture is policed in a variety of often contradictory ways, some of which may have been unrecognizable to the early moderns, others of which may have been quite familiar. The notion of emotionally cathartic (in the sense of purgative) grief (what we might casually call 'having a good cry') would not have been foreign to the early moderns. Even the Stoic Seneca admitted that there are traumas and losses to which we cannot help reacting by crying and, as we have seen in the subheading to this section, Burton quotes him thus: 'I know not how (saith Seneca) but sometimes 'tis good to be miserable in misery: & for the most part all grief evacuates itself by tears.'[30]

Conversely, the early modern concept that prolonged, 'immoderate' expression of sadness may lead not to emotional release but may be indicative of mental illness is not entirely strange to us either, though early modern figurations of the the excess of black bile in the body, which both indicates and causes sorrow and which overwhelms the griever, are of course foreign to modern science, as are, for many, the Christian and Classical notions that one is morally responsible for the moderation of one's own grief. The idea that 'overmuch sorrow' (see p. 201) could lead to – or actually is – mental illness resonates across the seventeenth century, and is echoed by Freud in the opening to his much-cited essay 'Mourning and Melancholia'; the essay explores what Freud considers to be the complex psychological differences between circumstantial grief and mental illness, and he does so first in temporal terms, recalling the instances I cite here of early modern people and dramatic characters being warned against mourning for too long:

> it never occurs to us to consider mourning as a pathological condition and present it to the doctor for treatment, despite the fact it produces severe deviations from normal behaviour. We rely on it being overcome after a certain period of time, and consider interfering with it being pointless, or even damaging.[31]

Ordinary mourning and pathological melancholia may be provoked by the same cause – loss. But the latter simply will not stop. Here, the difference between the cultural valuation of sorrow in the early modern period and the early twentieth century is a matter of timing: during the twentieth and twenty-first centuries, common sense suggests that mourning can – even should – last a very long time without the griever being considered mentally ill or insincere. In 1917, Freud can already assume that everyone understands him when he asserts that we 'consider interfering with [mourning] being pointless, or even damaging' until after 'a certain period of time'. Read any easily accessible advice on coping with loss today and one will be advised that while one's peers may tactlessly expect one to 'get over' the loss of a loved one in a matter of months, this is unrealistic and one should give oneself time to grieve.[32]

Ultimately, however, though one might compare the acceptable time limits placed on grief in both periods of history, the moral, religious and philosophical imperatives to moderate one's grief in cultural life – exhortations not to be passion's slave – that emerge in the sermons and treatises of the early modern period simply do not, I would argue, pressure the contemporary theatre-goer. The rest of this chapter, then, is divided into two different but related kinds of endeavours: the exploration of grief and its value as it emerges differently in the early modern drama; and examples of the ways in which two contemporary productions – one of *Richard III* and one of *Hamlet* – have staged what I will call the political dramaturgy of grief, in ways that are accessible to the theatre-goer today.

## GRIEF AND ACTION: *HENRY VI* AND *RICHARD III*

In Shakespeare's earliest historical dramas, the *Henry VI* plays, weeping is repeatedly figured as an obstruction to action, particularly to revenge. In the second play, Henry VI calls his own tears for his imprisoned uncle Gloucester 'unhelpful', comparing himself to a cow bereft of her slaughtered calf, who

[...] runs lowing up and down,
Looking the way her harmless young one went,
And can do nought but wail her darling's loss;
Even so myself bewails good Gloucester's case
With sad unhelpful tears, and with dimm'd eyes
Look after him, and cannot do him good;
(*2 Henry VI*, 3.1.214–19)

When Suffolk hypocritically laments Humphrey of Gloucester, having conspired to murder him, Queen Margaret makes an ironic statement on the unproductive nature of tears, where she insists that she does not blame Suffolk for crying and suggests she herself would cry if it could do any good; again, the audience will be well aware of the hypocrisy of the speech given Margaret's own collusion in the murder:

QUEEN
Why do you rate my Lord of Suffolk thus?
Although the duke was enemy to him,
Yet he most Christian-like laments his death.
And for myself, foe as he was to me,
Might liquid tears, or heart-offending groans,

> Or blood-consuming sighs recall his life,
> I would be blind with weeping, sick with groans,
> Look pale as primrose with blood-drinking sighs,
> And all to have the noble duke alive.
>
> (3.2.56–64)

In both cases grief disables, rendering the avenging agent a somatic mess of tears, sighs and pallor. If the self is an active agent in the world, grief makes one less oneself – less of an avenger with a purpose, more a mass of unfocused, reactive affect. The griever in Henry's speech is figured as a cow. The grieving body in Margaret's speech is consumed and made drunk by grief, and her assertion that she would let this happen would it save 'the noble duke' only serves to emphasize the fact that crying won't save anyone. Grief is anathema to the kind of action that redeems oneself from the self-obliteration of slight.

Later in the play, after the assassination of Suffolk, Margaret admits, as Macduff does when he hears of his wife and children's slaughter, that the loss of a loved one by violent means makes it impossible to avoid tears:

> QUEEN
> Oft have I heard that grief softens the mind
> And makes it fearful and degenerate;
> Think therefore on revenge and cease to weep.
> But who can cease to weep and look on this?
> Here may his head lie on my throbbing breast;
> But where's the body that I should embrace?
>
> (4.4.1–6)

She cradles Suffolk's head, and it is her throbbing breast, rather than the mind that might reason out a revenge, which controls her actions. Margaret's rhetorical question addressed to the audience produces a moment that in common parlance today might be called more 'human' than Margaret's other comments on crying and one cannot but imagine that her early audiences, too, would have responded 'who indeed?' and felt, like Macduff, that Margaret must also 'feel it as a [hu]man' (*Macbeth* 4.3.221). As we have seen, a complete lack of grief in the face of terrible troubles is a sign of an inhuman and un-Christian hardness for the early moderns. For Patricia Phillippy in *Women, Death and Literature in Post-Reformation England,* Shakespeare's Richard III, with his Machiavellian performances of mourning, and his declaration that his 'manly eyes did scorn a humble tear' at the deaths of young Rutland and his own father (*Richard III*, 1.2.168), demonstrates that a failure to mourn properly is as culturally problematic as excessive mourning. As we have seen, the ideal mean for grief is summed up in Phillippy's citation of Robert Southwell, who declares that to feel nothing at 'sorrowful chances' demonstrates a brutish lack of human understanding, whereas to fail to bear them with moderation is 'effeminate' (see p. 169). To mourn too little is to place oneself outside of the bounds of what it is to be human; to mourn too much is to place oneself outside of masculine subjectivity and an active agency in the world.

By the end of the third part of *Henry VI*, Margaret has hardened the mind that Suffolk's death had softened with grief and returns to the stock assertion that weeping simply delays revenge:

> QUEEN
> Great lords, wise men ne'er sit and wail their loss,
> But cheerly seek how to redress their harms.
> [. . .]
> We will not from the helm to sit and weep,
> But keep our course, though the rough wind say no,
> From shelves and rocks that threaten us with wrack.
> [. . .]
> Why, courage then! what cannot be avoided
> 'Twere childish weakness to lament or fear.
> (5.4.1–2, 21–3, 38–9)

The sailing metaphor is particularly significant here in contrast to Henry's cow image: the grieving cow runs, directionless, up and down with dimm'd eyes; the unweeping sailors keep a straight course through shelves and rocks. By this point in the *Henry VI* narrative, Margaret has become a 'woman of stone' to borrow from Lear's accusation in the face of what he sees as insufficient howling for Cordelia's death (*King Lear*, 5.3.255). In positing grief against action, these are plays that hold in tension two versions of what it is to be human that emerge again in *Hamlet*.

Richard of Gloucester, when his father the Duke of York is killed, demonstrates precisely the opposite somatic workings to the griever drowned in tears: he claims his body is too hot with avenging fury, either to weep or to speak:

RICHARD
I cannot weep, for all my body's moisture
Scarce serves to quench my furnace-burning heart;
Nor can my tongue unload my heart's great burden;
For self-same wind that I should speak withal
Is kindling coals that fires all my breast,
And burns me up with flames that tears would quench.
To weep is to make less the depth of grief:
Tears then for babes; blows and revenge for me.
Richard, I bear thy name; I'll venge thy death,
Or die renowned by attempting it.
(2.1.79–88)

The declaration that 'to weep is to make less the depth of grief' posits Richard's subjectivity in his name, inherited from his father: his heroic, aristocratic, adult male selfhood lies in family honour and reputation. Tears are for babies; to be fully mature is to revenge gross slights. His suggestion that to speak any more than he does of his heart's great burden would be similarly degrading to this sense of hot, male selfhood.

It is notable that the figures in the early history plays who favour vengeance over weeping are the most violent and villainous, fury-like in their vengeance (Margaret) or devil-like in their murderous plotting (Richard). Henry's cow-like grief, on the other hand, may be sympathetic but it figures him as a weak-minded and ineffectual monarch. Relentlessly directional pursuit of vengeance is hardly being held up as an ideal in these plays. But grief is most certainly unproductive. The tension is staged from the very first scene of *1 Henry VI*, in which Exeter demands to know why everyone is wearing the black of mourning for Henry V, when they should be 'mourn[ing] in blood' (1.1.17) and recovering his lands in France. At his funeral, Henry V is figured as an impossible, mythological figure of perfect manhood, both virtuous and wrathful (1.1.8–16) but 'Too famous to live long' (1.1.6). The living characters in the play are either virtuous or wrathful, grieving or acting.

Gender underpins the binaries of active revenge and inactive grief, where women are socially barred from violent action (Margaret and Joan La Pucelle are figured as both monstrous and sexually excessive in their violent, active womanhood). Beatrice in *Much Ado About Nothing* makes explicit the socially constructed expectation that women grieve while men get angry, when she is seen weeping for her cousin Hero, wrongly disgraced for unchastity at her wedding. Beatrice asks that Benedick avenge the young woman's wronged reputation as it is a 'man's office' (4.1.265), bursts into prolonged and furious invective at the effeminate court 'princes and counties' (313) whose manhood is 'only turned into tongue' (318) when he refuses, and rants that, were she a man, she would 'eat [Claudio's] heart in the market place' (304–5). The violence and the rhythm of her language recalls Laertes' cry that to revenge himself upon his father's killer he would 'cut his throat i'th'church' (4.7.126). But Beatrice is not a man, and her fury subsides in the declaration that if she cannot 'be a man with wishing, [she] will die a woman with grieving' (4.1.420–1). The Duchess of Gloucester in *Richard II*, too, angrily and actively demands that a man – this time her brother-in-law – avenge the death of a loved one, her husband. When he will not act for her, she declares that she is going home to die of grief (1.2.65–74). Again, grief echoes with grievance, a grievance a woman is not permitted to address. In *Richard III*, however, wherein it may seem to the modern actress that all the women in the play get to do is mourn, mourning becomes action. I am referring here not, of course, to the first instance of mourning in the play, that of Anne, who appears to be entirely acted upon by Richard: she begins 1.3 by following the corpse of her father-in-law who Richard killed and ends the scene engaged to be married to him. I refer rather to the turning point in Richard's fortunes, when he is met by the Senecan trio of mourning women in 4.4,[33] who intercept him, as he puts it, in his 'expedition' against his mustering enemies (4.4.136). Grief here turns not to impotent tears but to the linguistically performative as the women shift from the helpless language of mourning, which turns the women against one another in what amounts to a mourning competition, to the language of the curse, which Elizabeth explicitly asks Margaret to teach her (116–17). Whereas Gaunt's exhortation to the Duchess of Gloucester to ask God for vengeance where she cannot take it herself leads to her declaration that she will die of grief, Margaret in *Richard III* now speaks of woe as performative:

ELIZABETH
My words are dull: O quicken them with thine.

MARGARET
Thy woes will make them sharp and pierce like mine.
(124–5)

If Elizabeth mourns in excess of her causes of grief, deliberately imagining that her 'babes were sweeter than they were,/And he that slew them fouler than he is' (120–1), Margaret advises that her 'woes' will become effectual, piercing (125). Elizabeth suggests that even if this cannot be the case, they will at least be therapeutic: 'Let them have scope: though what they do impart/ Help not all, yet do they ease the heart' (130–1). But the Duchess of York, Richard's mother, is more of Margaret's optimism as to the effectivity of the linguistic expression of grief, replying,

If so, then be not tongue-tied; go with me
And in the breath of bitter words let's smother
My damned son, that thy two sweet sons smother'd.
(132–3)

Words of grief turn bitter; women's metaphors for words turn from those of wind and air (126–30) to a breath which smothers: words are figured as literally taking revenge. And sure enough, as many of Richard's audiences across history will know when they hear the Duchess's 'most grievous curse' (188) on Richard, it works. Bloody Richard is, as the Duchess curses, and bloody is his end (195); the ghosts he has created do indeed haunt him and 'whisper the spirit of [his] enemies' (193).

The sequence that follows this one, in which Richard persuades the mourning Elizabeth to permit his marriage to her daughter, looks set to prove the mirror sequence to his wooing of Anne. In their Senecan group of female mourners the women block Richard's path and almost silence him; once Elizabeth is left alone, however, she falls prey, as Anne does, to his Machiavellian machinations in a more theatrical realist vein. But rather than next taking the stage alone to crow at his success, as he does in 1.3, Richard begins what might be a similar speech – 'Relenting fool, and shallow, changing woman!' (431) – to be interrupted by messenger after messenger announcing the armies mustering against him. This is the turning point in Richard's fortunes, whereat his hot, tearless realism gives way to the metaphysics of the grief he has caused. Having been blocked in his determined journey to a firmer power base by the mourning women, having failed to block the sounds of their mourning with the sounds of war, Richard's tragedy begins its downward trajectory as the women's curses, Senecan tragic inevitability and Christian providence in the holy Richmond unite to defeat Richard.

A number of scholars have plausibly argued that the cultural losses and anxieties inscribed in the staging/writing of this scene's mourning, cursing women render them repeatedly in excess of religious and political hegemony. Their grief is subversive, both within the play and within the Protestant culture of late seventeenth-century England. I have found arguments about the memorialization of purgatory in this play convincing.[34] But the staging of residual Catholic practice is only part of a wider sense in which grief subverts by leaking back into political life in *Richard III*. Grief stops action in the *Henry VI* plays; here it stops Richard in his progression to power, and the play's mourning women can work through production to demonstrate the dramaturgy of grief and political power, even where audiences have no knowledge of the residual systems of mourning for the dead that may be being grieved for in the early modern period.

## 'WHO INTERCEPTS ME IN MY EXPEDITION?': *RICHARD III* (SWAN THEATRE 2012)

Roxana Silbert's *Richard III* at the Swan in 2012[35] was played by Jonjo O'Neill. This actor had previously played the Machiavellian Edmund in Rupert Goold's *King Lear* (Liverpool Everyman and Young Vic),[36] with horribly good-humoured direct address to what seemed like a delighted audience, and opposite a hopelessly innocent Gloucester and Edgar. There is no such contrast of foolish goodness and clever evil in *Richard III*, as it is peopled almost entirely by power-mongering members of the play's two

Figure 7: Richard III (Jonjo O'Neill) in *Richard III* dir. Roxana Silbert, Royal Shakespeare Company, 2012 (© Geraint Lewis)

central royal factions, many of whom appear entirely aware of Richard's machinations but do nothing about them, out of fear, or hope of self-advancement, or both.[37] The most ludicrous example of this is in 3.4, the scene in which Richard suddenly declares that Hastings must be executed because he has conspired with Mistress Shaw to wither Richard's arm, which the court must all surely know has been thus deformed since his birth (3.4.59–79).[38] The power of this play for audience members today, who are not necessarily particularly invested in the politics of a fifteenth-century civil war and its implications for a sixteenth-century monarchy, lies in the relationship between Richard and his audience: however much one might disapprove of the political murder of spouses and relatives, a Richard with deft comic timing, confiding to the auditorium what he is doing in the face of so little resistance from the other characters on-stage, can prove irresistibly funny, and give Richmond an uphill struggle in convincing us not to be somewhat disappointed when right triumphs and the new king removes Richard from the action.

This may be a transhistorical effect of the dramaturgy of this play, especially given the theatre history of the entertaining 'Vice' figure, whose lineage Richard acknowledges (3.1.82–3). What the play presumably relied upon in its first productions was the audience's ready-made bias for Richmond as founder of their own Queen's dynasty; like the Vice, Richard must have been able to seduce the audience into his grim comedy without any real danger of changing the average late Tudor theatre-goer's allegiance to Richmond's offspring.[39] As Silbert and her company found, though, Richard's blatant stage-management of power also offers a challenge to the play's women, whose formally structured speeches of mourning may seem both lengthy and excluding in comparison to Richard's swift wit and direct address. One element of this play – Richard, with his inheritance from the vice and the stage Machiavel – translates easily into comic traditions with which modern audiences are still familiar, while the formalities of Senecan tragedy from whence Shakespeare developed the carefully structured speeches of the mourning women are now perhaps less accessible and their proportional length in the drama[40] may seem excessive. It would have been easy, remarked Silbert when cutting the play for production, to have lost huge swathes of the women's speeches without losing any of the bare bones of the plot. She was keen not to do this, however, and to give the women the proportional presence they have in an uncut text.

Silbert's production is particularly pertinent for an examination of early modern theatrical grief in current production, given her ease with permitting modern actorly interest in character psychology and back-story into the rehearsal room, alongside a commitment to the staging of action over feeling (it is not, Silbert insists, how a character feels, and how that might be expressed through the language of the play, that is staged in an early modern drama but what a character does with the language, and to whom: language in Silbert's rehearsal room is usually performative, though she also acknowledges the limits of the Stanislavskian method of 'actioning').[41] Alongside an essentially performative analysis of the text and an openness to psychological discussion, Silbert has embraced the notion of a direct relationship between performer and audience, particularly for her productions in the intimacy of the RSC's Swan Theatre, and has an interest in the dramaturgical histories encoded in a play of this period. As a visitor to rehearsal, offering background material to the production in the last of these areas, it seemed strangely contradictory that I should speak to the actors about, say, the theatricality of Vice figure and Richard's consciousness (impossible in the realist theatre) that he is (pre-)determined to be a villain (1.1.30), and then that such a talk should be followed up by a psychologist's visit to rehearsals, in which the emotional damage done to a child rejected by its mother was discussed. But these different forms of knowledge were all ways into the play for this company and generated a range of theatrical effects which, far from ironing out its dramaturgy of sharp contrasts, reconfigured the politics of the women's grief in ways that potentially accessed that grief's subversiveness for an audience unaware of its original religious and political meanings.

While the mourning, cursing women of 4.4 in no way sobbed their way through their lines in this production, their physical actions were juxtaposed with the formal poetry of the speeches and the additional formality of the accoutrements of modern mourning – formal dress and wreathes put up against the walls of the 'tower' in mourning for the princes – to produce an effect of emotional reality that in turn foregrounded Richard's easy, natural way with the audience as theatrical convention. When Siobhan Redmond as Elizabeth lay on the floor of the Swan's thrust stage, catatonic with grief, she looked awkwardly *un*theatrical, her body refusing the angry grace of the lines she spoke. The Duchess of York and Margaret 'rest' on the ground in the scene as it is written (4.4.29, 34 – it is modern editors who interpret these internal stage directions as [*sitting*]), and as there is nothing for them to rest on but 'England's lawful earth' (4.4.29), this effect of awkwardness, one might argue, is already partially encoded in the play. But Silbert's eclectic rehearsal process, metatheatrical in ways appropriate to the play's history for some scenes, as we will see, but typically post-Stanislavskian in its initial table work and its permission for actors to find character journeys through the play, permitted theatrical styles and staging conventions to inhabit the play simultaneously and in contrast, in such as way as to reopen emotional expression as a site of political contest.

O'Neill's performance as Richard was of a witty playground bully who it is difficult not to find hilarious despite the all too evident effect his cruelty has on others – particularly when the others are not particularly likeable themselves. He recalled a previous Richard, Paul Hunter's, in an English Shakespeare Company production of 1998,[42] in which the whole cast were dressed as children; after his ascent to the throne and the interval, Richard was revealed from within the folds of a bouncy castle as it inflated before the audience. Both productions emphasized the amorally playful relationship between Richard and an audience for whom he evidently cared no more than for the characters he was plotting to kill. Hence his seductiveness: the audience, it is implied, should count themselves favoured to be in on the plot and lucky to be outside of it. Richard's rise to power was played by O'Neill with all the impermeable high theatrical status bestowed upon him by the humour of direct address to the audience; he shared with the auditorium his contempt for those who know he is a murdering con-man but who will not step out of line to stop him. It was one of the most consciously theatrical *Richard III*s I have seen, playing very fully on Richard's metatheatrical awareness of his theatre-history status as vice and stage Machiavel, particularly in his orchestration of the noise and bluster for the benefit of the Lord Mayor in 3.5 (which of course comes directly after Buckingham's assurances that he will be well able to 'counterfeit the deep tragedian' with Richard (3.5.5.)), and 3.7, in which he poses as reluctant king between two churchmen. As the farce of 3.5 commenced, Richard shouted 'action', and the lighting state changed to a firey red. The scene then featured a comical feigned battle, in which Ratcliffe's arm emerged from an opening upstage centre in the plain *frons*, holding three swords for Richard to clash against, as if Ratcliffe had been instructed to enact a whole army. The head of Hastings which is then presented to the Lord Mayor was not a stock theatrical head in a bag but an impressive likeness of the actor playing him (John Stahl). The realistic prop made for a ghastly theatre of comic cruelty but barely gave Ratcliffe time to prepare for his next role as churchman in 3.7. In this production, Richard has no real monks to accompany his staged praying, and so dresses up two of his men instead.[43] There was much comical running about and getting ready glimpsed through the *frons*, topped by Ratcliffe attempting to enter too soon, being told 'not yet!' and being stuffed back through the window where he and his other player friar were to pose with bible and rosary. Richard, then, constructed his rise to power metatheatrically, in the shared space of actor and audience; he was both visible stage manager and stand-up comedian, a theatrical figure who produces an effect of hyper-reality because he can so clearly occupy the 'real' world of the present as well as that of the fiction.

However, Roxana Silbert also discussed psychological backstory with this company and her staging of Richard's death was redolent of both the villain's personal and mythological past. At the end of the last scene, after a vigorous full-cast sword fight complete with dangerously authentic-looking clanging broad swords, Richmond killed Richard with two strokes of his sword, finishing him off by breaking his neck. The pair wrestled each other to the ground, until Richmond had Richard lying in his lap, the latter's head in an arm lock. It took some time for Richard to die there. He opened his mouth in a strangled choke, goggle-eyed, appearing like the baby his mother wishes she had strangled in the womb (4.4.137–8), choked to death with an umbilical chord. To work back from Richard's demise to that turning point of his fortunes, the 4.4 confrontation with the mourning women, their mourning turns him from a metatheatrical orchestrator of power and audience engagement into a vulnerable psychological being who is unsure about whether he can love himself, because, it has been openly declared, he was hated from the moment of his birth.[44]

As I have said, Silbert's actresses made no attempt to emote their way through the lines of 4.4. Elizabeth describes words as 'Windy attorneys to their clients' woes,/Airy succeeders of intestate joys,/Poor breathing orators of miseries' (4.4.127–9) but there is none of the excess of gasp and breath that one might usually associate with the performance of sorrow. The women rather played a physical excess of sorrow – lying on the floor to mourn at the beginning of 4.4 – while vocally underplaying the lines that speak of extreme grief: 'O who has any cause to mourn but we?' (34). As they bar Richard's way in this scene, the women's competitive grieving and talk of the performative power of excessive grief gives way to Richard's mother's description of his birth; she promises to be 'mind and gentle in [her] words' (161) and Sandra Duncan's tone was, when compared to the content of her speech. What this performance permitted was a certain alienation from the women's grief and the possibility for the audience to watch its effects rather than empathize kinesthetically with the breath and tears grief might usually be expected to produce. Grief became productive, finally, of Richard's downfall, rather than of winds, sighs and tears that prevent action in the

Henriad. When Richard calls for the sounds of war to blot out the sounds of grieving – more stage-management of plot and power – he suddenly seems ludicrous in his theatricality, while the women's grief reads as fine, full, perfect – in excess of Richard's politics, rather than excessively performed.

## *HAMLET*

In the Henriad, grief is excessive in that it prohibits action: it is impossible to channel it into action unless it changes in its physical nature and becomes anger. In *Richard III*, the excess of the women's grief becomes active. What happens to grief in *Hamlet*, the play so famously marked by inaction? It is not that Hamlet's grief simply prohibits action. A range of much-explored intellectual and religious questions play a part in Hamlet's delay in avenging his father, but it is certainly a play about arrested agency and one replete with questions about grief and action. I am going to argue that it is grief, and a particularly contradictory, continually contested form of the early modern state of melancholy in this play,[45] that both arrest Hamlet's action and are the instigators of a dangerous, intellectual agency. Hamlet's is a subversive, insightful grief – subversive first in the simple sense that Hamlet's continued state of mourning visually subverts his uncle's celebration of the marriage to Gertrude, and at a time when the state is at war and needs to present an illusion of unity. Hamlet begins the play in a state of mourning. Then the Ghost demands that Hamlet remember him as Exeter exhorts his fellow Lancastrians to remember Henry V: not through mourning but through vengeance, not through tears but through action, not through melancholy ('mourn[ing] in black') but through sanguinity ('mourn[ing] [...] in blood', *1 Henry VI*, 1.1.17). But his father's demand precipitates Hamlet not into the anger-against-slight that is the sense of grievance which leads to revenge. Instead he may be read as remaining in a state of melancholy which involves over-thinking, meditation upon the pointlessness of existence and suicide, and self-denigration. How may the stasis of melancholy be said to subvert Claudius' state? On one level it cannot, as of course it may be said to stop Hamlet killing Claudius until the very end of the play. But Hamlet's state of insightful grief posits him continually against a political state that is 'moving on', from marriage to marriage, and over little patches of conquerable land. Anger, as we have seen, produces motion; love, too, the concupiscable passion, produces a movement towards the lover – and a movement across nations for Helena and Cleopatra. Grief produces a subversive stasis.

Insightful grief cannot be equated precisely with melancholy, the early modern psychosomatic state that has given rise to much productive speculation about this play. That scholars differ so radically in their reading of Hamlet's melancholy suggests that melancholy itself is at a semantic and cultural turning point in *Hamlet*. In *The Poetics of Melancholy in Early Modern England*,[46] Douglas Trevor reads Hamlet as a humoral materialist, who makes reference to his own melancholic complexion, his melancholic disposition, his diseased wit. For Trevor, humoral melancholy is becoming a scholarly fashion as Shakespeare writes *Hamlet*. Mark Breitenberg centres part of his argument about anxious masculinity in early modern drama on the notion that melancholy is the state against which the male gender is defined.[47] David Schalkwyk, on the other hand, suggests that humoral theory is figured as residual and outmoded in Shakespeare's late Elizabethan work.[48] These equally plausible but opposing arguments are unsurprising given that, in fact, Hamlet is figured as tussling with the theories of subjectivity available to an Elizabethan intellectual, and with the contradictions inherent in melancholy at this time – melancholy as a disease and a choice, the passions as excessive material presences in the body over which the reasoning self must try to exert control. It is Descartes who can be credited with the first systematic explanation of mind/body dualism (see p. xxxi), but I am arguing that a kind of dualism is struggling to emerge fifty years beforehand in late Elizabethan and early Jacobean drama, as it interrogates the binaries of reason and passion, responsibility and predestination, psychological agency and somatic helplessness.

These binaries become particularly blurred in *Hamlet* and its staging of melancholy. On the one hand, the passions are always somatic in early modern discourse, so that feelings associated with grief and sorrow – heaviness, emptiness, tearfulness – are caused by the various activities of excessive black bile in the body and, when these feelings have an external cause, such as bereavement, these somatic phenomena are bound to be produced. A man may be of a melancholic disposition, as Hamlet describes himself, and be particularly susceptible to the emotions of sorrow and fear, even when there is no external cause, as Hamlet fears may be the case with the Ghost he has seen (2.2.600–605). For such a man, the dominant humour of his disposition, black bile, is always in danger of becoming excessive and resulting in madness. Another may become overwhelmed by a particular trauma – the death of a dear friend or relative, also Hamlet's case – or may become sick with melancholy by habit, again with danger to his health, as Burton suggests in the *Anatomy*, where he describes 'Passions and Perturbations of the Mind: How they Cause Melancholy':

> *Perturbations often offend the body, and are most frequent causes of melancholy, turning it out of the hinges of his health.* [...] Those which are light, easy, and more seldom, to our thinking, do us little harm, and are therefore contemned of us: yet if they be reiterated, *as the rain* (saith Austin) *doth a stone, so do these perturbations penetrate the mind*: and (as one observes) *produce a habit of melancholy at the last*, which having gotten the mastery in our souls, may well be called diseases.[49]

Burton also asserts that melancholy is a universal human condition, always and inevitably leading to some form of madness, because everyone is prey to the passions that can cause it:

> For indeed who is not a fool, melancholy, mad? [...] who is not brain-sick? Folly, melancholy, madness, are but one disease, *Delirium* is a common name to all. [...]'twas an old Stoical paradox [...] all fools are mad, though some

> madder than others. And who is not a fool, who is free from melancholy? Who is not touched more or less in habit or disposition? [...] for what is sickness, but [...] 'A dissolution or perturbation of the bodily league, which health combines:' and who is not sick, or ill-disposed? in whom doth not passion, anger, envy, discontent, fear and sorrow reign? Who labours not of this disease?[50]

Here, the passions are figured as both universally felt and always in danger of being in excess. Passion is sickness and we are all sick. Again, it is difficult for the modern reader to decide what was considered normative in terms of mental health here: how much grief is 'normal' grief, when does sorrow – one of the primary symptoms and external causes of melancholy for Burton – become habitual and then pathological? How much sorrow is too much? Perhaps it is unhelpful to apply modern scientific notions of the normative or healthy to early modern medical and philosophical discourses of the passions, since to do so is to tend to forget the religious premises on which some of the early modern notions of the passions are founded. As Gail Kern Paster has pointed out in her opening to *Humoring the Body*, for the early modern thinker, the only being ever to have felt any emotion in a way not contaminated with the potential for sickness and degeneration was Christ, whose passions 'were like the shaking of pure Water in a cleane Vessell, which though it be thereby troubled, yet is it not fouled at all', whereas man's passion always 'bringeth up mire and dirt'.[51] The mere human subject is always fighting the excesses of his passions even where Christian thought permits him or her to have them, and the ultimate healthy state, in which the passions may be felt but are always moderated by reason, seems impossible to achieve. Sorrow is no exception here. For Burton it is one of the most obvious causes and symptoms of melancholy – although to call it a cause or a symptom involves the modern scholar in an ultimately futile attempt to separate cause from effect:

> In this catalogue of passions, which so much torment the soul of man, and cause this malady [...] the first

> place in this irascible appetite, may justly be challenged by sorrow. An inseparable companion, 'The mother and daughter of melancholy, her epitome, symptom, and chief cause:' as Hippocrates hath it, they beget one another, and tread in a ring, for sorrow is both cause and symptom of this disease.[52]

Despite the somatic composition of melancholy, Burton's list of remedies 'Against sorrow for Death of Friends or otherwise' are all philosophical and commonsensical rather than medical: to prevent oneself from being overwhelmed with grief at bereavement one needs to remind oneself that one has other friends and pleasures, that it is cruel to desire that someone who died in sickness should return from everlasting life to worldly pain, that death for the righteous is the ultimate peace and, most exhaustively, that there are others who have suffered too, probably worse than you have.[53] The explicit link between sorrow and black bile was being loosened by the late seventeenth century, as Richard Baxter's sermon on 'the best Preservatives against Melancholy and Overmuch Sorrow' indicates:

> Such a black distinct humour called Melancholy which hath of old been accused, is rarely, if ever found in any, unless you will call either blood or excrementitious humours by that name, which are grown black by mortification, for want of motion and spirits.[54]

While an interest in the physical causes and manifestations of sorrow is still clear here, the word *melancholy* is, it seems, beginning to be used, in the title of the sermon, as a word for what we might call an emotion, as separate from 'a black distinct humour'. This is made yet clearer where Baxter differentiates between circumstantial and dispositional melancholy:

> But sometimes persons that are found, are suddenly cast into Melancholy by a fright, or by the death of a friend, or by some great loss or cross, or some sad Tidings, even in an hour; which shews that it cometh not always from

> any humour called Melancholy, or any foregoing Disease at all.[55]

An earlier and better-known (because linked to *Hamlet*) tract on Melancholy, such as Timothy Bright's of 1586,[56] concentrates on melancholy as a humoral imbalance which leads to irrational fears and sorrows. Bright does not dwell upon or exemplify bereavement or loss as a cause of melancholy as Burton does later: Bright's melancholics are primarily so by disposition rather than by circumstance. He is anxious to differentiate between the somatic disease of melancholy and its effects on the one hand and, on the similar effects of sorrow and fear that might overwhelm someone stricken with conscience and fearful of God's anger. For Bright, all who suffer the disease of melancholy do so because of humoral imbalance; external causes are either simply imaginary, or the melancholic's sickness means he reacts to them in irrational and exaggerated ways. The conscience-stricken, on the other hand, feels as he does 'upon cause'; it is quite reasonable that he should suffer because he feels his sinfulness; therefore he cannot be said to be melancholic:

> this [consciousness of sin] is a sorrow and fear upon cause, & that the greatest cause that worketh misery unto man: the other [melancholy] contrarily a mere fancy & hath no ground of true and just object, but is only raised upon disorder of the humour in the fancy.[57]

Bright's explanations of melancholy's causes are far more limited in scope than Burton's (and it is certainly a far shorter work). For Bright, physical disease is the primary cause of negative affect in the end; for Burton, causes range from devils to desire for revenge, from sleep disorders to sorrow, from self-love to too much studying, heredity to habit, bad diet to bereavement.[58] Of course, Burton shares with Bright an early modern sense of mind's inextricable reciprocity with body and both's porous openness to the outside world. But what I am more interested in here is that both share a faith in effortful cure by the inflicted themselves, through reason and imagination. For Burton, melancholy is very much part of the human condition and is often caused by traumatic accidents and poor upbringing; his cures are often meditative and philosophical, the *Anatomy* reading as a kind of group therapy to be shared with all the Classical and Christian exemplars of those who have also suffered. Even Bright, who seems to be more wholly interested in the somatic, recommends alongside physic the contemplation of 'examples of constancy and moderation'.[59]

Douglas Trevor lists many of the references to humoural theory in *Hamlet*, and cites, as his example of Hamlet's use of the term 'complexion', a term used to denote humoral type, the use of the word in the jokey exchange with the pretentious Osric:

HAMLET
But yet methinks it is very sultry and hot for my
complexion.
(5.2.99–100)

But Hamlet uses the word twice elsewhere: once in the conventional humoral sense, in the first part of his remembered Pyrrhus speech, where Pyrrhus is described as blackened with the humoral madness of warlike violence, then smeared with the even more dreadful red of his enemy's blood:

The rugged Pyrrhus, he whose sable arms,
Black as his purpose, did the night resemble
When he lay couched in the ominous horse,
Hath now this dread and black complexion smear'd
With heraldry more dismal.
(2.2.53–7)

Hamlet has also used it in a context that complicates this sense of 'complexion' in the contorted second half of a speech to Horatio, in which Hamlet condemns his uncle's revels. Hamlet explains how Claudius' court's drunken celebrations sully Denmark's reputation, then compares it to a man whose virtues are obliterated in the eyes of others by one fault:

So, oft it chances in particular men
That for some vicious mole of nature in them,
As, in their birth, wherein they are not guilty,
(Since nature cannot choose his origin),
By the o'ergrowth of some complexion,
Oft breaking down the pales and forts of reason,
Or by some habit that too much o'er-leavens
The form of plausive manners – that these men,
Carrying, I say, the stamp of one defect,
Being nature's livery, or fortune's star,
Their virtues else, be they as pure as grace,
As infinite as man may undergo,
Shall in the general censure take corruption
From that particular fault. The dram of evil
Doth all the noble substance often dout
To his own scandal.

(1.4.23–38)

Thus, the single faults so detrimental to the 'noble substance' of these putative men are defects of birth, of which they cannot be said to be guilty, or they are humoral imbalances – 'the o'ergrowth of some complexion' – or they are habitual. They are natural excesses or they are visited upon this man by the fates. The sense of the passage is repeatedly broken by qualifying clauses that give the impression of one attempting to convince himself. What Hamlet seems to be repeating is that something that is not the fault of a man may condemn him in the world's eyes, subject him to 'scandal'. He switches between nature and habit, nature and fate in deciding what might be to blame – but it is not the faulty agent himself. It is an odd choice of extended metaphor given the initial excesses he sets out to criticize. Claudius and his court are celebrating and drinking too much, and it is clear that Hamlet considers this no 'vicious mole of nature' but a conscious choice. Trevor is not quite right to suggest, then, that Hamlet's 'outlook' is essentially materialist,[60] based in humoral theory. Or at least, this is just one outlook Hamlet marshalls against the horrible notion that he may be responsible for his own actions in a time so out of joint.

When Hamlet watches Fortinbras' soldiers march across the stage to conquer a tiny patch of Poland, he witnesses the actions of a man who certainly never sits at the helm and weeps, but keeps his course, as Margaret encourages the 'Great lords' of *3 Henry VI* to do. As we have seen, *Hamlet* is full of people keeping their course after the death of his father, in ways that Hamlet finds he cannot. The audience first see him witness Laertes getting permission to travel, while Hamlet is told that he should stay where he is. They first see Claudius announcing that the whole court are to 'move on', to use an appropriate current cliché, after the death of their late king, by accepting that Gertrude and he are married; he then orders ambassadors abroad and generally seems to get on with the business of ruling in a swift and efficient manner, as a number of critics have noted.[61] In this second scene of *Hamlet*, everyone is either talking about moving, or actually moving on- and off-stage, leaving Hamlet as static and reluctant commentator. When Laertes' father is killed by Hamlet, Laertes declares he would happily cut Hamlet's throat 'i'th'church' (4.7.126); Hamlet finds the murderer of his father praying and finds reason not to do so, poising with the dagger frozen above the murderer like Pyhrrus in the Player's speech but without the eventual violent conclusion. I may seem to be returning here to Lawrence Olivier's assertion that *Hamlet* is 'a tragedy about a man who could not make up his mind'.[62] But Hamlet spends the play 'making up' his mind in another sense. He spends the play in a state of what I have called insightful grief, forging and producing a mind in dialogue with his audience, until he succumbs to the stock Protestant notion that there is a special providence in the fall of a sparrow and agrees to take part in Claudius' play fight.[63] This making up, or constructing, of his 'mind' is posited against the kind of assertive agency it takes to be a revenge hero. Grief, always in danger of being 'excessive grief, the enemy to the living' (*All's Well*, 1.155), produces a caesura in politically productive time; it produces insight rather than action, stillness or directionless movement rather than clear trajectory. Interestingly, Jonathan Hope and Michael Witmore's use of a software system set up to search text for linguistic constructions and tropes has tentatively concluded that Shakespeare's early work is more concerned with human action, his later work with human experience of action and being acted upon – with what characters feel, then, rather than with what they do.[64] This is certainly borne out by an examination of grief in the early histories and *Hamlet*, throughout which dramatic history, the expression of sorrow is anathema to action, so that in the earlier, 'active' plays, tears are repeatedly scorned by characters as they call for revenge, where in *Hamlet*, whose central character is called to revenge but cannot manage it, grief is central to his subjectivity, his language and his philosophical insights.

## 'THERE'S MATTER IN THESE SIGHS, THESE PROFOUND HEAVES': NICHOLAS HYTNER'S *HAMLET* AND THE POLITICS OF EMOTIONAL EXCESS[65]

A number of recent modern Hamlets have been far from physically inactive. David Tennant at the RSC leapt about the stage with boundless energy – but this seeming drivenness only emphasized his directionlessness: after swearing to the Ghost to take only one direction, Hamlet then fails to take it.[66] Rory Kinnear in the National Theatre's 2011 production, as we will see, emphasized the comic dimension of Hamlet's 'antic disposition' (1.5.180) and the unproductive aimlessness of the expression of grief. Michael Sheen's incarcerated Hamlet had the restless energy of paranoia: in the twentieth-century asylum setting at the Young Vic, it was hinted that Claudius, the director of the hospital, might not have been old Hamlet's killer and that Hamlet had staged the whole play's action, creeping about the asylum at night when he should have been still, stealing the coat of his dead father so as better to pretend to be the Ghost, emerging from behind Fortinbras' mask at the end of the play.[67] Dreamthinkspeak's heavily cut *Hamlet*,

Figure 8: Hamlet (Rory Kinnear) in *Hamlet* dir. Nicholas Hytner, National Theatre, 2010 (© Geraint Lewis)

*The Rest is Silence*, on the other hand, set behind a quadrangle of perspex windows, with the audience standing in darkness at its centre peering into the world of the play, centred on a static and often silent Hamlet, many of whose lines were cut. The 'To be or not to be' soliloquy was spoken by his uncle, mother and friends who had sneaked into his room to read it in his diary and who, in the case of Rosencrantz and Guildenstern, proceeded scornfully to read it aloud for their own amusement, jumbled to produce a comical range of meanings. Edward Hogg's Hamlet sat silently watching much of the action and seemed also to watch the audience; his voice was thin and reedy and there was a blankness about him suggestive of a theatricalized autism. The question I want to ask in the following analysis of the National Theatre's production is around what meaningful sense might be made of the early modern tensions between passion and its moderation, and between grief and action, when these tensions do not exist for the modern spectator in the urgent way they may have for early modern audiences. It is perhaps, partially, in the relationship between movement and stasis that early modern meanings can be opened up to a modern audience.

The National Theatre *Hamlet* of 2010, directed by the theatre's Artistic Director Nicholas Hytner, was most notably distinguished by its setting in a modern surveillance state, in which the play's conventions of dialogue and soliloquy are complicated by the constant presence of Claudius' state surveillance team, his Switzers, as Claudius refers to his personal guard in 4.5 (97) and as the stage-manager names these figures in the prompt copy.[68] Movement is foregrounded in this Elsinore, because it is always watched and followed. This was a *Hamlet* of exceptionally clear directorial decisions, some of which – particularly the death of Ophelia, who is fairly certainly murdered by the Switzers – did not emerge from the text but were logical extensions of the state and society that the production generated from the play. It was a *Hamlet* in which everyone's actions, relationships – and indeed passions – were policed most blatantly by the state. From the moment when Fransisco muttered that he was 'sick at heart' (1.1.9) after his watch and Barnado looked at him questioningly, as if somewhat disturbed, because one does not admit such things as a soldier in this Elsinore, we were clearly in a world where openly showing that one is unhappy could be politically dangerous. What this highlighted for this study was the emergence in this play of a subjectivity forged in the tensions between private passion and public expression, single subject and the needs of the state, tensions which again heighten questions around agency and responsibility within the holistic worldview in which the somatic passions take their place.

The state that dominated this production may be read as an explicitly Soviet or even contemporary Russian one, and one might argue that this rendered the production an easy critique of something of which many of its audiences were likely already to disapprove. The fact that, as several broadsheet reviewers and a large number of bloggers and less mainstream reviewers remarked, Patrick Malahide's Claudius looked rather like Vladamir Putin,[69] contributed to this sense of specific historical setting: *Hamlet* as the Russian leader's fantasy of returning to Soviet-style state surveillance, perhaps. Indeed, Jami Rogers entitled her review for *Internet Shakespeare Editions* 'Hamlet and Putin', and suggests that 'it was thought-provoking as a critique of the contemporary Russian regime'.[70] Two years later, as two young women are imprisoned for a critique of Putin's actual regime[71] (an artistic intervention similarly daft in its visuals to this Hamlet's smiley face campaign, of which more later), this narrow reading seems more plausible than it might have when I left the theatre after seeing the production. In conversation with Matt Wolf for a series of public interviews around the production, Rory Kinnear (Hamlet) makes reference only to a setting that might 'veer towards a Soviet satellite state'.[72] However, whether or not one read this Hamlet as 'set' in contemporary Russia or the old Soviet Union, the production took very seriously the question of how, in modern dress, one might portray a state with a leader who murders former leaders and pack future leaders off into exile. The answer was an excessively paranoid one which, as Peter Holland reminds us in his programme essay for this production, is how Shakespeare portrays Elsinore.[73] What ultimately prevented the production from being simply a satire on contemporary Russia or the former Soviet Union, if it was that at all, was the care it took in exploring the politics of emotion: this state policed emotion as if it were always dangerously excessive, endeavouring to follow it and cut it off – quite explicitly in the case of Ophelia.

Kinnear and Hytner, in an interview for the production's programme, are particularly concerned with Hamlet's 'authenticity': 'human authenticity is one of the play's chief concerns,' asserts Hytner. 'One of our jobs has been to find ways of making vivid Hamlet's grapple with his own authenticity.'[74] For the creators of this production, the fact that Hamlet finds himself surrounded by corruption, pretence and false friends leads him through a distraught quest for that which passeth show. However, I would argue that the production went beyond familiar binaries of honesty and social pretence, false show and authentic selfhood. What Kinnear made clear, through a performance of Hamlet's deepening 'depression', as he puts it,[75] is Hamlet's dawning realization that the expression of 'that within', however sincerely felt and self-authored, does not get him any closer to avenging his father but rather demonstrates the length the state will go to pry into and police that interiority.

Rory Kinnear's Hamlet risked his life in this production by showing he was miserable in a court where everyone is obliged to pretend to be happy – and when they are not, drown their sorrows in champagne and whiskey: Claudius and Gertrude drank liberally from the moment the cameras started filming what became Claudius' statement to the nation (1.2.1–25) It was a production which took the Ghost's accusation of Claudius' and Gertrude's adultery in a modern sense (in the play this is open to interpretation, of course, due to the religious and legal ambiguities around marrying one's dead spouse's sibling). The Ghost emphasized the word 'adulterate' in describing Claudius as 'that incestuous, that adulterate beast' (1.5.42) and Hamlet reacted in renewed surprise and horror. In this production, old Hamlet's son is clearly being told that the 'falling off' (47) of the love between his mother and his father happened before the old King's death. Thus Gertrude was already in conspiracy with Claudius before the play began, having hidden her illicit love for him when her husband was alive – and the love his mother had for his father has, for Hamlet, now been tainted with a falsehood yet worse than that demonstrated by her swift turn to Claudius after old Hamlet's death. Significantly, in 1.2, the re-announcement of the new King and old Queen's marriage was televised, complete with recording of a national anthem-like theme and cheering crowds, Claudius and Gertrude sitting before a large painting of old Hamlet draped in black, while the foreign policy issues with Norway and the organization of the ambassadors were kept from the viewing public, discussed when the broadcast was complete. This was a royal marriage which was supposed to lull and calm the nation at a time of encroaching war, chiming well with Claudius' suggestion of measure and balance in his personal actions – he weighed delight and dole (1.2.13) – while Hamlet figures the court as a place of excess. As soon as the broadcast was over, Gertrude took a tense swig from a glass of champagne. It was not suggested that she suspected her new husband of her former husband's murder – her exclamation in the Closet scene 'As kill a king?' (3.4.29) was as horrified as any Gertrude's at this idea (though her revulsion to Claudius' touch at the end of this scene suggests that she certainly believes Hamlet's accusation by this point). What the scene set up was the state's utilization of the personal to smooth the political, its use of that which reads as authentic emotion – love between the newly married – to soften and humanize the state in the eyes of the populace. This strong visual reminder of the public, state occasion of this speech fits particularly plausibly with the lines in which Claudius posits himself as a paradigm of the victory of reason over passionate excess of grief:

> Yet so far hath discretion fought with nature
> That we with wisest sorrow think on him
> Together with remembrance of ourselves.
> Therefore [...].
>
> (1.2.5–8)

The king's 'therefore' leads to the redeclaration of his marriage, which Claudius presented almost as a sacrifice of his natural desire to mourn his brother for the good of the state.

This Elsinore policed emotion and affect relentlessly. 'Switzers' lurked behind every panel of the set, a consciously bland and sinisterly shifting series of grey walls. The state followed, most literally, romantic relationships, friendship, art, all modes of what we might call 'self-expression'. When Ophelia was confronted by her father about her relationship with Hamlet in 1.3 and was forbidden to consort further with him, Polonius thrust at her a file of photographs of the couple seen together, taken by these not particularly shadowy agents; she was clearly horrified at the breach of privacy. The agents sprang forth after Hamlet's first soliloquy in 1.2, to hold Horatio and the men of the watch at the threshold until Hamlet approved their entry. These Switzers listened quite blatantly to Hamlet's request that the players play *The Murder of Gonzago*. The First Player appeared most unnerved by the request, as if this were potentially a subversive text in its own right; he appeared even more worried when Hamlet asked him to learn the newly inserted lines.

Ophelia was, the audience was undoubtedly to assume, finally murdered by the surveillance Switzers, justifying the terror with which she responded to Polonius' demand that they go to the King to tell of Hamlet's crazed entrance to her closet (2.1.117–18). Her father murdered, the Switzers prevented her from mourning him: his body in a clinical white bag was wheeled across the stage and she was prevented from following it. Her madness is explicitly feared as subversive by Horatio (4.5.14–15) and in this production she was given the treatment that is planned for Hamlet when he is sent off to England. The production also made the rare choice of having Gertrude see the Ghost in her closet: Clare Higgins stepped towards him, treading distractedly on to the painting of Claudius that Hamlet had removed from the wall to compare it to his father's portrait. Gertrude then denied seeing the Ghost, and later, though she had conspired with Hamlet in her promise not to reveal that he is only 'mad in craft' (3.4.190), colluded with her husband's government in a delivery of the description of Ophelia's drowning which implied that she at least suspected the murder.

Kinnear's was, from the outset, an emotionally expressive Hamlet, frustratedly tearful at his mother's rapid remarriage in the first soliloquy and very plausibly devastated to hear the Ghost's tale of the murder. He was clearly angry and frustrated after the humiliation of being refused a return to Wittenburg, which request he presented to his uncle as an official paper; he directed 'A little more than kin and less than kind' (1.2.65) directly at his uncle rather than to the audience or as if muttering to himself – not by any means the first time this has been done in production but a rarer choice, one which made the relationship between uncle and nephew very obviously confrontational.[76] In this Denmark, it also made Hamlet a very brave man – though it also suggested a critique of censorship and surveillance as crassly unsubtle mechanisms of state control. It was as if the authorities knew they needed to police passions and relationships but could only do so through their usual technologies for the surveillance of exterior shows and actions.

Interestingly, Kinnear's Hamlet reacted particularly furiously to Claudius' suggestion that his persistent mourning of his father was 'unmanly grief' (1.2.94) and stormed away from his uncle on this line. This may be read as contempt for the machismo underlying the suggestion that grief could be thus gendered – but to me it rather read as genuine offence at being called unmanly. This reading of the line suggested that Hamlet's melancholy might be circumstantial rather than dispositional, primarily produced by his father's death. Indeed, a number of critics commented on the ordinariness of this Hamlet[77] and certainly he spoke his lines within a realist tradition of acting that produced an effect of distress at bereavement which audiences might recognize from their own experience. Kinnear tried new meanings via odd emphases (more than one reviewer commented on the delivery of 'Soft you now, the fair Ophelia' as 'Soft! *You – now*! The Fair Ophelia' (3.1.88–9) as if to say 'and now *you* enter, the woman who is rejected me, just to cap the speech in which I've been contemplating suicide'). He had a cigarette in his hand through 'To be or not to be', producing an effect of spontaneous thought – though in fact he only smoked it before the line 'Thus conscience doth make cowards of us all' (83), a conventional enough point for an actor to move or change pace, as it marks a new thought or conclusion after the set of questions that precedes it. The smoking was not used to break up lines, so that I found no irritable complaints from reviewers about bad verse speaking. What his supposed ordinariness suggested was that in this surveillance state, any kind of emotional expression is in excess of what is permissible, because potentially disruptive. It is only legitimated if it can be displayed, like Claudius' and Gertrude's marriage, as part of the state's propaganda apparatus. Having that within which passeth show is highly subversive.

Kinnear's Hamlet did not give the impression of having been a melancholic outsider before the death of his father or even of having been an extraordinarily profound intellectual, one of the marks of the early modern melancholic. He is, like his father (a downbeat, vulnerable-seeming and very human Ghost played by James Laurenson), 'a man, take him for all in all' (1.2.187), devastated by his father's death, offended at being called unmanly and understanding, horribly suddenly, that he lives in a place where expressing 'that within which passeth show' is not regarded as legitimate.

Particularly passionate was Kinnear's delivery of the 'O what a rogue and peasant slave am I' soliloquy (2.2.550ff.). The exclamations of 'Bloody, bawdy villain!' (582) burst from Hamlet in fury and distress, as he knelt on the floor and desperately struck at it, underlining the fact that Hamlet's anger is impotent because it is conflated with his grief. My preferred interpretation of these lines has been that they are a desperate rehearsal of the stage revenge hero, a theatrical rant intended by Hamlet to force himself into the choleric state of the stage revenger who is, in action, as good as his word. Then 'Why what an ass am I! This is most brave,' (384) is the bathetic, often comic, self-reprimand at his poor and ineffectual performance. 'Bravery', after all, means showiness in early modern English. However, there was no sense of a conscious theatricality at this point in this production. Kinnear exclaimed with a seemingly spontaneous but impotent desperation: Hamlet proved here that he felt just as strongly as the Player in the latter's acted passion over the death of Hecuba, but that this makes no difference whatsoever to the fact that he, Hamlet, is still not an effective agent in the revenge tragedy the Ghost of his dead father commanded him to set in motion. It is significant that the production used a Q2-based text so that the words 'O vengeance!' were cut from the end of Hamlet's exclamations in this soliloquy. The Folio line may have been considered too archaically stagy for Kinnear's interpretation of the role, too far evocative of the archetypal revenger, which even in Shakespeare's lifetime was being parodied.[78] But Kinnear's delivery indicated that no matter how much Hamlet feels and how powerfully he expresses it, 'expression' of passion is how one makes up one's mind in the sense in which I have used it above (p. 205) – the way in which one constructs one's own subjectivity – whereas his father has demanded that he make up his mind, in the common, figurative sense, to action.

Hamlet now talks himself into one more prequel to the action of the revenge hero, the Players' performance, which he sets up to assure himself that his 'melancholy' has not misled him as to the nature of the Ghost (2.2.600–605). This, more than in any other production I have seen, read as a temporary burst of action before Hamlet falls back into the contemplative and interrogatory inaction of the 'To be or not to be' soliloquy. Kinnear and Ruth Negga signalled a sincere love between Hamlet and Ophelia, once expressed through the tokens Ophelia was now returning. They were both in tears when Hamlet declared that he 'did love [her] once' and she replied that she believed it (3.1.115–16). His warning against himself as 'proud, revengeful, ambitious' (125) was spoken as a performance he felt obliged to give in order to break the bonds between them, a pompous and implausible joke. As in many productions, Kinnear staged the realization that Hamlet is being spied on on his line 'where's your father?' (130–1), when he realized that the book Ophelia was holding was, in this production, bugged. After that, his disgust was palpable for the love he once believed sincere and his later innuendoes for Ophelia's benefit at The Mousetrap, crude and cruel. She became yet another of the court saps for whom Hamlet has been performing his ludicrous acts of madness – his silly weeping noises under the duvet for the benefit of Polonius in 2.2, the spoilt-brat whine with which he delivers 'I lack advancement' (3.2.342) for Rosencrantz and Guildenstern. Kinnear played madness as if Hamlet cannot quite believe anyone is falling for his charade. He played the rebellious iconoclastic artist producing The Mousetrap with similarly violent irony, giving out T-shirts with the iconic smiley face he has been posting up about Elsinore and which Gertrude and Ophelia dutifully donned for the Players' performance. He dropped his underpants, uttered obscenities (this Hamlet certainly put the 'c*nt' into 'country matters' (3.2.118)) and until the moment Claudius cried for lights, everyone patronizingly humoured the eccentric Prince. Hytner and Kinnear's concern with subjective authenticity came to fruition here: Kinnear's performance suggested that after Ophelia's betrayal, Hamlet reread every expression of feeling he had received or witnessed in Elsinore as having an ulterior and inauthentic motive; his maniacal glee at the court performance suggested that he simply could not believe the stupidity of the conniving and calculating court – were they really permitting him to do all this?

However, once the Ghost's authenticity was proven by Claudius' horror as he looked down upon the dead body of the player king (and the effect was intensified by a doubling of the Player with the Ghost of old Hamlet), this Hamlet developed a kind of hardened pragmatism in action that seemed far from 'authentic'. The audience had come to know a Hamlet who talks about how he feels and what he must do. When he actually acted, he ceased to be Hamlet-like. In his mother's closet he played a blunt lack of concern at her distress, until the Ghost came to upbraid him; his dry, comical reaction to his mistaken killing of Polonius seemed similarly determined in its performance of indifference. His pragmatic pleasure at his plan to send Rosencrantz and Guildenstern to their deaths startled Horatio. He was clearly affected by the uncovering of Yorick's skull, and here Kinnear movingly signalled Hamlet's memories of an age before he knew of betrayal and corruption and could simply play with a friend he loved. But when he challenged Laertes over the strength of their love for Ophelia, the bitter sarcasm of 'I'll rant as well as thou' (5.2.284) showed us a Hamlet for whom all declarations and deeds of love are meaningless show.

Hytner's own reading of Hamlet's 'We defy augury' speech to Horatio (5.2.218–23) is that here he suddenly and paradoxically reaches some profoundly spiritual conclusions about his – and all of humankind's – situation. Here he is in conversation with Kinnear during rehearsal:

> *Nick Hytner*: The other thing which is immensely engrossing – and releasing – is that everything you think you know, is simultaneously contradicted….For example, I think we're both pretty sure that, by the time Hamlet comes back after being rescued [he has experienced] something mysterious enough for him to be unable to explain it in a soliloquy. Famously, the soliloquies stop. When he tells Horatio 'Let be', he seems to be saying that he's letting go, relinquishing control, that he has discovered a truth that is unavailable to explanation. And yet, when he knows he's dying, not once but three times Hamlet tells Horatio that he must tell his story and tell it correctly. As he's dying, the thing that appears to be filling his thoughts most is the need to control the story that gets told after his dead. Now that's not letting be, not letting go. And yet, simultaneously, I believe he's genuinely discovered that there is a peace which passeth all understanding. I think both are true.[79]

Of course, early modern Protestant theology very much coheres with the notion that peace is to be found in the 'special providence in the fall of a sparrow' (5.2.218–9) which Hamlet cites from St Matthew's gospel. As John Curran reminds us, 'Calvinism often drew upon this passage to emphasize that we must take solace in God's steady and thorough control of the universe'; we must sprinkle Christian patience on our passions. Curran goes on to point out how the sparrow axiom comforts the Christian who must, of course, be of more importance to God than a mere sparrow.[80] It is interesting that Hytner also quotes from the Bible when he describes the 'peace' that Hamlet has discovered. But I would argue that predestination is not a satisfactory answer to this play's questions and it is significant that Hamlet speaks these lines so soon after telling Horatio about 'how ill all's here about my heart' (5.2.211–12). I have argued elsewhere that these lines may be more plausibly read as a relinquishing of life rather than a renewed understanding of it and the fact that 'famously the soliloquies stop', to quote Hytner again, speaks not so much of peace as of death-wish.[81] The fact that in this production, Osric was clearly high up in the hierarchy of the surveillance state, wearily humouring Hamlet as the latter teased him over his hat, and that he later helped Laertes to his poisoned sword, points even more clearly to a reading of this speech in which letting be is equivalent to giving up. Hamlet has fallen into somebody else's plot of active vengeance and relinquished his socially excessive, insightful grief, his self-construction, his making up of mind.

When Fortinbras claimed the Danish throne in this production, he did so in front of the television cameras that had broadcast Claudius' reassuring statement to the nation in 1.2. Fortinbras saluted to camera as he instructed his men to 'bid the soldiers shoot' (5.2.410); his statement that Hamlet should be born 'like a soldier to the stage' and was likely to have 'prov'd most royal' (5.2.403, 405) rang even more hollowly than it often does in modern production. The audience was left not with the impression that Hamlet's request to Horatio represented a reneging on the peace he has found in providence, but the sense that 'the need to control the story that gets told after he's dead' will be a pressing one in a new state, which seemed as keen to erase the real Hamlet and his untidy, inactive, unsoldierly passions from history, as Claudius was to eliminate him from the court.

This was a production that placed a highly plausible, emotionally expressive Hamlet in a state that clearly disapproved of most forms of emotional expression. The 'setting' was potentially problematic in that it gave rise to a possible reading as a Soviet-style state, an easy-to-read, repressive and distant 'other'. But Kinnear played Hamlet as an 'ordinary' man with an intensity of grief that I think will have prevented too easy a dismissal of a state that might be complacently and negatively compared with 'our' own. The spatial dramaturgy produced by the set, whose grey walls moved to enclose and reveal those who felt what they should not, successfully foregrounded the ways in which the state of Denmark is constructed to suspect all emotional expression as in excess of its rigidly defined needs, thus producing emotional expression as 'self' in opposition to state. This chimes interestingly with theories of early modern subjectivity that see interiority produced in historical moments of surveillance and religious interrogation. It also resonates with current concerns in the UK about literal surveillance on the one hand and, perhaps, state interventions into the happiness of its citizens on the other. We are at a point, in British culture, when we are once again struggling with questions of the value of emotional expression and self-control in explicitly political ways. To a degree, the emotions have been made a matter of personal psychology in popular self-help and therapeutic discourse. However, debates around the over-prescribing or otherwise of pharmaceuticals for depression and the UK goverment's current interest in the state of the nation's happiness are examples of emotion's recent and explicit politicization.[82] As Hytner and Kinnear state repeatedly, for them, Hamlet is about 'authenticity'. If one redefines the term as meaning self-authorship, without attaching to it moral abstractions around sincerity and binaries of inner truth versus social falsehood, Kinnear's Hamlet wrestles to produce a self in a place where the expression of self in grief is always regarded as excessive. Hamlet in its own period represents an intense struggle between the notion of the somatic passions as always in excess of the reason's attempts to keep it within 'natural' boundaries, and the passions as individuating and differentiating factors in the construction of self. Hamlet distrusts his melancholy and cannot become the directional avenger of the older history plays. The National Theatre production politicized emotion in such a way as to revivify these conflicts and contradictions for an audience in the early twenty-first century.

# CHAPTER FIVE

## CONCLUSION: EMOTIONAL AGENDAS

To bring together ideas about the passions and their perceived excesses that were circulating among the literate in early modern England with the plays that both recirculated, troubled and produced anew such ideas for a wider audience is a large enough endeavour for more than one book. To bring these ideas and plays into dialogue with discourses circulating about emotion and its perceived excesses today, particularly as they are recirculated, troubled and produced anew in contemporary theatre production, is a yet larger enterprise and one which inevitably remains unfinished with this Conclusion. I want to continue with this kind of comparative, transhistorical project, a project that is always historically contentious, as W. B. Worthen has so cogently explained.[1] What one 'discovers' about historical plays from current performance is always, to a degree, imposed and invented by the present, particularly if an uncritical naivety about what 'works' in the theatre now is brought to bear on what might have been performed and expressed 400 years ago. However, having begun to consider emotion and its excesses in the early modern period via recent production, I am optimistic that the kinds of comparison that arise from this book may productively alienate ideas of emotional excess in the study of both early modern and contemporary theatrical cultures, and provoke further thought about how emotion has been expressed, judged, disapproved or valorized, recently and historically.

I introduced this book by suggesting that the drama of the early modern period is a particularly rich theatrical site for the discussion of the ways in which our own society conceives of, celebrates and regulates emotion. In the UK, we are living through a period where a range of authorities are particularly interested in the way we feel. A 'Happiness Agenda' has recently been drawn up by a government keen to find ways other than the economic to improve the lives of its citizens. The ideological underpinnings of this 'agenda' have been summed up by commentator Suzanne Moore, who makes the blunt assertion that, at a time of economic recession, 'the happiness agenda is just a way of making huge social problems seem personal'. Moore continues, 'We do not have control over a globalised system that right now is in crisis, nor do we have full control over our own impulses, our own unfathomable psyches.'[2] The early modern period, before the discovery or invention of the unconscious, before the formal theorization of social and economic systems, appeared to understand this very well. The power of the passions, and the religious and socio-economic systems that attempted to regulate them, were staged starkly, excitingly, in tension and contradiction with each other in the early modern theatre. It was a theatre able to stage the passions, and debates about the passions, their place in society and the body, powerfully and explicitly, because certain modern assumptions about individual emotional expression and its social and psychological benefits had not yet been made. I hope that this book will provoke readers to consider ways in which 400-year-old plays might productively estrange us from ourselves and our supposedly inalienable right to emotional expression.

I also hope that this book can be part of (yet) another reconsideration of what we call the period in which Shakespeare and his contemporaries produced theatre. I have used 'early modern' here, 'hopelessly Whiggish' though the term is to some,[3] because it speaks to the mix of familiarity and strangeness of emotional expression that emerges in the plays of this period. A purpose-built theatre as a capitalist enterprise may be reasonably described as an 'early modern' phenomenon, as may early capitalist modes of trade and exchange. The notion of an 'early modern dramatic subjectivity', a concern (or invention?) of late twentieth-century Cultural Materialist scholarship, is more clearly in danger of imposing postmodern constructions of the self onto pre-modern culture. It still seems a productive concept to me, however: though I have not cited Stephen Greenblatt and Catherine Belsey on the subject here, their conceptions of self-fashioning and of the theatrical construction of agency[4] have inevitably informed this book as I have considered the ways in which the passions were shifting in the theatre and wider culture of this period, from dangerous and turbulent somatic forces to that which begins to define the individual in relation to his or her society. If the First Player had had the cause to act that Hamlet had, he would have obliterated the stage with his tears and un-selfed the audience: maddened them, confounded them, amazed them. But Hamlet is not going to do that, because his passions are not of the right kind for this sort of passionate action. He has a psychosomatic make-up which, in conjunction with the social ties and restrictions that limit him, the education which informs him and the violent incident that has just been revealed to him, make him feel – and therefore move, and act – differently from the stock revenge hero. How one expresses, controls and judges one's own passions, and how one's social environment controls and judges them, is at the root of the construction of the dramatic subject during this period. These building blocks of subjectivity are clearly conceived and staged in the work of early modern theatre. Their reproduction now can provoke current audiences, I think, to reconsider the building blocks of their own.

## ANGER

Rereading *Coriolanus* for Chapter 1 of this project, I was startled to be reminded of Volumnia's assertion that she had a brain that led her use of anger. This idea of the brain seems so modern, post-Cartesian, super-egoic. But the tension between personal feeling and social usage, between the somatic and the socially constructed, is both very much of the period and begins to generate the binaries of self and body, individual and social environment that are fully expressed in later periods. Caius

Martius' assertion that to compromise and suppress his fury at the Tribunes and Citizens is to prevent him from being the man he is has, naturally, led some actors and directors to wonder what made him that man. Why so angry? The play, I believe, is less concerned with what we may think of as psychological answers to that question, than with how his anger might be used by Martius' political community. Eventually, it can't be. Martius does not have a brain that leads his use of anger on to self-governance and resultant political power. His choler is himself, yet it is finally self-obliterating. In early modern writings on anger, drawing on the classics, anger is described almost unremittingly negatively; in *Coriolanus*, the choleric warrior can only make use of his anger in battle, has a moment of remittance from it in weeping before his family, then rekindles it and challenges his enemies to kill him, which they do.

In British culture at the time of writing, anger has an oddly ambiguous cultural status. Educational agendas around 'emotional literacy' and children's 'emotional and behavioural difficulties', psychological and legal concepts of 'anger management', all speak to a concern that anger's excesses are very much in need of control. Yet some expression of anger, it is assumed in therapeutic and self-help discourses, is necessary for mental health. These figurings of anger largely assume it is a personal trait or problem. The early modern period assumes it is partly that – albeit 'personal' to the whole body rather than to our modern psyche – but that it is also a socially constructed trait or problem. The productions I have outlined in closing Chapter One here seem particularly conscious of the notion that anger is a passion which moves people and bodies of people politically – something that is easy to forget in a society with a supposed 'happiness agenda'. In order for *Coriolanus* to speak this notion of anger as political movement, it does not have to be progressive or reactionary, to side with the plebeians or the patricians. It rather has to stage the anger of all who contain and express that passion, in terms of concrete proxemics as well as inner feeling, political movement as well as personal trauma. I hope that this book's somewhat

Brechtian agenda in this regard may renew debate about what a 'political' theatre might be if it is still interested in staging 400-year-old plays.

## LAUGHTER

As I have described in Chapter Two, London's South Bank is currently the site of a wide spectrum of attitudes to the past – a spectrum from alien cruelty to humanist kind-ness is staged, as one takes a walk from London Bridge to Shakespeare's Globe. My work on laughter here has renewed my interest in 'humanism', which was rather generally and ahistorically condemned as 'liberal humanism' in my early university education, when post-structuralist, post-humanist discourses were excitingly sweeping Arts and Humanities departments. I have been interested in the rehabilitation of humanism since reading Levinas on the ethics of recognition and otherness,[5] and it has seemed to me that the early modern dramas featuring mad figures, which I have examined here, offer a particularly productive way of considering moments of humanity and recognition in the theatre. Carol Neely's work on *Distracted Subjects* is a brilliant historicist and humanist rehabilitation of the purposes of the Bethlem hospital (see pp. 76–7), but it underestimates the power of the face-to-face encounter in the theatre to trouble monolithic meaning. What has surprised me about working on plays featuring the incarcerated mad, so disturbing and potentially distasteful to some of the theatre reviewers I have cited, is that they have had more to offer a 'humanist' agenda of recognition of the other than that the work of that supposed inventor of the human, Shakespeare, where he falsely imprisons Malvolio as a madman. Tim Crouch's desire to retell *Twelfth Night* from the point of view of an abused and abject Malvolio led me to scholars who have related the performance history of Malvolio as a history of the abuse of the social outcast, from the mid-nineteenth century onward (see pp. 254–5n. 118). This, is a performance history that may allow an audience member to congratulate herself on her kindly humanism, as she views poor Malvolio, battered and humiliated, and which allows her the *frisson* of theatrical shame, as Malvolio declares that he is to be revenged on the whole pack of us. However, in answer to Crouch's repeated question of 'Is that what you find funny?', I should say that, while reconsidering *Twelfth Night*, my answer must be, for the most part, 'Yes': Shakespeare does permit us to laugh at the 'good practice'[6] of the gulling of Malvolio, the social climber. It is the dramatists who stage the incarcerated mad as theatrical turns who have the greater potential for shifting and disturbing our secure positions within communities of laughter. Ironically, then, given the predominance of Shakespeare in this book, I hope that the work on laughter here, its potentially cruel excesses and its power as an expression of recognition, may also begin to shift and disturb Shakespeare's position as the most humane writer of comedy.

## LOVE

My hopes for love having written Chapter Three may seem perverse. It is the early modern passion connected to versions of the female that have pertained, most disturbingly, across 400 years. Ideas about unfathomable, seductive yet wayward and unreliable women, ideas about spendthrift women, ideas about women so desperate for a man that they would go anywhere, do anything, have emerged at every turn as I have considered the powerful passions of Cleopatra and Helena. I would like to see these two plays in production fully and uncompromisingly investigate love's selfish yet self-obliterating excesses, even at the expense of demonstrating that 'Shakespeare wrote strong women' – though partially because I think that releasing ourselves from the duty of rehabilitating early modern misogyny in this regard may actually still produce strong women. What has interested me in considering love' s excesses in these two plays has been love's amorality, during a period which clearly did differentiate love from 'mere' lust and had a powerful sense of the pure and selfless love that came from God. Production and reading since the early modern period has found problems in these plays – *Antony and Cleopatra* in feminist terms, *All's Well* in distinctly moral ones – which they have attempted to erase; in the process, they have often reinscribed Cleopatra and Helena within the gendered and moral boundaries from which the readings and productions were attempting to release them. It will be clear to the reader that one of the productions I enjoyed most while researching this book has been Arpana's Gujarati *All's Well*; this was because it managed to stage love in the most unabashedly excessive way, as Heli shared her passion for Bharatram with her Globe audience. Its setting in late nineteenth-century India permitted a range of historical and social commentary around colonialism, patriarchy and 'traditional' cultural mores, while also permitting love to be both in excess of these cultural phenomena and finally reassimilated by them.

As with all of the early modern passions – but perhaps more surprisingly for modern audiences and readers – love is far from an assumed good in the writings about it circulating during this period. In contemporary critical terms, moreover, it is impossible to release it from ideological constructions of gender and sexuality. But a love like Cleopatra's, in its theatrical amorality, cares little for these things and manages to be both of and in excess of its historical and cultural moment. In addition to hoping that there might be more stagings of shameless, amoral love in the future to entice and disturb theatre audiences, I hope that there may be more writing on this passion in early modern drama that is less concerned with finding love on the right side of a sex/spiritual transcendency binary than some recent work has been.

## GRIEF

In considering grief and its relationship to melancholy in Chapter Four, I have returned to the sense of emotion as motion that emerged in the Introduction and in Chapter 1. Grief produces stasis rather than action in the *Henry VI* plays, and this stasis acquires a political inflection in *Richard III* and *Hamlet*, as the mourning women disrupt Richard's political trajectory and Hamlet refuses to cease his mourning for the sake of his uncle's corrupted monarchy and, for most of the play, to become the simple avenging agent demanded by the ghost of his father. I have been drawn here to productions within mainstream British theatres which have been more clearly informed by the conventions of theatrical realism than those that have interested me elsewhere. Roxana Silbert's *Richard III* was a theatrically conscious production, with a clear performer/audience relationship – but the company were interested in a personal psychology for Richard as well as in his history as Vice and stage Machiavel. Nicholas Hytner's *Hamlet* was set in a political world of modern surveillance and was concerned with ideas of personal authenticity in the face of totalitarianism.

Here, I am interested in the place of the stage within stage realism, the stage whose presence realism tends to erase. In this RSC *Richard III*, the psychology of damaged self-esteem drove Richard in his jovial but ultimately contemptuous relationship with the audience and underpinned a theatricality finally undone by the excesses of female grief, as the women refused to play to either of the production's dominant theatrical conventions – open stage direct address or psychological realism – and lay on the ground. In the National's *Hamlet* a continuously moving set, and set of surveillance officials, hemmed Hamlet in at every turn, foregrounding movement as the dominant mode of a state for which any expression of grief was in excess of its regulatory forces. This chapter is, I think, an example of renewed scholarly interest by Cultural Materialist performance critics in the ways in which theatrical realism produces meaning in Shakespeare.[7] 'Naturalistic' acting – particularly, perhaps, the acting of sorrow and grief, with its production of the sobs, gasps and tears that indicate the spontaneous, somatic production of emotion – has, partially due to Brecht's critique, become associated with a privileging of personal psychology over political construction. These productions have defied this binary and foregrounded the politics of potentially disruptive, subversive emotion. I hope this book can continue the work of politicizing emotion, in the study of historical theatrical culture and of our own.

# NOTES

## INTRODUCTION

* All quotations are in modern spelling. Play quotations are from modern editions and I have rendered all other quotations into modern spelling, in order not to suggest that plays are somehow more accessible to the modern reader than other writings.

1. There is a wide range of early modern writing criticizing, in terms both highly serious and lightly satirical, the pure stoical position on the passions, whereby one rejects all feeling as inconsequential to a life of virtue. See Richard Strier, *The Unrepentant Renaissance* (Chicago, 2011), ch. 1, 'Against the Rule of Reason', in which he reads Erasmus' *In Praise of Folly* as a genuine celebration of the 'folly' of human passion and a satire on stoicism (32–6) and 37–42, where he cites Luther and Calvin as supportive of a place for the passions in Christian life.

   See also, as other early modern examples, James Sandford's *The Mirror of Madness* in which he satirizes the Stoic Zenocrates' position on anger and the contorted excuses a Stoic might make for indulging his own fury (London, 1576); Levinas Lemnias' *The sanctuary of salvation, helmet of health, and mirror of modesty and good manners* (London, 1592), in which even moderate levels of enjoyment are said to be 'reprehended [...] of the 'sour sad and unpleasant Stoic' (142); William Fulbeck's *Direction or Preparative to the Study of the Law* (London, 1600), which is particularly scathing of Stoic 'sourness', and which suggests that in seeking to overcome man's nature, those of the Stoic philosophy 'become beasts' (16); Joseph Hall's poem on the succession of James I, *The King's Prophecy*, which suggests that a passionate 'Weeping Joy' is the only appropriate response to the Queen's death and the coming of the new King, which opens:

   > What Stoic could his steely breast contain
   > (If *Zeno's* self, or who were made beside
   > Of tougher mold) from being torn in twain
   > With the cross Passions of this wondrous tide? (London, 1603)

   In Thomas Adams' sermons on *England's Sickness* (London, 1615) it is sinful to claim a Stoical immunity to the suffering imposed upon man by

God: 'But when God sees that thou digestest his Physic as diet, and with a strange kind of indulgency, wilt neither grieve that thou hast offended, nor that thou art offended: God will strike home, and sharpen at once both his blow & thy sense. Now thou shalt *feel*; even thy *seared heart* shall bleed. In a word, the wicked may be senseless Stoics, they cannot be insensible stones. There is in all men an impossibility of impassibility' (85).

James I's own *Basilicon Doron* in *James I, Works* (London, 1616) advises his son in a balance of feeling and self-regulation thus: 'Keep true Constancy, not only in your kindness towards honest men; but being also *invicti animi* against all adversities: not with that Stoic insensible stupidity, wherewith many in our days, pressing to wine honour, in imitating that ancient sect, by their inconstant behaviour in their own lives, belie their profession. But although ye are not a stock, not to feel calamities; yet let not the feeling of them, so over-rule and doazen your reason, as may stay you from taking and using the best resolution for remedy, that can be found out' (178).

2. A moving example of such advice comes from Ludvig Lavater's *The Book of Ruth Expounded in Twenty Eight Sermons* (London, 1586), which explains that 'Our saviour Christ himself wept often, therefore that Stoical senselessness is not approved of God. Yet as in other things so also in weeping their must be kept a mean, neither must we weep for every cause. For all kind of weeping cannot be excused. SENECA although he was a Stoic himself, yet he sayeth we may weep but not howl out. But this makes greatly to our comfort, that in this little book it is written down twice, that these poor women wept abundantly, for hereby we do gather, that God regardeth the tears even of them that be very poor' (34).
3. Thomas Playfere, *The Mean in Mourning* (London, 1595), 5–6.
4. See Louis Althusser, 'Ideology and Ideological State Apparatuses' in *Lenin and Philosophy and Other Essays*, trans. Ben Brewster (London, 1971, 174) for an explanation of this concept, whereby the social subject is created by the ideological call into being. While I do not hold Althusser's somewhat disempowering position, whereby the social subject appears to have no agency whatsoever in the world and is entirely a construct of the various ideological apparatuses that interpellate him or her into subjectivity, the idea of interpellation into *emotional* subjectivity usefully denaturalizes the notion of emotional expression and provokes us to consider what kinds of cultural historical moments value which emotions and why.
5. Jonas Barish's analysis of works such as Gosson's *Plays Confuted in Five Actions* (London, 1582), Stubbes' *Anatomy of Abuses* (London, 1595), and Prynne's *Histrio-mastix* (London, 1633) still provides a useful

introduction: *The Anti Theatrical Prejudice* (Berkeley and Los Angeles, CA, 1981), 82–96.

6. For an account of the emergence of the concept of emotional intelligence within the academic discipline of psychology and within self-help discourses, see the Introduction to Gerald Matthews, Moshe Zeidner and Richard D. Roberts, *Emotional Intelligence: Science and Myth* (Cambridge, MA, 2004), 1–21. The work that was largely responsible for the popularization of the concept was Daniel Goleman's *Emotional Intelligence* (New York, 1995).
7. A key work on the ambivalent status of the public theatre in early modern England is still Steven Mullaney's *The Place of the Stage: License, Play, and Power in Renaissance England* (Chicago and London, 1988).
8. See Alan Hunt, *Governance of the Consuming Passions: A History of Sumptuary Law* (Basingtoke, 1996).
9. *The Tudors* television series, dir. Michael Hurst, Peace Arch Entertainment for Showtime (2007–10). This series was a highly colourful costume drama, based on the life and loves of Henry VIII.
10. *Ian Hislop's Stiff Upper Lip: An Emotional History of Britain* (BBC, 2012). The first episode of this series offered some engaging examples of commentaries on English culture by European travellers such as Erasmus, who remarked on the English propensity for kissing visitors at every available opportunity; see Erasmus, *Epistola* 65, translated in *Retrospective Review* 5, 251.
11. See above, n. 1.
12. All references to the *Oxford English Dictionary* are to the 2000 online edition.
13. In fact the current OED entry for emotion (3) is fascinatingly ambivalent about the development of the word to its current usage. The whole definition of Emotion (3a) reads: 'Originally: an agitation of mind; an excited mental state. Subsequently: any strong mental or instinctive feeling, as pleasure, grief, hope, fear etc., deriving esp. from one's circumstances, mood or relationship with others.' Its list of citations begins with the 1602 example I have quoted above, then ranges through ten more, ending with '1992 *More* 28 October – 64/2 Lust is a powerful emotion and can often be mistaken for love'. However, the historical moment where 'original' usage shifts to 'subsequent' is not pinpointed.
14. See Thomas Dixon, *From Passions to Emotions: The Creation of a Secular Psychological Category* (Cambridge, 2003) for an analysis of how 'over time, affective psychologies became gradually less theological and more philosophical, and ultimately more "scientific"' and how terminology shifted correspondingly (20–5 and *passim*). See the Introduction

to Gail Kern Paster, Katherine Rowe and Mary Floyd-Wilson (eds), *Reading the Early Modern Passions: Essays in the Cultural History of Emotion* (Philadelphia, 2004) for a useful summary and problematization of the historical usage of 'passion' and 'emotion' among other relevant terms (1–20, 2). For an account of challenges to universalist scientific approaches to the production and meaning of emotion, see Barbara H. Rosenwein, 'Problems and Methods in the History of Emotions', *Passions in Context, an International Journal for the History of the Emotions* 1 (2010). Available online at www.passionsincontext.de/uploads/media/01_Rosenwein.pdf (accessed 1 April 2012).

15. It is still a current enough tension for the novelist Ian McEwan wittily to summarize, for example. See *Solar* (London, 2011) 130–2.
16. Michael C. Schoenfeldt, *Bodies and Selves in Early Modern England* (Cambridge, 1999).
17. Paster *et al.* (in *Reading the Early Modern Passions*), have pointed out that 'we now tend to associate' both the terms passion and affection 'with amorous or fond feelings' (2). 'Emotional excess' could mean 'an excess of emotion' or 'an excess which is emotional', where 'passionate excess' may just mean 'an excess which is passionate' to the reader.
18. Dixon, *Passions*, 35–6.
19. See Konstantin Stanislavski 'Emotion Memory' in *An Actor's Work* trans. Jean Benedetti (Abingdon and New York, 2008) 195–228. Affective Memory, as Lee Strasberg named it, became one of the most significant techniques for what came to be called The Method in the USA. Strasberg developed this technique, from Stanislavski's practice, at the Actors' Studio. Later in Stanislavski's own career he developed the 'Method of Physical Action', a set of techniques created to aid the actor in producing plausible realist performance – including the performance of emotion – via simple but rigorous physical tasks rather than the recollection of strong feeling. See e.g. 'Creating the Physical Life of a Role' in *Creating a Role* trans. Elizabeth Hapgood (London 1981) 131–50.
20. See e.g. Stanslavski, *Creating a Role,* 'Creative Objectives', 51–62; Jean Benedetti *Stanislavski and the Actor* (New York, 1998).
21. Strier, *The Unrepentant Renaissance* (Chicago, 2011), 17–18, citing Michael Schoenfeldt, *Bodies and Selves in Early Modern England* (Cambridge, 1996), 15–16.
22. Jonathan Dollimore, *Radical Tragedy: Religion, Ideology and Power* (Basingstoke, 2004), 'Introduction to the Second Edition', l–li.
23. Eve Kosofsky Sedgwick,*Tendencies* (Durham, NC, 1993), 1–20, 8.
24. I refer here to Mark Breitenberg, *Anxious Masculinity in Early Modern England* (Cambridge, 1996), Ania Loomba, *Gender, Race, Renaissance*

*Drama* (Manchester, 1989), and Kenneth Gross, *Shakespeare's Noise* (Chicago, 2001), respectively.

25. In their paper 'Language at Work: The Periods of Shakespeare' at the International Shakespeare Congress (Stratford-upon-Avon, 2012), Jonathan Hope and Michael Witmore demonstrated the ways in which sophisticated electronic search engines might be used to study linguistic patterns in Shakespeare. In this case, they were demonstrating tools for exploring the development of Shakespeare's language across period and through genre.
26. Andrew Gurr, *The Shakespearean Stage 1574–1642* (3rd edn) (Cambridge, 1992), 215.
27. See Christie Carson, 'Democratizing the Audience?', in Christie Carson and Farah Karim-Cooper (eds), *Shakespeare's Globe: A Theatrical Experiment* (Cambridge, 2008), 115–126.
28. Ben Jonson, 'To the Memory of my Beloved, the Author, Mr William Shakespeare and What He Hath Left Us', in William Shakespeare, *Mr William Shakespeare's Comedies, Histories and Tragedies* (the First Folio) (London, 1623).
29. For example, in Gary Taylor, *Reinventing Shakespeare: A Cultural History from the Restoration to the Present* (London, 1990); Michael D. Bristol, *Big-Time Shakespeare* (London, 1996); Barbara Hodgdon, *The Shakespeare Trade: Performances and Appropriations* (Philadelphia, 1998); Graham Holderness, 'Shakespeare-Land', in Willy Maley and Margaret Tudeau-Clayton (eds), *This England, That Shakespeare: New Angles on England and the Bard* (Farnham and Burlington, VT, 2010).
30. In attempting this dialogue across histories and theatres, I hope I have heeded the warnings contained in W. B. Worthen's *Shakespeare and the Force of Modern Performance* (Cambridge, 2003), where he troubles any possibility of a directly reproductive relationship between historical play text and current – or any – performance.
31. Gail Kern Paster, *Humoring the Body: Emotions and the Shakespearean Stage* (Chicago and London, 2004).
32. Christian M. Billing's *Masculinity, Corporality and the English Stage, 1580–1635* has recently done significant work to challenge recent scholarly assumptions about the fluid, indeterminate nature of early modern concepts of gender (Farham, 2008).
33. Dixon, *Passions*, 3.
34. In René Descartes, *The Passions of the Soul*, trans. anon. (London, 1650).
35. Though in terms of gender, women are repeatedly figured as unable to control their passions and thus as less reasonable, less human, than men.

36. Plutarch, trans. Thomas North, 'Life of Caius Martius Coriolanus', in Bullough, *Narrative and Dramatic Sources of Shakespeare* 5, *The Roman Plays* (London and New York, 1957–75).
37. Plutarch, 'Of Meekness, or How a Man Should Refrain Choler', in *The Morals*, trans. Philomen Holland (London, 1603); Seneca, 'A Treatise of Anger', in *The Workes of Lucius Annaeus Seneca, Both Moral and Natural,* trans. Thomas Lodge (London, 1614).
38. *Coriolanus*, dir. Dominic Dromgoole, Shakespeare's Globe (London, 2006).
39. *Coriolanus* (film), dir. Ralph Fiennes Icon Entertainment International and BBC Films (2011).
40. *Coriolanus*, dir. Ivo van Hove, in *The Roman Tragedies* (*Romeinse Tragedies),* Toneelgroep Amsterdam (Barbican, London, 2009).
41. *Coriolan/Us*, William Shakespeare and Bertolt Brecht, dir. Mike Pearson and Mike Brookes, National Theatre Wales, RAF St Athan (Wales, 2012).
42. Helen Freshwater, *Theatre and Audiences* (Basingstoke, 2009). I refer to the work of Penelope Woods, 'Globe Audiences: Spectatorship and Reconstruction at Shakespeare's Globe' (Ph.D. thesis, Queen Mary University of London, 2011), Jan Wozniak's work on Shakespeare for young people and Christine Twite's on cultures of spectatorship in the work of the Actors Touring Company.
43. I use this term, which makes 'audience' an active verb, from Cultural and Media Studies, for the very reason that it does suggest that there is something active to be done, some work to undertake, as an audience for the theatre. See e.g. John Fisk, 'Audiencing: A Cultural Studies Approach to Watching Television', *Poetics*, 21.4 (August, 1992), 345–59; See Penelope Woods, 'Globe Audiences' for an analysis of the 'work' of the audience at Shakespeare's Globe, London.
44. Separated culturally and medically in the early modern period as those experiencing mental illnesses and those with intellectual disabilities are today (See p. 250n. 76).
45. Thomas Middleton and William Rowley, *The Changeling* (1622), New Mermaids edition (London, 2006).
46. John Webster, *The Duchess of Malfi* (1614), Arden Early Modern Drama (London, 2009).
47. Thomas Dekker and Thomas Middleton, *The Honest Whore Part 1* (1604), in Fredson Bowers ed., *The Dramatic Works of Thomas Dekker* (Cambridge, 1964).
48. Tim Crouch, *I Malvolio*, in *I, Shakespeare: Four of Shakespeare's Better Known Plays Retold for Young Audiences by their Lesser-Known Characters* (London, 2011).

49. See e.g. for madness as a metaphor for the state of being in love, Shakespeare, *Love's Labour's Lost* (1.4.1–19), *As You Like It* (3.2.396–412), and *Troilus and Cressida* (1.1.47–62), in which Troilus describes his love for Cressida in the most violent terms, and *Hamlet* (1.1.85), where Polonius assumes that Hamlet has been literally driven mad for his daughter's love.
50. Robert Burton, *The Anatomy of Melancholy* (London 1621), Thomas C. Faulkner, Nicholas K. Kiessling, and Rhonda L. Blair (eds) (Oxford, 1989); James Ferrand, *Erotomania or A treatise discoursing of the essence, causes, symptoms, prognostics, and cure of love, or erotic melancholy* (London, 1640).
51. For a summary of neurobiological research into the ways in which the increase of hormones associated with love also deactiviates the parts of the brain that make social judgements, an article which also draws on a range of philosophical and literary accounts of love, see S. Zeki, 'The Neurobiology of Love', Federation of European Biochemical Societies (2007), particularly 2576–7, '2. Cortical De-activations and the Madness of love'.
52. For an argument that it is not an 'emotion' *per se*, see my discussion of David Schalkwyk's article on the subject, (p. 113).
53. Fay Bound Alberti, *Matters of the Heart* (Oxford, 2010).
54. Eric Langley, *Narcissism and Suicide in Shakespeare and his Contemporaries* (Oxford, 2009); see also p. 125, this volume.
55. See e.g. Clare Gittings *Death, Burial and the Individual in Early Modern England* (London and Sydney, 1984) 14, 197.
56. *Richard III*, dir. Roxana Silbert, Royal Shakespeare Company (Swan Theatre, Stratford-upon-Avon, 2012).
57. *Hamlet*, dir. Nicholas Hytner, National Theatre, Olivier Theatre (2010).

## 1: 'A BRAIN THAT LEADS MY USE OF ANGER': CHOLER AND THE POLITICS OF SPATIAL PRODUCTION

1. Daniel M. Gross, *The Secret History of Emotion: From Aristotle's 'Rhetoric' to Modern Brain Science* (Chicago, 2006).
2. Gross, *The Secret History*, 5.
3. Gross, *The Secret History*, 3.
4. Gross, *The Secret History*, 2.
5. William Shakespeare, *Coriolanus*, dir. Yukio Ninagawa, Ninagawa Company (Barbican, London, 2007).
6. Yukio Ninagawa, interviewed by Rachel Halliburton, *Time Out*, 16

April 2007. Availaibe at http://www.timeout.com/london/theatre/features/2809/Yukio_Ninagawa-interview.html (accessed 20 November 2012).

7. Nancy Sherman, 'Stoic Meditations and the Shaping of Character. The Case of Educating the Military', in David Carr and John Haldane (eds), *Spirituality, Philosophy and Education* (London, 2003), 68.
8. William Fulbecke, *A Direction or Preparative to the Study of the Law* (London, 1600), 16.
9. Seneca, 'A Treatise of Anger', in *The Workes of Lucius Annaeus Seneca, Both Moral and Natural,* trans. Thomas Lodge (London, 1614), Book 1, ch. 9, 516.
10. Seneca, 'A Treatise of Anger, Book 1, ch. 5, 514.
11. In *Shakespeare and the Constant Romans* (Oxford, 1996) Geoffrey Miles reads a critique of North's Plutarch and the notion of Roman constancy in Shakespeare's portrayal of Coriolanus, which 'explicitly links Coriolanus' stubbornness with the Stoic virtue of constancy [...]. He [Shakespeare] thus suggests an analogy which Plutarch would not have accepted. Coriolanus' stubbornness is not merely a fault in a bull-like character untempered by moral training; it is a moral ideal consciously followed in the belief that to be immovable and unyielding is "a token of magnanimitie" – a belief in which he is supported, up to a point by his society. If we see in him an absurd and self-destructive rigidity and pride, then that judgment (Shakespeare implies) reflects upon the noble Brutus and upon Roman virtue in general' (121).
12. Particularly virtuosic by British standards, Ninagawa suggests in his interview with Halliburton: 'With a glint in his eye, Ninagawa adds "He [Toshiaki Karasawa]'s also very good at sword-fighting. British actors don't do sword-fighting very often do they?"' (Ninagawa, *Time Out*).
13. Lyn Gardner, Review of *Coriolanus*, dir. Yukio Ninagawa, *Guardian,* 27 April 2007.
14. Howard Loxton, Review of *Coriolanus*, dir. Yukio Ninagawa. Available at http://www.britishtheatreguide.info/reviews/coriolanusnina-rev (accessed 12 December 2012).
15. For a brief and clear explanation of Galenic humoral theory and the basis of the belief that those of a choleric temperament should not eat burnt meat, see Melina Spencer Kingsbury, 'Kate's Froward Humour: Historicizing Affect in *The Taming of the Shrew*', *South Atlantic Modern Language Association* 69. 1 (winter 2004), 61–84 (65, 75).
16. For example, the RSC's production of 2008, dir. Connall Morrison, (Swan Theatre, Stratford-upon-Avon), and Propeller's all-male production, in which Kate is brutally treated throughout the 'taming': dir. Edward Hall, Old Vic (London, 2007).

17. For a wide-ranging list of twentieth-century performance choices for this moment, see Elizabeth Schafer ed., commentary on William Shakespeare, *The Taming of the Shrew, Shakespeare in Production* series (Cambridge, 2002), 230–231.
18. Bruce Smith, *Shakespeare and Masculinity* (Oxford, 2000), 1–2.
19. Seneca, 'A Treatise of Anger', Book 1, ch. 1, 510.
20. Nicholas Coeffeteau, *A Table of the Human Passions*, trans. Edward Grimeston (London, 1621), 598.
21. Plutarch, 'Of Meekness, or How a Man Should Refrain Choler', in *The Morals*, trans. Philomen Holland (London, 1603).
22. Plutarch, 'Of Meekness', 122.
23. Seneca, 'A Treatise of Anger', Book 1, ch. 7, 516.
24. Seneca, 'A Treatise of Anger', Book 2, ch. 3, 529.
25. Coeffeteau, *A Table* 608–69.
26. Michel de Montaigne, 'Of Anger and Choler', in *Essays*, trans. John Florio (London, 1613), 403.
27. Plutarch, 'Of Meekness', 123
28. Plutarch, 'Of Meekness', 123, and throughout, where Plutarch refers to choler as, and compares it to, a malady and a sickness.
29. Gross, *A Secret History*, 1.
30. Gross, *A Secret History*, 2.
31. Thomas Wright, *The Passions of the Mind in General* (London, 1604), 278.
32. Coeffeteau, *A Table*, 560.
33. Ibid., 569–70.
34. Ibid., 589.
35. Ibid., 570.
36. Ibid., 579.
37. Ibid., 579.
38. Seneca, 'A Treatise of Anger', Book 1, ch. 3, 512.
39. Coeffeteau, *A Table*, 620–621; see also Plutarch, 'Of Meekness', 121.
40. For a lucid account of 'The Stoic Montaigne' and his later repudiation of stoicism, see Geoffrey Miles, *Shakespeare and the Constant Romans* (Oxford, 1996), 86–109.
41. see pp. 10–11; Plutarch, 'Of Meekness', 122. Cf. Seneca, who likens the physiological manifestations of anger to those of the madman:

    Some therefore of the wiser sort have said that anger is a short madness, for she is as little Mistress of herself as the other [...]. And to the end thou mayest know that they who are surprised with anger are truly mad, consider a little their countenance, and the manner of their behaviour. For even as there are certain signs of confirmed madness, to have a bold

> and threatening countenance, a heavy brow, and dreadful face, a swift and disordered gate, unquiet hands, changed colour, and frequent and deep sighs: so those that are angry have the same signs. Their eyes sparkle and shine, their face is on fire through a reflux of blood that boileth up from the bottom of their breasts, their lips quiver, their teeth grate, their hair startleth and standeth upright, their breath is enforced and wheezeth, they wrest and crack their fingers, their speech is interrupted with plaints and groans and muttering, which a man may hardly understand.
>
> ('A Treatise on Anger', 510–11)

Nicholas Coffeteau's treatise on the passions seems to draw upon Seneca's outright condemnation of the passion as a near madness, likening it to a 'frenzy', and, as Seneca does, suggesting that the 'natural' constitution of man is distorted by it. He writes:

> of all the Passions of man, there is not any one more pernicious, no more dreadful than choler, which alters the graceful countenance and the whole constitution of men. For as furious and mad men show the excess of their rage, by the violent changes which appear in their bodies, even so a man transported with choler gives great signs of the frenzy that does afflict him: his eyes full of fire and flame.
>
> (*A Table*, 601–2)

42. Montaigne, 'Of Anger and Choler', 402.
43. Ibid.
44. Ibid.
45. Plutarch, 'The Life of Caius Martius Coriolanus', in *Lives of the Ancient Greeks and Romans*, trans. Thomas North, in Geoffrey Bullough ed., *Narrative and Dramatic Sources of Shakespeare 5, The Roman Plays* (London and New York, 1964).
46. M. W. McCullum in *Shakespeare's Roman Plays and their Background* (1967) thinks *Antony and Cleopatra* was influenced by the *Iris and Osiris* narrative from the Holland/Plutarch *Moralia* but does not touch upon the *Anger* essay.
47. Plutarch, 'Of Meekness', 118.
48. Ibid., 122.
49. Ibid., 125.
50. Ibid., 124.
51. Plutarch, 'Life of Caius Martius Coriolanus', 544.
51. Ibid., 125.
52. Robin Headlam Wells, *Shakespeare on Masculinity* (Cambridge and New York, 2000), 144.

53. Plutarch, 'Life of Caius Martius Coriolanus', 526.
54. Ibid.
55. Jonathan Cake in Guillaume Winter, 'An Interview with Jonathan Cake, Starring as Coriolanus at Shakespeare's Globe Theatre in 2006', in Delphine Lemmonier-Texier and Guillaume Winter (eds), *Lectures de Coriolan de William Shakespeare* (Rennes, 2006), 179.
56. Bridget Escolme, *Talking to the Audience: Shakespeare, Performance, Self* (London, 2005).
57. Plutarch, 'Life of Caius Martius Coriolanus', 505.
58. Ibid., 505–6.
59. Ibid., 506.
60. Ibid., 519.
61. Cake in Winter, 'Interview', 176.
62. Much has been made of Coriolanus' lack of subjectivity; see Peter F. Neumeyer, 'Not Local Habitation nor a Name: *Coriolanus*', *University Review* 32 (1966), 195–8; Constance C. Relihan, 'Appropriation of "The Thing of Blood": Absence of Self and the Struggle for Ownership in *Coriolanus*', *Iowa State Journal of Research* 62 (1988), 407–20.
63. Cake in Winter, 'Interview, 179.
64. Ibid.
65. Ibid., 180.
66. For Michael Billington, 'Initially [...], Cake seems less lonely monster than arrogant captain of the first 11. When he comes into his own is in his crumbling, little-boy-lost deference to Volumnia' ('*Coriolanus*: Shakespeare's Globe', *Guardian*, 12 May 2006). For Christopher Hart in *The Sunday Times* (14 May 2006), 'Coriolanus seems too much the cheerful, rugby-playing lad, Cake the beefcake'; Kate Bassett's *Independent on Sunday* review, *The Hotspur of Ancient Rome* (14 May 2006), makes explicit the class connotations of the rugby link: 'He races from one battle to the next...like a young sporting Henry VIII or a public school rugger champ. This Coriolanus has an almost ridiculously posh accent combined with a potentially thuggish physique, yet manages to be remarkably likeable, giving his loyal friends bearhugs', as does Paul Taylor in the *Independent* (11 May 2006), for whom Cake resembled 'a posh rugger bugger with his broken-nose profile and sounding like a clipped public-school toff'.
67. Quentin Letts, Review of *Coriolanus*, dir. Dominic Dromgoole, Shakespeare's Globe 2006, *Daily Mail* 12 March 2006.
68. For a lively account of the English public school system and its original political and cultural purposes, see Nick Duffell, *The Making Of Them: The British Attitude to Children and the Boarding School System* (London, 2000). Duffell explains that the fee-paying boarding-schools

that flourished in mid-nineteenth century England 'were the production centres for gentlemen destined and designed to run the new superpower, to export British values of civilization and justice to the world, while she imported cheap goods. Britain needed to equip herself with an unfailing supply of gentleman-leaders to run her Empire. They were required to set standards in moral behaviour for the rest of the world.... These gents needed to have a uniform code of values and to be tough enough to withstand discomfort, deprivation and conditions abroad. They were to be nominally Christian, unquestioningly loyal to Queen and country, well-educated but not so bright that they might question the rights and wrongs of the tasks they were set' (113). While their colonialist purpose no longer exists, and many of the schools have changed radically in outlook over 150 years, it is interesting that this 'type' still seemed instantly recognizable to the reviewers of the Globe's *Coriolanus*.

The use of sport to develop the patriotism, stoicism and 'team spirit' valued by the English public school is eulogized in Henry Newbolt's poem *Vitaï Lampada* (1892), in which those surrounded by the dying on the battlefield are heartened by the memory – or perhaps even the actual sound – of their old school cricket captain shouting 'Play up! Play up! And Play the game!' Cake is rather more of the stature associated with Rugby than cricket, as the reviewers repeatedly remark, but the association between war and the private school playing field is the same.

69. See, e.g. James Lee Calderwood, *Shakespeare and the Denial of Death* (Amherst, MA, 1987), 39; Cynthia Marshall, 'Shakespeare, Crossing the Rubicon', *Shakespeare Survey* 53 (2000), 83; entry for Volumnia in Alison Findlay, *Women in Shakespeare: A Dictionary* (London, 2010), 422.
70. *Pride and Prejudice*, dir. Joe Langton, adapted by Andrew Davies from the novel by Jane Austen (BBC, 1995).
71. For an an analysis of the concept of 'spin' and the publicly perceived untrustworthiness of UK politicians, see Kevin Maloney, 'The Rise and Fall of Spin: Changes of Fashion in the Presentation of UK Politics', *Journal of Public Affairs* 1.2 (May 2001), 124–135; for an analysis of the ways in which media coverage of the UK 2005 general election, the one before this production of *Coriolanus*, helped to generate the trope of untrustworthy politician and trustworthy expert, see Michael Billig, 'Politics as an Appearance and Reality Show: The Results of the Analysis of Qualitative Aspects of Coverage', in Deacon *et al.*, *Reporting the UK 2005 General Election* (Loughborough University Institutional Repository), 44–59. Lack of trust in politicians was widely seen to have been exacerbated by Tony Blair's involvement of the UK

in the war with Iraq in 2003 and the subsequent failure to discover the 'weapons of mass destruction' that Western citizens had been assured had been hidden by Saddam Hussein. See e.g. Martin Kettle, http://www.guardian.co.uk/commentisfree/2006/dec/30/comment.voterapathy (accessed 20 November 2012). Kettle argues that lack of trust in politicians is a much earlier British phenomenon but affirms the link in common perception.

72. Benedict Nightingale, review of *Coriolanus*, dir. Dominic Dromgoole, Shakespeare's Globe, London (12 May 2006).
73. Cake in Winter, 'Interview', 173–4.
74. Ibid., 174.
75. When they declared to the on-stage Citizens that they were 'at point to lose [their] "liberties" ', the Citizens were blocked close to the *frons scenae*, so that there was no opportunity for Sicinius and Brutus to include the audience in their warning against Martius. After a hugely enjoyable version of 3.2, in which Cominius and Volumnia try to persuade Martius that they can 'prompt' him in playing the conciliatory role he finally rejects outright, a round of applause occured in a number of performances at the absurd lack of mildness with which Martius speaks the last words 'mildly, be it then. Mildly!' (3.2.145). Sicinius and Brutus cut off the applause and the audience's enjoyment of the scene with their machinations. In 3.3, when Martius addresses the paying audience in the theatre and the fictional Citizens on the walkways and in the yard with 'What is the matter/That, being passed for consul with full voice,/, I am so dishonoured that the very hour/You take it off again?' (3.3.57–60), Sicinius blocked him from the greater part of the playgoers, standing between him and the audience to demand that he 'answer to us' (3.3.61). The move was made warily, as if Sicinius knew that Martius had our sympathies. Cake, as an actor, appeared to answer to us, the audience.
76. Peter Holland, '*Coriolanus* and the Remains of Excess', in Pierre Kapitaniak and Jean-Michel Déprats (eds), *Shakespeare et L'Excès: Actes du Congrès de la Société Francaise Shakespeare* (2007). Available at http://www.societefrancaiseshakespeare.org/document.php?id=1030 (accessed 18 November 2012).
77. Stephen Greenblatt, 'A Man of Principle', review of *Coriolanus*, dir. Ralph Fiennes, *New York Review of Books* (8 April 2012).
78. Slavov Žižek, 'Sing of the New Invasion', preview of *Coriolanus*, dir. Ralph Fiennes, *New Statesman* (12 December 2011).
79. Andreas Wiseman, 'Ralph Fiennes Blog: Coriolanus' Locations —Why Serbia?' Available at http://30ninjas.com/blog/ralph-fiennes-blog-coriolanus-locations-why-serbia (accessed 19 November 2012).

80. Ralph Fiennes, audio commentary to DVD release of *Coriolanus*, dir. Ralph Fiennes (2012).
81. A title early in the film, referencing John Osbourne's 1973 adaptation of *Coriolanus*.
82. Pearson et al., *Brith Gof: y llyfr glas: 1988–1995* (Cardiff, 1995), 51.
83. Greenblatt, 'A Man of Principle'.
84. For an alternative reading of Martius as a figure who excludes the audience, which better fits Fienne's psychologically unreadable Martius than Greenblatt's demand that the actor reveal the figure psychologically, see Janet Adelman's seminal *Suffocating Mothers: Fantasies of Maternal Origin in Shakespeare's Plays* (New York and Abingdon, 1992), ch. 6, 'Escaping the Matrix: The Construction of Masculinity in Coriolanus', 130–64, 163–4.
85. Greenblatt, 'A Man of Principle'.
86. Ralph Fiennes, audio commentary to DVD of *Coriolanus*, dir. Ralph Fiennes (2012).
87. Fiennes, in Wiseman, 'Ralph Fiennes Blog'.
88. Greenblatt reads this as a replacement for Martius' request to Cominius to spare the man who shelters him in Corioles and whose name he forgets; this reading is confirmed as intentional by Fiennes in the audio commentary available on the DVD rehease.
89. See also Bridget Escolme, 'Spatial Politics in Shakespeare's Rome.', *Shakespeare Survey 60* (2007), 170–83.
90. Slavov Žižek, 'Signs of the New Invasion'.
91. Rancière writes: 'The distribution of the sensible reveals who can have a share in what is common to the community based on what they do and on the time and space in which this activity is performed. Having a particular "occupation" thereby determines the ability or inability to take charge of what is common to the community; it defines what is visible or not in a common space, endowed with a common language, etc. […] Politics revolves around what is seen and what can be said about it, around who has the ability to see and the talent to speak, around the properties of spaces and the possibilities of time' (13). The cleaner has an occupation that banishes him to the non-space of the corridor while political power is being performed in the Senate; Fiennes' Martius places himself there too and they have a moment of eye contact that suggests that neither knows how to 'see' the other. Jacques Rancière, 'The Distribution of the Sensible: Politics and Aesthetics', in *The Politics of Aesthetics*, trans. Gabriel Rockhill (London, 2004).
92. Christian Billing, review of *The Roman Tragedies*, dir. Ivo van Hove, Toneelgroep Amsterdam (Barbican Theatre, 2009). *Shakespeare Quarterly* 61.3 (2010), 415–39. Also in *Shakespeare Quarterly*,

'Open Review: Shakespeare and New Media'. Available at http://mediacommons.futureofthebook.org/mcpress/ShakespeareQuarterly_NewMedia/shakespeare-performed/billing-the-roman-tragedies/ (accessed 1 December 2012).

93. In 2009, the British newspaper the *Daily Telegraph* published details of the expenses claims of British Members of Parliament, revealing a range of alleged misuses of their allowances and expenses system. Some of the allegations resulted in resignations and criminal convictions. The *Telegraph* story broke in May 2009 and van Hove's *Roman Tragedies* played at the Barbican in November of that year.
94. Michel de Certeau, 'Walking in the City', in Imre Szeman and Timothy Kaposy, *Cultural Anthropology: an Anthology* (Oxford, 2011), 264.
95. See also Bridget Escolme, 'Shakespeare, Rehearsal and the Site-Specific', *Shakespeare Bulletin* 30.4 (winter 2012), 505–22.
96. See Escolme, 'Living Monuments: The Spatial Politics of Shakespeare's Rome on the Contemporary Stage', *Shakespeare Survey* 60 (2007), 170–83.
97. See Mike Pearson and Michael Shanks, *Theatre/Archaeology* (London, 2001), 109, 117.
98. Bertolt Brecht, *Coriolanus*, trans. Ralph Manheim, in Ralph Manheim and John Willetts (eds), *Bertholt Brecht Collected Plays 9* (London, 1972).
99. Sarah Hemming, review of *Coriolan/US*, dir. Mike Brookes and Mike Pearson (National Theatre Wales at MOD St Athan), *Financial Times*, 12 August 2012.
100. There are a number of examples from recent productions of audience members in *Coriolanus* being called upon to join the Citizens. Michael Coveney, writing of the National Theatre's *Coriolanus* in 1984, enjoyed this casting of the audience: "A circular sandpit yields to structural hints of a Roman amphitheatre onstage populated by 90 paying customers who bolster the crowd, applaud the processional arrivals of Coriolanus and his mother, and are generally, rather excitingly, part of the action' (*Financial Times*, 17 December 1984), while others found the recalcitrant presence of non-actors somewhat embarrassing: Peter Holland describes them as 'sheepish' (Peter Holland, *English Shakespeares: Shakespeare on the English Stage in the 1990s* (Cambridge, 1997), 137) and his reaction recalls my own experience of this production. Holland suggests that Tim Supple's use of a rehearsed group of local amateur actors for his production at the Chichester Festival theatre in 1992 was more engaging: 'There was an exciting tension between the sense of the operatic chorus under directorial control and the realism of these people, their lack of professional skills producing an unactorish normality on stage; as soldiers, the men looked like a conscript army,

tall and short, overweight and thin, but their sheer weight of numbers had its own exhilaration' (137–8).

## 2: 'DO YOU MOCK OLD AGE, YOU ROGUES?' EXCESSIVE LAUGHTER, CRUELTY AND COMPASSION

1. Robert R. Provine, *Laughter: A Scientific Investigation* (London, 2004).
2. See http://www.peoplespalaceprojects.org.uk (accessed 2.7.2013).
3. The Universidade das Quebradas (University of the Broken) is an initiative set up by Brazil's Programa Avançado de Cultura Contemporânea (PACC), an organization dedicated to researching issues raised by the relationship between culture and development. It aims to promote knowledge production and artistic creation, stimulated by the encounter and dialogue between the academic community and cultural producers and artists from the periphery. See http://www.pacc.ufrj.br/universidade-das-quebradas/ (accessed 2.7.2013)
4. See Bridget Escolme, *Talking to the Audience: Shakespeare, Performance, Self* (London, 2005).
5. See Robert Darnton, *The Great Cat Massacre and Other Episodes in French Cultural History* (New York, 1985), ch. 2, 'Worker Revolt: The Great Cat Massacre of the Rue Saint Séverin', 75–106.
6. Bridget Escolme, 'Does Shakespeare Work Better Outside Britain?' Available at http://www.guardian.co.uk/commentisfree/2012/may/19/shakespeare-outside-britain-international (accessed 23 October 2012).
7. A sophisticated argument to this effect may, however, be found in Donna M. Goldstein, *Laughter Out of Place: Race, Class, Violence, and Sexuality in a Rio Shantytown* (Berkeley and Los Angeles, 2003).
8. Albrecht Classen, Introduction to Classen ed., *Laughter in the Middle Ages and Early Modern Times: Epistemology of a Fundamental Human Behavior, its Meaning and Consequences* (Berlin and New York, 2010), 3.
9. Provine, *Laughter*, 216.
10. See, as an example of where one might level such an accusation, Alan S. Miller and Satoshi Kanazawa, *Why Beautiful People Have More Daughters: From Dating, Shopping and Praying to Going to War and Becoming a Billionaire* (London, 2007), and the review of this work, 'Ten Politically Incorrect Truths about Human Nature'. Available at www.psychologytoday.com/articles/200706/ten-politically-correct-truths-about-human-nature (accessed 2.7.2013). I should add that I am not contending the scientific findings of works such as this so much as their implication that evolutionary biology makes particular gendered behaviours and hierarchies inevitable.

11. Philip Sidney, *An Apology for Poetry (or The Defense of Poesie)* (*c.*1579) (Manchester, 2002), 98.
12. Sidney, *Apology*, 112.
13. Ibid., 112–13.
14. Ibid., 113.
15. Laurent Joubert, *Treatise on Laughter* (*Traité du Ris*), trans. Gregory David de Rocher (Tuscaloosa, AL, 1980) 20. Joubert's French translation from the 1560 Latin edition of the Treatise was published in 1579.
16. Joubert, *Laughter*, 20
17. Jonas Barish's account of early modern Puritan anti-theatricality is still a useful one: see ch. 4, 'Puritans and Proteans', in *The Anti-Theatrical Prejudice* (Berkeley and Los Angeles, 1981), 80–131.
18. Indira Ghose, *Shakespeare and Laughter: A Cultural History* (Manchester, 2008).
19. Ghose opens her study of 'licensed laughter' in *Twelfth Night* with a historicization of the 'tradition of linking laughter to aggression, scorn and hostility that runs from Plato and Aristotle to the Judeo-Christian schools of thought', a strand which she argues culminates in Hobbes' theory of laughter emerging from a sense of superiority to the object of laughter (35). Although she states that a 'counter movement' to this attitude to laughter, in which philosophers defend it as 'joyous celebration and relief from tension' does not emerge in philosophy until the late seventeenth and eighteenth centuries (35), she suggests that 'as with most theories about laughter, one finds that they work and don't quite work at the same time' (35). Indira Ghose, 'Licence to Laugh: Festive Laughter in Twelfth Night', in Manfred Pfister ed., *A History of English Laughter: Laughter from Beowulf to Beckett and Beyond* (Amersterdam and New York, 2002), 35–46.
20. Ghose, *Laughter*, 108.
21. Ibid., 110.
22. What both my and Ghose's argument fail to take into account is possible female participation in cuckold jokes, tricks and rituals in early modern culture. See Pamela Allen Brown, *Better a Shrew than a Sheep: Women, Drama and the Culture of Jest in Early Modern England* (London and Ithaca, NY, 2003), ch. 3, 'Between Women, or All is Fair at Horn Fair' (83–117) for an account of women's performances of cuckold jests and the appeal to women of cuckold jokes in drama and other early modern writings.
23. Jaak Panksepp, 'The Riddle of Laughter: Neural and Psychoevolutionary Underpinnings of Joy', *Current Directions in Psychological Science*, 19, 6 (December 2000), 183.
24. Panksepp, 'The Riddle of Laughter', 183

25. Ibid., 184; see also J. Panksepp and J. Burgdorf, 'Laughing Rats? Playful Tickling Arouses High-frequency Ultrasonic Chirping in Young Rodents', in S. Hameroff, D. Chalmers and A. Kazniak (eds), *Towards a Science of Consciousness,* (Cambridge, MA, 1999) 231–44.
26. Joubert, *Laughter*, 81
27. Ibid., 94–5.
28. See also Provine, 1999.
29. Joubert, *Laughter*, 126.
30. Ibid., 103–4.
31. Matthew Gervais and David Sloan Wilson, 'The Evolutionary Functions of Laughter and Humor: A Synthetic Approach', *The Quarterly Review of Biology* 80.4 (December 2005).
32. Joubert, *Laughter*, 25.
33. Ibid., 21.
34. Ibid., 23.
35. Carol Neely, *Distracted Subjects.* See also pp. 00–00 (this volume).
36. Panksepp, 'The Riddle of Laughter', 184.
37. Joubert, *Laughter*, 22.
38. Panksepp, 'The Riddle of Laughter', 185.
39. Ghose, *Laughter*, 185
40. Panksepp, 'The Riddle of Laughter', 185.
41. Indeed, a wide range of recent evolutionary biological studies of laughter suggest that its function is primarily one of social bonding: a form of grooming for larger social groups, see R. I. M. Dunbar, 'Bridging the Bonding Gap: The Transition from Primates to Humans', *Philosophical Transactions of the Royal Society* (July 2012), 367, 1597, 1837–46; Pedro C. Marijuán and Jorge Navarro, 'The Bonds of Laughter: A Multidisciplinary Inquiry into the Information Processes of Human Laughter', Bioinformation and Systems Biology Group Instituto Aragonés de Ciencias de la Salud. Available at http://arxiv.org/abs/1010.5602 (accessed 27 November 2012); Guillaume Dezecache and R. I. M. Dunbar, 'Sharing the Joke: The Size of Natural Laughter Groups'. Availbale at www.grezes.ens.fr/reprints/dezecache&dunbar2012.pdf (accessed 28 November 2012); and a means of connecting individuals within groups, which 'increases social bonding and cooperation between strangers', and 'improves group functioning by increasing altruistic group contributions' Mark van Vugt, Charlie Hardy, Julie Stow and Robin Dunbar, 'Laughter as Social Lubricant: A Biosocial Hypothesis about the Pro-social Functions of Laughter and Humor'. Available at www.professormarkvanvugt.com/files/LaughterasSocialLubricant.pdf (accessed 20 November 2012), (12–17).

42. Jeremy Lopez, *Theatrical Convention and Audience Response in Early Modern Drama* (Cambridge and New York, 2003), 170.
43. Joubert, *Laughter*, 20.
44. Carol Neely, *Distracted Subjects*, 50.
45. As Kaara L. Petersen succinctly puts it in 'Performing Arts: Hysterical Disease, Exorcism, and Shakespeare's Theatre', in Stephanie Moss and Kaara L. Petersen, *Disease, Diagnosis and Cure on the Early Modern Stage* (Aldershot, 2004) 3–28, 'residual beliefs of any kind are slow to alter and culture is simply not always in agreement with itself over what it perceives' (22); thus so while Poor Tom quotes the invented names of demons from Harsnett's *Declaration of Egregious Popish Impostures* (London, 1603), it is difficult to know how ridiculous or how terrifying Edgar's evocations may have seemed to early modern audiences.
46. Joubert, *Laughter*, 21.
47. The Q1 stage direction for her first entrance in 4.5 is *Enter Ofelia playing on a Lute, and her hair down singing*. Queen Elizabeth in *Richard III* enters after the death of her husband 'with her hair about her ears'; rejected by Iarbus, Anna, sister to Dido Queen of Carthage, threatens to 'follow thee with outcries. [...] And strew thy walks with my dishevelled hair' (Marlowe, *Dido Queen of Carthage*, 4.2.).
48. Sidney, *Apology*, 113.
49. 'Fate' is cruel to Bardolph in *Henry V* (3.6.25); 'War' in the Prologue to *Troilus and Cressida*; 'Death' doubly cruel to Paris when he finds what he believes to be Juliet's dead body (*Romeo and Juliet* 4.5.56–7); 'Religious canons, civil laws' are cruel to *Timon of Athens*, (4.3.61).
50. http://www.shakespearesglobe.com/theatre/on-stage (accessed 9 February 2012).
51. http://www.clink.co.uk/Education.html (accessed 6 June 2010).
52. http://www.the-dungeons.co.uk/london/en/attractions/index.htm (accessed 6 June 2010).
53. http://www.the-dungeons.co.uk/london/en/attractions/index.htm (accessed 6 June 2010).
54. Torture exhibits are currently a popular museum attraction. There are torture museums, for example, in Prague, Vienna, San Gimignano (Italy) and in several towns in Germany. They commonly present the past as a generalized site of cruelty and corrupted power. The Torture Museum of Amsterdam's website is under development at the time of writing and presumably its 'History' section will eventually tell potential visitors to which period it refers when, in its 'instruments of torture: masks' section it explains that 'Particularly in times of turmoil, restriction of free speech was a normal police duty, the mouths of those who insulted the royal house or uttered blasphemous words

were literally stopped with iron gags.' Available www.torturemuseum.com (accessed 27 October 2012). The text on this site has a historically analytical bent and its images are all from primary sources; it currently offers no sense of specific historical period but rather a dark sense of the past as a site of torture. When a San Francisco museum borrowed exhibits from the Italian collection, it clearly wanted to demonstrate that its intentions were not sensationalist or prurient: 'Shown in many historical and prestigious venues all over Europe, in Tokyo, in Argentina and Mexico, the exhibit has always raised the interest of millions of visitors and the press, not only for its great visual impact, but also for its clear message against the violation of human rights'. Available http://www.torturamuseum.com/this.html (accessed 9 February 2012). The fact that a 'clear message' needs spelling out suggests anxieties around why a public may be interested in visiting such museums; I am not suggesting that they celebrate or glamorize violence so much as offer the violence of the past in such a way as to sanitize the present. As one blogger on a tourist review site comments: 'I'm not sure if I just started to notice this, but it seems that now more and more European cities are opening their own version of a medieval torture museum. Maybe coming clean about their own pasts? Perhaps letting people realize just how lucky they are not to be living in such a time? Cashing in perhaps.....or a bit of all of the above.' http://www.virtualtourist.com/travel/Europe/Czech_Republic/Hlavni_Mesto_Praha/Prague-400455/Things_To_Do-Prague-Torture_Museum-BR-1.html (accessed 27 October 2012).

55. Carol Neely writes that the analogy between early modern Bedlam and theatrical spectacle 'is firmly cemented in the twentieth century in two studies – Edward O'Donoghue's *Story of Bethlem Hospital* (1915) and Robert Reed's *Bedlam on the Jacobean Stage* (1952) – and it has stuck' (Neely, *Distracted Subjects*, 206); the connection continues to be assumed by Michael MacDonald in *Mystical Bedlam: Madness, Anxiety and Healing in Seventeenth Century England* (Cambridge, 1981) and Roy Porter in *Mind Forg'd Manacles: A History of Madness in England from the Restoration to the Regency* (London, 1990) (cited in Neely, *Distracted Subjects*, 208). 'Even *The History of Bedlam*' (by Jonathan Andrews *et al.*), writes Neely, 'committed to exposing 'pseudo-facts about the hospital and to separating the state of "Bedlam" from the institution, Bethlem, cannot completely abandon the analogy between the theatre's and the hospital's spectacle and the visitors who underwrite it' (209). Andrews, one of the scholars cited by Neely as perpetuating the myth of a theatrical show at Bethlem – and who indeed insists that the Percy story is 'the first undoubted reference to a real-life visit to "the shew

of Bethlem"' – also propounds another theory of Jacobean theatrical interest in madhouse scenes: the proximity of two early modern theatres to the hospital, the fact that Edward Alleyn's father was its keeper and that the family remained in the parish following his resignation, and the fact that Ben Jonson was a St Botolph's parishioner too: 'It is quite possible, therefore, that Alleyn's and Jonson's circles had a considerably greater acquaintance with Bethlem than most Londoners and visitors to the city' (Andrews *et al.*, *The History of Bedlam* (London 1997), 133).

56. Neely, *Distracted Subjects*, 185–6.
57. *Ibid.*, 202–3.
58. Neely, *Distracted Subjects*, 200, drawing on Jonathan Andrews, 'Bethlem Revisited: A History of Bethlem Hospital *c.* 1643–1770', Ph.D. Diss. (University of London, 1991), 11–133.
    In *Separate Theaters, Bethlem ('Bedlam') Hospital and the Shakespearean Stage* (Newark, NJ, 2005) (see esp. 156–5), Ken Jackson's argument about Bethlem, charity and poor relief supports Neely to a degree; he suggests that there was a 'show at Bedlam' whose first purposes were primarily charitable – but he argues that this became recreation or entertainment 'at precisely the historical moment when new theatrical categories, Shakespeare and Jonson's modern representational stage, became visible' (165). He cites in support of this history the changing registration of names at the hospital – from proper names in the 1598 census of Bethlem, to 'more theatrical monikers' such as '"Black Will, Welsh Harry, Old Madam, Joan of the Hospital"' in the 1607 census (Jackson, 165, citing Patricia Allderidge, 'Management and Mismanagement at Bedlam, 1547–1633', in Charles Webster ed., *Health, Medicine and Mortality in the Sixteenth Century* (Cambridge,1979), 141–64).
59. Neely, 'The Purposes of Confinement at Bethlem Hospital', *Distracted Subjects*, 169–84.
60. Neely, *Distracted Subjects*, 203.
61. Ibid., 184–98.
62. Ibid., 203.
63. Ibid., 1.
64. Ibid., 188.
65. Leah Marcus, Appendix 3 to *The Duchess of Malfi, Arden Early Modern Drama* (London, 2009), 403.
66. *The Duchess of Malfi* was a King's Men play, first performed c.1613, when the company owned both the Globe and the Blackfriars.
67. Brooke argues that in reading and watching Jacobean tragedies, 'we still suffer from the inhibiting effects of a tradition that goes back at least

to French classicism in the seventeenth century, requiring [tragedy and laughter's] absolute separation' (3) and that while Shakespeare's tragic endings seem to conclude in the 'unalloyed emotional satisfaction' of solemnity or tears (4), the plays of Tourneur, Webster, Middleton, Rowley and Ford which he explores 'end, again and again, with the grandeur and grotesquerie similarly perceived, tears and laughter equally projected' (9). Nicholas Brooke, *Horrid Laughter in Jacobean Tragedy* (London, 1979).

68. Matthew Steggle, in *Laughing and Weeping in the Early Modern Theatres* (Aldershot, 2007), does offer the multiply authored *Lust's Dominion* as evidence for audience laughter at non-comical moments in tragedy and suggests that this play opens other tragedies to readings 'not just to the implicit cues of audience laughter, but to the representation of stage weeping and laughter' (123).
69. Brooke, *Horrid Laughter*, 56.
70. Ibid., 57.
71. *The Duchess of Malfi*, dir. Jamie Lloyd (Old Vic Theatre, London, 2012).
72. Kim Solga, *Violence Against Women in Early Modern Performance. Invisible Acts* (Basingstoke, 2009), 133 on *The Duchess of Malfi*, dir. Phyllida Lloyd (National Theatre, 2003).
73. *The Duchess of Malfi*, dir. Gayle Edwards (Royal Shakespeare Company, 2001).
74. *Ten Thousand Several Doors, The Duchess of Malfi*, dir. Jane Collins and Peter Farley Prodigal Theatre, The Nightingale (Brighton, 2006).
75. The madmen in 1.2 shout about bread, cheese and onions; one madman calls a cat a whore, seemingly for failing to save his cheese (1.2.195–202).
76. In English law, 'natural fools' or 'idiots' – those with congenital intellectual disabilities – and persons '*non compos mentis*' are distinguished from the second half of the thirteenth century. See Richard Neugebauer, 'Medieval and Early Modern Theories of Mental Illness', *Archives of General Psychiatry* 36.4 (1979), 477–83, 478–79.
77. Neely, *Distracted Subjects*, 175.
78. As Peter Hyland demonstrates in *Disguise on the Early Modern Stage* (Farnham, 2011), 'As a general though not absolute rule, disguise had to be entirely opaque to characters on stage and entirely transparent to the audience' (42).
79. Joost Daalder, for example, accuses critics of 'giving up the subplot in despair' as Rowley's poorly written addition to Middleton's main plot, and failing to grasp that the play is 'a study, in dramatic form of folly and madness'; Daalder asserts that the subplot 'develops the concept of

madness which helps us to grasp its nature in the main plot' (1); 'Folly and Madness in *The Changeling*', *Essays in Criticism*, 38.1 (January 1988).

80. Michael Billington, Review of *The Changeling*, dir. Declan Donnellan, Cheek by Jowl and BITE Barbican, 2006, *Guardian*, 16 May 2006.
81. Susannah Clapp, Review of *The Changeling*, dir. Declan Donnellan, *Observer*, 21 May 2006.
82. David Benedict, Review of *The Changeling*, dir. Declen Donnellan, *Variety.Com*, 28 May 2006. Available at http://www.variety.com/review/VE1117930662?reCatld=33 (accessed 21 June 2010).
83. John Peter, Review of *The Changeling* dir. Declan Donnellan, *Sunday Times*, (21 May 2006).
84. Peter, *Sunday Times*, (21 May 2006).
85. Clapp, *Observer*, (21 May 2006).
86. Billington, *Guardian*, (16 May 2006).
87. Peter, *Sunday Times*, (21 May 2006).
88. *The Changeling*, dir. Joe Hill-Gibbons Young Vic Studio and Young Vic Theatre (London, 2012).
89. The lyrics of the chorus to Beyoncé Knowles' 2008 hit are as follows:

    Cuz if you liked it then you should have put a ring on it
    If you liked it then you shoulda put a ring on it
    Don't be mad once you see that he want it
    If you liked it then you shoulda put a ring on it.

    The 'it' seems to refer both to the ring finger of the female narrator and the narrator herself.
90. Zoe Svendson, '"A mad qualm within this hour": The dramaturgical challenges of Middleton and Rowley's *The Changeling* (1622) in modern production', paper given at conference, 'Confined Spaces: Considering Madness, Psychiatry, and Performance', AHRC Network: Isolated Acts (Cambridge, 2012).
91. Michael Billington, Review of *The Changeling*, dir. Joe Hill-Gibbons, *Guardian*, 3 February 2012.
92. Charles Spencer, Review of *The Changeling*, dir. Joe Hill-Gibbons, *The Times*, 3 February 2012.
93. Billington, *Guardian*, 3 February 2012.
94. Paul Taylor, Review of *The Changeling*, dir. Joe Hill-Gibbons, *Independant*, 3 February 2012.
95. Part I, considered here, by Dekker and Middleton, Part 2 by Dekker (1604); Fredson Bowers ed., *The Dramatic Works of Thomas Dekker* (Cambridge, 1964).
96. Ken Jackson has also noted that *The Honest Whore* 'assumes visiting the mad an acceptable practice, but it also seems to assume that some rules of decorum apply. The Duke and his men avoid being seen arriving in

a group.' Jackson goes on to suggest that visits to asylums during this period were charitable and that this scene registers 'the subtle rules governing the exhortation and distribution of charity at the hospital' (Jackson, *Separate Theatres*, 120).

97. Joost Daalder suggests that this is unsurprising, given the whippings with which Anselmo threatens his inmates and argues that 'By modern standards, the care offered is clearly insensitive and unintelligent' but that, importantly, 'it appears that Dekker sees it that way too'. Daalder, 'Madness in Parts 1 and 2 of *The Honest Whore:* A Case for Close Reading', *AUMLA* 86 (November 1996), 63–79, 73.
98. Joubert, *Laughter*, 21.
99. In his much-cited 'Letter to the Reader', Webster offers as a reason for publication of *The White Devil* the fact that 'it was acted in so dull a time of winter, presented in so open and black a theatre, that it wanted (that which is the only grace and setting-out of a tragedy) a full and understanding auditory'. John Webster, 'To the Reader', *The White Devil* (London, 2008), 5.
100. All places and dates of performance taken from Andrew Gurr, *The Shakespearean Stage* (Cambridge, 2009), Appendix A, 286–98.
101. Ben Jonson, *The Devil is an Ass* (1616) (Manchester, 1994), Prologue, 7–8.
102. Sarah Dustagheer, 'To see, and to bee seene [...] and possesse the Stage, against the Play': Blackfriars' actor/audience interaction in the repertory of the Children of the Queen's Revels and the King's Men', paper given at the 'Jacobean Indoor Playing Symposium', London Shakespeare Centre, King's College (London, 4 February 2012), citing Ben Jonson.
103. Tiffany Stern, 'Taking Part: Actors and Audiences on the Stage at Blackfriars', in Paul Menzer ed., *Indoor Shakespeare: Essays on the Blackfriar's Stage* (Selinsgrove, 2006), 35–53.
104. Ralph Cohen, 'The Most Convenient Place: The Second Blackfriars Theater and its Appeal', in Richard Dutton ed., *The Oxford Handbook of Early Modern Theatre* (Oxford, 2009), 209–24.
105. Nova Myhill, 'Taking the Stage: Spectators as Spectacles in the Caroline Public Theatres', in Nova Myhill and Jennifer Low, *Imagining the Audience in Early Modern Drama, 1558–1642* (Basingstoke, 2011), 37–54, 37.
106. Myhill, 'Taking the Stage', 52.
107. *Malvolio's Revenge*, Shakespeare Theatre Company Mock Trial (Sidney Harman Hall, Washington, DC, June 2009). Image taken from website publicity for the event. Available at http://www.shakespearetheatre.org/events/details.aspx?id=221 (accessed 24 May 2010).

108. See David Carnegie, '"Malvolio Within": Performance Perspectives on the Dark House', *Shakespeare Quarterly* 52.3 (Autumn 2001), 392–413 (395–96).
109. C. L. Barber, *Shakespeare's Festive Comedy: A Study of Dramatic Form and Its Relation to Social Custom* (Princeton, NJ, 1959).
110. Becky Kemper, 'A Clown in the Dark House: Reclaiming the Humor in Malvolio's Downfall', *Journal of the Wooden O Symposium* (2007), 42–50, 42.
111. Barnaby Riche's tale 'Of Apolonius and Silla' contains the obvious source for the narrative of the separated brother and sister and the cross-dressed love story. The incident Kemper cites is from 'Two Bretheren and Their Wives' from the same collection, Riche's *Farewell to Military Profession* (1581) (Ottawa, Canada, 1992). Scolded at every turn by his wife and unable to please her, one of the brothers, 'seeing that by no manner of fair means he was able to reclaim her, in the end he devised this way: himself with a trusty friend that he made of his counsel, got and pinioned her arms so fast that she was not able to undo them, and then putting her into an old petticoat which he rent and tattered in pieces of purpose, and shaking her hair loose about her eyes, tore her smock sleeves that her arms were all bare and scratching them all over with a bramble that the blood followed, with a great chain about her leg wherewith he tied her in a dark house that was on his backside [at the back of his house?], and then calling his neighbours about her he would seem with great sorrow to lament his wife's distress, telling them that she was suddenly become lunatic' (258). The wife proceeds to confirm her false diagnosis by becoming so angry that she does indeed seem mad, rather as Malvolio's complaints are used as proof of his madness by 'Sir Topaz'.
112. Kemper, 'Reclaiming', 42.
113. 'Only from about the middle of the nineteenth century can a consistent tradition of allowing Malvolio to be visible be firmly documented' (395); David Carnegie cites a note in a c.1850s prompt book which describes a central door revealing a cell with chain and straw for Malvolio; then, 'Most promptbooks from 1850 until well into the twentieth century record a version of this staging, with Malvolio seen in a straw-littered dungeon through the grating of a dark-house door' (396). Carnegie suggests that Irving's split-stage design, which seems to follow the illustration in the Rowe edition of 1709 (Carnegie argues that it is unlikely that Rowe was illustrating an actual stage setting of the play at this time (394)) was not much copied, if at all (397); however, he suggests that the staging led to the expansion of the possibilities 'for sentimental and piteous playing of Malvolio' and cites Edward

Aveling declaring that 'The mental and physical horror of darkness and the longing yearning for deliverance were never so realized, I think, before. And with all this agony (it is literally agony) there is the sense of the grevious wrong done to him' (Edward Aveling, *Our Corner*, July 1884, in Gamini Saldago, *Eyewitnesses of Shakespeare: First Hand Accounts of Performance*, 1590–1890 (London, 1975), 214, in Carnegie, '"Malvolio Within"', 396). Gayle Gaskill takes Irving's performance to be paradigmatic of pitiable late Victorian Malvolios. Gayle Gaskill, 'Overhearing Malvolio for Pleasure or Pity', in Laury Magnus and Walter W. Cannon, *Who Hears in Shakespeare? Auditory Worlds on Stage and Screen* (Madison, WI, 2012), 199–218, 210.

114. Gaskill, 'Overhearing Malvolio', 210.
115. According to the *Legal Times* blog, BLT, http://legaltimes.typepad.com/blt/2009/04/in-twelfth-night-mock-trial-malvolio-loses.html (accessed 26 November 2012).
116. For a reading of Antonio and Bosola, the Steward and Steward-like figures in Malfi, via Malvolio in Shakespeare's *Twelfth Night*, see Barbara Correll, 'Malvolio at Malfi: Managing Desire in Shakespeare and Webster', *Shakespeare Quarterly* 58.1 (spring 2007), 65–92.
117. John Fletcher, *The Pilgrim*, in Fredson Bowers, ed., *The Dramatic Works in the Beaumont and Fletcher Canon*, Vol. 6 (Cambridge, 1994).
118. See e.g. Thad Jenkins Logan, '*Twelfth Night*: The Limits of Festivity', *Studies in English Literature 1500–1900*, 22.2 (spring 1982), where Logan suggests that Malvolio's exit makes impossible the reconciliation essential to a 'Festive Comedy': 'Malvolio's exit is as disturbing as Mercade's entrance in *Love's Labours Lost*, with his message of death. We feel, in the audience, the necessity of somehow making peace with him, and he is gone. His last line must certainly include everyone in the theater' (237). Margret Fetzer entitles her contribution to *Deutsche Shakespeare-Gesellschaft 2006*, 'Staging Violence and Terror: Violence as the "Dark Room" of Comedy: Shakespeare's *Twelfth Night*' and aims to explore 'why audiences are still quite happy to laugh at the rather violent treatment Olivia's steward meets with'. She concludes by citing Manfred Pfister: 'in England [...] the mingling of laughter and tears, of the laughable and the pathetic or even the horrifying, and their tragicomic juxtaposition or conflation are the rule rather than the exception" (Fetzer, 'Violence', http://shakespeare-gesellschaft.de/en/publications/seminar/ausgabe2006/fetzer.html (accessed 26 November 2006), citing Pfister, *English Laughter*, vi-vii); Sean Benson, in '"Perverse Fantasies"? Rehabilitating Malvolio's Reading', argues that far from providing an easy satire on the Puritan solipsistic reader (Benson, '"Perverse Fantasies?"', *Papers on Language and Literature*

45.3 (Summer 2009), 261, citing Bevington, 336) *Twelfth Night* depicts Malvolio as 'every bit as careful' a social and semantic reader 'as Sebastian and Viola' and suggests that 'instead of reading Malvolio as one who is imprisoned because of his tortuous reading, we ought to regard him as one who, despite his careful hermeneutic, is tortured for it' (286).

119. I realize that such an assertion goes against the grain of recent criticism that has made similar assumptions about Malvolio's 'torture' to the ones Kemper critiques in production; for example, Alison P. Hobgood, in '*Twelfth Night*'s "Notorious Abuse" of Malvolio: Shame, Humorality, and Early Modern Spectatorship', (*Shakespeare Bulletin* 24.3 (2006), 1–22, assumes that the audience will see the marks of physical abuse on Malvolio's body: 'He acts out the ways he has, as Sir Toby predicted, been "fool[ed] … black and blue"' (2.5.9). The notorious abuse he verbally recounts verifies the troubling spectacle his person visually represents. In this moment, 'Malvolio uses his broken body to reveal the shame he has suffered thus far' (11). Malvolio, of course, is described by both himself and Olivia has having been 'notoriously abused' (4.2; 5.1); but it should be noted that though the transitive verb 'to abuse' is cited in the OED as meaning 'to mistreat (a person or thing); to injure, hurt; to wrong' from 1473, early modern usage is also cited as: 'to take advantage of wrongly', to 'misrepresent (a person or thing); 'to betray (a person's trust, confidence, etc.)' and in the passive 'to be deceived, mistaken'. The first citation of sense in which Hobgood suggests Malvolio has suffered abuse – 'to subject a person […] to physical, sexual or emotional abuse' – is from 1978.
120. Tim Crouch, interview for British Council Edinburgh Festival 2011 Showcase. Available at http://edinburghshowcase.britishcouncil.org/home/tim-crouch/ (accessed 24 November 2012).
121. Tim Crouch, *I Malvolio*, in *I, Shakespeare: Four of Shakespeare's Better Known Plays Retold for Young Audiences by their Lesser-Known Characters* (London, 2011), 26.
122. Crouch, *I, Malvolio*, 23–7.
123. The stage directions for this costume read:

> *Filthy long johns; the tattered remains of yellow stockings. Obscene stains down his front and around his groin. His face smeared with dirt. The word 'Bawcock' written on his forehead.*
>
> *Devil horns on his head. A turkey wattle crudely attached under his chin.*
>
> (Crouch, *I, Malvolio*, 18)

124. See Martin Ingram, 'Shame and Pain: Themes and Variations in Tudor Punishments', in Simon Devereaux and Paul Griffiths (eds), *Penal*

*Practice and Culture, 1500–1900: Punishing the English* (Basingstoke, 2004), and David Nash and Anne Marie Kilday, *Exploring Crime and Morality in Britain, 1600–1900*, ch. 2, 'Private Passions and Public Penance: Popular Shaming Rituals in Pre-Modern Britain' (Basingstoke, 2010), 26–46.

125. Crouch, *I, Malvolio*, 14.
126. *Ibid.*, 17.
127. *The Author*, which premiered at The Royal Court in 2009, took place entirely amidst the audience, where characters were placed, who spoke, often directly to audience members, of their involvement in the making of a violent piece of theatre. The piece implicated both performers and audience in the complacent use of violence as spectacle. *England*, which premiered at the Fruitmarket Gallery, Edinburgh, in 2007 and toured to other art galleries in the UK, opened with the audience standing amidst the gallery's artworks, addressed by two characters, one of whom was Crouch as a man in need of a heart transplant, the other his partner whose art dealing, it is hinted, has enabled him or her to buy him a heart from the family of a dead man in a developing country. The audience is implicated in the power and economic relationships between the rich, art-buying West and the developing world.
128. Robert H. Bell, *Shakespeare's Great Stage of Fools* (Basingstoke and New York, 2011), 90.
129. *Pace* Sean Benson (see p. 254n. 117) Malvolio is, for Justin A. Joyce, a poor reader of sartorial semiotics too. See Joyce, 'Fashion, Class, and Gender in Early Modern England: Staging *Twelfth Night*' in Cynthia Kuhn and Cindy Carlson (eds), *Styling Texts: Dress and Fashion in Literature* (New York, 2007), 49–66, for an account of the ways in which Malvolio's fantasy of the 'branch'd velvet gown' clearly breaches sumptuary law (61) and the negative associations of the colour yellow in early modern England (62).
130. Quoted in Celia Wren, 'As You Litigate It', *American Theatre* 26.6 (July–August 2009), 42–3, 43.

## 3: 'GIVE ME EXCESS OF IT': LOVE, VIRTUE AND EXCESSIVE PLEASURE IN *ALL'S WELL THAT ENDS WELL* AND *ANTONY AND CLEOPATRA*

1. David Schalkwyk, 'Is Love an Emotion?: Shakespeare's *Twelfth Night* and *Antony and Cleopatra*', *Symploke* 18.1–2 (2010), 99–130, 110.
2. Schalkwyk, 'Is Love an Emotion?', 107.
3. Wright, *The Passions of the Mind in General* (London, 1604), 193.

4. Wright, *The Passions* (193) cited in Schalkwyk, 'Is Love an Emotion?' (107).
5. Schalkwyk, 'Is Love an Emotion?', 107.
6. Coeffeteau, *Human Passions*, 18.
7. Ibid., 103.
8. Ibid., 99–100.
9. James Ferrand, *Erotomania or A treatise discoursing of the essence, causes, symptoms, prognostics, and cure of love, or erotic melancholy* (London, 1640), 3.
10. Ferrand, *Erotomania*, 4.
11. For explorations of love as disease in early modern writing, see Nancy Frelick, 'Contagions of Love: Textual Transmission', in Claire L. Carlin (ed.), *Imagining Contagion in Early Modern Europe* (Basingstoke, 2005), 47–62; Carol Thomas Neely, 'Hot Blood: Estranging Mediterranean Bodies in Early Modern Medical and Dramatic Texts', in Stephanie Moss and Kaara L. Peterson (eds), *Disease Diagnosis and Cure on the Early Modern Stage* (Aldershot, 2004), 55–68; Neely, 'Destabilizing Lovesickness, Gender and Sexuality', *Distracted Subjects*, 99–135.
12. Paul A. Kottman, 'Defying the Stars: Tragic Love as the Struggle for Freedom in *Romeo and Juliet*', *Shakespeare Quarterly*, 63.1 (2012), 1–38 (2).
13. Stanley Wells, *Shakespeare, Sex and Love* (Oxford, 2010), 67.
14. Wells, *Shakespeare, Sex and Love*, 67.
15. Dympna Callaghan, 'The Ideology of Romantic Love: The Case of Romeo and Juliet', in Dympna Callaghan, Lorraine Helms and Jyotsna Singh (eds), *The Weyward Sisters: Shakespeare and Feminist Politics* (Oxford, and Cambridge, MA, 1994) pp. 59–101.
16. Wells, *Shakespeare, Sex and Love*, 167.
17. Ibid., 147.
18. Ibid., 250.
19. Maurice Charney, *Shakespeare on Love and Lust* (New York, 2000), 211.
20. David Scott Kastan, '*All's Well That Ends Well* and the Limits of Comedy', *ELH* 52.3 (autumn 1985), 575–89, 575. Kastan cites Philip Sidney,*The Apology for Poetry*, ed. Geoffrey Shepherd (London, 1965), 117; and Heywood, *Apology for Actors* (London, 1814), 54.
21. Kastan, '*All's Well*' 576, citing Francis Bacon, 'Of Love', in 'Francis Bacon: *A Selection of his Works*, ed. Sidney Warhaft (New York, 1965), 68.
22. Kastan, '*All's Well*', 579.
23. Frederick S. Boas, 'The Problem Plays', in *Shakespeare and his Predecessors* (London, 1896), 344–408.
24. W.W. Lawrence, *Shakespeare's Problem Comedies* (New York, 1931).

25. Peter Ure, *Shakespeare: The Problem Plays* (London, 1961), 7.
26. Ure, *Problem Plays*, 7, citing E.M.W. Tillyard, *Shakespeare's Problem Plays* (London, 1951), 9–10.
27. Tillyard, *Problem Plays*, 10.
28. Boas, 'The Problem Plays', 345.
29. Anne Barton, Introduction to *All's Well That Ends Well*, Riverside Shakespeare (New York, 1976), p. 502.
30. G. Beiner, *Generic Tension as Exploratory Mode: Shakespeare Among Others* (Saarbruken, 2010), back cover.
31. *All's Well That Ends Well*, dir. John Dove (Shakespeare's Globe, 2011).
32. Harold Bloom, *Bloom's Shakespeare through the Ages* (New York, 2010), 23.
33. However, *All's Well That Ends Well* has certainly been described as an undiluted problem in a range of negative senses at various points of its critical history. It has been famously excoriated by luminaries from Dr Johnson (Samuel Johnson, *Notes to Shakespeare I, The Comedies, All's Well that Ends Well*, 'General Observation' to 5.3 (London, 1765)) whose view of Bertram as the play's central problem had 'never been answered' according to Carl Dennis in 1971 ('*All's Well that Ends Well* and the Meaning of Agape', *Philological Quarterly* 50.1 (January 1971), 75–84), to Katherine Mansfield, whose 'problem' is primarily Helena but much of whose contempt for her character stems from her 'pegging away after the odious Bertram' (*The Journal of Katherine Mansfield*, ed. J. M. Murray (New York, 1921), 200). Twenty- and twenty-first-century critics have engaged with the play in terms of the unease it might produce in its audiences: 'I can only guess how it might work on stage' muses Nicholas Brooke, who by 1977 had seen it once. '[A]lthough I believe it could work and be very sharply interesting as well as uncomfortably amusing, I do not suppose it would be exactly popular' (Nicholas Brooke,'*All's Well that Ends Well*', *Shakespeare Survey* 30 (1977), 20). Thirty years later, Helena's 'pursuits inspire uneasy responses both onstage and off' according to Kathryn Schwarz ('My Intents are Fix'd: Constant Will in *All's Well that Ends Well*', *Shakespeare Quarterly* 58.2 (Summer 2007) 200–29, 200).
34. Charles Spenser, Review of *All's Well that Ends Well*, dir. John Dove, Shakespeare's Globe, *Daily Telegraph*, 9 May 2011.
35. Paul Taylor Review of *All's Well that Ends Well*, dir. John Dove, *Independent*, 10 May 2011.
36. Michael Billington, Review of *All's Well that Ends Well*, dir. John Dove, *Guardian*, 6 May 2011.
37. Susannah Clapp, Review of *All's Well that Ends Well*, dir. John Dove, *Guardian*, *Observer*, 8 May 2011.

38. Billington, Review of *All's Well*.
39. Taylor, Review of *All's Well*.
40. Sarah Hemming, Review of *All's Well That Ends Well*, dir. John Dove, *Financial Times*, 8 May 2011.
41. Giovanni Boccaccio, *Amorous Fiammetta*, trans. Bartholomew Young (London, 1587), 4–5.
42. 'Love therefore having abused the eyes, as the proper spies and porters of the mind, maketh a way for itself smoothly to glance along through the conducting guides, and passing without any perseverance in this sort through the veins into the liver, doth suddenly imprint a burning desire to obtain the thing, which is or seemeth worthy to be beloved, setteth concupiscence on fire, and beginneth by this desire all the strife and contention.' André du Laurens, *A discourse of the preservation of the sight: of melancholic diseases; of rheums, and of old age*, trans. Richard Surphlet (London, 1599), 118.
43. Robert Burton, 'Other Causes of Love Melancholy, Sight, Beauty from the Face, Eyes, other Parts and how it pierceth', *Anatomy*, Part 3, 66.
44. Johannes Kepler, *Optics: Paralimpomena to Witelo and Optical Part of Astronomy*, trans. William H. Donahue (1604) (Santa Fe, NM, 2000).
45. Eric Langley, *Narcissism and Suicide in Shakespeare and his Contemporaries* (Oxford, 2009), 54–5.
46. Langley, 56–7, citing Anon., *A Pleasant and Delightful Poeme of Two Lovers: Philos and Licia* (London, 1624), repr. in Miller ed., *Seven Minor Epics* (Gainsville, 1967) 33.
47. William Painter, 'Giletta of Narbona', in *The Palace of Pleasure* (London, 1566), 95–101.
48. *Oxford English Dictionary* online, 2000.
49. Schwartz, 'Intents', 200.
50. Painter, 'Giletta', 95.
51. See e.g. Ian Frederick Moulton, 'Fat Knight, or What You Will: Unimitable Falstaff', in Richard Dutton and Jean E. Howard (eds), *A Companion to Shakespeare's Works: The Comedies* (Malden, MA, and Oxford, 2003), 223–242 (231).
52. Ewan Fernie, 'Shakesperience 3: Helena's Fantasies (Part Two)'. Available at http://bloggingshakespeare.com/shakespearience-3-helenas-fantasies-part-two (accessed 1 December 2012).
53. Andrew Dickson, Review of *All's Well that Ends Well*, dir. Sunil Shanbag, Arpana Theatre, Shakespeare's Globe, *Guardian* 1 June 2012.
54. Susan Bennett and Christie Carlson (eds), *Shakespeare Beyond English* (Cambridge, 2013), in press.
55. Peter Kirwan, '*All's Well That Ends Well*: Arpana', in Bennett and Carlson (eds), *Shakespeare Beyond English*.

56. Web publicity for the Globe to Globe Festival, Shakespeare's Globe 2012. Available at http://globetoglobe.shakespearesglobe.com/plays/alls-well-that-ends-well/english-34 (accessed 5 June 2012).
57. Sunil Shanbag, interview with Andrew Dickson. Available at http://firstpageonlineuknews.co.uk/world-shakespeare-festival-around-the-globe-in-37-plays-3707 (accessed 5 November 2012).
58. Sunil Shanbag, personal correspondence.
59. Millie Taylor, *Musical Theatre, Realism and Entertainment* (Farnham, 2012), 168.
   See also Millie Taylor, 'Don't Dream It, Be It: Exploring Signification, Empathy and Mimesis in Relation to The Rocky Horror Show', *Studies in Musical Theatre* 1.1 (2007), 57–71 for an account of mimesis and empathy in a musical where 'the physical responses of the audience can be easily discerned' (57). Taylor defines empathy in an interestingly somatic way: 'To feel empathy is to feel the emotional state of another body' (63), and although this assertion does not take into account the tropes and conventions that might lead an audience member to imagine that this somatic reciprocity is what he or she is feeling, the use of Heli's songs, movements and facial expressions to suggest that audience members, even those who do not understand Gujarati, might feel what she feels, opens up interesting parallels between anxieties of emotional contagion in responses to the early modern theatre and cultural snobbery about musicals. David Savran's defence of the study of musical theatre is interesting here, particularly in its assertion that American musical theatre raises questions around the 'politics of pleasure' 'and offers an important site for an analysis of anti-theatricality' ('Towards a Historiography of the Popular', *Theatre Survey* 45.2 (November 2004), 211–17, 216). My sense is that both David Scott Kastan's distaste for the selfishness of Helena's love and Andrew Dickson's slight objection that Arpana's *All's Well* was not enough of a 'problem' actually express anxieties around pleasure in closure as both too easily pleasurable and too middle-brow.
60. Sohailia Kapur, 'Musical Theatre in India'. Available at http://shekharkapur.com/blog/2011/05/musical-theatre-in-india-guest-column-by-sohaila-kapur/ (accessed 1 December 2012).
61. Sunil Shanbag notes: 'Bharatram's family are traders – Bhatias (singular form: Bhatia) – and are higher up in the caste structure than Heli's family who are Kansaras (singular form Kansara), a craftsman caste. It was not unusual for a person from the craftsman caste to study traditional medicine, as Heli's father did. So one would immediately imagine that the issue of higher caste and lower caste would operate in this situation. But we are in Gujarat, where there was a strong reformist

tradition, and so caste prejudices were significantly less than in many other parts of the country. As Mihir Bhuta, our writer, told me, there is more horizontal caste tension than vertical, even in modern day Gujarat. Basically this means that there is no fundamental caste tension between Bharatram's and Heli's family, so if Bharatram is not interested in Heli it's not because of caste. It was common for a lower caste girl to be married into a higher caste family. So again, Kunti is not burdened by this taboo.' Personal correspondence, 29 September 2012.

62. Much has been made of *All's Well*'s mix of folk tradition and realism in criticism of the play; see e.g. Alexander Leggatt, '*All's Well that Ends Well*: The Testing of Romance', *Modern Language Quarterly* 32 (1971), 21–41; G. A. Wilkes, '*All's Well that Ends Well* and 'The Common Stock of Narrative Tradition', *Leeds Studies in English* 20 (1989), 207–16; G.K. Hunter, Introduction, *All's Well that Ends Well*, Arden Second Series (London, 2006), xxxiii–xxxiv; Regina Buccola, '"As Sweet as Sharp': Helena and the Fairy Bride Tradition', in Waller ed., *All's Well That Ends Well: New Critical Essays* (New York and Oxford, 2007), 71–84; and Anne Barton's essay in the Globe's own journal at the time of the 2011 production, 'Happy Ever After', *Around the Globe: The Magazine of Shakespeare's Globe* 48 (2011), 6–7.
63. See Plutarch, 'Life of Marcus Antonius', in *Lives of the Ancient Greeks and Romans*, trans. Thomas North, in Bullough, *Narrative and Dramatic Sources of Shakespeare*, 5, The Roman Plays, 276, where North marks a passage as 'The excessive expenses of Antonius and Cleopatra in Egypt'.
64. See Plutarch, 'Life of Marcus Antonius', 274; Shakespeare, *Antony and Cleopatra*, 2.2.200–28.
65. I refer to Cecil B. de Mille's 1934 *Cleopatra*, Gabriel Pascale's film version of George Bernard Shaw's *Caesar and Cleopatra* (1945) with Claude Rains and Vivien Leigh as the leads, and Joseph Mankiewicz's *Cleopatra* (1963) starring Elizabeth Taylor and Richard Burton. The iconic image of Cleopatra from the Mankiewicz film spawned one of the best known in the British 'Carry On' comedy series, made in 1964: *Carry On Cleo*, a close parody of the Mankiewicz film; Mankiewicz relocated to Rome mid-production, leaving a range of sets and costumes at the British Pinewood studios for the Carry On team's use.
66. Susan Osmond, '"Her Infinite Variety": Representations of Shakespeare's Cleopatra in Fashion, Film and Theatre', *Film, Fashion and Consumption* 1.1 (February 2011), 55–79.
67. Laurie N. Ede, *British Film Design: A History* (London, 2010), 67.
68. George Bernard Shaw, *Caesar and Cleopatra in Three Plays for Puritans* (London, 1901), 130.

69. Keith Lodwick, 'The Film Work of Stage Designer Oliver Messel', *V&A Online Journal* 1 (autumn 2008). Available at http://www.vam.ac.uk/content/journals/research-journal/issue-01/the-film-work-of-stage-designer-oliver-messel/ (accessed 4 December 2012).
70. *Antony and Cleopatra*, dir. Janet Suzman, Chichester Festival Theatre, (Chichester, 2012) (first produced, with some of the same cast, for the Liverpool Playhouse in 2010).
71. *Antony and Cleopatra*, dir. Peter Hall, Royal Shakespeare Company (Royal Shakespeare Theatre, Stratford-upon-Avon, 1987).
72. Steve Grant, Review of *Antony and Cleopatra*, dir. Peter Hall, *Time Out*, 15 April 1987.
73. *Antony and Cleopatra*, dir. Adrian Noble, Royal Shakespeare Company (The Other Place, Stratford-upon-Avon, 1983).
74. Steve Grant, Review of *Antony and Cleopatra*, dir. Adrian Noble, *Plays and Players*, November 1982.
75. *Antony and Cleopatra*, dir. Peter Brook, *Royal Shakespeare Company* Royal Shakespeare Theatre (Stratford-upon-Avon, 1978).
76. Richard Proudfoot, *Peter Brook and Shakespeare*, in James Redmond ed., *Themes In Drama 2: Drama and Mimesis* (Cambridge, 1980), 157–89, 175.
77. For a detailed account of Victorian pictorial production of the play and its adaptations, see Richard Madeleine's account of its performance history in *Shakespeare in Production: Antony and Cleopatra* (Cambridge,1998), 34–61.
78. Osmond, 'Her Infinite Variety', 56.
79. I take the phrase from Linda Charnes' *Notorious Identity: Materializing the Subject in Shakespeare* (Cambridge, MA, 1993), a study of Shakespeare's staging of notorious figures and the effects of agency and contingency this produces. See esp. ch. 3, 'Spies and Whispers: Exceeding Reputation in *Antony and Cleopatra*', 103–47.
80. Osmond, 'Her Infinite Variety', 59.
81. *Antony and Cleopatra*, dir. Janet Suzman (Chichester Festival Theatre, 2012).
82. Lyn Gardner, review of *Antony and Cleopatra*, dir. Janet Suzman, Chichester Festival Theatre, 2012, *Guardian*, 16 September 2012.
83. *Antony and Cleopatra*, dir. Janet Suzman (Liverpool Playhouse, 2012).
84. Claire Brennan, Review of *Antony and Cleopatra*, dir. Janet Suzman, Liverpool Playhouse 2010, *Observer*, 17 October 2010.
85. Paul Taylor, Review of *Antony and Cleopatra*, dir. Janet Suzman, Chichester Festival Theatre, *Independent*, 18 September 2012.
86. Suzman, in Dominic Cavendish, 'Suzman Interview for *Antony and Cleopatra*', *Daily Telegraph*, 28 September 2010.

87. Janet Suzman, 'A Word from the Director', programme note to *Antony and Cleopatra* (Chichester Festival Theatre, 2012).
88. Adrian Goldsworthy, *Antony and Cleopatra* (London, 2010), 308.
89. Janet Stacy Schiff, *Cleopatra: A Life* (New York, 2010), 2.
90. *Antony and Cleopatra*, dir. Trevor Nunn, Royal Shakespeare Company, Royal Shakespeare Theatre (Stratford-upon-Avon, 1972–1973).
91. *Antony and Cleopatra* television film, dir. Jon Scholfield, based on the Royal Shakespeare Company production, dir. Trevor Nunn (ATC, 1974).
92. L.T. Fitz, 'Egyptian Queens and Male Reviewers: Sexist Attitudies in *Antony and Cleopatra* Criticism', *Shakespeare Quarterly* 28.3 (Summer 1977) 375–97, 379.
93. Gardner, Review of *Antony and Cleopatra*, 16 September 2012.
94. Taylor, Review of *Antony and Cleopatra*, 18 September 2012.
95. Ernest Schanzer, *The Problem Plays of Shakespeare* (1963) (Oxford, 2005), 134–7.
96. Paster, *Humoring,* 77–100.
97. Helkiah Crooke, 'Of the Temperament of Women', *Microcosmographia* (London, 1615), 272–7.
98. Crooke, *Microcosmographia*, 273.
99. Ibid., 276.
100. Her temperate speech is so divinely calm,
 And from her Ruby portals, spring a Balm
 So precious, and invaluably Pure
 That Love makes every kiss become a Cure:
 She's never Jealous, 'cause she doth not know
 By what strange means 'tis planted or doth Grow:
 Yet (rightly) thinks they cannot be without
 The Guilt of Soul, who deal too much in Doubt;
 And therefore (piously) doth well prevent
 The Plague of both, by being Innocent.
 (Thomas Jordan, 'The Virtuous Wife', in *Pictures of Passions, Fancies and Affections, Poetically Deciphered in a Variety of Characters* (London, 1641))
101. 'I have been a traveller this thirty & odd years, and many travellers live in disdain of women; the reason is, for that their affections are so poisoned with the heinous evils of unconstant women, which they happen to be acquainted with in their travels' (Epistle 'Neither to the best, nor yet to the worse; but to the common sort of women', Joseph Swetnam (1615), in F. W. Van Heertum ed., *A Critical Edition of Joseph Swetnam's The Arraignment of Lewd, Idle, Froward, and Unconstant Women* (Nijmegen, 1989), 190.

102. Thomas Dekker, *The Bachelor's Banquet* (London, 1604).
103. Stephen Mullaney, 'Mourning and Misogyny: *Hamlet*, the *Revenger's Tragedy* and the Final Progress of Elizabeth I, 1600–1607', in Robert D. Newman ed., *Centuries' Ends, Narrative Means* (Stanford, CA, 1996), 238–60, 240.
104. See Samuel Taylor Coleridge, 'Notes on *Antony and Cleopatra*', in *The Literary Remains of Samuel Taylor Coleridge*, ed. Henry Nelson Coleridge (London, 1836): 'This play should be perused in mental contrast with *Romeo and Juliet*; as the love of passion and appetite opposed to the love of affection and instinct. But the art displayed in the character of Cleopatra is profound; in this especially, that the sense of criminality is lessened by our insight into its depth and energy, at the very moment that we cannot but perceive that the passion itself springs out of the habitual craving of a licentious nature' (143).
105. For positive accounts of Cleopatra's changeability, see Phyllis Rackin, 'Shakesepeare's Boy Cleopatra, the Decorum of Nature, and the Golden World of Poetry', *PMLA* 87 (1972), 201–12; Francesca T. Royster, *Becoming Cleopatra: The Shifting Image of an Icon* (Basingtoke, 2003): 'An image always still in formation, Cleopatra slides out of the poet's and scholar's grasp. It is not for nothing that Shakespeare's most memorable description of Cleopatra is put in the mouth of one of his most articulate cynics of love and politics. What Enobarbus sees and what Antony does not is that Cleopatra "makes hungry where she most satisfies." She can never satisfyingly be described or explained because she is always shifting. To attempt a history of the Cleopatra Icon is always to leave something out' (1–2).
106. Jonathan Gil Harris, '"Narcissus in thy Face": Roman Desire and the Difference it Fakes in *Antony and Cleopatra*', *Shakespeare Quarterly* 45.4 (Winter 1994), 408–25, 422.
107. See Bridget Escolme, 'Costume, Disguise and Self-Display' in Farah Karim-Cooper and Tiffany Stern (eds) *Shakespeare's Theatre and the Effects of Performance* (London, 2013) pp. 118-140 (136).
108. Plutarch, 'Life of Marcus Antonius', 276.
109. Ibid., 261.
110. Ibid., 276.
111. Ibid., 257.
112. *Antony and Cleopatra*, dir. Giles Block Shakespeare's Globe (London, 1999).
113. See Ingram, and Nash and Kilday (p. 255–6, n.124).
114. 'Bravery', or fine clothing, often epitomizes female immorality in early modern discourse; the courtesan Lamia, in Whetstone's *Promos and Cassandra* (1579) (in Geoffrey Bullough, *Narrative and Dramatic*

*Sources of Shakespeare*, vol 2, *The Comedies*), Shakespeare's source for *Measure for Measure*, dupes her clients into buying her clothes and begins a song 'All aflaunt now, vaunt it! Brave wench cast away care' (Part I, 1.2.1); her first concern when she is arrested for prostitution is that her captors should not tear her clothes (Part I, 3.6.1); for Thomas Bentley in his '*Mirror* for all sorts of wicked women', such women are 'with Jezabel, in all their bravery' to '[...] be thrown headlong down into the street out of their own window, and be eaten and devoured of dogs, and so want the honour of christian burial' (Thomas Bentley, 'To the Christian Reader' (3), in *The Monument of Matrons* (London, 1582); 'Bravery in ancient English was called Baudry', states D.T. bluntly in *Asylum veneris, or A sanctuary for ladies* (London, 1616), 54. As in Dekker's *The Bachelor's Banquet* (see p. 154), it is the cost of apparel to poor, duped men, as much as the seductiveness of women's 'bravery' that concerns the anonymous author of the broadside 'The Phantastick Age' (London, 1634):

The women will not be at quiet,
their minds will still be crost,
Til Husbands, Friends, or Fathers buy it,
what ever price it cost.
Thus wide mouth'd pride insatiately,
devoures all thoughts of piety.

(2)

## 4: STOP YOUR SOBBING: GRIEF, MELANCHOLY AND MODERATION

1. Robert Southwell, *The Triumphs Over Death: Or, A Consolatory Epistle, for Afflicted Minds, in the Affects of Dying Friends* (London, 1595), cited in Patricia Phillippy, *Women, Death and Literature in Post-Reformation England* (Cambridge, 2002), 129.
2. Mavericke Radford, *Three Treatises Religiously Handled and Named According to the Several Subject of Each Treatise: The Mourning Weed. The Morning's Joy. The King's Rejoicing* (London, 1603), 1.
3. Thomas Playfere, *The Mean in Mourning. A Sermon Preached at Saint Mary's Spittle in London on Tuesday in Easter week 1595* (London, 1596), 5–6.
4. G. I. Pigman III, *Grief and the Renaissance Elegy* (Cambridge, 1985), ch. 2, 'The Emergence of Compassionate Moderation', 27–39.
5. Charnes, *Notorious Identity*, ch. 2, 'So Unsecret to Ourselves: Notorious Identity and the Material Subject in *Troilus and Cressida*', 70–102.

6. See also Adam H. Kitzes, *The Politics of Melancholy from Spenser to Milton* (New York and Abingdon, 2006). I hope that this chapter is a theatrically inflected complement to his exploration of melancholy as a political phenomenon in early modern literature and culture.
7. *Richard III*, dir. Roxana Silbert, Royal Shakespeare Company, Swan Theatre, Stratford upon Avon, 2012; *Hamlet*, dir. Nicholas Hytner, National Theatre (London, 2010).
8. I have chosen the title of the Kinks' song as my subtitle here (*Stop Your Sobbing*, Ray Davis, 1964) because it is such an unusually direct exhortation in a twentieth-century popular music lyric, and seems appropriate to Claudius' and Lafew's exhortations to Hamlet and Helena (see p. 174).
9. Sarah Tarlow, *Ritual, Belief and the Dead in Early Modern Britain and Ireland* (Cambridge, 2011), 139.
10. Tarlow, *Ritual*, 138.
11. Clare Gittings, 'Sacred and Secular: 1558–1660' in Peter C. Jupp and Clare Gittings (eds), *Death in England an Illustrated History* (Manchester, 1999), citing John Chamberlain, *The Letters of John Chamberlain,* ed. N. E. M. McClure (Philadelphia, PA, 1939), 164.
12. Lucinda M. Becker, *Death and the Early Modern Englishwoman* (Aldershot, 2003), 138.
13. Note to to *All's Well That Ends Well* (1.1.53), Riverside Shakespeare (New York, 1976).
14. Indeed, the *Arden Shakespeare Complete Works* editors gloss 'affect' as to 'impersonate, put on' (London, 2011).
15. See esp. Katharine Eisamann Maus, *Inwardness and Theater in the English Renaissance* (Chicago, IL, 1995).
16. See e.g. *2 Henry VI* (2.1.174); *3 Henry VI* (2.5.20, 94); *Richard II* (3.3.184–5); *The Tempest* (5.1.215).
17. At the time of writing, this ballad appears on a range of websites, complete with its Collier additions unquestioned. For an account of the authenticity of the original and the Collier forgeries, see 'A Burbage Ballad and John Payne Collier', *Review of English Studies* 40.159 (August 1989), 393–97.
18. Aristotle, *Poetics*, trans. Malcolm Heath (London, 1996).
19. See Leon Golden for a lucid account of the ways in which sixteenth-century understandings of catharsis of purgation have influenced later thinking: 'The Purgation Theory of Cartharsis', *Journal of Aesthetics and Art Criticism* 31.4 (Summer 1973), 473–79.
20. John Milton, *Sampson Agonistes*, cited in Golden, 'Purgation', 473.
21. Tobias Doring, *Performances of Mourning in Shakespearean Theatre and Early Modern Culture* (Basingstoke, 2006), 102.

22. Doring, *Performances*, 102.
23. For an account of *Hamlet* that suggests an anti-Stoical line in the therapeutic valuing of grief is being debated and affirmed in the play, see Michael Schoenfeldt, 'Give Sorrow Words: Emotional Loss and the Articulation of Temperament in Early Modern England', in Basil Dufallo and Peggy McCracken (eds), *Dead Lovers: Erotic Bonds and the Study of Premodern Europe* (Ann Arbor, 2006),143–64.
24. Stephen Pender, 'Rhetoric, Grief and the Imagination in Early Modern England', *Philosophy and Rhetoric* 43.1 (2010), 54–85, 66.
25. Burton, 'Against Sorrow for Death of Friends or Otherwise Vain Fear etc', *Anatomy*, Vol. 2, 180.
26. Pender 'Rhetoric', 66, citing Cicero, *Those Five Questions, which Marke Tully Cicero, Disputed in his Manor of Tusculanum*, trans. John Dolman (1561).
27. Burton, 'Against Sorrow for Death of Friends', *Anatomy* Vol. 2, 177.
28. Ibid.
29. Burton, *Anatomy*, cited in Pinder, 'Rhetoric', 57.
30. Seneca in Burton, *Anatomy*, Vol. 2, 80.
31. Sigmund Freud, 'Mourning and Melancholia', trans. Shaun Whiteside, in *On Murder, Mourning and Melancholia* (London, 2005), 204.
32. For example, this from the BBC's 'Emotional Health' website:

    > How long does grief last?
    > Unfortunately, there's no definitive answer because each of us is different. Recovery time may take months, a few years or even longer. Our friends may think we should've 'got over it' by six months, but this is usually an unrealistic expectation. A severe physical wound takes time to heal, and so it is with bereavement. However, the acute pain you feel in the beginning will lessen and life will gradually seem less bleak and meaningless.
    >
    > (http://www.bbc.co.uk/health/emotional_health/bereavement/bereavement_helpourselves.shtml) (accessed 20.6.2012)

    As this advice from the UK National Health Service demonstrates, normative grief must, as in Freud, have some time limit, or it will be suspected of becoming an illness, and this is a notion that seems to have lasted, in various forms, across 400 years. Their current website on bereavement lists symptoms usually associated with depression:

    - you can't get out of bed;
    - you neglect yourself or your family, for example, you don't eat properly;
    - you feel you can't go on without the person you've lost;
    - the emotion is so intense it's affecting the rest of your life, for

example, you can't face going to work or you're taking your anger out on someone else.

(http://www.nhs.uk/Livewell/bereavement/Pages/coping-with-bereavement.aspx) (accessed 20.6.2012)

The site then asserts that 'These feelings are normal as long as they don't last for a long time'. '"The time to get help depends on the person," says Sarah [Smith, bereavement counsellor]. "If these things last for a period that you feel is too long."' Interestingly here, the bereaved person is supposed to self-diagnose in terms of what is a 'normal' time for 'these things [to] last' and the first example given that grief is negatively affecting 'the rest of your life' is if 'you can't face going to work'. The website has a compassionate and not overly patronizing tone and would no doubt be of comfort to a bereaved person whose insensitive peers were telling them to 'snap out of it'. Ultimately, though, it is up to the bereaved to decide when the length of their mourning is preventing them from becoming an economically productive citizen.

33. For an account of the influences of Seneca on the mourning women in this play, see Harold Brookes, '*Richard III*, Unhistorical Amplifications: The Women's Scenes and Seneca', *Modern Language Review 75* (1980), 721–137; Robert S. Miola, *Shakespeare and Classical Tragedy: The Influence of Seneca* (Oxford, 1992), 74–82 (this section is a revision of Brookes' findings); M.L. Stapleton, *Fated Sky, The Femina Furens in Shakespeare* (Newark, DL and London, 2000) (particularly for an account of Seneca's influence on Shakespeare's depiction of Margaret).
34. For Paige Martin Reynolds, given that 'early modern Protestantism demanded a decisive separation between [the living and the dead]', drama after the English Reformation retains the efficacious performative function that praying for the dead once had. 'Female memory and mourning in *Richard III*', asserts Reynolds, 'replace purgatory' (19). The liminal position of Henry VI's corpse, on its way to burial at Paul's, Anne's belief that her dead father's wounds reopen in the presence of his murderer, based, for Reynolds, in Catholic-like superstition, and her address to the corpse, all 'indicate a resistance to entirely abandoning superstition and a pre-Reformation understanding of the dead' (22). After this scene, Reynolds reminds us that the audience never again sees any of the many bodies mourned by the women in the play: 'That the play insists' on this absence 'reinforces the Protestant privileging of the soul over the body' but the women always mourn in excess of religious hegemony and continue to 'refuse to let them be forgotten' (22). The women disappear from the play to be replaced by the ghosts of the dead who lead Richmond to hope for victory and Richard to 'despair and die' as his mother wishes, so that 'insofar as they have borne the

burden of memory throughout the play, the women of *Richard III* bring about Richard's downfall'. As has been argued about revenge tragedy, then, this reading of *Richard III* offers the play as a kind of therapeutic replacement for the sense of agency a mourner might have had when he or she was permitted to pray for dead loved ones in purgatory. Patricia Phillippy shares Reynolds' conviction that Catholic mourning practices are being referenced in Anne's formal lament of her father-in-law and addressed to his body: 'The king's ritualized funeral procession carries the trace of the Catholic practice in which the cortege made frequent stops at public crosses, shrines, and taverns' and prayers for the dead were spoken (she also cites accounts of drunkenness and disorder at these assemblies) (131). Indeed, Reynolds' article draws on Phillippy's connection between *Richard III's* lamenting women and Catholic practice 'in which women took a prominent role' (132). According to this reading, the kind of theatrical grief which calls upon the dead as though they were present on-stage is always in excess of the grief permitted by Protestant doctrine – and masculine power more broadly. Katharine Goodland, too, explores *Richard III* in terms of post-Reformation grief and women's mourning, in *Female Mourning and Tragedy in Medieval and Renaissance English Drama: From the Raising of Lazarus to King Lear* (Aldershot, 2005). See also Thomas Rist, *Revenge Tragedy and the Drama of Commemoration* (Aldershot, 2008). Tobias Doring usefully sums up a scholarly turn in the examination of this scene, whereby the women's laments 'have been described as paradigmatic of the ways in which female passions are principally articulated in excess of social relations' (Doring, 55). See also Isabel Karremann, 'Rites of Oblivion in Shakespeare's History Plays', *Shakespeare Survey* 63 (2010), 24–36.

35. *Richard III*, dir. Roxana Silbert, Royal Shakespeare Company, (Swan Theatre, Stratford-upon-Avon, 2012).
36. *King Lear*, dir. Rupert Goold, Liverpool Everyman, (Young Vic, London, 2009).
37. As Donald G. Watson points out in *Shakespeare's Early History Plays* (Basingstoke, 1990), 'First, not everyone in the play is fooled, in fact very few are. Second, though Richard does dominate the play, often he must share the stage, and more than once he loses control of the scene [...] and at other times controls it through sheer power or threats rather than the subtleties of deception' (102).
38. Shakespeare's source, Edward Hall, *The Union of the Two Noble and Illustre Families of Lancaster and York* (London, 1548), which incorporates Thomas More's *History of King Richard the Thirde* (London, 1513), makes this explicit: 'there was no man there but knew that his arm was ever such sith the day of his birth' and the deformity is

mentioned in *3 Henry VI* (3.2.155–7), where Gloucester speaks of it occurring in his mother's womb.

39. For analyses of Richard III as Vice and Machiavel, see William E. Sheriff, 'The Grotesque Comedy of Richard III', *Studies in the Literary Imagination* 5.1 (1972), 51–64; Wolfgang G. Muller, 'The Villain as Rhetorican in Shakeaspeare's *Richard III*', *Anglia* 102 (1984), 37–59; Ralph Berry, '*Richard III*: Bonding the Audience', in Berry, *Shakespeare and the Awareness of the Audience* (London, 1985); Katharine Eisaman Maus, *Inwardness and Theater in the English Renaissance* (Chicago, IL, and London, 1995), 48–54; Robert Weimann and Douglas Bruster, *Shakespeare and the Power of Performance* (Cambridge, 2008), ch. 2, 'Performance, Game and Representation in *Richard III*', 42–56.
40. Roxana Silbert, conversations in rehearsal, March 2012.
41. Silbert first developed ways of working with the Stanislavskian 'Method of Physical Action' in her time with Max Stafford-Clark at the Royal Court. Stafford-Clark writes a Forward in support of Bella Merlin's *Beyond Stanislavski: The Psycho-physical Approach to Actor Training* (London, 2001). He uses the method of 'actioning' whereby actors attach a transitive verb to each of their lines, thereby deciding not what feelings are being expressed through the lines but what is being done with them. Merlin, in an education pack for students about Stafford-Clark's methods, describes the technique thus: 'Basically, with "actioning", you pinpoint (very specifically through an active verb) what it is that you want to do to your on-stage partner. For example: "I excite you", "I challenge you", "I woo you", "I belittle you". (Merlin, in Maeve McKeown, 'Max Stafford-Clark Education Work Pack'. Available at http://www.outofjoint.co.uk/wp-content/uploads/2010/09/Max-Stafford-Clark-Workpack.pdf (accessed 11 December 2012). In agreement with Stafford-Clark and Merlin, Silbert likes to avoid the lack of precision and physical energy that privileging emotion over action can produce. Her work produces emotion through action and recalls early definitions of emotion as motion (see pp. xxi–xxiii). She has also suggested that insisting on an action for every line of every speech can lead to an energetic but sometimes overly aggressive style of performance (Interview with Roxana Silbert, 5 March 2012).
42. *Richard III*, dir. Michael Bogdanov, English Shakespeare Company, The Pleasance (Edinburgh, 1998).
43. In this production, Ratcliffe (Neal Barry) is not doubled as, but is, one of the murderers of Clarence; the impression given is that Richard has given away titles to those who have carried out his will and Ratcliffe is one of Richard's cronies throughout the rest of the play, also playing the part of churchman for him in 3.7.

44. Silbert's interest in an emerging psychology for Richard III through the play chimes significantly with Steven Mullaney's analysis of the affect of conscience (and of audience pity) which he argues is produced in Richard's last soliloquy, as he imagines that the actual ghosts that have cursed him in his sleep are the products of his conscience. Steven Mullaney, 'Affective Technologies: Toward an Emotional Logic of the Elizabethan Stage', in Mary Floyd-Wilson and Garrett A. Sullivan, Jr. (eds), *Environment and Embodiment in Early Modern England* (Basingstoke, 2007), 71–89, 85–7.
45. As I have suggested by footnoting recent discussions of *Richard III* and mourning/purgatory (see n. 34), I am not primarily concerned here with tensions between Catholic and Protestant forms of mourning and how the public and private signify and are figured in opposing religious discourses. For an engaging account of these tensions see Kate Welch, 'Making Mourning Show: *Hamlet* and Affective Public-Making', *Performance Research* 16.2 (2011), 74–82. Her idea of the theatre as a discursive space in which grief and mourning may be explored and evaluated is of interest here.
46. Douglas Trevor, *The Poetics of Melancholy in Early Modern England* (Cambridge, 2004).
47. Mark Breitenberg, *Anxious Masculinity in Early Modern England* (Cambridge, 1996).
48. David Schalkwyk,, 'Is Love an Emotion', *Symploke* 18 (2011), 1–2, 99–130.
49. Burton, *Anatomy*, Vol. 1, 248.
50. Burton, 'Democritus Junior to the Reader', *Anatomy*, Vol. 1, 25.
51. Gail Kern Paster, *Humoring*, 1, citing Edward Reynolds, *A Treatise on the Passions and Faculties of the Soul of Man* (London, 1647).
52. Burton, *Anatomy*, Vol. 1, 203.
53. Burton, *Anatomy*, Vol. 2, 176–86.
54. Richard Baxter, 'What are the Best Preservatives against Melancholy and Overmuch Sorrow?', in *A Continuation of Morning-Exercise Questions and Tales of Conscience, Practically Resolved by Sundry Ministers, in October 1682* (London, 1683), 297.
55. Baxter, 'Melancholy', 297.
56. Timothy Bright, *A Treatise of Melancholy* (London, 1586).
57. Bright, *Melancholy*, 188.
58. As first, the sites of the disease of melancholy on the one hand and religious dread on the other – respectively the body and the mind – are very much in binary opposition here; in the case of religious dread, 'it first proceedeth from the mind's apprehension'; in the case of melancholy, symptoms come 'from the humour, which deluding the

organical actions, abuseth the mind' (189). There is no medicinal cure for a stricken conscience, whereas melancholy can be cured by physic. It is important for Bright to make this distinction, because to believe that 'the soul's proper anguish' (197) is curable is heretical: to have a distressed conscience is a proper part of the human condition and is 'according to the good pleasure of God' (193), whereas melancholy is a degenerate somatic disease. He complicates the issue somewhat by admitting that the melancholic is particularly susceptible to such religious anguish. The mind seems to act as the portal for the soul in Bright's account of the soul's anguish, and the mind and body are inextricably connected in the rest of his treatise. However, here he is anxious to keep the soul untouched by the body: the soul can be anguished, sorrowful, fearful but it cannot be contaminated by the workings of black bile. Circumstantial causes of melancholy as are occasionally cited in Bright, broadly categorized as 'such accidents as befall us in this life against our wills, and unlooked for' (242), but these are rendered categorizable under Bright's taxonomy of physical causes of disease by considering them all part of our 'diet': 'Our diet consisteth not only (as it is commonly taken) in meat and drink: but in whatsoever exercises of mind or body: whether they be studies of the braine, or affections of the hart, or whether they be labours of the body, or exercises only' (242–3). Thus Bright, as well as Burton, can cite too much study as 'procuring' or causing melancholy (Bright, 24, Burton vol 1, 302–27), and advise the melancholic to avoid it, so that the spirits may be freed up to thin the blood. However, the overwhelming sense one gets from Bright is that melancholy is a physical disease with physical causes that one should eschew in order to keep in good health, albeit what he regards as somatic would not be connected so directly with the body today.

59. Bright, *Melancholy*, 242.
60. Trevor, *Poetics of Melancholy*, 64.
61. Kathleen O. Irace makes the point in her introduction to *The First Quarto of Hamlet* that 'the opening 27 lines in Act 1, Scene 2 of Q2 and F [...] are absent, undermining a possible first impression of the king as an efficient, gracious ruler'. Introduction, *The First Quarto of Hamlet* (Cambridge,1998), 12.
62. An assertion offered by Olivier in voiceover at the opening of his 1948 film. *Hamlet*, (film) dir. Lawrence Olivier (Two Cities, 1948).
63. See 273n. 79.
64. Jonathan Hope and Michael Witmore, 'Language at Work: The Periods of Shakespeare', paper given at the International Shakespeare Congress, Stratford-upon-Avon, 2012.

65. *Hamlet*, dir. Nicholas Hytner (National Theatre, London, 2010).
66. *Hamlet*, dir. Gregory Doran, Royal Shakespeare Company (Swan Theatre, Stratford-upon-Avon, 2008).
67. *Hamlet*, dir. Ian Rickson (Young Vic, London, 2011).
68. Held at the National Theatre Archive, London.
69. See e.g. James Woodall, review of *Hamlet*, dir. Nicholas Hytner, 8 October 2010. Available at http://www.theartsdesk.com/theatre/hamlet-national-theatre (accessed 10 October 2011); Maggie Constable, http://www.thepublicreviews.com/national-theatre-hamlet-milton-keynes-theatre/ (accessed 10 October 2011); Caroline McGinn, *Time Out*, 13 October 2010. Available at http://www.timeout.com/london/theatre/event/81883/hamlet (accessed 10 October 2011).
70. Jami Rogers, Review of *Hamlet*, dir. Hytner, *Internet Shakespeare Editions*, 3 October 2010. Available at http://isechronicle.uvic.ca/index.php/Ham?cat=114 (accessed 11 October 2011).
71. Two members of the Moscow punk rock band Pussy Riot, whose signature costume is a colourful balaclava, were imprisoned in 2012 for performing an anti-clerical, anti-government song in an Orthodox church.
72. Rory Kinnear, interview with Matt Wolf. Available at http://www.nationaltheatre.org.uk/video/rory-kinnear-talks-about-playing-hamlet (accessed 1 December 2012).
73. Peter Holland, Programme, *Hamlet*, dir. Nicholas Hytner, 2010.
74. Nicholas Hytner, Programme, *Hamlet*, dir. Nicholas Hytner, 2010.
75. Rory Kinnear, Programme, *Hamlet*, dir. Nicholas Hytner, 2010.
76. Particularly direct was Christopher Eccelstone's delivery of the line to Claudius in the West Yorkshire Playhouse production of 2002 (dir. Ian Brown). Both of these *Hamlet*s gave the initial impression that no matter how clearly they expressed their resentment of their uncle's marriage, Claudius had ways of recuperating the moment.
77. See David Lister, review of *Hamlet*, dir. Hytner, *Independent*, 8 October 2010; Charles Spenser, *The Daily Telegraph*, 8 October 2010; and, in a negative commentary on this Hamlet's 'ordinariness', Charles Weinstein, *Internet Shakespeare Editions*, 2 February 2011. Available at http://isechronicle.uvic.ca/index.php/Ham (accessed 10 October 2011).
78. Famously, by Thomas Lodge in *Wit's Misery and the World's Madness* (London, 1596), where he describes 'the ghost, which cried so miserably at the Theatre, "Hamlet, revenge!" ' (signature H4).
79. Nicholas Hytner, Programme, *Hamlet*, dir. Nicholas Hytner, 2010.
80. John E. Curran, Jr., Hamlet, *Protestantism, and the Mourning of Contingency: Not to Be* (Aldershot and Burlington, VT, 2006), 205.

81. Bridget Escolme, *Talking to the Audience: Shakespeare, Performance Self* (London, 2005), 73, 90–92; for an account of Hamlet's fatalism as read by Walter Benjamin in his comments on *Hamlet* as *Trauerspiel*, see Hugh Grady, *Shakespeare and Impure Aesthetics* (Cambridge, 2009), 'Hamlet as Mourning Play', 154–60, 156.
82. See Conclusion (p. 221).

## CONCLUSION: EMOTIONAL AGENDAS

1. In Chapter 2 of W. B. Worthen, *Shakespeare and the Force of Modern Performance* (Cambridge, 2003), 'Performing History', 28–78.
2. Suzanne Moore, 'Despite its promises, this government can't make you happy. In times of austerity, you are on your own.' Available at http://www.guardian.co.uk/commentisfree/2012/feb/08/government-cannot-make-you-happy (accessed 18 December 2012).
3. See Richard Strier, *The Unrepentant Renaissance* (2, n. 3); also, in *Resistant Structures: Particularity, Radicalism and Renaissance Texts* (Berkeley and Los Angeles, CA, 1995), Strier suggests that the term 'early modern' flatters and idealizes our own moment: 'the earlier period is seen to take its orientation from how it leads to "modern" culture' (6, n.5). I take his point but hope I have managed to historicize what he may regard as a dangerously presentist position in this book about 'modern' performance of 'early modern' drama.
4. In Stephen Greenblatt, *Renaissance Self-Fashioning from More to Shakespeare* (Chicago, IL, 1980), and Catherine Belsey, *The Subject of Tragedy: Identity and Difference in Renaissance Drama* (London, 1985).
5. Emmanuel Levinas, *Humanism of the Other* (1972), trans. Nidra Poller (Chicago, IL, 2003).
6. This is, famously, how John Manningham describes the gulling of Malvolio, after a performance at court in 1602. John Manningham, *The Diary of John Manningham of the Middle Temple* (1602–3), ed. R.P. Sorlien (Hanover,1976), 48.
7. At the time of writing, for example, an edition of *Shakespeare Bulletin* on 'Naturalism and Early Modern Performance' is in preparation (ed. Roberta Barker and Kim Solga, 2013).

# BIBLIOGRAPHY

## PRIMARY WORKS CITED

All original dates of publication of plays refer to dates of first production, where known. All plays by Shakespeare are from the *Arden Shakespeare Complete Works*, ed. Richard Proudfoot, David Scott Kastan and Ann Thompson (London and New York, 2011).


Adams, Thomas, *England's Sickness, Comparatively Conferred with Israel's. Divided into Two Sermons* (London, 1615).

Anon., *Elegy on the Death of Richard Burbage* (1619).

Anon., *A Pleasant and Delightful Poem of Two Lovers: Philos and Licia* (London 1624), repr. in Miller ed., *Seven Minor Epics* (Gainsville, 1967).

Bacon, Francis, 'Of Love' (1612), in *Francis Bacon: A Selection of his Works*, ed. Sidney Warhaft (New York, 1965).

Baxter, Richard, 'What are the Best Preservatives against Melancholy and Overmuch Sorrow?', in *A Continuation of Morning-Exercise Questions and Tales of Conscience, Practically Resolved by Sundry Ministers, in October 1682* (London, 1683).

Boccaccio, Giovanni, *Amorous Fiammetta*, trans. Bartholomew Young (London, 1587).

Bright, Timothy, *A Treatise on Melancholy* (London, 1586).

Burton, Robert, *The Anatomy of Melancholy* (1621), Thomas C. Faulkner, Nicholas K. Kiessling and Rhonda L. Blair (eds) (Oxford, 1989).

Chamberlain, John, *The Letters of John Chamberlain* (1597 to 1626), ed. N. E. M. McClure (Philadelphia, PA, 1939).

Cicero, Marcus Tullius, *Those Five Questions, which Marke Tully Cicero, Disputed in his Manor of Tusculanum*, trans. John Dolman (London, 1561).

Coeffeteau, Nicholas, *A Table of the Human Passions*, trans. Edward Grimeston (London, 1621).

Coleridge, Samuel Taylor, 'Notes on *Antony and Cleopatra*' in *The Literary Remains of Samuel Taylor Coleridge*, ed. Henry Nelson Coleridge (London, 1836).

Crouch, Tim, *England* (London, 2007).
—*The Author* (London, 2009).
—*I Malvolio*, in *I, Shakespeare: Four of Shakespeare's Better Known Plays Retold for Young Audiences by their Lesser-Known Characters* (London, 2011).
Dekker, Thomas and Thomas Middleton, *The Honest Whore Parts I and II* (1604–5), in Fredson Bowers (ed.), *The Dramatic Works of Thomas Dekker*, vol. 2 (Cambridge, 2009).
Dekker, Thomas and and John Webster, *Northward Ho* (1605), in Fredson Bowers ed., *The Dramatic Works of Thomas Dekker*, vol. 2 (Cambridge, 2009).
Descartes, René, *The Passions of the Soul*, trans. anon. (London, 1650).
Erasmus, Desiderius, 'Epistola 65' (1499), translated in *Retrospective Review* 5, ed. Henry Southern (London, 1822), 251.
Ferrand, James, *Erotomania or A treatise Discoursing of the Essence, Causes, Symptoms, Prognostics, and Cure of Love, or Erotic Melancholy* (London, 1640).
Fletcher, John, *The Pilgrim* (*c.*1621), in Fredson Bowers ed., *The Dramatic Works in the Beaumont and Fletcher Canon*, vol. 6 (Cambridge, 1994).
Fulbecke, William, *A Direction or Preparative to the Study of the Law* (London, 1600).
Gosson, Philip, *Plays Confuted in Five Actions, Proving They Are Not to be Suffered in a Christian Commonweal* (London, 1582).
Hall, Edward, *The Union of the Two Noble and Illustre Families of Lancaster and York* (London, 1548).
Hall, Joseph, *The King's Prophecy: or Weeping Joy Expressed in a Poem, to the Honor of England's too Great Solemnities* (London, 1603).
Harsnett, Samuel, *Declaration of Egregious Popish Impostures* (London, 1603).
James I, *Basilicon Doron*, in *James I, Works*, (London, 1616).
Jonson, Ben, 'To the Memory of my Beloved, the Author, Mr William Shakespeare and What He Hath Left Us', in William Shakespeare, *Mr William Shakespeare's Comedies, Histories and Tragedies* (First Folio) (London, 1623).
—*The Devil is an Ass* (1616) (Manchester, 1994).
Jordan, Thomas, 'The Virtuous Wife', in *Pictures of Passions, Fancies and Affections, Poetically Deciphered in a Variety of Characters* (London, 1641).
Joubert, Laurent, *Treatise on Laughter* (*Traité du Ris*) (1579), trans. Gregory David de Rocher (Tuscaloosa, AL, 1980).
Kepler, Johannes, *Optics: Paralimpomena to Witelo and Optical Part of Astronomy*, trans. William H. Donahue (1604) (Santa Fe, NM, 2000).
Laurens, André du, *A Discourse of the Preservation of the Sight: of Melancholic*

*Diseases; of Rheums, and of Old Age*, trans Richard Surphlet (London, 1599).

Lavater, Ludvig, *The Book of Ruth Expounded in Twenty Eight Sermons* (London, 1586).

Lemnias, Levinas, *The Sanctuary of Salvation, Helmet of Health, and Mirror of Modesty and Good Manners* (London, 1592).

Lipsius, Justus, *His First Book of Constancy*, trans. John Stradling (London,1594).

Lodge, Thomas, *Wit's Misery and the World's Madness* (London, 1596).

Manningham, John, *The Diary of John Manningham of the Middle Temple* (1602–1603), ed. R.P. Sorlien (Hanover, 1976).

Marlowe, *Dido, Queen of Carthage* (c. 1586) (Manchester, 1974).

Middleton, Thomas and William Rowley, *The Changeling* (1622) (London, 2006).

Milton, John, *Sampson Agonistes* (1671) (Cambridge, 1912).

Montaigne, Michel de, 'Of Anger and Choler', in *Essays*, trans. John Florio (London, 1613).

Painter, William, *The Palace of Pleasure* (London, 1566).

Plato, *Republic*, trans. G.M.A. Grube (Indianapolis, 1992).

Playfere, Thomas, *The Mean in Mourning. A Sermon Preached at Saint Mary's Spittle in London on Tuesday in Easter Week* 1595 (London, 1596).

Plutarch, Lucius Mestrius, 'Life of Caius Martius Coriolanus', *Lives of the Ancient Greeks and Romans*, trans. Thomas North (1579), in Geoffrey Bullough, *Narrative and Dramatic Sources of Shakespeare*, 8 vols (London and New York, 1957–75), vol. 4, *The Roman Plays*.

—'Life of Marcus Antonius', *Lives of the Ancient Greeks and Romans*, trans. Thomas North, in Geoffrey Bullough, *Narrative and Dramatic Sources of Shakespeare*, 8 vols (London and New York, 1957–75), vol. 4, *The Roman Plays*.

—'Of Meekness, or How a Man Should Refrain Choler', in *The Morals*, trans. Philomen Holland (London, 1603).

Prynne, William, *Histrio-mastix*, *The Players Scourge or Actors Tragedy* (London, 1633).

Radford, Mavericke, *Three Treatises Religiously Handled and Named According to the Several Subject of Each Treatise: The Mourning Weed. The Morning's Joy. The King's Rejoicing* (London, 1603).

Reynolds, Edward, *A Treatise on the Passions and Faculties of the Soul of Man* (London, 1647).

Riche, Barnaby, *Farewell to Military Profession* (1581) (Ottawa, Canada, 1992).

Sandford, James, *The Mirror of Madness* (London, 1576).

Seneca, Lucius Annaeus, 'A Treatise of Anger', in *The Workes of Lucius Annaeus Seneca, Both Moral and Natural*, trans. Thomas Lodge (London, 1614).

Sidney, Philip, *An Apology for Poetry (or The Defense of Poetry)* (1595) (Manchester, 1965).
Shakespeare, William, *All's Well that Ends Well* (c. 1602).
—*Antony and Cleopatra* (1608).
—*As You Like it* (1599).
—*Coriolanus* (1608).
—*Hamlet* (1601).
—*Hamlet* First Quarto (1603) (Cambridge, 1998).
—*Henry VI Parts I, II and III* (c. 1590; c. 1592–3).
—*King Henry V* (1599).
—*Love's Labours Lost* (c. 1594).
—*Richard II* (1595).
—*Richard III* (c. 1593).
—*Romeo and Juliet* (c. 1594).
—*The Taming of the Shrew* (c. 1593).
—*The Tempest* (1610).
—*Timon of Athens* (c. 1607).
—*Troilus and Cressida* (c. 1601).
—*Twelfth Night* (1600).
Southwell, Robert, *The Triumphs Over Death: Or, A Consolatory Epistle, for Afflicted Minds, in the Affects of Dying Friends* (London, 1595).
Stubbes, Philip, *Anatomy of Abuses* (London, 1583).
Webster, John, *The Duchess of Malfi* (1614), *Arden Early Modern Drama* (London, 2009).
Webster, John, *The White Devil* (1612) (London, 2008).
Wright, Thomas, *The Passions of the Mind in General* (London, 1604). Reprint based on the 1604 edition, ed. Thomas O. Sloan (Urbana, Chicago, IL, London, 1971).

## SECONDARY WORKS CITED

Alberti, Fay Bound, *Matters of the Heart* (Oxford, 2010).
Allderidge, Patricia, 'Management and Mismanagement at Bedlam, 1547–1633', in Charles Webster ed., *Health, Medicine and Mortality in the Sixteenth Century* (Cambridge,1979), 141–64.
Allen Brown, Pamela, *Better a Shrew than a Sheep: Women, Drama and the Culture of Jest in Early Modern England* (London, Ithaca, NY, 2003).
Althusser Louis, 'Ideology and Ideological State Apparatuses', in *Lenin and Philosophy and Other Essays*, trans. Ben Brewster (London, 1971).
Andrews, Jonathan 'Bethlem Revisited: A History of Bethlem Hospital c.1643–1770', Ph.D. Diss. (University of London, 1991).

Andrews, Jonathan, Asa Briggs, Roy Porter, Penny Tucker and Keir Waddington, *The History of Bedlam* (London, 1997).

Barber, C. L., *Shakespeare's Festive Comedy: A Study of Dramatic Form and its Relation to Social Custom* (Princeton, NJ, 2012).

Barish, Jonas, *The Anti-Theatrical Prejudice* (Berkeley and Los Angeles, CA, 1981).

Barton, Anne, Introduction to *All's Well that Ends Well*, Riverside Shakespeare (New York, 1976), 499–503.

Bassett, Kate, 'The Hotspur of Ancient Rome', Review of *Coriolanus*, dir. Dominic Dromgoole, Shakespeare's Globe *Independent on Sunday*, 14 May 2006.

British Broadcasting Corporation, http://www.bbc.co.uk/health/emotional_health/bereavement/bereavement_helpourselves.shtml (accessed 1 December 2012).

Becker, Lucinda M., *Death and the Early Modern Englishwoman* (Aldershot, 2003).

Belsey, Catherine, *The Subject of Tragedy: Identity and Difference in Renaissance Drama* (London, 1985).

Benedetti, Jean, *Stanislavski and the Actor* (New York, 1998).

Benedict, David, Review of *The Changeling*, Cheek by Jowl, Variety. Com, 28 May 2006. Available at http://www.variety.com/review/VE1117930662/?refCatId=33 (accessed 20 October 2010).

Bennett, Susan and Christie Carlson (eds), *Shakespeare Beyond English* (Cambridge, 2013).

Benson, Sean, 'Perverse Fantasies?', *Papers on Language and Literature* 45.3 (summer 2009).

Berry, Ralph, *Shakespeare and the Awareness of the Audience* (London, 1985).

Billing, Christian, *Masculinity, Corporality and the English Stage 1580–1635* (Farnham and Burlington, VT, 2008).

Billington, Michael, Review of *Coriolanus*, dir. Dominic Dromgoole, Shakespere's Globe *Guardian*, 12 May 2006.

—Review of *The Changeling*, dir. Declan Donnellan, Cheek by Jowl and BITE: 2006, Barbican, *Guardian*, 16 May 2006.

—Review of *All's Well that Ends Well*, dir. John Dove, Shakespeare's Globe, *Guardian*, 6 May 2011.

—Review of *The Changeling*, dir. Joe Hill-Gibbons,Young Vic, *Guardian*, 3 February 2012.

Bloom, Harold, *Bloom's Shakespeare through the Ages* (New York, 2010).

Boas, Frederick S., *Shakespeare and his Predecessors* (London, 1896).

Bowers, Rick, *Radical Comedy in Early Modern England* (Aldershot, 2008).

Brady, Angela, *English Funerary Elegy in the Seventeenth Century* (Basingstoke, 2006).

Breitenberg, Mark, *Anxious Masculinity in Early Modern England* (Cambridge, 1996).

Brennan, Claire, Review of *Antony and Cleopatra*, dir. Janet Suzman, Liverpool Playhouse, *Observer*, 17 October 2010.

Bristol, Michael D., *Big-Time Shakespeare* (London, 1996).

Brooke, Nicholas, '*All's Well that Ends Well*', *Shakespeare Survey* 30 (1977).

—*Horrid Laughter in Jacobean Tragedy* (London, 1979).

Brookes, Harold, '*Richard III*, Unhistorical Amplifications: The Women's Scenes and Seneca', *Modern Language Review* 75 (1980), 721–37.

Bullough, Geoffrey, *Narrative and Dramatic Sources of Shakespeare*, 8 vols (London and New York, 1957–75).

Cake, Jonathan, 'Interview with Guillaume Winter', in Delphine Lemmonier-Texier and Guillaume Winter, *Lectures de Coriolan de William Shakespeare* (Rennes, 2006).

Calderwood, James Lee, *Shakespeare and the Denial of Death* (Amherst, MA, 1987).

Carlin, Claire L. ed., *Imagining Contagion in Early Modern Europe* (Basingstoke, 2005).

Carnegie, David, '"Maluolio Within": Performance Perspectives on the Dark House', *Shakespeare Quarterly* 52.3 (Autumn 2001).

Carson, Christie, 'Democratising the Audience', in Christie Carson and Farah Karim-Cooper (eds), *Shakespeare's Globe: A Theatrical Experiment* (Cambridge, 2008).

Carson, Christie and Farah Karim-Cooper (eds), *Shakespeare's Globe: A Theatrical Experiment* (Cambridge, 2008).

Cavendish, Dominic, 'Suzman Interview for *Antony and Cleopatra*', *Daily Telegraph*, 28 September 2010.

Certeau, Michel de, 'Walking in the City', in Imre Szeman and Timothy Kaposy, *Cultural Anthropology: an Anthology* (Oxford, 2011).

Charnes, Linda, *Notorious Identity: Materializing the Subject in Shakespeare* (Cambridge, MA, 1993).

Charney, Maurice, *Shakespeare on Love and Lust* (New York, 2000).

Clapp, Susannah, Review of *The Changeling*, dir. Declan Donnellan, Cheek by Jowl and BITE: 2006, Barbican, *Observer*, 21 May 2006.

—Review of *All's Well that Ends Well*, dir. John Dove, Shakespeare's Globe, *Guardian*, *Observer*, 8 May 2011.

Classen, Albrecht ed., *Laughter in the Middle Ages and Early Modern Times: Epistemology of a Fundamental Human Behavior, its Meaning and Consequences* (Berlin, New York, 2010).

Clink Museum, London, 'Education', http://www.clink.co.uk/Education.html (accessed 6 June 2010).

Cohen, Ralph, 'The Most Convenient Place: The Second Blackfriars Theater and its Appeal', in Richard Dutton ed., *The Oxford Handbook of Early Modern Theatre* (Oxford, 2009), 209–224.

Constable, Maggie, review of *Hamlet*, dir. Hytner, National Theatre, 2 March 2011. Available at http://www.thepublicreviews.com/national-theatre-hamlet-milton-keynes-theatre/ (accessed 10 October 2011).

Correll, Barbara, 'Malvolio at Malfi: Managing Desire in Shakespeare and Webster', *Shakespeare Quarterly* 58.1 (Spring 2007), 65–92.

Crouch, Tim, Interview for British Council Edinburgh Festival 2011 Showcase. Available at http://edinburghshowcase.britishcouncil.org/home/tim-crouch/ (accessed 24 November 2012).

Curran, John E. Jr., *Hamlet, Protestantism, and the Mourning of Contingency: Not to Be* (Aldershot, Burlington, VT, 2006).

Daalder, Joost, 'Folly and Madness in *The Changeling*', *Essays in Criticism* 38.1 (January 1988).

—'Madness in Parts 1 and 2 of *The Honest Whore*: A Case for Close Reading', *AUMLA* 86 (November 1996), 63–79.

Darnton, Robert, *The Great Cat Massacre and Other Episodes in French Cultural History* (New York, 1985).

Deats, Sarah Munson, *Antony and Cleopatra: Routledge New Critical Essays* (London and New York, 2005).

Dennis, Carl, '*All's Well that Ends Well* and the Meaning of Agape', *Philological Quarterly* 50.1 (January 1971), 75–84.

Devereaux, Simon and Paul Griffiths (eds), *Penal Practice and Culture, 1500–1900: Punishing the English* (Basingstoke, 2004).

Dezecache, Guillaume and R.I.M. Dunbar, 'Sharing the Joke: The Size of Natural Laughter Groups'. Available at www.grezes.ens.fr/reprints/dezecache&dunbar2012.pdf (accessed 28 November 2012).

Dickson, Andrew, Review of *All's Well that Ends Well*, dir. Sunil Shanbag, Arpana Theatre, Shakespeare's Globe, *Guardian*, 1 June 2012.

Dixon, Thomas, *From Passions to Emotions: The Creation of a Secular Psychological Category* (Cambridge, 2003).

Dollimore, Jonathan, *Radical Tragedy*, 3rd edn (Basingstoke, 2004).

Doring, Tobias, *Performances of Mourning in Shakespearean Theatre and Early Modern Culture* (Basingstoke, 2006).

Dufallo, Basil and Peggy McCracken (eds), *Dead Lovers: Erotic Bonds and the Study of Premodern Europe* (Ann Arbor, MI, 2006).

Dunbar, R. I. M., 'Bridging the Bonding Gap: The Transition from Primates to Humans', *Philosophical Transactions of the Royal Society* 367 (July 2012), 1597, 1837–46.

Dustagheer, Sarah, 'To see, and to bee seene [...] and possesse the Stage, against the Play': Blackfriars' actor/audience interaction in the repertory of the Children of the Queen's Revels and the King's Men', paper given at the 'Jacobean Indoor Playing Symposium' (London Shakespeare Centre, King's College, London, 4 February 2012).

Dutton, Richard, ed., *The Oxford Handbook of Early Modern Theatre* (Oxford, 2009).

Dutton, Richard and Jean E. Howard (eds), *A Companion to Shakespeare's Works: The Comedies* (Malden, MA and Oxford, 2003).

Ede, Laurie N., *British Film Design: A History* (London, 2010).

Ellis, David, *Shakespeare's Practical Jokes: An introduction to the Comic in his Work* (Lewisburg, 2007).

Escolme, Bridget, *Talking to the Audience: Shakespeare, Performance, Self* (London, 2005).

—'The Spatial Politics of Shakespeare's Rome in the Contemporary Theatre', *Shakespeare Survey* 60, 2007.

—'Shakespeare, Rehearsal and and Site-Specific Performance', *Shakespeare Bulletin*, special edition, 'Rehearsing Shakespeare: Alternative Strategies in Process and Performance', 30.4 (Winter 2012).

—'Does Shakespeare Work Better Outside Britain?' Available at http://www.guardian.co.uk/commentisfree/2012/may/19/shakespeare-outside-britain-international (accessed 23 October 2012).

—'Costume, Disguise and Self-Display' in Farah Karim-Cooper and Tiffany Stern (eds) Shakespeare's Theatre and the Effects of Performance (London, 2013) pp. 118-140 (136).

Fernie, Ewan, 'Shakesperience 3: Helena's Fantasies (Part Two)'. Available at http://bloggingshakespeare.com/shakespearience-3-helenas-fantasies-part-two (accessed 1 December 2012).

Fetzer, Margret, 'Violence as the 'Dark Room' of Comedy: Shakespeare's *Twelfth Night*', *Deutsche Shakespeare-Gesellschaft* 2006, 'Staging Violence and Terror'. Available at http://shakespeare-gesellschaft.de/en/publications/seminar/ausgabe2006/fetzer.html (accessed 26 November 2006).

Findlay, Alison, *Women in Shakespeare: A Dictionary* (London, 2010).

Fisher, Philip, *The Vehement Passions* (Princeton, NJ, 2002).

Fisk, John, 'Audiencing: A Cultural Studies Approach to Watching Television', *Poetics* 21.4 (August 1992), 345–59.

Fitz, L. T., 'Egyptian Queens and Male Reviewers: Sexist Attitudies in *Antony and Cleopatra* Criticism', *Shakespeare Quarterly* 28.3 (Summer 1977), 375–97.

Floyd-Wilson, Mary and Garrett A. Sullivan, Jr (eds), *Environment and Embodiment in Early Modern England* (Basingstoke, 2007).

Frelick, Nancy, 'Contagions of Love: Textual Transmission', in Claire L.

Carlin ed., *Imagining Contagion in Early Modern Europe* (Basingstoke, 2005), 47–62.

Freshwater, Helen, *Theatre and Audiences* (Basingstoke, 2009).

Freud, Sigmund, 'Mourning and Melancholia', trans. Shaun Whiteside, in *On Murder, Mourning and Melancholia* (London, 2005).

Gardner, Lyn, Review of *Coriolanus*, dir. Yukio Ninagawa, *Guardian*, 27 April 2007.

—Review of *Antony and Cleopatra*, dir. Janet Suzman, Chichester Festival Theatre, 2012, *Guardian*, 16 September 2012.

Gaskill, Gayle, 'Overhearing Malvolio for Pleasure or Pity: The Letter Scene and the Dark House Scene in Twelfth Night on Stage and Screen', in Laury Magnus and Walter W. Cannon, *Who Hears in Shakespeare? Auditory Worlds on Stage and Screen* (Madison, NJ, 2012), 119–217.

Gervais, Matthew and David Sloan Wilson, 'The Evolutionary Functions of Laughter and Humor: A Synthetic Approach', *The Quarterly Review of Biology* 80.4 (December 2005), 395–430.

Ghose, Indira, *Shakespeare and Laughter*, (Manchester, 2008).

—'Licence to Laugh: Festive Laughter in Twelfth Night', in Manfred Pfister ed., *A History of English Laughter: Laughter from Beowulf to Beckett and Beyond*, (Amsterdam and New York, 2002)

Gittings, Clare, *Death, Burial and the Individual in Early Modern England* (London and Sydney, 1984).

—'Sacred and Secular: 1558–1660' in Peter C. Jupp and Clare Gittings (eds), *Death in England: An Illustrated History* (Manchester, 1999), 147–173.

Golden, Leon, 'The Purgation Theory of Cartharsis', *The Journal of Aesthetics and Art Criticism* 31.4 (Summer 1973), 473–9.

Goldstein, Donna M., *Laughter Out of Place: Race, Class, Violence, and Sexuality in a Rio Shantytown* (Berkeley and Los Angeles, CA, 2003).

Goldsworthy Adrian, *Antony and Cleopatra* (London, 2010).

Goleman, Daniel *Emotional Intelligence* (New York, 1995).

Goodland, Katharine, *Female Mourning and Tragedy in Medieval and Renaissance English Drama: From the Raising of Lazarus to King Lear* (Aldershot, 2005).

Grady, Hugh, *Shakespeare and Impure Aesthetics* (Cambridge, 2009).

Grant, Steve, Review of *Antony and Cleopatra*, dir. Adrian Noble, Royal Shakespeare Company, *Plays and Players*, November 1982.

—Review of *Antony and Cleopatra*, dir. Peter Hall, Royal Shakespeare Company, *Time Out*, 15 April 1987.

Greenblatt, Stephen, *Renaissance Self-Fashioning from More to Shakespeare* (Chicago, IL, 1980).

—'A Man of Principle', Review of *Coriolanus* (film), dir. Ralph Fiennes, *New York Review of Books*, 8 March 2012.

Gross, Daniel M., *The Secret History of Emotion: From Aristotle's 'Rhetoric' to Modern Brain Science* (Chicago, IL, 2006).

Gross, Kenneth, *Shakespeare's Noise* (Chicago, IL, 2001).

Gurr, Andrew, *The Shakespearean Stage 1574–1642* (3rd edn) (Cambridge, 1992).

Hamer, M., *Signs of Cleopatra: Reading an Icon Historically* (Exeter, 2008).

Harris, Jonathan Gil, '"Narcissus in thy Face": Roman Desire and the Difference it Fakes in *Antony and Cleopatra*', *Shakespeare Quarterly* 45.4 (Winter 1994), 408–25.

Hart, Christopher, Review of *Coriolanus*, dir. Dominic Dromgoole, Shakespeare's Globe, *Sunday Times*, 14 May 2006.

Headlam Wells, Robin, *Shakespeare on Masculinity* (Cambridge and New York, 2000).

Hemming, Sarah, Review of *All's Well that Ends Well*, dir. John Dove, Shakespeare's Globe, *Financial Times*, 8 May 2011.

Hobgood, Allison P., '*Twelfth Night*'s "Notorious Abuse" of Malvolio: Shame, Humorality, and Early Modern Spectatorship', *Shakespeare Bulletin* 24.3 (2006), 1–22.

Hodgdon, Barbara, *The Shakespeare Trade: Performances and Appropriations* (Philadelphia, PA, 1998).

Holderness, Graham, 'Shakespeare-Land', in Willy Maley and Margaret Tudeau-Clayton (eds), *This England, That Shakespeare: New Angles on England and the Bard* (Farnham and Burlington, VT, 2010).

Hope, Jonathan and Michael Witmore, 'Language at Work: The Periods of Shakespeare', paper given at the International Shakespeare Congress, Stratford-upon-Avon, 2012.

Hunt, Alan, *Governance of the Consuming Passions: A History of Sumptuary Law* (Basingtoke, 1996).

Hunter, G. K., Introduction to *All's Well that Ends Well*, Arden Second Series (London, 2006), xxxiii–xxxiv.

Hyland, Peter, *Disguise on the Early Modern Stage* (Farnham, 2011).

Ingram, Martin, 'Shame and Pain: Themes and Variations in Tudor Punishments', in Simon Devereaux and Paul Griffiths (eds), *Penal Practice and Culture, 1500–1900: Punishing the English* (Basingstoke, 2004).

Irace, Katherine, Introduction to *The First Quarto of Hamlet* (Cambridge,1998).

Jackson, Ken, *Separate Theaters, Bethlem ('Bedlam') Hospital and the Shakespearean Stage* (Newark, NJ, 2005).

Jenkins Logan, Thad, '*Twelfth Night*: The Limits of Festivity', *Studies in English Literature 1500–1900* 22.2 (spring 1982).

Johnson, Samuel, *Notes to Shakespeare I, The Comedies: All's Well that Ends Well* (London, 1765).

Jones, G. P., 'A Burbage Ballad and John Payne Collier', *The Review of English Studies* 40.159 (August 1989), 393–7.

Joyce, Justin A., 'Fashion, Class, and Gender in Early Modern England: Staging *Twelfth Night*', in Cynthia Kuhn and Cindy Carlson (eds), *Styling Texts: Dress and Fashion in Literature* (New York, 2007), 49–66.

Kapur, Sohailia, 'Musical Theatre in India'. Available at http://shekharkapur.com/blog/2011/05/musical-theatre-in-india-guest-column-by-sohaila-kapur/ (accessed 1 December 2012).

Karremann, Isabel, 'Rites of Oblivion in Shakespeare's History Plays', *Shakespeare Survey* 63 (2010), 24–36.

Kastan, David Scott, '*All's Well that Ends Well* and the Limits of Comedy', *ELH* 52.3 (autumn 1985), 575–589.

Kemper, Becky, 'A Clown in the Dark House: Reclaiming the Humor in Malvolio's Downfall', *Journal of the Wooden O Symposium* (2007), 42–50.

Khan Coppelia, *Shakespeare's Roman Plays: Warriors, Wounds and Women* (London and New York, 1997).

Kirwan, Peter, '*All's Well that Ends Well:* Arpana', in Susan Bennett and Christie Carlson (eds), *Shakespeare Beyond English* (Cambridge, 2013).

Kitzes, Adam H., *The Politcs of Melancholy from Spenser to Milton* (New York and Abingdon, 2006).

Kottman, Paul A., 'Defying the Stars: Tragic Love as the Struggle for Freedom in *Romeo and Juliet*', *Shakespeare Quarterly* 63.1 (2012), 1–38.

Kuhn, Cynthia G. and Cindy Carlson, *Styling Texts: Dress and Fashion in Literature* (Youngstown, NY, 2007).

Langis, Unhae, '*Coriolanus*: Inordinate Passions and Powers in Personal and Political Governance', *Comparative Drama* 44.1 (2010), 1–27.

Langley, Eric, *Narcissism and Suicide in Shakespeare and his Contemporaries* (Oxford, 2009).

Laroque, Francois, 'Slaughter and Laughter: Cruel Comedy in Fin de Siècle Tudor Drama', in Centre D'etudes Superieures de la Renaissance, *Tudor Theatre: For Laughs? Round Tables on Tudor Theatre and Drama* vol. 6 (Berne, 2002), 161–75.

Lawrence, W.W., *Shakespeare's Problem Comedies* (New York, 1931).

*Legal Times*, 'BLT', 'In *Twelfth Night* Mock Trial, Malvolio Loses'. Available at http://legaltimes.typepad.com/blt/2009/04/in-twelfth-night-mock-trial-malvolio-loses.html (accessed 26 November 2012).

Letzler Cole, Susan, *The Absent One: Mourning Ritual, Tragedy and the Performance of Ambivalence* (University Park and London, 1985).

Levinas, Emmanuel, *Humanism of the Other* (1972), trans. Nidra Poller (Chicago, IL, 2003).

Lister, David, Review of *Hamlet*, dir. Hytner, National Theatre, Olivier Theatre, London, 2010, *Independent*, 8 October 2010.

Lodwick, Keith, 'The Film Work of Stage Designer Oliver Messel', *V&A Online Journal* 1 (autumn 2008). Available at http://www.vam.ac.uk/content/journals/research-journal/issue-01/the-film-work-of-stage-designer-oliver-messel/ (accessed 4 December 2012).

London Dungeons, 'Attractions'. Available at http://www.the-dungeons.co.uk/london/en/attractions/index.htm (accessed 6 June 2010).

Loomba, Ania, *Gender, Race, Renaissance Drama* (Manchester, 1989).

Lopez, Jeremy, *Theatrical Convention and Audience Response in Early Modern Drama* (Cambridge and New York, 2003).

Loxton, Howard, *British Theatre Guide*, Review of *Coriolanus*, dir. Yukio Ninagawa. Available at http://www.britishtheatreguide.info/reviews/coriolanusnina-rev (accessed 4 April 2011).

http://www.britishtheatreguide.info/reviews/coriolanusnina-rev (accessed 20 November 2012).

McCallum, M. W., *Shakespeare's Roman Plays and their Background* (London, 1967).

McEwan, Ian, *Solar* (London, 2011).

McGinn, Caroline, Review of *Hamlet*, dir. Hytner, National Theatre, Olivier Theatre, London, *Time Out*, 13 October 2010. Available at http://www.timeout.com/london/theatre/event/81883/hamlet (accessed 10 October 2011).

McKeown, Maeve, 'Max Stafford Clerk Education Work Pack'. Available at http://www.outofjoint.co.uk/wp-content/uploads/2010/09/Max-Stafford-Clark-Workpack.pdf (accessed 2.7.2013)

MacDonald, Michael, *Mystical Bedlam: Madness, Anxiety and Healing in Seventeenth Century England* (Cambridge, 1981).

Madeleine, Richard, *Shakespeare in Production: Antony and Cleopatra* (Cambridge,1998).

Magnus, Laury and Walter W. Cannon, *Who Hears in Shakespeare? Auditory Worlds on Stage and Screen* (Madison, WI, 2012).

Maley, Willy and Margaret Tudeau-Clayton (eds), *This England, That Shakespeare: New Angles on England and the Bard* (Farnham and Burlington, VT, 2010).

Mansfield, Katherine, *The Journal of Katherine Mansfield*, ed. J. M. Murray (New York, 1921).

Marijuán, Pedro C. and Jorge Navarro, 'The Bonds of Laughter: A Multidisciplinary Inquiry into the Information Processes of Human Laughter', Bioinformation and Systems Biology Group Instituto Aragonés de Ciencias de la Salud. Available at http://arxiv.org/abs/1010.5602 (accessed 27 November 2012).

Marshall, Cynthia, 'Shakespeare, Crossing the Rubicon', *Shakespeare Survey* 53 (2000), 73–88.

Matthews, Gerald, Moshe Zeidner and Richard D. Roberts, *Emotional Intelligence: Science and Myth* (Cambridge, MA, 2004).

Maus, Katharine Eisaman, *Inwardness and Theater in the English Renaissance* (Chicago, IL, and London, 1995).

Menzer, Paul ed., *Indoor Shakespeare: Essays on the Blackfriar's Stage* (Selinsgrove, 2006).

Merlin, Bella, *Beyond Stanislavski: The Psycho-physical Approach to Actor Training* (London, 2001).

Miles, Geoffrey, *Shakespeare and the Constant Romans* (Oxford,1996).

Miller, Alan S., 'Ten Politically Incorrect Truths About Human Nature', Psychology Today. Available at http://www.psychologytoday.com/articles/200706/ten-politically-incorrect-truths-about-human-nature (accessed 12 December 2011).

Miller, Alan S. and Satoshi Kanazawa, *Why Beautiful People Have More Daughters: From Dating, Shopping and Praying to Going to War and Becoming a Billionaire* (London, 2007).

Miola, Robert S., *Shakespeare and Classical Tragedy: The Influence of Seneca* (Oxford, 1992).

Moss, Stephanie and Kaara L. Petersen, *Disease, Diagnosis and Cure on the Early Modern Stage* (Aldershot, 2004).

Moulton, Frederick, 'Fat Knight, or What You Will: Unimitable Falstaff', in Richard Dutton and Jean E. Howard (eds), *A Companion to Shakespeare's Works: The Comedies* (Malden, MA and Oxford, 2003), 223–242.

Mullaney, Steven, *The Place of the Stage: License, Play, and Power in Renaissance England* (Chicago, IL, and London, 1988).

—'Affective Technologies: Toward an Emotional Logic of the Elizabethan Stage', in Mary Floyd-Wilson and Garrett A. Sullivan, Jr (eds), *Evironment and Embodiment in Early Modern England* (Basingstoke, 2007), 71–89.

Muller, Wolfgang G., 'The Villain as Rhetorican in Shakeaspeare's Richard III', *Anglia* 102 (1984), 37–59.

Myhill, Nova, 'Taking the Stage: Spectators as Spectacles in the Caroline Public Theaters', in Nova Myhill and Jennifer Low, *Imagining the Audience in Early Modern Drama, 1558–1642* (Basingstoke, 2011), 37–54.

Myhill, Nova and Jennifer Low, *Imagining the Audience in Early Modern Drama, 1558–1642* (Basingstoke, 2011).

Nash, David and Anne Marie Kilday, *Exploring Crime and Morality in Britain, 1600–1900* (Basingstoke, 2010).

National Health Service, 'Bereavement'. Available at http://www.nhs.uk/Livewell/bereavement/Pages/coping-with-bereavement.aspx (accessed 2.7.2013)

Neely, Carol Thomas, 'Hot Blood: Estranging Mediterranean Bodies in Early Modern Medical and Dramatic Texts', in Stephanie Moss and Kaara L. Peterson (eds), *Disease Diagnosis and Cure on the Early Modern Stage* (Aldershot, 2004), 55–68.

—*Distracted Subjects: Madness and Gender in Shakespeare and Early Modern Culture* (Ithaca, NY, and London, 2004).

Neugebauer, Richard, 'Medieval and Early Modern Theories of Mental Illness', *Archives of General Psychiatry* 36.4 (1979), 477–83.

Nightingale, Benedict, Review of *Coriolanus*, dir. Dominic Dromgoole, Shakespeare's Globe, London, 12 May 2006.

Ninagawa, Yukio, interviewed by Rachel Halliburton, *Time Out*, 16 April 2007. Available at http://www.timeout.com/london/theatre/features/2809/Yukio_Ninagawa-interview.html (accessed 20 November 2012).

O'Donoghue, Edward, *The Story of Bethlem Hospital* (London, 1915).

Osmond, Susan, '"Her Infinite Variety": Representations of Shakespeare's Cleopatra in Fashion, Film and Theatre', *Film, Fashion and Consumption* 1.1 (February 2011), 55–79.

Panksepp, Jaak, 'The Riddle of Laughter: Neural and Psychoevolutionary Underpinnings of Joy', *Current Directions in Psychological Science* 19.6 (December 2000).

Panksepp, J. and J. Burgdorf, 'Laughing Rats? Playful Tickling Arouses High-frequency Ultrasonic Chirping in Young Rodents', in S. Hameroff, D. Chalmers and A. Kazniak (eds), *Towards a Science of Consciousness* (Cambridge, MA, 1999).

Paster, Gail Kern, *Humoring the Body: Emotions and the Shakesperean Stage* (Chicago, IL and London, 2004).

Paster, Gail Kern, Katherine Rowe and Mary Floyd-Wilson (eds), *Reading the Early Modern Passions: Essays in the Cultural History of Emotion* (Philadephia, PA, 2004).

Pender, Stephen, 'Rhetoric, Grief and the Imagination in Early Modern England', *Philosophy and Rhetoric* 43.1 (2010), 54–85.

Peter, John, Review of *The Changeling*, dir. Declan Donnellan, Cheek by Jowl and BITE: 2006, Barbican, *Sunday Times* 21 May 2006.

Petersen, Kaara L., 'Performing Arts: Hysterical Disease, Exorcism, and Shakespeare's Theatre', in Stephanie Moss and Kaara L. Petersen, *Disease, Diagnosis and Cure on the Early Modern Stage* (Aldershot, 2004).

Pfister, Manfred ed., *A History of English Laughter: Laughter from Beowulf to Beckett and Beyond* (Amsterdam and New York, 2002).

Phillipy, Patricia, *Women, Death and Literature in Post-Reformation England* (Cambridge, 2002).

Pigman, G. W. III, *Grief and the English Renaissance Elegy* (Cambridge, 1985).

Porter, Roy, *Mind Forg'd Manacles: A History of Madness in England from the Restoration to the Regency* (London, 1990).
Proudfoot, Richard, 'Peter Brook and Shakespeare', in James Redmond ed., *Themes In Drama 2: Drama and Mimesis* (Cambridge, 1980).
Provine, Robert R., *Laughter, A Scientific Investigation* (London, 2004).
Redmond, James (ed.), *Themes In Drama 2: Drama and Mimesis* (Cambridge, 1980).
Reed, Robert, *Bedlam on the Jacobean Stage* (London,1952).
Reynolds, Paige Martin, 'Mourning and Memory in *Richard III*', *ANQ* (2008), 19–25.
Rist, Thomas, *Revenge Tragedy and the Drama of Commemoration* (Aldershot, 2008).
Rogers, Jami, Review of *Hamlet*, dir. Hytner, National Theatre, *Internet Shakespeare Editions*, 3 October 2010. Available at http://isechronicle.uvic.ca/index.php/Ham?cat=114 (accessed 11 October 2011).
Rosenwein, Barbara H., 'Problems and Methods in the History of Emotions', *Passions in Context, an International Journal for the History of the Emotions* 1 (2010) Available at www.passionsincontext.de/uploads/media/01_Rosenwein.pdf (accessed 1 April 2012).
Royster, F. T., *Becoming Cleopatra: The Shifting Image of an Icon* (Basingstoke, 2003).
Rublack, Ulinka, 'Fluxes: The Early Modern Body and the Emotions', *History Workshop Journal* 53 (2002), 1–16.
Rutter, Carol Chilllington, *Enter the Body: Women and Representation on Shakespeare's Stage* (London, 2001).
Saito, Fumikazu, 'Perception and Optics in the 16th Century: Some Features of Della Porta's Theory of Vision', *Circumscribere* 8 (2010), 28–35.
Saldago, Gamini, *Eyewitnesses of Shakespeare: First Hand Accounts of Performance*, 1590–1890 (London, 1975).
Schafer, E., 'Shakespeare's Cleopatra, the Male Gaze, and Madonna: Performance Dilemmas', *CTR* 2.3 (2002), 7–16.
Schafer, Elizabeth, Commentary on William Shakespeare, *The Taming of the Shrew*, *Shakespeare in Production* series (Cambridge, 2002).
Schalkwyk, David, 'Is Love an Emotion?: Shakespeare's *Twelfth Night* and *Antony and Cleopatra*', *Symploke* 18.1–2 (2010), 99–130.
Schanze, Ernest, *The Problem Plays of Shakespeare* (Oxford, 2005).
Schiesari, Juliana, *The Gendering of Melancholia: Feminism, Psychoanalysis and the Symbolics of Loss* (Ithaca, NY, 1992).
Schiff, Stacy, *Cleopatra: A Life* (New York, 2010).
Schoenfeldt, Michael, *Bodies and Selves in Early Modern England* (Cambridge, 1996).
—'Give Sorrow Words: Emotional Loss and the Articulation of Temperament

in Early Modern England', in Basil Dufallo and Peggy McCracken (eds), *Dead Lovers: Erotic Bonds and the Study of Premodern Europe* (Ann Arbor, MI, 2006), 143–164.

Schwarz, Kathryn, 'My Intents are Fix'd: Constant Will in *All's Well that Ends Well*', *Shakespeare Quarterly* 58.2 (Summer 2007), 200–229.

Scodel, Joshua, *Excess and the Mean in Early Modern Literature* (Princeton, NJ, 2002).

Sedgwick, Eve Kosofsky, *Tendencies* (Durham, NC, 1993).

Shanbag, Sunil, Interview with Andrew Dickson. Available at http://firstpageonlineuknews.co.uk/world-shakespeare-festival-around-the-globe-in-37-plays-3707 (accessed 5 November 2012).

Shakespeare's Globe, http://www.shakespearesglobe.com/theatre/on-stage (accessed 9 February 2012).

Sheriff, William E., 'The Grotesque Comedy of Richard III', *Studies in the Literary Imagination* 5.1 (1972), 51–64.

Sherman, Nancy, 'Stoic Meditations and the Shaping of Character. The Case of Educating the Military', in David Carr and John Haldane (eds), *Spirituality, Philosophy and Education* (London, 2003), 65–78.

Smith, Bruce, *Shakespeare and Masculinity* (Oxford, 2000).

Solga, Kim, *Violence Against Women in Early Modern Performance. Invisible Acts* (Basingstoke, 2009).

Spargo, R. Clifton, *The Ethics of Mourning: Grief and Responsibility in Elegiac Literature* (Baltimore, MD and London, 2004).

Spencer Kingsbury, Melina, 'Kate's Froward Humour: Historicizing Affect in "The Taming of the Shrew"', *South Atlantic Modern Language Association* 69, 1 (winter 2004), 61–84.

Spenser, Charles, Review of *Hamlet*, dir. Nicholas Hytner, National Theatre, *Daily Telegraph*, 8 October 2010.

—Review of *All's Well that Ends Well*, dir. John Dove, Shakespeare's Globe, *Daily Telegraph*, 9 May 2011.

Stapleton, M. L., *Fated Sky, The Femina Furens in Shakespeare* (Newark, DE and London, 2000).

Stanislavski, Konstantin, *An Actor's Work*, trans. Jean Benedetti (Abingdon and New York, 2008).

—*Creating a Role*, trans. Elizabeth Hapgood (London 1981).

Steggle, Matthew, *Laughing and Weeping in the Early Modern Theatre* (Aldershot, 2007).

Stern, Tiffany, 'Taking Part: Actors and Audiences on the Stage at Blackfriars', in Paul Menzer ed., *Indoor Shakespeare: Essays on the Blackfriar's Stage* (Selinsgrove, 2006), 35–53.

Strier, Richard, *Resistant Structures: Particularity, Radicalism and Renaissance Texts* (Berkeley and Los Angeles, CA, 1995).

—*The Unrepentant Renaissance* (Chicago, IL, 2011)

Suzman, Janet, 'A Word from the Director', programme note to *Antony and Cleopatra*, Chichester Festival Theatre, 2012.

Svendsen, Zoe, '"A Mad Qualm Within this Hour": The dramaturgical Challenges of Middleton and Rowley's *The Changeling* (1622) in Modern Production', paper given at 'Confined Spaces: Considering Madness, Psychiatry, and Performance', AHRC Network: Isolated Acts (Cambridge, 2012).

Tarlow, Sarah, *Ritual, Belief and the Dead in Early Modern Britain and Ireland* (Cambridge, 2010).

Taylor, Gary, *Reinventing Shakespeare: A Cultural History from the Restoration to the Present* (London, 1990).

Taylor, Millie, 'Don't Dream It, Be It: Exploring Signification, Empathy and Mimesis in Relation to The Rocky Horror Show', *Studies in Musical Theatre* 1.1 (2007), 57–71.

Taylor, Paul, Review of *Coriolanus*, dir. Dominic Dromgoole, Shakespeare's Globe, *Independent*, 11 May 2006.

—Review of *All's Well that Ends Well*, dir. John Dove, Shakespeare's Globe, *Independent*, 10 May 2011.

—*Musical Theatre, Realism and Entertainment* (Farnham, 2012).

—Review of *Antony and Cleopatra*, dir. Janet Suzman, Chichester Festival Theatre, *Independent*, 18 September 2012.

—Review of *The Changeling*, dir. Joe Hill-Gibbons, Young Vic, 3 February 2012.

Tillyard, E. M. W., *Shakespeare's Problem Plays* (London, 1951).

Torture Museum, Amsterdam, www.torturemuseum.com (accessed 27 October 2012).

Torture Museum, 'Tortura, Inquizione, Pena de Morte'. Available at http://www.torturamuseum.com/this.html (accessed 9 February 2012).

Trevor, Douglas, *The Poetics of Melancholy in Early Modern England* (Cambridge, 2004).

Ure, Peter, *Shakespeare: The Problem Plays* (London, 1961).

van Vugt, Mark, Charlie Hardy, Julie Stow and Robin Dunbar, 'Laughter as Social Lubricant: A Biosocial Hypothesis about the Pro-social Functions of Laughter and Humor'. Available at www.professormarkvanvugt.com/files/LaughterasSocialLubricant.pdf (accessed 20 November 2012).

Virtualtourist.com, http://www.virtualtourist.com/travel/Europe/Czech_Republic/Hlavni_Mesto_Praha/Prague-400455/Things_To_Do-Prague-Torture_Museum-BR-1.html (accessed 27 October 2012).

Watson, Donald G., *Shakespeare's Early History Plays* (Basingstoke, 1990).

Webster, Charles ed., *Health, Medicine and Mortality in the Sixteenth Century* (Cambridge, 1979).

Weimann, Robert and Douglas Bruster, *Shakespeare and the Power of Performance* (Cambridge, 2008).

Weinstein, Charles, Review of *Hamlet*, dir. Nicholas Hytner, National Theatre, Olivier Theatre, London, 2010, *Internet Shakespeare Editions* 2 February 2011. Available at http://isechronicle.uvic.ca/index.php/Ham (accessed 10 October 2011).

Welch, Kate, 'Making Mourning Show: *Hamlet* and Affective Public-Making', *Performance Research* 16.2 (2011), 74–82.

Wells, Stanley, *Shakespeare, Sex and Love* (Oxford, 2010).

Wiles, David, *The Shakespearean Clown* (Cambridge, 1987).

Woodall, James, Review of *Hamlet*, dir. Nicholas Hytner, 8 October 2010. Available at http://www.theartsdesk.com/theatre/hamlet-national-theatre (accessed 10 October 2011).

Woods, Penelope, 'Globe Audiences: Spectatorship and Reconstruction at Shakespeare's Globe' (Ph.D. thesis, Queen Mary University of London, 2011).

Worthen, W. B., *Shakespeare and the Force of Modern Performance* (Cambridge, 2003).

Wren, Celia, '"As You Litigate It"', *American Theatre*, 26.6 (July–August 2009), 42–43.

Zeki, S. 'The Neurobiology of Love' (Federation of European Biochemical Societies, 2007).

Žižek, Slavov, 'Signs of the New Invasion', *New Statesman*, 12 December 2011.

## THEATRE PRODUCTIONS AND FILMS CITED

Crouch, Tim, *I Malvolio*, Unicorn Theatre (London, 2012).

de Mille, Cecil B., dir. *Cleopatra* (film), Paramount Pictures (1934).

Hislop, Ian, *Ian Hislop's Stiff Upper Lip: An Emotional History of Britain* (television series) BBC (2012).

Hurst, Michael, dir. *The Tudors* (television series), Peace Arch Entertainment for Showtime (2007–10).

Mankiewicz, Joseph, dir. *Cleopatra* (film), 20th Century Fox (1963).

Middleton, Thomas and William Rowley, *All's Well That Ends Well*, adapted by Mihir Bhuta, dir. Sunil Shanbag, Arpana Theatre, Shakespeare's Globe, London 2012.

—*Antony and Cleopatra*, dir. Trevor Nunn, Royal Royal Shakespeare Company, Shakespeare Theatre, (Stratford-upon-Avon, 1972–1973).

—*Antony and Cleopatra* (television film), dir. Jon Scholfield, Incorporated Television Company (1974); based on the Royal Shakespeare Company production, dir. Trevor Nunn (Stratford-upon-Avon, 1972).

—*Antony and Cleopatra*, dir. Peter Brook, Royal Shakespeare Company, Royal Shakespeare Theatre (Stratford-upon-Avon,1978).
—*Antony and Cleopatra*, dir. Adrian Noble, Royal Shakespeare Company, The Other Place (Stratford-upon-Avon, 1983).
—*Antony and Cleopatra*, dir. Peter Hall, Royal Shakespeare Company, Royal Shakespeare Theatre (Stratford-upon-Avon, 1987).
—*Antony and Cleopatra*, dir. Giles Block, Shakespeare's Globe (London, 1999).
—*Antony and Cleopatra*, dir. Janet Suzman, Chichester Festival Theatre (Chichester, 2012); first produced, with some of the same cast, for the Liverpool Playhouse (Liverpool, 2010).
—*The Changeling*, dir. Declan Donnellan, Cheek by Jowl and BITE: 2006, Barbican Theatre (London, 2006).
—*The Changeling*, dir. Joe Hill-Gibbons, Young Vic (London, 2011). Shakespeare, William, *All's Well That Ends Well*, dir. John Dove, Shakespeare's Globe, London 2011.
—*Coriolanus*, dir. Tim Supple, Chichester Festival Theatre and Renaissance Theatre Company (Chichester, 1992).
—*Coriolanus*, dir. Dominic Dromgoole, Shakespeare's Globe (London, 2006).
—*Coriolanus*, dir. Yukio Ninagawa, The Ninagawa Company, Barbican Theatre (London, 2007).
—*Coriolanus*, dir. Ivo van Hove, in *The Roman Tragedies* (*Romeinse Tragedies*), Toneelgroep Amsterdam, Barbican Theatre (London, 2009).
—*Coriolanus* (film), dir. Ralph Fiennes, Icon Entertainment International and BBC Films (2011).
—and Bertolt Brecht, *Coriolan/Us*, dir. Mike Pearson and Mike Brookes, National Theatre Wales (RAF St Athan, Wales, 2012).
—*Hamlet* (film), dir. Lawrence Olivier, Two Cities (1948).
—*Hamlet*, dir. Ian Brown, West Yorkshire Playhouse (Leeds, 2002).
—*Hamlet*, dir. Greg Doran, Royal Shakespeare Company, Swan Theatre (Stratford-upon-Avon, 2008).
—*Hamlet*, dir. Nicholas Hytner, National Theatre, Olivier Theatre (London, 2010).
—*Hamlet*, dir. Ian Rickson, Young Vic Theatre (London, 2011).
—*The Rest is Silence* (*Hamlet*), dir. Tristan Sharps, Dreamthinkspeak, Riverside Studios (London, 2012).
—*Richard III*, dir. Malachi Bogdanov, English Shakespeare Company, The Pleasance (Edinburgh, 1998).
—*Richard III*, dir. Roxana Silbert, Royal Shakespeare Company, Swan Theatre (Stratford-upon-Avon, 2012).
—*The Taming of the Shrew*, dir. Connall Morrison, Royal Shakespeare Company, Swan Theatre (Stratford-upon-Avon, 2008).

—*The Taming of the Shrew*, dir. Edward Hall, Propeller Theatre Company, Old Vic Theatre (London, 2008).
—*Twelfth Night*, Henry Irving, Manager, Lyceum Theatre (London, 1884).
—*Twelfth Night*, dir. Bill Alexander, Royal Shakespeare Company, Royal Shakespeare Theatre (Stratford-upon-Avon,1987).
—*Twelfth Night* (film), dir. Trevor Nunn, BBC Films/Circus Films/Fine Line Features (1996).
Shakespeare Theatre Company, *Malvolio's Revenge*, Shakespeare Theatre Company Mock Trial, Sidney Harman Hall (Washington, DC, 2009).
Shaw, George Bernard, *Caesar and Cleopatra* (film), dir. Gabriel Pascale, Gabriel Pascale Productions (1945).
Thomas, Gerald, *Carry on Cleo* (film), Pinewood Studios/Anglo-Amalgamated (1964).
Webster, John, *The Duchess of Malfi*, dir. Gale Edwards, Royal Shakespeare Company, Royal Shakespeare Theatre (Stratford-upon-Avon, 2001).
—*The Duchess of Malfi*, dir. Phyllida Lloyd, National Theatre, Lyttleton Theatre (London, 2003).
—*The Duchess of Malfi* (*Ten Thousand Several Doors*), dir. Jane Collins and Peter Farley, Prodigal Theatre, Nightingale Theatre (Brighton, 2006).
—*The Duchess of Malfi*, dir. Jamie Lloyd, Old Vic Theatre (London, 2012).

# INDEX